DATE		

THE SERPENT
AND
THE ROPE

THE SERPENT

AND

THE ROPE

RAJA RAO

THE OVERLOOK PRESS

WOODSTOCK, NEW YORK

First published in 1986 by
The Overlook Press
Lewis Hollow Road
Woodstock, New York 12498

Copyright © 1960 by **Raja Rao**

Library of Congress Cataloging in Publication Data

Rao, Raja
The serpent and the rope.

I. Title.

PR9499.3.R3S47   1985   823   85-13628
ISBN 0-87951-220-2

Waves are nothing but water. So is the sea.

Sri Atmananda Guru

THE SERPENT

AND

THE ROPE

There is a GLOSSARY *at the end of the book*

I WAS BORN a Brahmin—that is, devoted to Truth and all that. "Brahmin is he who knows Brahman," etc., etc. . . . But how many of my ancestors since the excellent Yagnyavalkya, my legendary and Upanishadic ancestor, have really known the Truth excepting the Sage Mādhava, who founded an empire or, rather, helped to build an empire, and wrote some of the most profound of Vedantic texts since Sri Sankara? There were others, so I'm told, who left hearth and riverside fields, and wandered to mountains distant and hermitages "to see God face to face." And some of them did see God face to face and built temples. But when they died—for indeed they did "die"—they too must have been burnt by tank or grove or meeting of two rivers, and they too must have known they did not die. I can feel them in me, and know they knew they did not die. Who is it that tells me they did not die? Who but me.

So my ancestors went one by one and were burnt, and their ashes have gone down the rivers.

Whenever I stand in a river I remember how when young, on the day the monster ate the moon and the day fell into an eclipse, I used with *til* and kusha grass to offer the manes my filial devotion. For withal I was a good Brahmin. I even knew Grammar and the Brahma Sutras, read the Upanishads at the age of four, was given the holy thread at seven—because my mother was dead

3

and I had to perform her funeral ceremonies, year after year, my father having married again. So with wet cloth and an empty stomach, with devotion, and sandal paste on my forehead, I fell before the rice-balls of my mother and I sobbed. I was born an orphan, and have remained one. I have wandered the world and have sobbed in hotel rooms and in trains, have looked at the cold mountains and sobbed, for I had no mother. One day, and that was when I was twenty-two, I sat in a hotel—it was in the Pyrenees—and I sobbed, for I knew I would never see my mother again.

They say my mother was very beautiful and very holy. Grandfather Kittanna said, "Her voice, son, was like a *vina* playing to itself, after evensong is over, when one has left the instrument beside a pillar in the temple. Her voice too was like those musical pillars at the Rameshwaram temple—it resonated from the depths, from some unknown space, and one felt God shone the brighter with this worship. She reminded me of Concubine Chandramma. She had the same voice. That was long before your time," Grandfather concluded, "it was in Mysore, and I have not been there these fifty years."

Grandfather Kittanna was a noble type, a heroic figure among us. It must be from him I have this natural love of the impossible—I can think that a building may just decide to fly, or that Stalin may become a saint, or that all the Japanese have become Buddhist monks, or that Mahatma Gandhi is walking with us now. I sometimes feel I can make the railway line stand up, or the elephant bear its young one in twenty-four days; I can see an aeroplane float over a mountain and sit carefully on a peak, or I could go to Fathe-Pur-Sikri and speak to the Emperor Akbar. It would be difficult for me not to think, when I am in Versailles, that I hear the uncouth voice of Roi Soleil, or in Meaux that Bossuet rubs his snuff in the palm of his hand, as they still do in India, and offers a pinch to me. I can sneeze with it, and hear Bossuet make one more of his funeral orations. For Bossuet believed—and so did Roi Soleil—that he never would die. And if they've died, I ask you, where indeed did they go?

Grandfather Kittanna was heroic in another manner. He could manage a horse, the fiercest, with a simplicity that made it go where it did not wish to go. I was brought up with the story of how Grandfather Kittanna actually pushed his horse into the Chandrapur forest one evening—the horse, Sundar, biting his lips off his face; the tiger that met him in the middle of the jungle; the leap Sundar gave, high above my Lord Sher, and the custard-apples that splashed on his back, so high he soared—and before my grandfather knew where he was, with sash and blue Maratha saddle, there he stood, Sundar, in the middle of the courtyard. The lamps were being lit, and when stableman Chowdayya heard the neigh he came and led the steed to the tank for a swish of water. Grandfather went into the bathroom, had his evening bath—he loved it to be very hot, and Aunt Seethamma had always to serve him potful after potful—and he rubbed himself till his body shone as the young of a banana tree. He washed and sat in prayer. When Atchakka asked, "Sundar is all full of scratches . . . ?" then Grandfather spoke of the tiger, and the leap. For him, if the horse had soared into the sky and landed in holy Brindavan he would not have been much surprised. Grandfather Kittanna was like that. He rode Sundar for another three years, and then the horse died—of some form of dysentery, for, you know, horses die too—and we buried him on the top of the Kittur Hill, with fife and filigree. We still make an annual pilgrimage to his tomb, and for Hyderabad reasons we cover it up with a rose-coloured muslin, like the Muslims do. Horses we think came from Arabia, and so they need a Muslim burial. Where is Sundar now? Where?

The impossible, for Grandfather, was always possible. He never—he, a Brahmin—never for once was afraid of gun or sword, and yet what depth he had in his prayers. When he came out, Aunt Seethamma used to say, "He has the shine of a Dharma-raja."

But I, I've the fright of gun and sword, and the smallest trick of violence can make me run a hundred leagues. But once having gone a hundred leagues I shall come back a thousand, for I do not really have the fear of fear. I only have fear.

I love rivers and lakes, and make my home easily by any waterside hamlet. I love palaces for their echoes, their sense of never having seen anything but the gloomy. Palaces remind me of old and venerable women, who never die. They look after others so much—I mean, orphans of the family always have great-aunts, who go on changing from orphan to orphan—that they remain ever young. One such was Aunt Lakshamma. She was married to a minister once, and he died when she was seven or eight. And since then my uncles and their daughters, my mother's cousins and their grandchildren, have always had Lakshamma to look after them, for an orphan in a real household is never an orphan. She preserved, did Lakshamma, all the clothes of the young in her eighteenth-century steel and *sheesham* trunk, in the central hall, and except when there was a death in the house these clothes never saw the light of the sun. Some of them were fifty years old, they said. The other day—that is, some seven or eight years ago—when we were told that Aunt Lakshamma, elder to my grandfather by many years, had actually died, I did not believe it. I thought she would live three hundred years. She never would complain or sigh. She never wept. We never wept when she died. For I cannot understand what death means.

My father, of course, loved me. He never let me stray into the hands of Lakshamma. He said, "Auntie smells bad, my son. I want you to be a hero and a prince." Some time before my mother died, it seems she had a strange vision. She saw three of my past lives, and in each one of them I was a son, and of course I was always her eldest born, tall, slim, deep-voiced, deferential and beautiful. In one I was a prince. That is why I had always to be adorned with diamonds—diamonds on my forehead, chest and ears. She died, they say, having sent someone to the goldsmith, asking if my hair-flower were ready. When she died they covered her with white flowers—jasmines from Coimbatore and champaks from Chamundi—and with a lot of kunkum on her they took her away to the burning ghat. They shaved me completely, and when they returned they gave me Bengal gram, and some sweets. I could not understand what had happened. Nor do I understand now. I know my mother, my Mother Gauri, is not dead, and yet I am an orphan. Am I always going to be an orphan?

That my father married for a third time—my stepmother having died leaving three children, Saroja, Sukumari, and the eldest, Kapila—is another story. My new stepmother loved me

6

very dearly, and I could not think of a home without her bright smile and the song that shone like the copper vessels in the house. When she smiled her mouth touched her ears—and she gave me everything I wanted. I used to weep, though, thinking of my own mother. But then my father died. He died on the third of the second moon-month when the small rains had just started. I have little to tell you of my father's death, except that I did not love him; but that after he died I knew him and loved him when his body was such pure white spread ash. Even now I have dreams of him saying to me, "Son, why did you not love me, you, my Eldest Son?" I cannot repent, as I do not know what repentance is. For I must first believe there is death. And that is the central fact—I do not believe that death is. So, for whom shall I repent?

Of course, I love my father now. Who could not love one that was protection and kindness itself, though he never understood that my mother wanted me to be a prince? And since I could not be a prince—I was born a Brahmin, and so how could I be king?—I wandered my life away, and became a holy vagabond. If Grandfather simply jumped over tigers in the jungles, how many tigers of the human jungle, how many accidents to plane and car have I passed by? And what misunderstandings and chasms of hatred have lain between me and those who first loved, and then hated, me? Left to myself, I became alone and full of love. When one is alone one always loves. In fact, it is because one loves, and one is alone, one does not die.

I went to Benares, once. It was in the month of March, and there was still a pinch of cold in the air. My father had just died and I took Vishalakshi, my second stepmother, and my young stepbrother Sridhara—he was only eleven months old—and I went to Benares. I was twenty-two then, and I had been to Europe; I came back when Father became ill. Little Mother was very proud of me—she said, "He's the bearing of a young pipal tree, tall and sacred, and the serpent-stones around it. We must go round him to become sacred." But the sacred Brahmins of Benares would hear none of this. They knew my grandfather and his grandfather and his great-grandfather again, and thus for seven generations—Ramakrishnayya and Ranganna, Madhava-swamy and Somasundarayya, Manjappa and Gangadharayya—and for each of them they knew the sons and grandsons (the daughters, of course, they did not quite know), and so, they stood on their rights. "Your son," they said to Little Mother, "has been to Europe, and has wed a European and he has no sacred thread. Pray, Mother, how could the manes be pleased?" So Little Mother yielded and just fifty silver rupees made everything holy. Some carcass-bearing Brahmins—"We're the men of the four shoulders," they boast—named my young brother Son of Ceremony in their tempestuous high and low of hymns—the quicker the better, for in Benares there be many dead, and all the dead of all the ages, the successive generations of manes after manes, have accumulated in the sky. And you could almost see them layer on layer, on the night of a moon-eclipse, fair and pale and tall and decrepit, fathers, grandfathers, great-grandfathers, mothers, sisters, brothers, nephews; friends, kings, Yogis, maternal uncles—all, all they accumulate in the Benares air and you can see them. They have a distanced, dull-eyed look—and they ask—they beg for this and that, and your round white rice-balls and sesame seed give the peace they ask for. The sacred Brahmin too is pleased. He has his fifty rupees. Only my young brother, eleven months old, does not understand. When his mother is weeping—for death takes a long time to be recognized—my brother pulls and pulls at the sari-fringe. I look at the plain, large river that is ever so young, so holy—like my mother. The temple bells ring and the crows are all about the white rice-balls. "The manes have come, look!" say the Brahmins. My brother crawls up to them saying "Caw-caw," and it's when he sees the monkeys that he jumps for Little Mother's lap. He's so tender and fine-limbed, is my brother. Little Mother takes him into her lap, opens her choli and gives him the breast.

The Brahmins are still muttering something. Two or three of them have already washed their feet in the river and are coming up, looking at their navels or their fine gold rings. They must be wondering what silver we would offer. We come from far—and from grandfather to grandfather, they knew what every one in the family had paid, in Moghul gold or in rupees of the East India Company, to the more recent times with the British Queen buxom and small-faced on the round, large silver. I would rather have thrown the rupees to the begging monkeys than to the Brahmins. But Little Mother was there. I took my brother in my arms, and I gave the money, silver by silver, to him. And gravely, as though he knew what he was doing, he gave the rupees to the seated Brahmins. He now knew too that Father was dead. Then suddenly he gave such a shriek as though he saw Father near us— not as he was but as he had become, blue, transcorporeal. Little Mother always believes the young see the dead more clearly than we the corrupt do. And Little Mother must be right. Anyway, it stopped her tears, and now that the clouds had come, we went down the steps of the Harishchandra Ghat, took a boat and floated down the river.

I told Little Mother how Tulsidas had written the *Ramayana* just there, next to the Rewa Palace, and Kabir had been hit on the head by Saint Ramanand. The saint had stumbled on the head of the Muslim weaver and had cried *Ram-Ram,* so Kabir stood up and said, "Now, My Lord, be Thou my Guru and I Thy disciple." That is how the weaver became so great a devotee and poet. Farther down, the Buddha himself had walked and had washed his alms-bowl—he had gone up the steps and had set the Wheel of Law a-turning. The aggregates, said the Buddha, make for desire and aversion, pleasure and ill, and one must seek that from which there is no returning. Little Mother listened to all this and seemed so convinced. She played with the petal-like fingers of my brother and when she saw a parrot in the sky, "Look, look, little one," she said, "that is the Parrot of Rama." And she began to sing:

O parrot, my parrot of Rama

and my little brother went to profoundest sleep.

My father was really dead. But Little Mother smiled. In Benares one knows death is as illusory as the mist in the morning. The Ganges is always there—and when the sun shines, oh, how hot it can still be . . .

I wrote postcards to friends in Europe. I told them I had come to Benares because Father had died, and I said the sacred capital was really a surrealist city. You never know where

9

reality starts and where illusion ends; whether the Brahmins of Benares are like the crows asking for funereal rice-balls, saying "Caw-caw"; or like the Sadhus by their fires, lost in such beautiful magnanimity, as though love were not something one gave to another, but what one gave to oneself. His trident in front of him, his holy books open, some saffron cloth drying anywhere— on bare bush or on broken wall, sometimes with an umbrella stuck above, and a dull fire eyeing him, as though the fire in Benares looked after the saints, not the cruel people of the sacred city—each Sadhu sat, a Shiva. And yet when you looked up you saw the lovely smile of some concubine, just floating down her rounded bust and nimble limbs, for a prayer and a client. The concubines of Benares are the most beautiful of any in the world, they say; and some say, too, that they worship the wife of Shiva, Parvathi herself, that they may have the juice of youth in their limbs. That is why Damodhara Gupta so exaltedly started his book on bawds with Benares. "O Holy Ganga, Mother Ganga, thou art purity itself, coming down from Shiva's hair." When you see so many limbs go purring and bursting on the ghats by the Ganges, how can limbs have any meaning? Death makes passion beautiful. Death makes the concubine inevitable. I remembered again Grandfather saying, "Your mother had such a beautiful voice. She had a voice like Concubine Chandramma. And that was in Mysore, and fifty years ago."

I could not forget Madeleine—how could I? Madeleine was away and in Aix-en-Provence. Madeleine had never recovered— in fact she never did recover—from the death of Pierre. She had called him Krishna till he was seven months old. Then when he began to have those coughs, Madeleine knew: mothers always know what is dangerous for their children. And on that Saturday morning, returning from her Collège Madeleine knew, she knew that in four weeks, in three and in two and in one, the dread disease would take him away. That was why from the moment he was born—we had him take birth in a little, lovely maternity home near Bandol—she spoke of all the hopes she had in him. He must be tall and twenty-three; he must go to an Engineering Institute and build bridges for India when he grew up. Like all melancholic people, Madeleine loved bridges. She felt Truth was always on the other side, and so sometimes I told her that next time she must be born on the Hudson. I bought her books on Provence or on Sardinia, which had such beautiful ivy-covered bridges built by the Romans. One day she said, "Let's go and see this bridge at Saint-Jean-Pied-de-Port," that she had found in a book on the Pays Basque. We drove through abrupt, arched Ardèche, and passing through Cahors I showed her the Pont de Valentré. She did not care for it. It was like Reinhardt's scenario at Salzburg, she said. When we went on to the Roman bridge of Saint-Jean-Pied-de-Port she said, "Rama, it makes me shiver." She had been a young girl at the time of the Spanish Civil War, so we never could go over to Spain. Then it was we went up to some beautiful mountain town—perhaps it was Pau, for I can still see the huge château, the one built by Henri IV—and maybe it was on that night, in trying to comfort Madeleine, that Krishna was conceived. She would love to have a child of mine, she said— and we had been married seven months.

At that time Madeleine was twenty-six, and I was twenty-one. We had first met at the University of Caen. Madeleine had an uncle—her parents had died leaving her an estate, so it was being looked after by Oncle Charles. He was from Normandy, and you know what that means.

Madeleine was so lovely, with golden hair—on her mother's side she came from Savoy—and her limbs had such pure unreality. Madeleine was altogether unreal. That is why, I think, she had never married anyone—in fact she had never touched anyone. She said that during the Nazi occupation, towards the end of 1943, a German officer had tried to touch her hair; it looked so magical, and it looked the perfect Nordic hair. She said he had brought his hands near her face, and she had only to smile and he could not do anything. He bowed and went away.

It was the Brahmin in me, she said, the sense that touch and untouch are so important, which she sensed; and she would let me touch her. Her hair was gold, and her skin for an Indian was like the unearthed marble with which we built our winter palaces. Cool, with the lake about one, and the peacock strutting in the garden below. The seventh-hour of music would come, and all the palace would see itself lit. Seeing oneself is what we always seek; the world, as the great Sage Sankara said, is like a city seen in a mirror. Madeleine was like the Palace of Amber seen in moonlight. There is such a luminous mystery—the deeper you go, the more you know yourself. So Krishna was born.

The bridge was never crossed. Madeleine had a horror of crossing bridges. Born in India she would have known how in Malabar they send off gunfire to frighten the evil spirits, as you cross a bridge. Whether the gunfire went off or not, Krishna could never cross the bridge of life. That is why with some primitive superstition Madeleine changed his name and called him Pierre from the second day of his illness. *"Pierre tu es, et sur cette pierre . . ."* she quoted. And she said—for she, a Frenchwoman, like an Indian woman was shy, and would not call me easily by my name—she had said, "My love, the gods of India will be angry, that you a Brahmin married a non-Brahmin like me; why should they let me have a child called Krishna? So sacred is that name." And the little fellow did not quite know what he was to do when he was called Pierre. I called him Pierre and respected her superstition. For all we do is really superstition. Was I really called Ramaswamy, or was Madeleine called Madeleine?

The illness continued. Good Dr. Pierre Marmoson, a specialist in child medicine—especially trained in America—gave every care available. But bronchopneumonia is bronchopneumonia, particularly after a severe attack of chickenpox. Madeleine, however, believed more in my powers of healing than in the doctors. So that when the child actually lay in my arms and steadied itself and kicked straight and lay quiet, Madeleine could not believe that Pierre was dead. The child had not even cried.

We were given special permission by the Préfet des Bouches-du-Rhône to cremate Pierre among the olive trees behind the Villa Sainte-Anne. It was a large villa and one saw on a day of the mistral the beautiful Mont Sainte-Victoire, as Cézanne must have seen it day after day, clear as though you could talk to it. The mistral blew and blew so vigorously: one could see one's body float away, like pantaloon, vest and scarf, and one's soul sit and shine on the top of Mont Sainte-Victoire. The dead, they say in Aix, live in the cathedral tower, the young and the virgins do—there is even a Provençal song about it—so Madeleine went to her early morning Mass and to vespers. She fasted on Friday, she a heathen, she began to light candles to the Virgin, and she just smothered me up in tenderness. She seemed so far that nearness was farther than any smell or touch. There was no bridge—all bridges now led to Spain.

So when my father had said he was very ill, and wished I could come, she said, "Go, and don't you worry about anything. I will look after myself." It seemed wiser for me to go. Madeleine would continue to teach and I would settle my affairs at home. Mother's property had been badly handled by the estate agent Sundarayya, the rents not paid, the papers not in order: and I thought I would go and see the University authorities too, for a job was being kept vacant for me. The Government had so far been very kind—and my scholarship continued. Once my doctorate was over I would take Madeleine home, and she would settle with me—somehow I always thought of a house white, single-storied, on a hill and by a lake—and I would go day after day to the University and preach to them the magnificence of European civilization. I had taken history, and my special subject was the Albigensian heresy. I was trying to link up the Bogomilites and the Druzes, and thus search back for the Indian background—Jain or maybe Buddhist—of the Cathars. The "Pure" were dear to me. Madeleine, too, got involved in them, but for a different reason. Touch, as I have said, was always distasteful to her, so she liked the untouching Cathars, she loved their celibacy. She implored me to practise the ascetic *brahmacharya* of my ancestors, and I was too proud a Brahmin to feel defeated. The bridge was anyhow there, and could not be crossed. I knew I would never go to Spain.

India was wonderful to me. It was like a juice that one is supposed to drink to conquer a kingdom or to reach the deathless—juice of rare jasmine or golden myrobalan, brought from the nether world by a hero or dark mermaid. It gave me sweetness and the *délire* of immortality. I could not die, I knew; and the world seemed so whole, even death when it was like my father's. So simple: when it came he said, "I go," and looked at us, with just one tear at the end of his left eye; then stretched himself out, and died.

The smell of India was sweet. But Madeleine was very far.

Little Mother, when she saw the photographs of Madeleine and the baby, did not say anything, but went inside to the sanctuary to lay flowers on her *Ramayana*. She never spoke about it at all, but whenever she saw me sad she said, "Birth and death are the illusions of the non-Self." And as though before my own sorrow her unhappiness seemed petty and untrue, she seemed suddenly to grow happier and happier. She started singing the whole day; she even brought out her *vina* from the box where it had not been touched for three years, and started singing. My father who was still alive then said, "Oh, I suppose you want to show off your great musical learning to the Eldest." Even so he laid his book aside, a rare act for him to do, and started to listen to the music.

My grandfather said Father had such a wonderful voice when young—just like a woman's voice. "Later, when that Mathematics got hold of him—for figures are like gnomes, they entice you and lead you away, with backward-turned faces, to the world of the unknown——" he continued, "your father never sang a single *kirtanam* again. Oh, you should have heard him sing *Purandaradasa*." I never heard my father sing, but this I know: he had a grave and slow-moving voice such as musicians possess. His mathematics absorbed him so deeply that you saw him more with a pencil—his glasses stuck to the end of his nose (he had a well-shapen but long and somewhat pointed nose)—than with a *vina* on his arm. Father was a mathematician, and when he was not able to solve a problem he would turn to Sanscrit Grammar. Panini was his hobby all his life, and later he included Bharthrihari among the great Grammarians. Father had no use for philosophy at all—he called it the old hag's description of the menu in paradise. For him curry of cucumber or of pumpkin made no difference to your intestines. "The important fact is that you eat—and you live."

Father's greatest sorrow was that I did not take his mathematical studies a little further. He would say, "The British will not go till we can shame them with our intelligence. And what is more intellectual than mathematics, son?" He worshipped Euler, and quoted with admiration his famous saying on the algebraic proof of God. That Father's work on Roger Ramanujam's identities or on Waring's problem were accepted by the world only made him feel happy that it made Indian freedom so much the nearer. He was happy, though, that I had taken the Albigensian heresy as a subject for research, for he thought India should be made more real to the European.

He had never been to Europe. First, Grandfather was against the eldest son-in-law going across the seas. Then when Grandfather was reconciled with the changing values of the world there were too many responsibilities at home. And Father, in any case, did not care for travel. Like many persons of his generation I think he could not forget his bath and the Brahmin atmosphere of the house—the ablutions in the morning, with the women singing hymns, the perfume of camphor, and the smell of garlic and incense when the daughter came home for child-birth. He disliked my marriage, I think chiefly because my wife could not sing at an *ārathi;* but before the world he boasted of his intellectual daughter-in-law, and had a picture of me and Madeleine on his table.

He never thought he would die, so he never thought of the funeral ceremonies. Grandfather must have thought of it, for when I went to ask his advice as to where and what should be done Grandfather had all the answers ready: the ceremony had to be in Benares, and it had to be in my brother's name. "Not that I do not love you, Rama. How can I not love my daughter's own eldest born? But that is what the elders have laid down; and it has come from father to son, generation after generation. Why change it today? Why give importance to unimportant things? God is not hidden in a formula, nor is affection confined to funeral ceremonies. Be what you are. I like the way you go about thinking on the more serious things of Vedanta. Leave religion to smelly old fogeys like me," he concluded, and I almost touched his feet. He was so noble and humble, Grandfather was.

It was not the same thing with my uncles, but that is a different story.

Thus Benares was predestined, and as I went down the river with Little Mother, Sridhara on her lap, I could so clearly picture Madeleine. She would be seated at the left window of the

Villa Sainte-Anne, patching some shirt of mine, and thinking that as the sun sets and the sun rises, she would soon have the winter out. Then the house had to be got ready, and before the house was ready I would be there, back in Aix. Not that it gave her any happiness—but it had to be, so it would be. I was part of the rotation of a system—just as July 14 would come, and she would spend the two weeks till the thirtieth getting the house in order before we went to the mountain for a month. After that we would go to see her uncle for three days on a family visit, take a week off in Paris, and then come down to Aix before the third week of September. On October 1 term begins and on waking up she would see my face.

Affection is just a spot in the geography of the mind.

For Madeleine geography was very real, almost solid. She smelt the things of the earth, as though sound, form, touch, taste, smell were such realities that you could not go beyond them—even if you tried. Her Savoyard ancestry must have mingled with a lot of Piedmontese, so that this girl from Charente still had the thyme and the lavender almost at the roots of her hair. She said that when she was young she loved to read of bull-fights, and the first picture she had ever stuck against the wall of her room was of Castillero y Abavez, who had won at the young age of nineteen every distinction of a great *torero*. She hated killing animals, however, and I did not have to persuade her much to become a vegetarian. But sometimes her warm Southern blood would boil as never my thin Brahmin blood could, and when she was indignant—and always for some just cause—whether about the injustice done to teachers at the Lycée de Moulin, or the pitiful intrigue in some provincial miners' union at Lens or Sainte-Étienne, she would first grow warm and then cold with anger, and burst into tears, and weep a whole hour. This also explains how during the Occupation she was closer to the communists than to the Catholics or socialists, though she hated tyranny of all sorts. What I think Madeleine really cared for was a disinterested devotion to any cause, and she loved me partly because she felt India had been wronged by the British, and because she would, in marrying me, know and identify herself with a great people. She regretted whenever she read a Greek text not having been born at the time of the Athenian Republic; which also explained her great enthusiasm for Paul Valéry. I, on the other hand, had been brought up in the *gnya-gnyaneries* of Romain Rolland, and having read his books on Vivekananda and Ramakrishna, I almost called him a Rishi and a saint. Valéry seemed to be too disdainful, too European. For me, the Albigensian humility seemed sweeter, and more naturally Indian.

Loving Valéry, Madeleine, who taught history at the Collège, loved more the whole of ancient Greece. And when I introduced her to Indian history her joy was so great that she started researching on the idea of the Holy Grail. There is an old theory that the Holy Grail was a Buddhist conception—that the cup of Christ was a Buddhist relic which the Nestorians took over and brought to Persia; there the legend mingled with Manichaeism, and became towards the end of the Middle Ages the strange story of the Holy Grail. The Holy Grail also gave Madeleine's sense of geography a natural movement. She loved countries and epochs not our own.

Whereas I was born to India, where the past and the present are for ever knit into one whole experience—going down the Ganges who could not imagine the Compassionate One Himself coming down the footpath, by the Saraju, to wash the mendicant-bowl?—and so for me time and space had very relative importance. I remember how in 1946, when I first came to Europe—I landed in Naples—Europe did not seem so far nor so alien. Nor when later I put my face into Madeleine's golden hair and smelt its rich acridity with the olfactory organs of a horse—for I am a Sagittarian by birth—did I feel it any the less familiar. I was too much of a Brahmin to be unfamiliar with anything, such is the pride of caste and race, and lying by Madeleine it was she who remarked, "Look at this pale skin beside your golden one. Oh, to be born in a country where tradition is so alive," she once said, "that even the skin of her men is like some royal satin, softened and given a new shine through the rubbing of ages." I, however, being so different, never really noted any difference. To me difference was inborn—like my being the eldest son of my father, or like my grandfather being the Eight-Pillared House

Ramakrishnayya, and you had just to mention his name anywhere in Mysore State, even to the Maharaja, and you were
offered a seat, a wash and a meal, and a coconut-and-shawl adieu.
To me difference was self-created, and so I accepted that
Madeleine was different. That is why I loved her so. In fact, even
Little Mother, who sat in front of me—how could I not love
her, though she was so different from my own mother? In
difference there is the acceptance of one's self as a reality—and
the perspective gives the space for love.

In some ways—I thought that day, as the boat, now that
evening was soon going to fall, was moving upstream, with a fine,
clear wind sailing against us—in some ways how like Madeleine
was Little Mother. They both had the same shy presence, both
rather silent and remembering everything; they loved, too,
more than is customary. Both knew by birth that life is no
song but a brave suffering, and that at best there are moments of
bridal joy with occasionally a drive over a bridge—and then
the return to the earth and maybe to widowhood.

I remember very well that day, just three days before our
marriage. We had been to Rouen, just because we had nothing
better to do, and Madeleine seemed so, so sad. She said, "I have
a fear, a deep fear somewhere here; I have a fear I will kill you,
that something in me will kill you, and I shall be a widow. Oh,
beloved," she begged, "do not marry me. Let us part. There is
still time." She was twenty-six then, and I twenty-one. I did
not care for death and I said to her, as one does with deep
certitude at such moments, "I will never die till you give me permission, Madeleine." She stopped and looked at me as though
she were looking at a god, and turning laughed, for we were by
the statue of Henriette de Bruges, who for the birth of her son
Charles, later to become the Dark Hero of the Spanish Wars,
had a statue erected to herself. The child Charles, with the
crown of Burgundy already on his small plump head, was lying
on her lap. The statue was stupid, but it seemed somehow an
answer. And when we got back to Paris and were married at the
Mairie of the VIIth Arrondissement—for I then lived in the Rue

Saint-Dominique—we bought ourselves a book on Bruges that is still with me. It is one of the few things I could save for myself when the catastrophe came.

Bruges must be beautiful, though. I have never been to that city of canals and waterfronts, but the ugly, fat face of Henriette de Bruges will always remain a patron saint of some mysterious and unperformed marriage.

Little Mother, having recovered her peace, started reciting as at home Sankara's *Nirvana-Astakam*. I have loved it since the time Grandfather Kittanna returned from Benares and taught it to me. I would start on *"Mano-budhi Ahankara . . ."* with a deep and learned voice, for after all I had been to a Sanscrit school. Little Mother followed me, and verse after verse: *"Shivoham, Shivoham,* I am Shiva, I am Shiva," she chanted with me. All the lights in Benares were by now lit, and even the funeral pyres on the ghats seemed like some natural illumination. The monkeys must have gone to the treetops, and the Sadhus must be at their meals. Evening drums were beating from every temple, and one heard in the midst of it a train rumble over the Dalhousie Bridge. It was the long Calcutta Mail, going down to Moghul Sarai.

On the other side lay Ramnagarh—a real city for Rama. Every year people still came down to see the festival of Rama, and men and women and the royal family with horses, fife and elephants enacted the story of Rama. Little Mother felt unhappy we were too late for it this year. I told her I would soon come back to India and take her on a long pilgrimage. I promised her Badrinath and even Kailas. I knew there would be no Himalayas for me. Sridhara woke and as Little Mother started suckling the child again, I chanted to her the *Kāshikapurādinātha Kalā-bhairavam bhajé:*

> I worship Kalabhairava, Lord of the city of Kashi,
> Blazing like a million suns;
> Our great saviour in our voyage across the world,
> The blue-throated, the three-eyed grantor of all desires;
> The lotus-eyed who is the death of death,

The imperishable one,
Holding the rosary of the human bone and the trident
Kāshikapurādinātha Kalābhairavam bhajé.

Benares is eternal. There the dead do not die nor the living live. The dead come down to play on the banks of the Ganges, and the living who move about, and even offer rice-balls to the manes, live in the illusion of a vast night and a bright city. Once again at the request of Little Mother I sang out a hymn of Sri Sankara's, and this time it was *Sri Dakshinamurti Strotram.* Maybe it was the evening, or something deeper than me that in me unawares was touched. I had a few tears rolling down my cheeks. Holiness is happiness. Happiness is holiness. That is why a Brahmin should be happy, I said to myself, and laughed. How different from Pascal's, *"Le silence éternel des grands espaces infinis m'effraie."*

The road to the infinite is luminous if you see it as a city lit in a mirror. If you want to live in it you break the glass. The unreal is possible because the real is. But if you want to go from the unreal to the real, it would be like a man trying to walk into a road that he sees in a hall of mirrors. Dushasana* is none other than the *homme moyen sensuel.*

For the bourgeois the world, and the bank, and the notary are real; and the wedding ring as well. We spent, Madeleine and I, the last few thousand francs we had, to buy ourselves two thin gold wedding rings the day before our marriage. I still remember how they cost us 3,700 francs apiece, and as we had a little over 9,000 francs we went up the Boulevard Saint-Michel to eat at the Indochinese Restaurant, Rue Monsieur. We had rice for dinner and Madeleine felt happy. It was her recognition of India.

The next day at eleven we went up to the Mairie with two witnesses. One was Count R., an old and dear friend of Father's who had worked with de Broglie; unable to go back to Hungary because of the communist revolution there, he had settled in Paris. The other, from Madeleine's side, was her cousin Roland, who was an officer in the French Marine. Having seen a great

---

* A character in the *Mahabharatha,* humiliated because he had walked into a mirror thinking it was a path in the park.

deal of the world, an Indian was for him no stranger—he even knew Trichinopoly and Manamadurai—and he came to the marriage in his brilliant uniform.

Madeleine's uncle, of course, disapproved of all this outlandish matrimony. Oncle Charles was settled as a *notaire* at Rouen and he would not admit of any disturbance in his peaceful provincial existence. It was said of him that when he married his second wife—she was a *divorcée*—he married her without telling his old mother. It would have upset old Madame Roussellin too much— she lived in Arras. His second marriage was a most unhappy one, but he was proud of his brilliant wife; she made his position secure, and he loved her. Madeleine was her favourite, but lest the child should see too much of his married life the uncle very studiously avoided sending for her.

Madeleine was brought up by an unmarried aunt at Saintonge, in the Charente, but she saw her cousins from time to time, and they were gay with her. They teased her and said she would end up in a convent. Roland even discovered some mysterious tribe in the Australasian isles—they were called the Kuru-buri, I think—and said that on one of his expeditions he would land her on that blessed isle. "Your virtue will be appreciated there, Mado," he would say, "and imagine adding twenty thousand more to Christendom, before some Gauguin goes discovering the beauty of their virgins and peoples the island with many blue-eyed children." Such things were never said in front of me, but one day Madeleine, finding what a prude I was, told me the story with generous detail. "Imagine me a Catholic Sister," she said; "I who love the Greeks. Tell me, Rama, am I not a pagan?"

I was the pagan, in fact, going down the Ganges, feeling such worship for this grave and knowing river. Flowers floated downstream, and now and again we hit against a fish or log of wood. Sometimes too a burnt piece of fuel from some funeral pyre would hit against the oars of the boat. People say there are crocodiles in the Ganges, and some add that bits of dead bodies, only half-burnt, are often washed down by the river. But I have never seen these myself. Night, a rare and immediate night, was covering the vast expanse of the Benares sky. Somewhere on these very banks the Upanishadic Sages, perhaps four, five or six thousand years ago, had discussed the roots of human understanding. And Yagnyavalkya had said to Maiteryi, "For whose sake, verily, does a husband love his wife? Not for the sake of his wife, but verily for the sake of the Self in her." Did Little Mother love the Self in my father? Did I love the Self in Madeleine? I knew I did not. I knew I could not love: that I did not even love Pierre. I took a handful of Ganges water in my hand, and poured it back to the river. It was for Pierre.

I CANNOT REMEMBER anything more about Benares. We spent a further two or three days there, and while Little Mother went to hear *pārāyanams* in a private temple I wandered, like a sacred cow, among the lanes and temples of the Holy City.

What I loved most were the shops, with their magnificent copperwork, inlaid with lacquer and ivory; the many bunches of false hair hanging from the roof; the multicoloured bangles; and the rich, fervid smell of *bhang*, as it was given mixed with buttermilk and spice. The Benares silk shops too were splendid, with saris of such intricate designs as to make one marvel that people still prepared such wonders and sold them for money. One day I went out alone and bought a rose-coloured sari, with pistachio-green mango-leaf *pallo* for Madeleine—the pistachio would be so splendid against her gold. For Saroja I bought a simple white knitted sari from Lucknow. I wanted to buy bangles, too, but I was afraid they would break, and thought besides that when Little Mother had had to break them but the other day, to carry them would have been improper.

I wandered also among the cows tied up inside the temples, and touched their grave and fervent faces and fed them with green grass. What wonderful animals these be in our sacred land —such maternal and ancient looks they have. One can understand why we worship them. I bought some kunkum one day and decorated the faces of all the cows in a temple, then went out and bought Bengal gram and fed the monkeys. Evening was falling. I went back to Harishchandra Ghat and collected Little Mother where she sat on the bank of the river, talking away to Sridhara. I hired an ekka somewhere in the outskirts of the Brahmin quarter and took Little Mother to the Annapurna temple for worship.

23

How beautiful the Devi looked, in her saffron sari and with dark forehead bejewelled, and what strength emanated from her, what depth of peace.

> O Thou who hast clothed Thyself in cloth of gold,
> Decked in ornaments made of many and varied gems;
> Whose breasts rounded like a water-jar
> Are resplendent with their necklace of pearls;
> Whose beauty is enhanced by the fragrance of the Kashmir aloe;
> O Devi who presidest over the city of Kashi,
> O vessel of mercy, grant me aid.

"*Annapurné Sadapurné*," I recited with Little Mother, and when the camphor was lit Sridhara was so absorbed and quiet that I knew this last child of my family could gather the holiness of generations. Maybe one day he would answer my questions; for I had serious questions of my own and I could not name them. Something had just missed me in life, some deep *absence* grew in me, like a coconut on a young tree, that no love or learning could fulfil. And sitting sometimes, my hand against my face, I wondered where all this wandering would lead to. Life is a pilgrimage, I know, but a pilgrimage to where—and of what?

Everyone, for thousands of years, every one of the billion billion men and women since the Paleolithic ages, feels that something is just being missed. One in ten million perhaps knows what it is, and like the Buddha goes out seeking that from which there is no returning. Yet what is the answer? Not the monkhood of the Sadhu, or the worship of a God. The Ganges alone seemed to carry a meaning, and I could not understand what she said. She seemed like Little Mother, so grave and full of inward sounds.

I was anxious about something, anxious with an anxiety that had no beginning, and so no maturity. Lying on the stone floor of the big Brahmin house where we were staying I could hear the bells ring all the hours of the day, and pilgrims, muttering mantras to themselves, going down the steps. Sometimes, too, a fish caught something in the water, and you could almost feel the night tear with its swish and plunge.

Little Mother slept. Her hands on the head of Sridhara, pressed gently against her breast, Little Mother slept. She slept as though the waters of the Ganges were made of sleep and each one of us a wave. But she would suddenly open her eyes and ask, "Rama, are you sure you are not cold? I am frightened of your lungs, son."

Though the damp entered the very pores of my body the mosquitoes were worse. Little Mother had given me her mosquito curtain that I at least should have real rest. Under the net I felt so much apart that sleep seemed unnecessary. Perhaps it was the damp, or perhaps I did not eat enough, but I started to cough again. Little Mother was frightened. By the next afternoon we had left for Allahabad. Getting down at the station Little Mother said, "I fear everything now."

But she was warmed by the presence of Venktaraman on the platform. Venktaraman was a colleague of my father's in Hyderabad. He now taught English at Allahabad University, and we had sent him a wire. Little Mother felt comforted too when a South Indian spoke to her in Telugu; and when we reached home, Oh, it was so wonderful to have *rasam* with asafoetida in it, and chutney with coconut and coriander leaf! In the morning, when *dosé* came with filter-coffee, Little Mother really smiled. How much we are dependent on familiar things for our feelings of sorrow or joy. In this new-found ambience, Little Mother almost discovered her old spirits. Benares seemed hateful to her: the whole of the North, but for the Ganges, was one desolation of dirt. Lakshamma agreed. And they could talk of children and marriages, and who gave what and at which wedding. One daughter of Lakshamma was married to an I.F.S. in Delhi, and the other to someone in the railway services. The son was studying engineering in Benares, but he had come home for the holidays. Hints were thrown that though we belonged to two different communities Lakshamma would not mind thinking of Saroja for her first daughter-in-law. Little Mother noted all this in silence, and simply said, "It's a pity Rama is married already. Otherwise he would be so splendid for Kaumudi." Kaumudi, the third daughter, was sixteen and was studying for the Intermediate. "It may still happen," said Lakshamma, blowing away at the kitchen fire. I was unconcerned.

But I, too, was happy in these South Indian surroundings.

25

Since I left for Europe, I had never had an opportunity to live with other Indian families. We played—Kaumudi, Lakshamma, Little Mother and I—country chess that afternoon. In the morning Mother and I went down to the Triveni for the ceremonies and later I showed her Ananda Bhavan.* One day I took her to the museum.

It must have been on the second or third evening of our arrival, while sitting in the drawing room and reading some book on mathematics—for I had my father's interest as well—something happened which was to change the whole perspective of my life. Venktaraman came from the University Club, bringing along a former student of his, Pratap Singh, to the house. Pratap Singh, as I was soon to learn, had been a very bright student at Osmaina University. He had taken English Honours, and indeed did so well that Venktaraman had given him special coaching for the I.C.S.

Pratap was a posthumous son—his family were Jagirdars of Mukthapuri in Aurangabad District. Of a melancholy temperament, Pratap at least wished to brighten other people's lives. So he worked hard to brighten his mother's solitary existence. He sat for the examination but the competition was too severe: they took only seven Indians that year, and he was but the twenty-sixth or twenty-seventh on the list. The British Resident, however, immediately recommended him for nomination into the Political Services. He was a Raja Sahib of sorts; besides, he was such a clever lad, and the family had always been loyal to the Crown. He was of course chosen, and was sent over to England, being one of the last batch of civil servants to do this. His mother was so happy she went to live with her daughter in Parbhani.

One thing, however, remained to be done. If only the boy could be affianced, of course on his return, to the right party, then even if his mother should die before her time, she would breathe her last with peace in her soul. Pratap not only came from an ancient, if impoverished, family—they only owned some six or seven villages now—he also had a certain gravity of bearing. He was naturally virtuous. He was steady, and he was devoted.

* The home of the Nehru family.

That the choice should fall on the daughter of Raja Raghubir Singh of Surajpur—on the daughter who had just been sent to Europe for her education—seemed neither strange nor impossible. That the Raja Sahib was a tyrant and even his servants were afraid to go anywhere near him made no difference to the choice. On the contrary, having such a manly father—he had once tied one of his servants to a pillar and given him such a licking that his wounds took a month to heal in hospital—all this made the marriage even more desirable. A manly father has a gentle daughter always. Her mother was the gentlest of creatures, ever bent over her *Ramayana* and *Gita*. Her fasts and *kirtanas* were known everywhere. She had lost a young son, her first-born, while she was only eighteen—and it had given her such a shock that nobody had heard her speak a loud word nor seen her make a quick gesture the many long years since. Dignified in carriage, she was a contrast to the whip-bearing, *pān*-spitting father, who was known to have other and more common vices. But music is, after all, as much mine as yours, and if dancing girls are more learned in the art the fault is not theirs but that of our own women!

Savithri, for that was the daughter's name, was the eldest. She was sent to England as soon as the war was over, with the Lord Sahib's own recommendation. And so to be eventually married to a civil servant would be no real humiliation, even if the young man did not come from so good a family. After all, to be in the Political Services was to belong to the most exclusive cadres of the Government of India: you were not quite an Englishman or a Maharaja, but about equidistant from both, and sometimes superior, because you played polo. You ruled Maharajas, who ruled Indians, and the British received you at the Club. Thus an Assistant Resident was still a highly respected party in the marriage market of North India. The British Governor's presence, music and a few Maharajas would do the trick in the end. And then Pandit Nehru could pat his bald pate as long as he liked. And hurrah for the Congress Raj!

The story is too long to relate. Sufficient that the girl did not agree. She came home on holiday and was shown him, and he her—and she suggested he marry Pushpāvathi, her younger sister. It was nevertheless agreed that the engagement would be between

Pratap and Savithri, for Savithri was still very young and she might yet change her mind. If in a few years she did not, Pushpāvathi would certainly be ready to marry him. Pushpāvathi did not care for her studies anyway, and she longed for a large family and a good mother-in-law. Pratap's mother actually liked the second daughter, but the first was the girl Pratap chose, and on the auspicious star, with coconut and kunkum, Savithri was officially engaged to Pratap. There were drum-beats and a lot of music. The best dancing girls had come from Lucknow, Rampur and Benares, and the Raja Sahib of Surajpur had special illumination arranged on the dome of the palace. Guns popped off announcing the *fiançailles* and some ten soldiers of the army, for that was what protocol permitted, marched in front of the palace. Horses and elephants were adorned; the temple of Amba Devi was lit with a thousand lights. Even the children at the local school were given sweets. Altogether it was a splendid occasion for all concerned.

When the family came back to their city home in Allahabad the girl refused to see Pratap. She said it was just her official engagement: nothing had been promised and nothing would ever take place. She had, besides, an aversion to British rule in India, and though Britain was giving up India, in Great Britain the mood had not changed. That Pratap had served the British so faithfully during the terrible war years was a point against him. There was no question of marriage. Months had passed since then, and there had been no letter from her. When she came back again from Cambridge she still said she would not see him. It was here that I was to come in and unweave the whole mystery. Why did she not want to see him? Why?

Living in Europe as I did, and having a French wife, seemed in their eyes to give me some special privilege in the understanding of love, which I did not, of course, possess. But when Pratap invited me over with him to the Raja Sahib's house I, who hate all this decayed and false modernity of our small Rajas and Maharajas, went with some apprehension. That the whole set-up of Kumara Villa was in the bad taste I had anticipated did not surprise me. It is often difficult to be wrong about modern India. The crust is so superficial—it lies about everywhere but you can remove it, even with a babul-thorn.

The Rani Saheba received us in one of those modern drawing rooms hung with huge oil portraits of British ex-Governors and sundry Maharajas. There were a few Ravi Varma lithographs on the walls, too, with paper flowers round them. There were three tiger skins, one of them almost a nine-footer that the Raja Sahib had killed in Kumaoan, and there were English-speaking servants. The tea set was suburban, the English babu-English, and then came Savithri. There was nothing in her round, almost plump face and her thick spectacles to show but the most ordinary upper-middle-class Indian. Apart from France, and all that, the fact that I was a Brahmin by birth and a South Indian seemed to have given me a natural superiority. Though Pratap was at least four or five years my senior he fumbled at every step and looked up to me for explanation and support. It seemed that even if my father's death had served for nothing else, it would serve to bring Pratap and Savithri together.

Savithri came with that sweep and nervousness of the modern girl and sat near me. She was fascinated with the idea that I was working on the Albigensians; she would herself have taken history, but her father had recommended English. So she was doing the English Tripos, and asked if I knew Cambridge. I told her I did not, but would take the earliest opportunity to go there when I was next in London. I also invited her to Aix-en-Provence, showed her a picture of Villa Sainte-Anne and spoke feelingly of Madeleine. I never mentioned the child. And the only curious thing I remember about Savithri that day was—I said to myself: Here is a very clever person, but she never says anything that really matters. We had one thing in common: we both knew Sanscrit, and could entertain each other with *Uttara Rama Charita* or *Raghuvamsa*.

Her presence never said anything, but her absence spoke. Even when she went to speak on the telephone one felt she had a rich, natural grace, and one longed for her to be back. I felt I did not like her, she was too modern for me; she had already started smoking. If I remember right she was fixing up a dance engagement on the telephone. I could not understand these Northerners going from strict purdah to this extreme modernism with unholy haste. We in the South were more sober, and very distant. We lived by tradition—shameful though it might look. We did not mind quoting Sankaracharya in law courts or marrying our girls in the old way, even if they had gone abroad. The elder brother still commanded respect, and my sisters would never speak to me as Savithri spoke to her father—the Raja Sahib had just come to say good-bye and he felt his future son-in-law and family were in good company.

When I went back home, what could I tell Little Mother? I told her I saw a strange family and dropped the subject there. We spoke of other and more urgent things. I told her about going to Hardwar and described to her the beauty of Dehra Dun and the foothills of the Himalayas, whence Mother Ganga surges out to purify mankind. You cannot have so much Sanscrit in your being and not feel,

> *Devi Sureshvari Bhagavathi Gange . . .*
> Saviour of the three worlds of restless waves,
> Clear is Thy water circling upon the head of Shiva,
> May my mind ever repose at Thy lotus-feet.

Venktaraman spoke of the past and of Father. He said how much my father had loved me, and how he had wept showing him some of my letters from Europe. I tried to be sincere and told him I had a great respect for Father, but that somehow since Mother's death he could not inspire my love. Venktaraman knew some of my former sentences by heart and I could have wept for such brutality of language. Partly it was a defence of Madeleine; I think Madeleine hated my father because she wanted all of me. She loved India, for India was a cause to love. My father? Oh, no, why should one love him? She had a veneration for my mother, and hung her picture in my bedroom, my mother with her thick black hair and the central parting, and the big round kunkum on her forehead. It was already when the disease had eaten deep into her that the picture was taken. She was beautiful even so, and you almost felt that for her breathing's sake at least her nose-pendant should be removed from her face. It seemed heavy, incongruous, and somehow very self-conscious.

But Father had died now, and Mother was dead long ago. "You must remember his mother," said Little Mother to Lakshamma when they were praising me for things I did not possess:

dignity, deference towards elders and a deep seriousness towards life. "Only such a mother could have borne such a son," added Little Mother again, and Sridhara looked at me as though he recognized my own mother in myself.

I laughed and recited, *"Kupathu jayathā, kachadapé kumāta nachavathu:* A bad son may sometimes be born, but a bad mother never."

On the morning of our departure for Hardwar I received via Cooks in Delhi a letter from Madeleine. I did not open it. I knew: one can know in the moment of any event the whole nature of that event, if only we let our minds dwell upon it—meaning, in fact, is meaningful to meaning. I put the envelope into my right pocket, where I kept all her letters.

When we had said good-bye to the Venktaramans—the father and Kaumudi had come to see us off at the station—and Little Mother had wiped her tears, Sridhara began to look out and see the girders of the Ganges Bridge; he looked back at his mother to ask what it meant. Suddenly, without reason, Little Mother shook with sobs. She shook and shook with such violent sobs that I sat there, hands on my knees, with no understanding. Long after the bridge had passed it was that I guessed: perhaps for the first time she realized, Little Mother realized, that Father was really dead. Something in the big look of the child perhaps, or perhaps it was the Ganges, with her sweet motherliness that one was unhappy to quit, who said it, for she it was, from age to age, who had borne the sorrows of our sorrowful land. Like one of our own mothers, Ganga, Mother Ganga, has sat by the ghats, her bundle beside her. What impurity, Lord, have we made her bear.

I sang the *Gangāstakam* again. Little Mother was very sensitive to Sanscrit hymns, being herself brought up the granddaughter of a learned Bhatta.

> *Kāshi kshétram, sharīram tribhuvana jananīm . . .*
> And nigh the riverbank Thy water is strewn
> With kusha grass and flowers,
> There thrown by Sages at morn and even.
> May the waters of the Ganges protect us,

I chanted. Then it was I understood: Little Mother must have remembered the ashes and bones of Father that we let down into the Ganges at Benares. The Ganges knew our secret, held our patrimony. In leaving the Ganges she felt Sridhara was an orphan.

After the next station she looked towards me reassuringly. I was there, heir and protector and companion. By now a common pain had knit us together, and in the daily pressure of the unexpected, in which two humans thrown together have to live side by side, Sridhara became our means of understanding. We both of us played with him—what a lovely child he was!—and in that common language we communicated with each other. Little Mother was a shy and silent person. I used to say she spoke as though she were talking to the wall or to a bird on a tree. She always spoke to herself as it were. She spoke to me sometimes, with long silences, in simple sentences that she could not formulate, for her education was meagre. But her voice was infinite in accent and tone, as though it were some primitive musical instrument, that could make some noise, which having been used from age to age had learnt the meaning of sound. And sound is born of silence.

So rich and natural was Little Mother's silence that she often lay with her eyes closed, almost motionless. She now stretched herself out on the berth, for we were alone in the whole compartment, and with Sridhara against her breast she lay almost asleep. Only when the child moved you could see her hand cover his head with the fringe of the sari. Little Mother must later have fallen sleep, for I heard her snore once, and then she did not wake for many hours.

Meanwhile Manduadih, Balapur, Hardatpur, Rajatalab, Nigatpur passed by: little hamlets with green all around and clusters of ancient trees by pond or on mound, that seemed to guard the tradition of the race. One remembered that it was here that the Aryans, when they first entered the country, camped under the ancestors of these trees, and the Ganges flowing by brought them the richness of green wheat-stalks, the yellow of sesame and the gold of sugar cane. It was somewhere here, too, that Gargi and Yagnyavalkya must have walked, and out of their discussions by wood-fire and by river-steps was our philosophy born, and that noble, imperial heritage of ours, Sanscrit, the pure, the complete, the unique. He who possesses Sanscrit can possess himself.

A signal, a flag and the clang of the train carried us towards the holy, thrice holy Himalayas. It was thither, when the work in the plains was over, or when one needed the integrity of selfness, that my Aryan ancestors went up the Ganges to seek the solitude of the snows and the identity of Truth. Somewhere over against the sky should Kailas stand, and Shiva and Parvathi besport themselves therein, for the joy of mankind. Nandi, the vehicle and disciple of Shiva, that bull without blemish, would wander round the world, hearing the sorrows of this vast countryside, hearing of painful birth and death, of litigation, quarrel and paupery. Parvathi would know of it, for Nandi would never dare tell his master in speech, and Parvathi would plead with Shiva that orphan, beggar and widow should have the splendour of life given unto them. You never knew when the door would open, and the sack of gold be found at your threshold.

The whole of the Gangetic plain is one song of saintly sorrow, as though Truth began where sorrow was accepted, and India began where Truth was acknowledged. So sorrow is our river, sorrow our earth, but the green of our trees and the white of our mountains are the affirmation that Truth is possible; that when the cycle of birth and death is over, we can proclaim ourselves the Truth. Truth is the Himalaya, and Ganges humanity. That is why we throw the ashes of the dead to her. She delivers them to the sea, and the sun heats the waters so that, becoming clouds, they return to the Himalaya. The cycle of death and birth goes on eternally like the snows and the rivers. That explains why holy Badrinath is in the Himalaya: it proclaims the Truth.

Sri Sankara again came to my mind.

> Shines forth does the Devi, born in the snowy mountains;
> Her beautiful hands are like a red leaf.
> It is She with whom Shiva seeks shelter,
> Who stoops from the weight of her breasts,
> Whose words are sweet;
> Tender creeper of intelligence and bliss.

Reciting the hymn I slipped into one of those curious moods that fill us in the vastness of India; we feel large and infinite, compassion touching our sorrow as eyelashes touch the skin. Someone behind and beyond all living things gave us the touch, the tear, the elevation that make our natural living so tender. If there were no barbarian beyond our borders the Hindu would have melted into his nature, grown white as some women in the zenana, and his eyes have seen the splendour of himself everywhere. He might have grown emasculated, but he would have played in the garden of the Ganga.

My thoughts were, as you see, very Indian, and I thought it right, now that the evening was slowly stretching itself down, that in this atmosphere I should read the letter from Madeleine.

"*M'ami,* my friend," she wrote. The letter was dated the twenty-ninth of March, 1951.

"*M'ami,* my friend. Will I give you pain if I tell you I went down last week end to Bandol? Somehow I had to visit it. You could never understand what Pierrot's birth was to me. You in your masculine isolation—I could almost say your Indian aloneness—can never understand what it is for a mother, and a French mother, to bear a child. It is the birth of the god in a chalice, the Holy Grail; you know, Christian or not, one feels *the birth,* and even one who is not a Christian would almost look around and see the stable and the *Rois-Mages* bringing offerings to the Lord.

"I bore him, your son, with such love, for he was a child of love; but you were more interested in his sonship than in his being my son. The feminine to the Indian must always be accessory, a side issue. Yet I loved my son from the time I felt him kicking inside me, for he was your son. You thought of his future: I thought of the present. You told me how in India you had to have different hymns and diet according to whether you wanted the child to be a hero, a wise man, a doctor or a grammarian. I just wanted a man: my son.

"Your impersonal approach was strange to me, you yourself so impersonal. I loved you for it, for in touching you I smelt, as it were, some mountain air, the honey-pine of the heights, the smell of incense while the mist rises. Your heart was so like a mountain stream, its tenderness so pure. I loved to bathe in it. But how cruel it can be, how exasperating for a European. You people are sentimental about the invisible, we about the visible. And to me you were the invisible made concrete, so visible, incarnate, beside me—and my husband.

"You will never know, *m'ami,* dear husband, what it was to have your little child beside me; how, as he lay against my breast, I told him a million silly things that I always wanted to tell you, but could never tell you. You make the simple too big, and everything human seems ridiculous before you. You remember how we laughed one day when you told me, 'Madeleine, why put that nasty powder—some chemical—on your skin; it cannot make the skin more beautiful than it is. I hate to touch the chemical; I want the true.' Then I told you a feminine lie, I said it protected the skin in our climate; and how satisfied you were with my answer. You were cruel, as you would have been to a Hindu wife. But months later, when I told you the truth, instead of becoming angry you laughed and laughed at yourself. It is so easy to fool you: you have no understanding of woman at all, dear Rama. I thought I was the innocent one, but you are more foolish than me. No wonder Oncle Charles thinks it served me right to have married such an outlandish creature.

"The child in the cradle. And the cradle against the Mediterranean, the Mediterranean the cradle of our civilization. I slept, Rama, night after night in the nursing home, not thinking of Pierre or of you but of Demeter and Poseidon and the voyage of Ulysses. In fact at first I thought a second name for Krishna would be Ulysses. How I rounded the names on my tongue: Krishna Ulysses Ramaswamy. Absurd, absurd, said something to me, but I repeated them so often together, thinking that with familiarity it might become natural. No, the name seemed so absurd. Then I thought of Achille, as I told you; Achille was the name of one of the servants in the clinic, but I thought it too heroic for the son of a Brahmin. Well, there was no hurry and Krishna was Krishna. Krishna. Krishna, Krishna, I said to myself, as one repeats a mantra, and I was so filled with delight. He would be copper-coloured, and with your eyes. He would have your limbs, but not your heavy lips or your big nose. A little bit of my nose might not do him any harm. And I prayed and I prayed to some unknown divinity that he should be just a son—not yours or mine, just ours.

"One night, the night before his birth, a great sweep of mistral cleared the air, and we could see as far as Corsica. Far away against the horizon lit boats went across the Mediterranean—to Africa perhaps, and to farthest America. The world moved. Fishing boats were all about the place, for the fishes come up to the surface on moonlit nights; and as the hill went rolling down with the olives and the lone cypress stood against the tower by the Hôtel de Ville I wondered who I was: what I was doing there? You were away in the hotel, but I told you later of the vision I had that night. Demeter, with fruits and stalks in her hand, rose out of the invisible sea, as though she were made more of silken thread than of substance. It was as if you could see beyond her and she could vanish into herself, as some birds hide their faces in their down. Do you know that beautiful Homeric hymn? *Demeter Kourotrophos,* I thought to myself, and she not even the daughter of Poseidon. But the sea was auspicious and the whole world bathed in simple delight. There was no sorrow, no place for imperfection, no death or misery for man. The corn grew, the gods played, the fife filled the valley, the girls danced before the altars and flowers grew everywhere—roses, crocuses, violets, narcissus. Beauty filled the magnanimity of creation and I was happy, Rama, happy as I have never been.

"The next morning at five the pains started, and by eleven the little baby was born. I was neither happy nor sorry to see him, and when I saw your glowing face I wondered why such a lump of flesh which gave me so much pain should give you so much joy. For you it was not a child, a son, your son and my son; but your heir. For me it was just a something—but then *suddenly* when I took him in my arms and held him against my breast the whole of creation shone in a single second—the nativity, I repeat, the first and only birth, the proud proof of happiness. Yes, for me Pierre was happiness, he did not make me happy. He was proof that man *is,* and cannot be happy but be happiness itself.

"The olive trees still go down to the sea. Achille is still at Bandol, but he's become a *garçon-de-café*. There are no rich English people coming to have their babies in the South of

36

France. I went down to the port; the jetty was still unrepaired, as it was during the German-Italian occupation. I bought flowers *chez* Henriette, where you said you bought me fresh tulips every morning. I wanted to sleep again in Bandol, so I went to your hotel, the Hôtel des Pêcheurs, and got the selfsame room. The *patron* did not recognize my name; he probably thought it was Russian. I put the tulips into a vase, put the car in the garage and went out again into the night. I was not sad, I was just empty. Would I see Demeter again?

"The moon was still in the sky. I felt so pagan. I wish there were an Aliscamps, as in Arles, and that I could write a beautiful epitaph to my dead son. It would read something like this: 'He was born to the cypress, he was born to the syllable, he the child of silence and of Woman.' Or some such thing. He had your silence, Rama, and his hair smelt of thyme.

"The Greek gods are jealous. They are jealous of happiness. My votive offerings brought no answer. No Demeter came in vision with polos and veil, nor did the sea throw up a broken raft on which was to be found the golden child. Like Penelope I sat on the seashore, weaving my web. When will you come, O Ulysses?

"Strange, Rama, nowadays I often go to church. I love ruins, and especially the ruins of cathedrals or chapels. On my way here I passed by Saint-Maximin and visited the Dominican monastery. That is, I went to the chapel for Mass, and Oh, how deeply it affected me, that *'Regina coeli, laetare.'* I wandered all over the place, visited the crypt and saw the relic of holy Marie-Madeleine. The smell of incense that used to hurt me now gives me a pained delight. I hate to kneel and yet sometimes I half bend my knees and remember what my mother always said: 'Never kneel without cotton on your knees; God knows what infection may lie there.' I still have such a fear of bacteria—how shall I ever stand India?

"You say you are going to Benares with your mother. Of Benares all I know is the bits of floating human flesh and the pyres of the dead, and that the Ganges water when chemically examined shows no bacteria. We Europeans are not yet holy enough to have crypts with no bacteria.

"I hated going to Saint-Maximin, though. I could not visit the church without you; I almost felt you by my side and often turned back to see if by chance you had not suddenly come back, and missing me in Aix had followed me by that terrible intuition of yours. These days with aeroplanes everything is possible. And how sad, Rama, is a lonely woman. Without a man she can see nothing great or holy. There the Hindus are right. Man must lead woman to the altar of God.

"I love you, Rama, with a strange, distant, impenitent love—as though in loving you I say I do not in fact love you. I wish I had an assurance of love, that I did not love you for your purity, your inner strength—the wall, the stone wall that will never yield, 'celui qui ne décevra jamais,' as the astrologer in the Boulevard Saint-Germain told me. I wondered whether I could really love you—whether anyone could love a thing so abstract as you. Sometimes you seem almost here, and I have such delight that I think I will go down to teach at the Collège, almost singing, when you have given me my morning coffee. You the most choice, the most noble, the most unhuman husband. I wonder if Indians can love.

"I can. And therefore I await you, you my young love.

"MAD.

"P.S. How Indian sometimes I have become—I see and I wonder. India is infectious, mysterious and infectious."

Even the Indian trains seem to chant mantras: "Namasthethu Gangé twadangé bhujangé; Hari-Hari-Ram-Hari-Ram, Ram-Haré"; and going uphill, "Shiva-Shiva, Hara-Hara, Shiva-Shiva-Hara"; and so to the morning. The night was quickly over; the child woke up only once or twice, and Little Mother said something incomprehensible in sleep. "Saroja," she seemed to say, "bring me a glass of white water." Then came the silence, the long empty silences of the stations, the cry of hawkers, the sound of pilgrims, and then up again, and towards the mountains. The compartment was getting cold. I rose up to cover Little Mother's uncovered feet. She was awake, and said, "Oh, I cannot bear to hear you cough like that." Was I coughing?

The morning mists were already against the windowpane when the restaurant-car boy came to wake us up. The coffee was warm but very bad. The birches and the deodhars of the Himalayas spread before us. Isolated forest bungalows came, and now and again a whole tribe of deer jumped away across the pools of the forest, so frightened were they of the train. The parrots had slender and very lovely yellow rings round their throats, and the Himalayas shone above them, simple, aware, vibrant with sound. The Ganges, a small stream, flowed gently against us, but her freshness was so mature. Whether young or older in years the Ganges is ever so knowing, so wise. If wisdom became water the Ganges would be that water, flowing down to the seven seas.

Somewhere between the interstices of those trees, somewhere in the movement of the hinds, in the mountain stillness of Hardwar did I feel a new knowledge. I felt *absence*.

The mountains must know, I thought, and so I looked up towards the bridge and mountain path that, winding through the pines, led to Rishikesh and Badrinath. There beyond the folds of the snow was Gangotri, where the holy mother took her birth; and the barbarian began where she started. Tibet lay beyond, where Sister Brahmaputra cuts herself gorges in the Himalaya to feed the barbarian; then mingling with the Ganga and become holy she enters the sea conjointly. Duality is anti-Indian; the non-dual affirms the Truth.

I dipped in the Ganges and felt so pure that I wondered anyone could die or go to war, that people could weep, or that Hindus and Muslims had cut each other's throats and genitals. Indeed the refugees in Hardwar, innocent creatures, had seen the barbarities of an alien religion. One could expiate for the kidnapped and the forsaken, dipping and dipping in Ganges by the Himalaya. One could expiate also in the Ganges for the dead. Pierre was never dead: I could feel him in my loins.

There is no absence if you have the feel of your own presence. The mountain echoed an absence that seemed primordial, a syllable, a name.

We went to Dehra Dun in the evening. Next morning I took Little Mother to Mussoorie, and showed her the snows from the Hamilton Point. White and beautiful in their simplicity were they, peaks, bare glaciers and the sounding emptiness of sky. Sridhara clung to his mother as if he saw something too big to understand, and Little Mother simply muttered away some prayers. When she was moved she always understood herself reciting a hymn. Ultimately the far and the awesome is divine; it destroys the barriers of body and mind, no, rather of mind and body, and reveals the background of our unborn, immaculate being. That is why Shiva lives in the Himalaya.

What happened afterwards is still very hazy in my mind. Little Mother and I left the mountains and the Ganges with immeasurable pain, as though we had been visiting some venerable relations and had to leave them, with a broad kunkum on our faces and their hands on our heads, the perfume of their feet in our nostrils. Mother Ganga had her feet all yellowed with turmeric, and she carried the flowers of our evenings in her hair. The Himalaya was like Lord Shiva himself, distant, inscrutable, and yet very intimate there where you do not exist. He was like space made articulate, not before you but behind you, behind what is behind that which is behind one; it led you back through abrupt silences to the recesses of your own familiar but unrecognized self. The Himalaya made the peasant and the Brahmin feel big, not with any earthly ambition, but with the bigness, the stature of the impersonal, the stature of one who knows the nature of his deepest sleep. For in the deepest sleep, as every pilgrim knows, one is wide awake, awake to oneself. And the Himalaya was that sleep made knowledge.

Coming down the ravines by the silent rivulets that ran with us one had the sense of innocence great mountains never give. One felt indeed that neither tiger nor scratching bear, neither python nor porcupine could ever do the smallest hurt; as the epics say, here in this auspicious refuge the deer and the lion drink of the same waters, and the jackal and the elephant are friends. However, one could not forget, for newspapers never let you forget, that not far from Dehra Dun, in the Tarai, the man-eaters still roamed, and villagers were just caught in their fields and taken away with the ease that boys catch wagtails in spring. You shoot the tigers, so the Government said, and get five hundred rupees. And yet how tame and wise-eyed the deer under the trees looked, and when the peacocks danced the world seemed touched by the music of the flute.

Oh where shall I go, oh where, thou source of virtue, Kanhayya;
Oh where when the flute plays, and the cattle come to thee?

Mira the poetess is so Northern. She, a Rajput princess, could treat God, could treat Sri Krishna, her Kanhayya, as she would a Rathor. She could count the jewels of his howdah, admire the rings on his fingers, whisper that the cavalry move quicker and the drums beat as royalty advances. And by pool and archway would the women await, with kunkum-water and coconut and flower in hand, to welcome this great God, this Principle, this Presence amidst them. The pools suddenly grew lotuses, the parrots suddenly sang, "Hari is come. Sister, Hari is come," and the peacocks would pull their tails and offer that he wear a crown of their feathers. The black deer, hearing the sound of music, came to him as in the Rajput paintings, their heads lifted and their ears laid back, listening to the music that came from the flute.

Muraré, I have brought thee the butter of my heart,
And when the pyre is ready, Lord, light it thyself;
Let my ashes serve as tilak on thy brow.

At Muradabad on the way back the train jerked away from the main line and took us down to Delhi. There the green, virginal Jumna greeted us not as sister of the Ganga, but as it were her daughter, Kalindanandini. Delhi was so sad, with the refugees and the dirt on the streets and the stories one heard of what had happened on the border. Mothers had lost their daughters and fathers their wives, but when the Women's Commission went to recover the abducted women some of them laughed. "Sisters, you call us. What sisters are we to you, O respectable ones? The Muslims took us and here we are of their harems; they treat us better than the cowards that left us and ran for their lives. Tell my daughter, I am happy. And tell that man called my husband I spit on his face . . ."

Some women that were brought back had no tale to tell: they never opened their mouths. They spun cotton, or made baskets at the refugee centres, past thinking. Some had left their fathers behind, some their husbands. Once in a while someone escaped from Pakistan and told tales that could never be heard to the end.

Some, too, there were, the true Gandhians, who spoke of the horrors we had committed on the Muslims, and pointed at the fanaticism that led to the sacrifice of him whom we so tenderly called Father of the Nation.

Little Mother naturally wanted to visit the Jumna Ghat, where the last mortal remains of the Mahatma were cremated. She did not weep, she did not even pray. She went down to the Jumna and washed her feet and face. She just could not understand what death was. And yet death was everywhere about—a fanatic shoots a saint, a tiger carries away a peasant woman cutting grass in the fields, or the Muslims kill a thousand, ten thousand, a hundred thousand, on the banks of the Ravi, for their God, they say, is different from our God. It is good, Little Mother must have told herself, to belong to the far South. No barbarian will ever come to us.

The train ran straight down south, and looping through the Vindhyas brought us directly to Bombay. By now Sridhara had had too much of travel and he developed a slight fever. Our friends in Bombay—we stayed in Mathunga, and with South Indians of course—were most kind to us. We had a car to go about in, but this barbaric city simply had no meaning for a Brahmin like me. It spoke a language so alien, had a structure so improper, made a demand so vehement and secondary, that one had no business to be there. Bombay had no right to exist. Marseille is certainly horrible, with its wide dark windows and its singsong tramways, its underground world of ruffians, *quemandeurs, bicots,* and its sheer smelly natural vulgarity; but at least it has the old port and the beauty of Notre-Dame-de-la-Garde. Once you go up the hundred and seventeen steps and see the majesty of the sea from the portico of the cathedral the whole of the Greek conquest comes to your mind, and not far from there one can almost see to the right Saintes-Maries-de-la-Mer, where the first Christians landed in Gaul.

Alas, nobody landed in Bombay but merchants and the vulgarity had no naturalness about it, save it were in the Hindu area, where you almost felt you were back in Benares. Somebody suggested we go to Bhan Ganga, and the idea that the Ganga had arisen even in this unholy territory gladdened the heart of Little Mother. "Look, look!" she cried, showing the sea behind Bhan Ganga. "It's just like Benares." Beyond was the burning ghat, of course, and a little farther away Little Mother and I sat by the sea and spoke of family affairs. She was worried about Saroja and Sukumari. One was seventeen years of age and the other fourteen.

"You, Rama, though borne by another woman and a blessed soul at that, you are like my own son. But they are different. Their mother was different, too, and they still have strong links with their mother's family. And after all, what am I? A poor court clerk's daughter. I am twenty-six, and these girls are already taller than me; they go to school and college and know more than I do. As long as *He* was there, there was someone to look after the house, and now I ask and wonder what will happen to everything. Night after night I cannot close my eyes, and your cough worries me even more. How can men understand the pained heart of woman?"

In between the smells of the sea there came sudden wafts of incense, as though absence was no more an absence, but just a presence invisible, unincarnate. Little Mother blew her nose, and I said, "I am your son. It is for you to say, and for me to obey."

There was a small clear moon and I can still feel the auspicious sense of the evening. We had just rung the bells at the Shiva temple and had put flowers on the Three-Eyed's head. The Walkeshwar temple was filled with the smell of sandalwood and camphor. Women were saying prayers in a corner; the Sadhus were lost in their sacred books. Little Mother knew I spoke the sacred truth. I could hear her weep into the edge of her sari, gently and undramatically. She put her hand on the head of Sridhara, as though now she was sure he was protected. I can still remember how immediately her trembling voice became steadier. Then after a long while of silence she said, "Promise me one thing, Rama?"

"And what may I promise you, Little Mother?"

"Promise that we will never interfere in your life. Your father once said, Rama, 'He's always been an independent child. He never will obey anyone unless he can be convinced. Let him lead

43

his own life.' That was what He said to us again when your letter came announcing your marriage. What your father respected I shall respect, Rama."

In the car, just as we had left the sea and were going up Malabar Hill, I said:

"And how shall I be of help—so far away, and with so alien an existence?"

"Simply by writing to us often; and coming to us every two or three years. So that they know there's a head of the household, an elder brother; so that the children feel they are protected, and there's one whom they have to obey."

"Well, for marriages and initiation ceremonies!" I said and laughed.

"And when Sridhara is big like you he will take charge of the household. Won't you, you foolish little baby?" she said, and laughed too. Sridhara was asleep.

It was late when we arrived home, but the *prasād* of the Walkeshwar temple was wonderful to bring back and we all ate happily, and later the eldest daughter of Venkatasubbayya sang some film-songs.

From that evening on Little Mother spoke more simply to me. She would say, "Now I must take dates for Sukumari, and chocolate for Saroja," or she would talk of Kapila, the eldest daughter, who had quarrelled with Father and had never set foot in the household again. Since she married into a "big house" in Mysore and became a daughter-in-law with golden girdle and diamond earrings her very nature seemed to have changed. She was, of course, my sister, but there was as much in common between us as between jasmine and tamarind. Let the tamarind grow, I said, and become the village-gate tree.

The whole family was at the station when we arrived, including the Other-House people, Seena, Kitta and even Uncle Seetharamu. Grandfather Kittanna, too, had sent us his benediction: I would go and see him the next day. Everybody was happy to see me, and so impressed with the dignity and serenity of Little Mother. She had left such a helpless and broken-down woman— almost a girl—and now she returned with natural dignity. She

walked as though space was not something unreal and undependable, but this was her own earth, her own home, her own
back yard, with the moon-guava and the well.

Saroja was the first to remark, "Oh, Little Mother, you seem so
changed. You have grown thinner, but you look more like
Brother Rama's sister than our mother."

"Yes," I told Saroja, "I have become the head of the family
now. And since I must return to Europe soon, Little Mother will
be my representative, with the power of the baton and the bank
account."

"We obey," said Saroja, looking at me shyly.

That evening everyone vied with the others to make Little
Mother's bed, and then mine. The whole house seemed to have
banished sorrow from the world. Here someone sang, there others
had their faces in their books. Sridhara already lay on his
mother's bed, as if he, too, felt the world was a safe and good
place, and that when he grew up Little Mother would have nothing to bend and break, nor a thing to carry. Milk would flow in
the house and the cattle would fill the courtyard with holiness.

Till late in the night lying on the veranda—for it was so hot
already—Little Mother told of all her experiences in the North.
I nearly fell asleep, but she woke me up and said, "Do you remember, Rama, that meal in Calcutta? You know what they did,
Saroja? We bought meal tickets at the station Hindu restaurant.
'Brahmin or non-Brahmin?' they asked. 'Brahmin,' we answered.
And when I went to the Brahmin section the whole place looked
funny. It was not that I had not been to restaurants before—I
have even eaten in Brahmin hotels at Bangalore—but there it was
different. They started serving. I put my hand into the curry. It
seemed very soft to touch, but yielded with such difficulty. 'Brinjal
it must be,' I said, and looked at Rama. Rama, who's been all
over the world, he also proceeded with care. Saroja, thank God
I did not put it into my mouth. You know what it was—it was
fish. 'Ayyappa!' I said, and rose hastily. I would have thrown the
whole of my stomach out. They laughed at us and explained that
in Bengal Brahmins do eat fish; they call it 'the vegetable of the
sea.' Ayyayyo," said Little Mother, "I could have put my hand
into fire, as we do impure vessels, to get the touch of it out of my

skin. Thoo!" spat Little Mother. and how Saroja laughed. "Say what you will, Saroja, the Northerners haven't the sensibility of living such as we have. You can see married women without kunkum on their faces, or men spitting on the floor. And as for dirt, well, the less said the better. It is something, Saroja, to be born a Brahmin," she said, and became silent.

Sleep came with the fresh breeze that blew from the crackling palm trees, and now and again the smell of jasmine wafted above us. I knew I was home.

It was Saroja in fact who made me feel I was back home and in India. When I first came back after Father's illness I was too busy with doctors and visitors to think of being back home. I took Little Mother to the North, not to see India myself, but to show India to her and make her "inauspiciousness" familiar to herself. Now here I was, back again on the veranda of Vishnu Bhavan, quiet, on my own, with the sound of the toddy palms at the back, and the smell of jasmine coming with the midnight breezes. The tap in the street still purred, despite changes of government and municipal constitution, and the blind Tiger, my father's favourite dog, still hunted the fleas on his back, even at night.

"How does a blind thing know night from day?" Little Mother asked.

Tiger always had fleas, so one day some four or five years before I had bought a bottle of phenol and given him such a scrub that some of the liquid entered his eyes. He could hardly see anything afterwards, and he transferred his loyalties. He went to my father, he treated me as secondary in the scale of human importance. For Tiger I still existed, but just as a member of the household, albeit the eldest. One fact, however, must be said in his favour. For three days before my father's death he never touched any food. On the day of Father's death he howled at the moon a great deal. And the next day he let Sridhara pull his tail as much as the child liked. But Tiger never got reconciled to me. He always looked at the gate, as though the doors would open and Father would come in again.

Saroja had grown so lovely. At seventeen, Lord, how beautiful the world could be! She was tall and was fair in a family where most of us are fair. And her silence had a quality that made living cervine. Saroja would never say anything important to anyone, and yet by some abrupt inconsequentiality she would say something you had been waiting to name. She had a deep and a noble wisdom. And she could talk so much, tell such stories, read your hand or invent a tale about her class-companions; but always it was to hide something of her own.

Sukumari was different; she was afraid of something, so she always quarrelled. What was red to Saroja was always pink and white to Sukumari, and the discussion usually ended in a long-drawn sobbing. "What an inauspicious thing to be doing, and of an evening, when the lights are being lit," Little Mother would say, and Saroja would go into the kitchen to help her with frying the mustard for the *rasam*.

Each evening before the meal the younger children would recite hymns, and once the camphor was lit Saroja would sing an *ārathi* song and I would begin "*Rājhādhi-Rājāya . . .*" After the circumambulations we would eat quickly and rush back to the veranda, and the talk of what happened with the Venktaramans in Allahabad or with the Vikrams in Delhi would begin again. There had been one miserable little child of Vikram's—Vikram had married for the fourth time at fifty-five and she eighteen—who was so ugly, such a bunch of carrots and coriander leaves, that nobody seemed to care for it. Sridhara looked a prince beside that Vithal, and at the mention of Vithal everybody laughed. Later Little Mother wrote to me that Vithal had died, of cholera.

Saroja was a strange sensation for me. Here was a mystery which I had never observed before: the girl becoming woman, and the thousand ways it shows itself, in shyness, in language, in prime presence. I had left India too young to know the sensibilities of a Brahmin girl. Saroja was thirteen when I left, and Sukumari but nine years old. Saroja's presence now obsessed me sometimes, like one of those nights with the perfume of magnolia. Rich and green seemed the sap as it rose, and it had a night of its own and a day. That Saroja was my sister made the knowledge of her womanhood natural to me—natural to see, to observe and even to breathe. I would myself pluck flowers for her hair and take her out on long walks and speak to her of Europe and of Madeleine. She too wanted to come and study in Europe; she would be a doctor, and later she would get Little Mother to live with us, she said. I was intoxicated with Saroja's presence, like a deer could be before a waterfall, or an elephant before a mountain peak; something primordial was awakening in a creature, and I felt that maturity in a girl was like the new moon or the change of equinox, it had polar affinities. There was something of the smell of musk, of the oyster when the pearl is still within, of the deep silent sea before the monsoon breaks. There was, too, a feeling of a temple sanctuary, and I could now understand why primitive peoples took the first blood of menstruation for the better harvesting of their fields. And why the Indians gave such beautiful names to their women, and told us how Malavika when she poured water made the asoka flower, or Shakunthala the karnikar blossom. What a deep and reverential mystery womanhood is. I could bow before Saroja and call her Queen.

She gave me one of her own saris for Madeleine as I left. I prayed for Saroja, and knew in the eye of my eye, somewhere in the interstices of my being, I had named something I had not known yet—it was the absence that had become presence again; it was not Saroja I felt and I smelt, but something of the Ganges and the Jumna that rose into my very being. Benares was indeed nowhere but inside oneself: *"Kāshi kshétram, sharīram tribhuvana jananīm."* And I knew: all brides be Benares born.

THE TRIP BACK to Aix started somewhat inauspiciously. My plane, after being five hours in flight and almost halfway to Cairo, returned to Bombay Airport with engine trouble. Here they tinkered away on the tarmac, but somewhere in the middle of the night they put us into a new plane, and off we were again. We did not land at Cairo till midday, and at Rome I missed my connection for Nice. I sent a cable to Madeleine immediately—I had begged her anyway not to come to the airport, for I wanted to see her first against the *vénitienne* in her own room, in her beige-green suit, with her hair falling on her shoulders and the back of it seen in the mirror. I took a plane straight to Geneva, and finding nothing there to take me to Marseille went on to Paris. Here, there would be a plane, only not until the morning, so leaving my baggage I wandered from midnight till five of dawn aimlessly by the Seine, absorbing Paris into my being.

Paris somehow is not a city: it is an area in oneself, a Concorde in one's being, where the river flows by you with an intimacy that seems to say the divine is not in the visible architecture of the Orangerie or the presence of the Pont des Arts, but where the trees would end; and even when the lorries have trundled over the cobbled streets—with potato and onion, geese, lard, margarine and cows' flesh; oranges, birds, Roquefort; *poireaux de Saint-*

Germain, carottes de Crécy, petits pois de Clamart; bottes de persil, romarin d'Antibes; sugar, mint and pepper—there opposite, begirt in her isle of existence, is the Mother of God, to whom man has built a sanctuary, a convocation of stone, uttered truly as never before. For it was the Word of God made actual, in prayer and fast, in dedication and in pain, that raised layer after layer of that white intimacy of thought, and this once made high and solid and pointed at space, man wanted to withdraw, to gaze inwards through tower and *arc-boutant* to see how the Virgin sat the Son of God on her lap. I might have led a cow to her altar had I been in Benares.

Dawn was already breaking over the city, and from bridge to bridge one could see the awareness of oneself made more acute, and that the day would soon hide from our own immaculateness. Paris is a sort of Benares turned outward, and where but in Benares would Baudelaire be more real, more understandable, more perfect, and in every dimension?

> Insouciants et taciturnes,
> Des Ganges, dans le firmament,
> Versaient le trésor de leurs urnes
> Dans des gouffres de diamant.

I sat among workmen in some bistro, drank hot, steaming coffee, stood up and walked again. Where was I? Once at Le Bourget and in the plane I was happy again. France seemed such a rolling garden of carrots and turnips, of plane trees that made diagonal approaches to river and castle, and of long, white roads that went to the infinity of the three seas. For all roads in France, I remembered, started from Notre-Dame.

Beyond Lyon the weather was rough, but at Marignane it seemed as though I was returning home from one of my usual trips to Paris. Henri the taxi-driver recognized me, and remarked, "Monsieur has a lot of luggage." I told him I had been to my country. "It must be a beautiful country," he said, with the same feeling as once before, when seeing a bunch of flowers at some tram station he had stopped the car, bought them for fifteen or twenty francs, and offered them to Madeleine saying, "These azaleas will go with Madame's grey-green suit. We call them the flowers of the Queen, for they say Azalais des Baux wore one on the day she saw Gui Guerjerat." Everywhere in the South you meet with this civilized attention, which shows how man has been informed of the sainthood of natural living. Those who live truly are the pure of heart.

Strange, I thought to myself, as the car twisted and roared through the hills of the Alpilles, that I seem to be returning not to my home, some spot of earth known and felt with limb and breath, but to some quarter in myself that, as in a psychoanalyst's chamber, shows itself with such foreknown unfamiliarity. It is as though somewhere I had stored away impressions of a possible becoming, and that on finding this the day had changed its dimensions—the sun had hidden himself and let shadow play on the hills, or the mistral bent the cypress so, and a curve of pain had managed to steal itself into my being. Yet there was in me the awareness of a new continuity, as though now that I had seen India and had told her of Madeleine, and now that Little Mother had given me, as her parting gift and as her blessing to her daughter-in-law, two little toe-rings of my own mother's—"From mother to daughter-in-law, as from father to son, is the race created," she had said, quoting some verse—I felt at last I was going to make Madeleine mine.

Jewels bear a lore of one's genealogy, and you know when the gold and diamond mango-garland is hung round the neck, or the ruby ring has been passed on to her finger, how you have invaded a new area of her presence; and how, like some old eunuchs in the palace, the ruby and the moonstone looked after your beloved, and gave her sweet thoughts and obedience to her Lord, once the right jewel shone at the parting of her breasts. Thus the King gave jewels to his vassals, and the Kingdom was run on the power of the seal.

The toe-rings, I thought; what a sweet thought of Little Mother's! My mother had them from my grandmother, and when my father married Saroja's mother the toe-rings went to her. They had to be enlarged, for she was a big woman. When Little Mother was brought to the house they were naturally given to her, and now they would go to her who bore Krishna to me. Would not Pierre have loved the bells that sounded with each footstep, and would he not have known they spoke of things his own and so old?

All these thoughts I knew were only subterfuges for some other predicament. I thought of Villa Sainte-Anne with the spreading pine tree, under which opened like two frank eyes the two rooms of Madeleine and myself. Behind the house beside the high pine wood was a grove of mirabelles, and beyond, against the blue sky, Mont Sainte-Victoire itself. There was a sainthood about that elevation of the mountain, not for any sanctuary of saint or martyr but because the good Cézanne saw it day after day; and it carried such a message of strength, and of the possible, that it was something of a Kailas for us. Often on walks when the air was very still and not a leaf moved, and a strange note of music seemed to fill the valley, I would say, "Madeleine, there, there! Parvathi is singing to Shiva." And Madeleine would burst out laughing, as if her unbelief itself was the proof of my truth.

Madeleine had never participated at first in my superstitions, though I had in hers. We used to go up the Hautes-Alpes, and would lie in the sun amidst the pines somewhere on the Durance. One day I started building a miniature temple, stone laid beside stone in respectful uniformity, and when the three outer walls had been built and the inner sanctuary made I said, "And now I must find a statue of Shiva, a *linga*." I told her how in the city of Belur, when the god's image comes floating down the river, the whole town hears the *OM* as though sounded on a conch, and men and priests go with fife and drum and palanquin to get him to his sanctuary—and of course he is there, the Channaa Keshava, the God of Beautiful Hair. So would the Durance, I said, give me my *linga*. And one morning as we wandered on her banks in search of gems for the temple—jasper and agate and marmoreal stone—there he was, our round and oval *linga,* on the bed of the river, and though I could not give him moon-flower and tulasi I gathered marguerites and harebells and installed him with Madeleine pouring holy water on Shiva's head. "Here is your Ganges," she said, *"Shiva, Shiva, Hara, Hara,"* and she trembled as she had that day on the Seine at Rouen, saying she loved me. On the way home that evening through the Gorge du Loup, with the swish of the river, she said, "You would make me a Hindu, would you, my love? I tell you that if marriage to you meant only the wearing of a sari I would still have married you." I told her the gods were neither Hindu nor Greek; being creations of your own mind they behaved as you made them—if Shiva was what I wanted, Shiva himself would come to the Durance. After all, I said, the Greek gods were made by the Greeks, but when the Romans and the Christians came they often metamorphosed into Saints of Christ. The world, I told her, was as you made it. She was lost in thought; she could not understand this anthropocentricity.

When we reached home I said, "Look, here's Shiva's bull at our door!" and I showed her the huge flat stone that lay like a squat Nandi at the edge of our garden.

"True, how very like a bull he is. You thought of Shiva, and so here is Nandi," she said, with unconvinced assurance. And she plucked some grass and gave it to him, saying, "Now, Bull, eat!"

And from then on Madeleine never passed by the door of the garden without either touching the huge hump of the bull, or caressing him and saying, "Here, Bull, here is your feed today." Sometimes coming from market she would lay a flower or two on his head and add, "Be happy, Bull." Seeing it from my window, the Hindu in me used to be so happy.

Then there was the elephant too at the top of the hill. A huge, gently curved rock lay almost flat on the ground, and if you sat on him of an evening, very still, you could hear him move. You could actually feel him shake and change sides, one foot first and then the other. When Madeleine and I had questions we could not solve, and she wished to avoid getting irritable and angry, she would say, "I will go and consult the elephant." Half an hour later there she used to be, her face beaming with wonder that man and woman could live in such harmony. Sometimes as I trudged my heavy-breathing way upwards she would shout and say, "Rama-Rama," like cow calling to calf at the fall of dusk, when the lamps are just being lit. There was not one question the elephant did not answer. When rarely we saw some schoolchild on a Thursday or Sunday seated on our elephant, or some soldier resting before he reached his barracks, how unhappy we used to feel. On such days we did not give him grass or pine-fruits, but flowers. I have never heard the resonance of Sanscrit so noble as on the back of the elephant. The Ganges flowed at our feet, and Krishna would soon be born.

It was one day almost a year later, as we came down from the elephant, that a telegraph-boy ran up our goat-path bringing us the wire to say that Father had been struck with apoplexy, and that I should come home at once. How tender Madeleine was to me that evening! Despite my lack of love for Father, tears came to my throat; I felt the beginnings of my biological presence on the earth disappear one by one. Not that he was my father, I felt; but like the wine in the cellars of Champagne that ferments when spring comes to the vineyard outside, and sinks and bubbles back at the fall of autumn, the sap in me, the continuity in me, was being strained, was being broken. I would be an orphan again.

That evening Madeleine was like my own mother. She said had my mother still been alive she would have flown with me to be beside her in her pain. Death and birth mean different things to different peoples of the earth; to me Madeleine's presence would have meant the daughter-in-law coming home, the division of family responsibility; truly it would have been "the crossing of the threshold." I almost felt if she came Father could not die, he would not die. How, when the first daughter-in-law came home, could the father die?

Auspicious, so auspicious—with kunkum, coconut and choli-piece, bangles on the arm, the necklace of black beads—is life.

Once again my thoughts had wandered away. "*Voici*, we're already at Brigonne," said Henri, and I woke up to the sudden reality that Aix was indeed there down in the valley. There was the cathedral, proclaiming not that Christ was the Son of God, but that the King of France was the Son of Christ.

This old Royalist city, with its spread, low trees, and inward *hôtels* with narrow, decorated entrances—this city of flowers and music was somehow not frank and open, but as if any day Zola's *sans-culottes* would invade her Place Publique again, and dragging her countesses on to the streets, not shoot them but make them dance, as if it were the fourteenth of July, curtseying to them each time and saying, "Pardon, Madame la Comtesse, we are the

54

shepherds of the mountains; we have beheld the Magian Kings and we come down the valleys that King Christ be anointed and crowned." For the Provençaux all is a festival of joy, and they live by the stars.

Madeleine was not at home. The house was securely closed, the blinds drawn; how anxious it looked. I could see from the grass which had fallen down the back of the bull that Madeleine must have gone the previous day; the grass had turned yellow under the sun. Neither did the house allow any mistake; it spoke to me and gave me the same information.

When I went down to the garage the assistant, Hector, said "Oh, Monsieur's car has not come back since yesterday evening. Madame has probably gone out somewhere."

The postman gave me two letters, one from Oncle Charles, the other from an Indian friend in London. I told Henri to take me to the Hôtel du Roi Jean. When Madame Patensier saw me, how she beamed.

"Madame must have gone to Nice to meet me," I told her. "And I missed my connection in Rome."

Madame Patensier had known us from the first time we came to Aix; before we managed to find a villa we had stayed with her. She knew all my needs, shouted that a bath be made ready for me and instructed Jeanne that I be served with vegetables. "Monsieur never, never eats meat," she said with such pride. Jeanne shook her head and said nothing, as though Madame la Patronne had become groggy.

After my bath and my lunch served in bed I walked about the familiar place, not like one who lived there, but like someone who was going to live there. It makes all the difference in the world whether the woman of your life is with you or not; she alone enables you to be in a world that is familiar and whole. If it is not his wife, then for an Indian it may be a sister in Mysore, or Little Mother in Benares.

Love is a way of looking at things. If you love you forget yourself, and perceive the object not as you see it, but rather as the seen. The woman therefore is the priestess of God.

There was no way I could contact Madeleine. Where, in Nice, would I find her? We never knew anyone there; besides,

55

Madeleine did not like to see anybody unless I liked to do so myself. She felt that between the Villa Sainte-Anne and the elephant on the hill was the space of joy. Beyond was barbary.

I was anxious, however. I knew she would wait for the next plane, and then return. Hoping against hope I walked back again: the shutters were as firmly closed. The grass on the bull's back had grown drier. I gave him some more fresh grass, hoping that if Madeleine came while I went to pay a visit to the elephant she would see and know I had returned. I knew she would be unhappy first, then angry, knowing that Indians are so undependable. If a European says he comes by such and such a plane he will come by it; if he misses his connection he will sleep in a hotel, and come by the next. But this Indian haphazardness, like the towels in the bathroom that lay everywhere about, was exasperating to Madeleine.

I put my hand through the gate and with difficulty opened the postbox. With wind and rain it had lost all integrity, and with a little coaxing it always yielded. Inside was the *Journal de Genève*—and my telegram. I searched every corner I could reach, but there was no message for me. So with anxious footsteps I went up the goat-path, through the bends in the pine wood to the elephant on the hill.

To feel that beyond the orchard of mirabelles and the slope of olives was the valley, and beyond that the plain stretched out to the sea, gave me a sense of comfort. Space is a comforter of sorrow, and the Mediterranean presence has a human richness that no ocean can give. One never thinks of the galley slaves; one thinks of the ships of Saint Louis, going out with hero and priest to conquer the Holy Land. And silently the Durance poured her mountain waters to the sea.

It must have been late in the evening, when the day had ended but the night not yet begun, that I heard the steady big footsteps of Madeleine. I was seated on the bull, looking down the pine wood to the little stream that ran at the end of the valley. Madeleine was heavy-laden with her purchases—she had bought two new brooms for the house, a basin, towels, boot-polish, and a summer hat for me, all from the Galeries Lafayette.

"You," she said, almost with a fright, and she stood there helpless, as though she now knew she had lost me. At such moments my breathing always grows faster and heavier, and I cough.

"Poor dear," she said, clinging to my arms, and seated on the bull she cried and cried.

I had no words for her, and when slowly I took the key from her bag and opened the gate, and led her up the Provençal steps of Villa Sainte-Anne, she said, "I just do not know why, I do not want to enter the house, I do not want to." I put on the light, and when she saw me now she said, with a touch of astonishment, "I, I never remembered you were so dark. It must be the sun of India," and kissed me for the first time. She said, months later, it was like kissing a serpent or the body of death.

When I led her to her room, I found her hair was all dishevelled; she had opened the hood of the car to have more air and to forget her disappointment. How man can disappoint a woman, how with a look or by an absence kill the very root of a woman's flowered awaiting!

She looked to me for help. I said, "Come, we'll go and get my luggage," and she, "Rama, you go and get your bags while I go and cook something for you."

With Madeleine in such a mood where she was like a woman who had seen her logic go wrong and had no logic left to connect events with, the best thing, I thought, was to leave her alone. I did not even ask for the key of the car. I walked down in that perfumed spring air, breathing the many herbs and flowers and the warm smell of human flesh as it passed, myself lost. For once I felt a foreigner in France.

When I took my luggage out I waited long before asking for a taxi, and went into great detail about all sorts of things Indian, as if it were urgent for Madame Patensier to know everything about my country. She seemed more like a confessor than the *patronne* of the Hôtel du Roi Jean, and I felt the lighter after talking to her of the interminable Indian journeys; the thousands of miles one travels; the Ganges, nearly two thousand miles long; and of the Himalayas, the highest mountains in the world.

"Bigger than the Alps and Mont Blanc?" she asked, surprised, in the same voice as two years before, when I said I did not eat meat.

"Oh, much bigger."

"But you have no snow there, so what grows on the top of the mountains?" she asked.

"Himalay itself means 'the abode of snow,'" I told her very proudly. *La demeure des neiges;* to her Provençal ear it sounded right and beautiful.

Having convinced Madame Patensier of the snow on the Himalayas I convinced myself that all was well with the world. Getting into the taxi, now ready at the door, I went to Villa Sainte-Anne with a feeling as if, having crossed evil spittle, I had crossed back three times in expiation; now the road went straight and to Benares. For what is holiness but the assurance man has of himself? The sacred is nothing but the symbol seen as the "I."

I shall never forget as long as I live that evening, with the luggage in the corridor, and the smell of thyme and parsley that came from the kitchen. Wanting to feel that nothing had changed, Madeleine called out from the kitchen:

"I've made risotto for you, and the apple semolina, and here I am your wife." She was in her thin blue summer dress, with a near-mango design on it, that we had bought in Paris the summer before.

"And smell me now," she said. She smelt of eau-de-Cologne, for that was the first smell I had smelt on her in Rouen.

I said an awkward "Thank you," and she went on: "Take the new towels I bought today. I bought a dozen so that your Brahminism, renewed and affirmed, can wash itself as often as it likes. Meanwhile your Brahmin wife will cook you your rice."

No, things were not going too well. There was nothing we could say to one another which would not sound like something the departing say to each other at a railway station. I remember so clearly how my big white suitcase and the smaller blue one lay on one another. Madeleine went to open them—for that was her habit—and tried to hang my clothes, but she did not go any further than my blue striped suit.

"The risotto will get burnt," she said, "and your family will not like me for having given you burnt rice on the night of your

58

arrival home. Rama," she warmed up, "you know I've become a good cook. I have been learning many new dishes from Hélène Berichon."

Hélène was the wife of the Professor of History in the Collège de Garçons, and since she was half English, on her mother's side, she liked to come to us and speak English.

"She says her father—or rather her mother's father—was a colonel in the Indian Army. So now I'll make you the right curry."

If speech were born it must have been on a woman's lip, just as hair if it were born must have sprung from a woman's pudendum to hide her shame. For women are great hiders of the unsayable; their gossip is only their own sorrow turned downside up.

I went over to my cases, but just could not take anything out, neither books nor dhoti, nor even the sari for Madeleine that Saroja had so carefully folded and put in a corner, with a silver kunkum-box, sacred coconut and betel leaves. The customs official had wanted to see whether, being an Oriental, I did not carry opium; he took the lid off the kunkum, and the powder fell on the sari, as at a marriage, or at the seven-month pregnancy adoration. Auspicious the sari looked, and I thought it best to take it out first. "I've a gift for you," I said.

"Show it to me," she shouted from the kitchen.

"Here is a gift of a sari from Saroja."

She was disappointed: she wanted it to be from me. But Saroja's sari was the one at the top, and it was the one which had the kunkum on, so I took it out. "Let me put it on you," I said.

As she undressed I could see the contours of her beautiful body, so simple, so erect, so unopened. I tried to dress her, and she let me do it, for she wanted to be touched by me, to be held by me, to know the knowing that has made knowing a single presence. But I was far away, my hands slipped, and several times I had to make and remake the folds. When I had at last tightened her at the waist, I said, "Now I'll go and have my bath." She answered, "Come quick; the food will be cold, love."

As the bath-water ran I just did not know what I was thinking or doing. Noise somehow gives one a feeling of rest, noise that is steady and familiar. I went to the bathroom window and saw that the sickly olives had been removed—planted in the days of the Romans, Hector had said—and the open land already showed the emergence of fireflies. They were just beginning to shine here and there and soon, I thought, I would see their dance, as we saw it every summer in the dark of the olives. I slipped into my bath and scrubbed myself dutifully, feeling that I might have more courage thus. A clean body seems full of wisdom.

The fireflies did not start dancing in the back yard. But far away in Monsieur Thibaut's olive groves they made such a pattern of beauty that I shouted "Madeleine, Madeleine!" There was no answer. I slipped into my pyjamas and went to Madeleine's room, where we usually moved our table to eat, and there she was lying on her sofa, silent. She must have been crying, but she put on a brave face. Tears came rarely to Madeleine; she seemed to have a power to stop them.

"Shall we eat?"

"Oh, yes. Everything is ready. I have only to make a salad dressing."

"No garlic for me, please!" I shouted, once again to say something.

I can remember as though it happened but the other day how we started our meal rather easily: I told Madeleine about Little Mother, and her wonderful promise on the Bombay beach. "You Indians seem full of wonderful gestures," she said, without bitterness, but with a certain objectivity.

"We are a sentimental people," I said. "We weep for everything."

"Yes; so much so that with Tagore's novels alone you could make a Ganges."

"There's much sorrow in my land, Madeleine, but such beauty between man and man. Even between man and woman," I added.

"Did you hate the Europeans very much when you were there?" she asked.

"Hate them? You know the Englishman is more loved in India than foreigner has ever been. We forget evil easily. Naturally we love the good."

"So that the pariah may have his separate well, and the woman slave for men."

This was an unexpected, a new bitterness. She added, as though to hide her thoughts:

"Georges has been asking me a great deal about India. You know, Rama, he's a nice fellow, though a little fanatical. Fanatic as he is his Catholicism makes him understand India more than I do, pagan that I am. He would convert the whole of India to the Roman Church, make of India an august gift to the Pope. He can see no salvation otherwise. But there you are, he's studied Ramakrishna and Vivekananda, and he's also studied Vedanta, and that is more than I have done. He wants to see you very much. When shall we ask him home?"

"Whenever you like," I said, and added somewhat self-consciously: "You know it was I who first discovered him."

Georges was one of those brilliant young White Russian intellectuals, brought up in the best of European and Orthodox traditions—his father was a well-known critic, belonging to the group round Berdiaev. Georges had joined the Maquis, and had his left arm shattered in some gun battle; thus he walked, with the awkward assurance of a mystic, and taught Latin at the Collège de Garçons. He read with ease several European languages, and had lately started learning Chinese and Sanscrit. He had come under the influence of the unfortunate Ségond tradition in Aix, but the Maquis and the confusion after led him more and more to visit the Dominicans at Saint-Maximin.

During the Occupation—before Georges joined the Maquis— he had gone to the monastery on a visit; Father Zenobias, the young Austrian monk who took him round, spoke French haltingly, and whenever he hesitated for a word Georges was ready to help him. The Austrian, being quite lost in this southern land, was so happy to meet someone who could speak German with him. A friendship thus casually made grew with the years, and when the Maquisards wanted to hide their ammunition in the region the Dominican Fathers were most helpful: three of them gave their life for it. Georges thus started becoming involved in Catholicism. His father was already a convert to Catholicism and worked at the Theological Seminary in Munich, besides working at the Russian Institute of the University. But Georges, brought up in exile, clung to his Orthodox fold, for in loving his church he felt he was more faithful to his motherland. To him even Mount Athos was part of Russia: for the Slavs it will continue to be so as long as they feel their religion was born on the mountains of the pagan Greeks.

Georges loved his father, the more so as he had lost his mother at an early age, in fact in Russia, and before the exile: his clinging to Orthodoxy had brought no difficulty in the relationship between father and son. They loved each other deeply, and the old man wrote such long and wise letters to his son. It was perhaps an act of loyalty to his father that had made Georges become kinder to Catholicism, and as soon as the Germans had occupied the whole country Georges simply went over to Saint-Maximin and asked for baptism. He spent three weeks in prayer and meditation, and they say he came out a new man. He did not seem to belong to this world.

He took his Agrégation in Latin because it mattered little what he taught. He could just as well have taken a History or Philology Agrégation. The more difficult a thing, the more he liked it: which explains the reasons for his taking up Chinese. But Sanscrit he started learning, I think, truly for the sake of understanding Indian philosophy.

Georges and I had met at the University library. We had heard of each other, or rather he had heard of me; I was more visible, as it were, being an Indian, and being married to a colleague of his from the Women's Collège. He came to us with that Slav simplicity and earnestness that makes contact with the Russians so enriching.

"Yes, I would be happy to see Georges," I said.

"You know he was the first to take me to Saint-Maximin. I have met Father Zenobias," she added, somewhat timidly.

I said, "I am happy that at last religion is not such a fearful monster for you."

"But I'll always be anticlerical," she insisted.

"Why, Madeleine, did you think I was going to defend the Pope?"

"Well, from joint-family to community and from community to Church isn't such a big leap, is it? I would rather a cowl on your head than an Ave Maria on my lip. I hate the *cagots*," she said, as if to reassure herself of her faith. "In fact I think I hate all religions, and would to God man simply lived intelligently."

"Intelligence, I suppose, must lead you to socialism and all that. Or to being fat and a buffoon like Edouard Herriot, or a washerman's beast like Daladier."

She nodded and was silent.

"Or why not Maurice Thorez?" I persisted.

"He's too crude for me," she remarked, and went into the kitchen to bring the risotto.

I can remember even today, so clearly, the risotto on our plates: the thyme and the lavender removed and laid on one side, the tomato right in the middle, disembowelled and flat, and when Madeleine had put one spoonful to her mouth, my hand just would not lift. There was a wide area of vivid space all around one, as though some magic circle had been drawn; the night seemed to stand heavy on the world. I said, almost in suffocation:

"Mado, something has happened."

She, who was half-filling her spoon with rice, stopped, and said: "Yes, something has."

I was quiet. Then she said, slowly, "To whom?"

"To everything," I answered, and laid my spoon down.

I just did not know where I was and what I meant. Madeleine left her spoon in the plate as well, and slowly came nearer me, pushing herself on my lap. She tried to pass her hand through my hair, knowing how much I loved her touch, and she put her face against my skin. She had the Charentaise smell of burnt apple, her smell rising through my nose, almost intoxicant. Her limbs became fervent, and in her pain she thrust her breast against my face, a vocable of God. Lord, how her breath went up and down! Her breast seemed to swell with love, as we say in my own land.

There is in pain something almost physical: the body seems to rise and say for the inarticulate, "Here is the speech beyond all speech, the knowledge beyond all knowledge." In that moment, for once Madeleine seemed to have intuited womanhood, as if the hair had grown rich and the belly had heaved high; as though the outer turning had slipped back inward, and she saw herself woman. Womanhood has eyes and sees itself in a splendour that man will never know, for his discovery is the outer, hers the inner which widens into a whole world. Childbirth is not the creation of a body; it is for woman, as Madeleine had said, the creation of the world. What she sees she keeps within her womb, as the emperor penguin the egg between its feet; and when the time comes she does not offer you an heir, a son, but her whole regnum of creation.

She might then have taken me into herself as never before, not with the knowledge that she knew me, but with the conviction that she would make me know myself in the shine of annihilation. But I'm a Brahmin, and for me touch and knowledge go with the holiness of surrender, of woman not taking me there, but I revealing to her *that*. Pain is not of love. Pain could never be incarnate but in the dissimulation of love. The lost lover is the passionate lover. The true man takes woman to his silence and stays in her for her recognition.

Now it was I who had tears. I could not take so much beauty proffered, because man should not do what a woman would do.

She said, "My love."

And I said, *"M'amie,* my friend."

"What is it?" she asked, drawing herself a little away.

"Oh, nothing," I answered; for that nothing, she knew, was the all.

"I have failed your gods?" she said.

"No," I said, looking at her; and for some un-understandable reason I added, "You've failed me."

She stood up in the full stature of her presence, her sari looking curious against that evening, and suddenly laughing she said, "Come, I'll change, and we'll go and say hullo to the elephant."

I could not tell her, in spite of all my truth, that I had been up already. She felt that if nothing else worked our superstitions would work.

We went into the night like two ghosts who had sold their lives not to win some paradise, however brief, but as if telling themselves they were going to heaven; a red-hot star had forked the path, yet through twists and wrong turnings we had been brought where only the flesh is true. But men, all men, walk with something more than flesh, till one becomes like Circassier, to die in front of Moscow and have a cross put up: *"Mort pour la patrie."* Only the dead in battle ever die a true death. All of them die for a purpose, and they have a right to a permanent cross.

"You know," said Madeleine on the way up, "your Holy Grail is not such a mysterious affair. The more I read the Church Fathers—and Georges has been a great help to me—the more I realize that it came from the Nestorian heresy, sister to your Albigensian one. Some Orientalists I have been reading do confirm my theory that it was a Buddhist relic that came via Persia to Christendom, and that the Chalice is only the mendicant alms-bowl upturned."

"Very poetic indeed."

"Why not, pray?"

"History should not be poetic; it is poetry without events."

"What remains then?"

"Well, facts. Every fact in its place is pure poetry like your broomstick and your towels from Galeries Lafayette. But let us go on to your Holy Grail."

"You see there is another, more plausible hypothesis, that it was the cup in which the Mother of God gathered, one by one, the dripping globules of our Lord's blood. When the Muslims came, naturally it had to be hidden and brought away on some galley to Gaul; yet they say this sacred cup shone like the 'moon of God,' and enchanted the winds to holy beckonings, while the idea that it came from Persia was one of the Church's tricks to steal a march on the Saracen. There are others who say it is the cup of gold that the Chaldeans took to the Temple of Ninurta, and that after they had slain a handsome slave some Semiramis, Queen of the Earth and Mother of Fertility, would drink of it, then call her hero and give it to him with musk and porphyry, that in their procreation the world might see the light of plenty. I read the other day that in some primitive tribes they spread the first menses of a woman with the first rains, so that the crops rise yellow as gold, and there's a glowing hearth in every hut."

"In some parts of India, you know, we still do that. In fact I was thinking of it just the other day. But surely there need be no connection between country and country to have a common

65

belief? Otherwise the Mayas of Mexico, who were the only people in the world apart from the Hindus that knew zero, could only have got it from them. Absurd," I said, "and thus everything good came from India!" And I laughed.

"Everything good for me has only come from India," she said, with that humility women know to soften the heart of the cruellest male.

"And evil," I said, and fortunately for me I started such a heavy cough that I had to sit down on a rock beside the path, and let Madeleine massage me on the back. It did us good, this cough, for my helplessness made her position more urgent: she was the wife, the protector of the household hearth. It reminded me of one day, during the early months of our marriage, when I was put out by something, and she brought me a hot-water bottle to be thrust into my bed. It burst over my blanket in such a way that we rolled and rolled on the bed with laughter, happy that so small a thing could bring us together. From that day we always called it the holy hot-water bottle, *"la sainte bouillotte."*

A hazy moon rose over the hills, but the stars right above us were very gay. We laughed to each other like children making up after a lost quarrel. I tore thyme as we went up, just to smell it, I a Brahmin from South India; Madeleine gathered hyacinths among the rocks and poured them over my head. We could be happy again.

We sat on the elephant and I told Madeleine all the inconsequent things—about Venktaraman's daughter Kaumudi, who wondered how we could live without an aunt or a mother-in-law at home, or about the Benares Brahmin who asked what sort of hymns the Brahmins in Europe chanted.

"He did not ask what they get paid for a funeral; nor would I know."

"A funeral is a costly business," said Madeleine knowingly. "I am happy I shall die in India. You will burn me, won't you, Rama? But not by the Ganges, for I hate the thought of the dogs that wait to gobble you before you're burnt up fully."

"I'll burn you on the Himavathy," I said, "like we did Grandfather. I shall pile up pieces of sandalwood one over the other, and I shall sing a special hymn for you. It will be called 'Hymn to the Goddess of the Golden Skin.' I will have carried some special heather and thyme from this elephant's back, and I shall perfume the river so that the fishes and the deer will come to see what is happening. Once you have been reduced to white ash, the river will rise and carry you away—as it did Grandfather. Thus you will become a Brahmin at last."

But Madeleine was away, her thoughts were far away, and we fell into an easy, a distant silence. The elephant did not seem to know anything or say anything. The stars were perfect: they were so beautiful you wanted to count them, just to cool your heart. Man is so far from perfection that all that is far seems wondrous bright to him.

We came down slowly and as we opened the door my half-opened case still lay there with its question unanswered. We could tell lies to people, but we could not tell lies to animals or things. When we went to bed we were so tired that I only said, "So, Madeleine, tomorrow the Prince will bring the Professor her coffee."

"Don't you be silly," she said, "you must be so tired. Now that the holidays are soon coming I have little work. Besides, to-morrow is Friday, and my classes begin at ten."

Next morning, when Madeleine had gone to Collège, I closed my case and left it at the other end of the corridor. Neither of us spoke about it, and when Madame Jeanne came to *"faire le ménage"* she dusted it and put it into the cupboard.

In the afternoon Georges came to have tea with us, and we had many interesting things to tell each other. His Chinese had made progress, and he was in contact with some Jesuit Fathers in Belgium about the exact philosophical equivalents of certain Chinese metaphysical expressions. Georges had a congenital contempt for Orientalists, and all unreligious writers as such: thus he hated Gide and loved Claudel. He read Romain Rolland, however, because he wanted to know more about India. How he wished some more well-informed and balanced mind had written about these great saints of modern India, Sri Ramakrishna, Vivekananda, Aurobindo and Dayananda.

A little later, Lezo joined us. Lezo was a clever young Basque refugee who knew some eighteen languages. He had been the youngest elected president of the Basque Academy, but when he made his first inaugural speech about the need for teaching in the mother tongue, and substantiated it with multiple quotations from the Church Fathers, Franco's henchmen were there to listen. After three months of prison he was given *liberté surveillée,* but he escaped and was now doing linguistics at Aix University. His father sent him a little money in secret, which he supplemented by giving lessons in languages. He it was who taught Georges Sanscrit.

Lezo was deeply interested in Buddhism. He had been to Heidelberg to study Sanscrit, and there he had come under the influence of Badenspeizer, who preferred Buddhism to every other religion in the world. During the war Badenspeizer was a prisoner of war, first in Shanghai and later in Ceylon. He preferred the Little Vehicle, and so did Lezo. Of Vedanta Lezo knew but the name of Sankara.

The Sanscrit language has a *gambhiryatha,* a nobility that seems rooted in primary sound. For hour after hour I chanted verses, especially those of Bharthrihari, Kalidasa or Sankara, which created, as it were, an aura of emptiness around one and one felt the breath of oneself, saw the sight as it were of oneself. Even Georges, who seemed so angry with Indian incursions into Christendom and with Massis and others, was frightened of this new Catharism, even he used to sit lost in this primordial rhythm. Lezo, to exasperate his friend, once said, "You can hear how your church services came from this rhythm, just as the Christian monasticism of the Thebaid hermits rose in Alexandria at the same time as Buddhism was being preached. 'Since the time of good king Antiochus, and yet beyond Antiochus from other kings, to wit, Ptolemy, Antigonus, Mages and Alexander, thus too in the Empire of the Greeks, everywhere they follow the Law and the friend of the Law, that is to say the Buddha Sakyamuni,' " and so on. He would quote abstruse, and often absurd, texts. He was at once so learned and so boyish that nobody could take them too seriously or not give them any consideration at all. When someone quotes an unknown Nestorian text in Pahlevi and links it up with a more ancient tablet in Kharosthi; and when, coming down through the Greeks, he talks to you of the school of Alexandria and of Apollonius of Tyana, who went to India to meet the Brahmins and returned with his belly full of Vedantic wisdom; and when he concludes by saying that Saint Ambrose of Milan (333–97) wrote a treatise *De Moribus Brachmanorum* addressed to a certain Palladius, a Greek; you feel convinced that even if all this were true it should not be true. Georges, on the other hand, would rather, it might have seemed, go upward, vertically—for he was hungry for God, and this he preferred to the three-dimensional and historical excursuses of his colleague. It was Vedanta that really attracted Georges, the *Neti-Neti,* the "not-this, not-thisness," as he called it. Some of my most memorable experience of France is having sat hour after hour before this nervous, indrawn, grey-blue-eyed Georges, with his right hand always trembling as if he held the sword of the Crusader and his, "But God, but God, where is He, when Sankara says, '*Shivoham, Shivoham;* I am Shiva, I am Shiva'?"

"There is no one to say anything then," laughed Lezo. Though that was the only answer, coming as it did from Lezo, it gave one the impression he was quoting an author. And of course to prove that it was true he quoted some Buddhist saying of Vasubandhu or Nagarjuna, as if it were an answer from the Vedanta of Sri Sankara himself. The trouble with Lezo was he knew too much, and he understood little. I think the person who learnt most of all during these discussions was Madeleine.

For Madeleine knew the time had come for an important decision: there were many roads out of the forest—which was the one that led most naturally to where she should be? The war had given her the feeling that change is inevitable for man, and that whether you took one road or the other, whether the Germans were behind this hill or in that hamlet, lying beside the broken bridge and the river down below, the *chemin de cristal,* as she called it, depended not on some preconceived logic but on the logic of the moment: a strange, almost pure reasoning power, that gave you the answer and commanded your step. All it needed was to stay time for a while, and then walk down to your *clairière.*

So this Sanscrit recitation was like hearing one's own silence. Madeleine spoke little, partly from timidity, partly in pride, and whatever she said would always be the unexpected. In this she resembled Lezo, for both spoke from an irregular sense of logic, an inaccuracy not of knowledge but of decision.

And during the months that followed (for Lezo and Georges joined us at Montpalais, in Gascony, where we soon went for the summer) the impression remained with me that indecision brought out the most heroic in both of them. Lezo always said the most unusual thing spontaneously, like, "The Buddhists were surrealist—or let us say Dadaist?" and this would send Georges into a holy fury. Such frivolity should have been pardoned for, apart from the learning behind it, it was not so absurd. But in exasperation Georges would say something like, "You should be a journalist of philology or a trader in vocables!" Moved by the helplessness of Lezo, for he was innocent as a child, Madeleine would go into the kitchen and make some hot coffee.

But when Georges spoke, even if she sat cross-legged, Madeleine would bend forward, bring her two feet together and listen as one would to a hero, to a saint. For Georges spoke with the noble anguish of the believer, with the feeling that if God is not true he must be made true, and that if God could not be made true then must impious man be made to go through hellfire so that God might be, and in the image Georges had given the Supreme Being. Like Shatov, Georges could have said "I must, must believe in God."

His sincerity was moving: one felt he bore the heavy history of humanity on his bent back. He carried our sorrows and our stupidities, rags that we threw on his back, as he went along the street; the more you threw, the more he blessed, for in the earth, deep in the mud, in the shine of the dung-lice and in the wound of the dog, in spittle and in dustbin-bone, in the face of a wriggling pink prostitute, would Georges find his proof of God. For him, to be was to know evil existed, to acknowledge sin was to be already at the ladder of the divine. *"Dieu est, parce que le mal est,"* he used to repeat. And I often thought Georges was like some municipal street-cleaner in the Middle Ages, who after carrying the dirt on his back would make a bonfire on the other side of the rampart, and having warmed himself would look into the round space, cross himself and see God. That

Georges had seen God you could see from the pleroma of his face.

Madeleine threw all her rags on Georges, as though she were helping someone to be himself. And she felt much lighter after this performance. She hated him to be so impervious: Georges seemed to have only metaphysical interests. When, at Montpalais, we went out on our evening walks Lezo would stick to me, for Lezo wanted to know more of India, of Sanscrit, Buddhism, Jainism, the Lingayats; even the religion and the language of the Todas; and he knew more about India than I did myself. Georges and Madeleine would go off on some quiet mountain footpath, step by step, as if Georges had not only one arm but one leg as well. Sometimes when he stood before a boulder on the path, lost in some discourse of his own, Madeleine would help him as she would a father—though he was only thirty-one—and give him a hand to cross over to the other side.

She cared for his presence a great deal, did Madeleine, and the respect she showed him was not altogether happy for a Brahmin husband to bear. She felt that here was a man that possessed a secret knowledge of something, some magic that could make mountains move, or the seas recede. And Georges was too distant and too whole to think he had any other feeling for Madeleine but the most brotherly; he almost felt a paternal affection for her, and besides he liked being with her. Her agnosticism was childish, he knew, for her innocence was so great. God could not but inhabit where innocence was. In fact the moment Madeleine acknowledged her innocence God would shine on her soul. He was there already. "You are not a saint, you are not a heathen—you're a girl," he would remark, just to exasperate her.

But when Georges went off on some abstruse theory of docetic Christology, or the theory of incarnation among the Monophysites, she would enjoy his tortuous logomachy as though it was so much time gained, and so much argument against some unnameable enemy.

MONTPALAIS is a little château on the top of a sharp *monticule,* as they say in France, a lone, eleventh-century bastion, with many gaping eyes and hands and feet, all torn to bits, first of all by the Saracens against whom it was built. The Comtes de Montpalais were cousins and vassals of the Ducs de Montségur, and when the Cathar heresy came the Comte rose against his own overlord, joined the Dominicans—he had meanwhile married Isobel de Navarre—and fought with such violence that even today, in the region, they say "courageous as Celuy de Montpalais," meaning headstrong as an ass.

The castle was fortified again during the wars of religion, Comte Henri de Montpalais having joined Henri IV, and when this liberal-hearted prince went to Paris and was crowned King, there was Monseigneur Henri, Comte de Montpalais, first as Adjutant-General in the Royal Cavalry, and later as Minister of Marine. He enriched himself thus with booty from the Spaniards, but because of some strange streak of cruelty in him his wife left him and ran away; later he was shut up in the tower, on the second floor, where they say he still walks about in the costume of the Grenadiers.

Apart from Isobel de Navarre the women in the château were never very interesting, it would seem, except another Isobel, daughter of Louis de Montpalais; Isobel who though so near to Spain would visit Montaigne in his country house, write verses in the Italian manner, and was known to have ridden a horse in battle. The story of her lovers is the stuff of all the poetry round Montpalais, and when a girl is beautiful they call her Isobel-Marie, for by adding the name of the Virgin they feel she will remain in virtue. All she did for the château was to give it an

Italian entrance, but when the Revolution came they just couldn't tolerate anything outlandish; thus of the famous Italian double curve of steps there is nothing left but a bit of stone that juts out of the first floor right beneath the central balcony of the main hall.

Today you enter the château from the kitchen, for after the Revolution nothing very much remained of the castle. The estate was bought by some bourgeois from Condom, and from generation to generation the family added horrors to make themselves feel at home, till mercifully one day a little daughter playing in the stables set fire to the hay outside, and for days on end, they say, Montpalais was one block of fire; you can still see the charred steps at the back and many charred beams. They offered the place then to anyone who wanted it, and some rich peasants from La Romieu bought the hill and the land, almost for nothing. The buildings served to keep hay and wheat and bottles of armagnac. But during the Occupation, like many such old châteaux that came to life again, it was bought by some northern refugees from Laon, who made it comfortable with doors, windows and balustrade. They must have had such nice taste: it was difficult to realize that only forty years before the whole structure had gone up in flame.

When the war was over, Robert Fern, an English painter, bought it, to be in the sunshine of France but not among the "Picassos"; he fitted it up with the necessary modern conveniences, and added to it all the English sense of comfort. He did not live there much, except in winter, for in summer he preferred to go yachting all over the Mediterranean. We had met Robert at Saint-Rémy among the Cubists and Madame Férrol had such love for India that she often asked us over. When we wanted to go somewhere for the summer she suggested Montpalais, and Robert Fern was only too happy to let it to any decent people. He took only a nominal rent—all we could afford—and left us his servants, his horses, his cows, and even his canvases to admire. Cubism is not entirely in my line of understanding, but Madeleine and Georges would stand for hours before some portrait of a lady in a tub, which had nothing to say for itself other than that its quadrangles and its pentagons were of the most curious and coloured admixture. But Robert was a fine person for all that, so civilized, so noble-spoken; the whole castle felt him and his clear presence.

I slept in the chapel. There was nothing left of the sanctuary but its niche for *l'eau bénite,* and over my door was a very lovely cross. Lezo jumped to the conclusion—for the cross had here and there some little twists and scratches making it look like a swastika—that the chapel must secretly have been used by the Cathars. The swastika, that emblem of the Aryans, was brought from Central Asia by the Nestorians, the Bogomils and the Cathars, so that before Hitler had any knowledge of it, all the Basque and many Béarnais houses had this noble symbol on their outer walls.

"Your anti-heretic, Henri de Montpalais, must have been pretty much of a heretic, like all the people in these parts at one time; and like many noblemen who preferred when the battle was lost to save their skin rather than be burnt at the stake, he must have joined the Bishop of Auch as an afterthought. As for his heroism, it must have come, as with so many others of his kind, not from conviction, but from wanting to be convinced. *Veni, Creator Spiritus . . .*"

Lezo was an incorrigible cynic, to whom human history, indeed mankind, was one large question of grammar and dates. For the rest he believed, like most Spaniards, that man is a fine animal. There is something of the Arab tradition in this division of life into enjoyment—and God.

Lezo occupied the large northern room, the one used by Henri de Montpalais himself, and he always had curious dreams there. How much of it was his own invention—for like most Latins he could enjoy a story simply for its own sake—or how much of it was true, was difficult to say. He would sometimes call in Marie, the maid, to bear witness, and Marie would describe in the most elaborate and emphatic way how she had a similar dream of the Comte riding wildly into battle, stopping suddenly and shouting, "Cowards, give me a glass of water." Water, of course, could only have meant death—for wine meant life.

Georges had a small room in the corner by the stables. He liked to live near the animals—it came, he said, from his Russian sense of intimacy with all living things. But I think that like people who love concentration he wanted the isolation in which one feels the intimacy of one's own presence. In a larger place you become one with the fields and the sky, and your eyes seek the height of the mountains.

For the Pyrenees were only a hundred kilometres away, and on a good summer day it would look from Montpalais as though you had only to go right ahead on the white charger to come to this straight wall of white mountain and the heavy Saracen.

> Au porz d'Espagne en est passet Rollanz
> Sur Veillantif sur son cheval curant . . .
> Vers Sarrazins regardent fierement
> Et vers Français humle et dulcement,
> Si leur ad dit un mot curteisement.

From the tower room, where Madeleine slept, you could contemplate the withdrawn arrogance of a mountain that seemed more a bastion of Spain than a fortress of France.

Outside in the fields such lovely blue and green vines stood, and aubergines grew in the garden behind. Sometimes, as in India, the heat rose and one smelt the acridity of grass. Often when my cough did not trouble me much I woke early; then I would jump on Blanche, the mare, and go romping down to the river. It was as if Blanche could speak to me what no man could. Not that she understood my problem, but she could tell me to contemplate the Guadelupe, the little white stream that meandered with such tranquillity on the yellow countryside.

What after all was the problem? Where exactly did it begin? For Madeleine had never been sweeter. There was nothing I needed which she did not know beforehand, and bring to me: my medicine after lunch, my handkerchief when I started on a walk, my pencil, duly sharpened and laid on my notebook—for I continued to work on my Albigensians. Yet she herself was not there. She was nowhere. Sometimes she used to incarnate in a glance, in the smile of a second—when Georges spoke.

But Lezo she began to detest, and wished to God he had never come. For Lezo, like all Spaniards—though he hated being called a Spaniard and insisted he was a Basque—could not help being somewhat frivolous, either with Madeleine or sometimes even with Marie, the healthy-looking servant girl. Marie's young man came only on Sunday afternoons and in between Lezo had his little moments of innocent fun. Sometimes while on a walk he would sing, *"Oh, ciel d'amour!"* at the sight of a young girl with her pail under a tap and then suddenly would make eyes at Madeleine, as though to say, "Isn't she splendid?" The more Lezo felt isolated, the more his vulgarity appeared. But he was no fool. One evening when he said something quite crude—at coffee after dinner—Madeleine went straight up to her room. He understood, and in a few days left with a stupid excuse. He said he was too near the Spanish frontier, and one never knew with the French police . . . Of course, we all knew that Franco's henchmen had better things to do—bigger fish to capture than this poor philologist Lezo.

Lezo's departure, though it seemed so inevitable, created an entirely new situation. Looking back at my diaries of those days —for I started writing down things to myself about myself, at Montpalais; it gave some mental relief to see myself in black handwriting against white paper; it made me more objective to myself—I was saying, looking over those diaries I have come across some bewildering remarks.

August 3. "Virtue is more difficult to accept than vice. Vice has a way of saying, 'Here I am; take me, and forget the rest.' Virtue has a way of saying, 'Here I am; you cannot take me, and you cannot forget me.' Virtue seems to defeat itself, whereas vice conquers.

"This is not strictly true. Lezo, before he left, seemed so intimate, so personal, so generous; as though if you asked he would give his cloak, and bow before you in homage to your presence. But Madeleine is like the choking in my breath. The doctors say the less I cough the better, but when I have coughed little, one day it rushes up with such a burst that my whole bed is covered with blood. And then Madeleine, like her saintly namesake, sits me back and, with such beautiful eyes, wipes the blood off my face, and carries the basin as though she were carrying the blood of a martyr. Sainthood, I think, is natural to man or woman— not virtue.

"Yesterday when Madeleine had tucked me back to bed and had stayed a while to see whether my breathing were regular and normal, and went back to the central hall, I could hear her whispering voice all through the night talking to Georges. I heard them discuss my illness with deep concern: not for three years had such an effusion of blood appeared. Georges has a voice so grave and deep, especially at night; it makes one think it's the walls that speak a prophecy.

"Madeleine looks much more beautiful now: her virtue makes her conspicuous. She reads a great deal out of Saint John of the Cross, and about Buddhism. She feels happier with the latter, but prefers to read the Christian mystic with Georges. Now it is I who give her Sanscrit lessons. She had begun to loathe Sanscrit, she said, because of Lezo. But Georges has a different opinion: he thinks I 'feel' Sanscrit, I do not 'know' Sanscrit. Lezo, on the other hand 'knew' a language—and did not care whether it were Icelandic or Hebrew. The classical mind has a grandeur I shall never possess. I am too weak, so I see stars where others see planets."

August 17. "This week has been a glorious interlude. Georges has come so near to me. His gentle, vibrant, withdrawn presence makes one feel so selfish, so crude. How the Christian humility has beauty—even as some lovely women wear mourning because it makes them beautiful. The Brahmin, the Vedantin, has such arrogance. It was Astavakra who said, 'Wonderful, wonderful am I'; he with the eight deformations. Yes, one is wonderful— when one is not *one,* but the 'I.'

"Strange, as I myself go away from Buddhism it is Madeleine who gets deeper into it. She is moved by Buddhist compassion and poetry: it has, as she said, Christian humility without stupidity and blind belief; it has poetry without the smell of the crypt. Oh, the Christian love of relics! This body seems more worthy to the Christian after death than in life. Those who have no roof over their heads still buy space for a *caveau de famille,* says Madeleine. She knows what she is saying, for the family is talking a great deal about the famous *caveau de famille* at Saint-Médard. '*Caveau* for *caveau,*' says Madeleine, 'I would rather my bones felt the warmth of the southern sun than that the mist, penetrating through the earth, should form round globules of perspiration on my non-existent body. Oh!'

"For Madeleine there is an area which is not me that she fills with Christian longings, but she will not admit it. She thinks it is betraying me to praise Saint John of the Cross. But sometimes when they sit in the sun of the courtyard, and Georges and she discuss the Spanish mystic, she seems so tender and understanding that it is she who would teach Georges. Catholicism is in her blood. Not all Georges's fervour can give him the *instinct*—and religion is an instinct—that gives illumination to a line, a reference. Just the same way when she talks of Buddhism I feel the word *dukka* almost with the entrails dropping into my hand, whereas for her it is mere sorrow. *Dukka* is the very tragedy of creation, the sorrow of the sorrow that *sorrow is.*"

August 23. "Madeleine today came and sat near me on my bed. Outside the day was glorious—I could almost hear the parrots cry, or the monkeys leap from branch to branch of the peepul tree. She saw how happy I was. But it was with a happiness that knows life is a continuous jump from awareness to awareness, like a straight line is from point to point. In between is the knowledge of the perpetuity of life. Sorrow is the background of all moments, for moment means the transitory and the transitory is always sorrowful. I remembered Rilke.

"She was so happy herself; she kissed me on the lips as never she had. She gave the whole of herself to me, as though it were a gift that my life might be spared. But I am not so ill—that is the wonder of it. I was told that when Mother was ill they needed to have a basin and a towel always by her. Mine is only a minor relapse. There is nothing to worry about.

"Madeleine does not love me. She wants me to be big and true that she may pour her love on me, as some devotee would want her Shiva or Krishna to be big and grand, that she might make a grand *abhishkea* with milk and honey and holy Ganges water. To anoint oneself in worshipping another is the basis of all love. We become ourself by becoming another."

August 24. "That Georges is leaving in three or four days oppresses me. Something in him was like a solid stone wall, on which Madeleine leant to love me. He must have prayed to his God a great deal. But Madeleine is happy; she hates confusions. She thinks Georges's God is something of a carnival god, with big teeth and terrible to see. 'In the Middle Ages,' she said, 'Georges would have been like that famous bishop who started counting his rosary the louder, that the torture of the heretic might be adequate. For the excellent bishop had said to the torturers, "He should be tortured until I hear his cry." So the bishop went on shouting to his Father that the sins of the Church might be forgiven.'

"Fanaticism is such a force. It takes you to sublimities and gives you the sense of the heroic, the impossible. The fanatics today become mountain-climbers. It is ultimately a form of spiritual vanity.

"Truth must be simple, natural and sweet."

August 26. "Georges came to me on Saturday, when Madeleine had gone down to Auch to buy provisions. He sat with ease and reverence as though he had long communed with God. He said:

" 'You know, Rama, I have a last request to make. I say it from the depths of my sinful heart. I am a Russian, you are an Indian. We both have the messianic madness of the race in us— for us only the Absolute counts. Living beside you, as I do these days, you cannot imagine how much your Brahminical "aura," as it were, helps to make me a better Christian. What we do with such an effort, such a desire for virtue, you do so spontaneously. What I admire is the frugality of your food, the generosity with which you open yourself to everyone and everything. Above all, and for a Christian what is fascinating, is your relationship with Madeleine. I have never seen a European couple act and behave with such innocence. The sin of concupiscence . . .' After that my mind went black. I would never have thought any intelligent man in the year 1951 could use such a crude word. It spoke more of Georges's deeper mind than anything he had said. I can still remember him saying, 'The sin of concupiscence!' I looked out into the sky, and saw the birds pecking away at the figs. I almost felt I should rise and throw a stone at them.

"There was a long silence. Then Georges said:

" 'Salvation is only for the baptized. You know how Maritain brought Péguy back to the Church. I tell you, Rama, there is no salvation, none, but in the Church of Christ.'

"He burst into tears, and his face shone as did Alyosha Karamazov's when *staritz* Zossima rose from his dead body and appeared to him, hallowed.

" 'I will always pray for you. Father Zenobias already prays for you. There is no hope but in the Church of Christ.' "

August 29. "Strange that *this* has left so deep a mark on me. Night after night I have opened my eyes and looking out of the window have seen the night birds active in the trees; far away some light has shone, even as it might from the Pyrenees, and I have been filled with a longing for God—to kneel, yes, to kneel and worship something that has such a nearness of presence, such intimacy, such historical authenticity.

"I can now understand the Muslim, for Mohammed was the last historical prophet of God. I realize that when the son of man comes to earth, he gives us the proof of God in a way that no religion of the pagans, be it Hindu or Greek, could ever offer. Shiva and Vishnu live in Kailas or Vaikuntha, and you may see them or not see them; and once seen they may again disappear. But religion with a prophet gives God a place in time, gives him a mother and father, even were he Virgin-born, and gives him friends and enemies. Judas more than Saint John made Christ holy. You know Saint John in the same way that in some families they say, 'Oh, the grandmother of Saint Louis was a La Rochefoucauld,' and it is immediately understood that Saint Louis must have been true, and that you yourself had fought in the Crusades and won back the oriflamme of Jerusalem. Historicity is part of human certainty—it makes man real. If Christ—or Mohammed—were not historical there could be no God."

August 30. "I came to work on my Albigensians and unknowingly my mind wanders away and I start speaking of myself to myself. And history makes involutes to prove me. Lord, how can one ever get out of oneself!

"The historical presence of Christ and Mohammed, I was saying, is implicative of God. This is the true explanation, if ever, of Christian heresy. The Cathars, when pressed to answer if they did indeed believe in Christ, were not always so sure as when asked if they believed in the Holy Ghost. What is uncertain is an enemy of the people. It is a sort of spiritual Darwinism. Christianity, Islam and Judaism belong here, but Taoism, Buddhism and Vedanta live in the chaos of the present: the present seen as present could never be chaos. That is why Indians wrote no history; even Buddhism was too historical, and therefore too psychological, for India. Vedanta triumphed like Mahayana Buddhism—so near to Vedanta—did, and Taoism against Confucianism.

"The Cathars, were they Vedantins? They feared no death, they believed in the Pure, they believed in Truth. The Church believed in God.

"For these few days how happy I feel in the ancient fold of the Church. I feel protected, I feel confirmed in my humaneness. I feel truly happy.

"Georges has lent me Berdiaev's book on Dostoevsky and this is what I fell upon tonight:

Tuer Dieu, c'est en même temps tuer l'homme. . . . Ni Dieu ne dévore l'homme, ni l'homme ne disparaît en Dieu; il reste lui-même jusqu'à la fin et pour la consommation des siècles. C'est ici que Dostoievsky se montre chrétien au sens le plus profond du mot.

"How I wish I could tell Madeleine I have begun to worship her God."

August 31. "Yesterday as evening was falling Madeleine brought me home and went out again to have a longer walk. I came back to my room, remembered it was an old chapel, and turning towards the window knelt and prayed, saying inconsequent things. (My Latin is too poor to make a prayer, and only in Latin can one feel truly Christian.) Madeleine must have felt something, for she came back unexpectedly, saying she'd forgotten her cane and didn't want to be bitten by Monsieur Robert's dogs, but when she came she knew she knew me. There was a common area where we were together, and for the first time. I almost felt she would give me some cotton and say, 'Rama, there are a lot of bacteria here. Take care.' Then she would kneel by me—just my bride. Yesterday I felt married to her as never before.

"Which explains why she came to me last night. Perhaps, too, because Georges has left she knew that apart from the innocent servants nobody would think of Monsieur and Madame in bed together. Madeleine felt the thought of another was even more vile than the look of another. I think she has liked Georges less these last few days; when talking of Saint John of the Cross he dwelt so much on temptation. Womanhood has been swelling up in her for some days. Last night she rose as she always has, with a single gesture, and on my sickbed in the chapel of Montpalais, when the night was clear as one's knowledge of oneself, she became my wife again and I called her many sweet names. I also called her my Isobel, and she gave a laugh that the mountains might have seen as a ripple of lightning.

"I am such a different man today. For to wed a woman you must wed her God."

While we were at Montpalais Oncle Charles came to us on his annual visit: pilgrimage to the Brahmins, he called it. This sounded all the more absurd as we were on the main route to Saint-Jacques de Compostelle, and down below in the Val de Biran you could see many a black cross of pilgrims who must have lost their lives with the fever of the marshes, or from hunger; or even the wolves might have jumped on them and eaten them for Friday lunch, as the *curé* would say. The whole district was filled with little chapels, opened but once a year when the *curé* brought the chalice and the cross, and clothed Sainte Élise or Sainte Rosalie for another year. Old peasants from the country, with lace bonnets and beards on their faces—one woman was ninety-seven years old—came murmuring things to the patron goddess of their fields. Under the loop of sky that covered the yellow of the land and the snow on top of the mountains, ran a series of small *pogs*—as they call little hills in those parts—and by tree and rivulet goats browsed as the prayers were said. We would take fresh-cut grass and a few violets to Sainte Rosalie. Oncle Charles was to be with us at the *fête du pays.*

"We leave Place Saint-Nicolas at nine in the morning," he had written, "and the house will be in charge of Catherine this time. She has to finish her exams the coming year—she is twenty-three, and she cannot go on studying any longer. She never looks at a man; she never looks at a thing; everything is jurisprudence for her. She loves to look after my work, so she will manage the office while I am away. She's happy Madeleine will come back with us. Though Madeleine is just five years older, Catherine talks of her as if she were her mother.

"Strange, sensitive child. That she should be mine . . .

"Well, as for our arrivals and departures. We leave Place Saint-Nicolas, as I said, at nine in the morning. Zoubie may make it a little late—you know what she is like. By one o'clock anyway we should be at Angoulême. And by four or half past, you should see our 'angel of resurrection' mount up your *puy.* I am excited to be back in clear pure sunshine again, with the smell of mountain all about one. Tell Madeleine if she's not more beautiful this time Oncle Charles will make her eat a *foie-de-veau*—the *veau* slit in the garden, under her nose. *Oh, la Brahmine . . .*! Zoubie and I kiss you both tenderly. Charles."

He is the whole of himself, is Oncle Charles, whatever he does. Pity he did not take more to music, for they say even today he could go and sit in the cathedral and play the organ, if the organist were ill. He was always dressed impeccably; and for his age—he was fifty-seven then—he looked clearly fifteen years younger. Zoubie was a fat, big bunch. She was called Zoubeida because her father, an employee in the railways, had gone to Paris for his honeymoon, and that was in the curious nineties of the last century; he chanced on an operetta called *Zoubeida ou l'Esclave de Perse,* and it was about a slave girl, Zoubeida, who wished to wed the Prince Soulieman one day—and she did.

Zoubie was a great lady, once divorced, for her husband had run off with someone much younger. He was seven years younger than herself. Oncle Charles was a timid widower. He courted Zoubie for five or six years before she yielded to his requests and married him. But Tante Zoubie had such fantasy, such generosity. It was she who welcomed Madeleine back to the family, not Oncle Charles. He was always afraid of what his old crone of a mother in Arras would say.

"She will never understand this, never. And after all she's so near the grave. Let her die in peace."

Though this was partly the truth, Madeleine once said to me, "You will never understand us, the French. There is piety, of course, and compassion. But Lord, there is so much calculation. I tell you, virtue is a part of French bourgeois economy."

Oncle Charles knows well, for that is his job, how some old women when the fear of death comes nearer simply transfer their "goods" to the holy Church; just to make sure, not only that Paradise awaits them on the other side, but also that there will be a nice sermon pronounced at their funeral, and the right novena said in their name ever after. Whether this be true or not, Oncle Charles was frightened to hurt his old mother. Whatever happened and wheresoever he might be, on September the twenty-eighth, Oncle Charles had to be in Arras to kiss his mother and spend a week in her company. During that week she would never mention her daughter-in-law, and all letters to Oncle Charles from Zoubie had to be addressed poste restante. Strange the way Oncle Charles—he who held such an important position in Haute Normandie—should tremble as he talked of his mother. How different, I thought, was Grandfather Kittanna.

Of course "the dark angel of resurrection"—that huge Citröen *quinze-chevaux*—sang herself up the hill before Madeleine had had time to dress. She had become so beautiful, had Madeleine, as though you could pluck riches out of her face, that had I been superstitious I should have been afraid to take her out of an evening. She was so childlike that no sooner did she hear the car outside than she ran to the window, pins in hand, and her golden hair actually fell out of the window like a bunch of grapes. For an Indian this golden hair seemed always something unearthly, magical, made of moonbeam and of raven-silver.

Once the vegetables and honey and butter of Normandy were spread out on the kitchen table—the kitchen being on the ground floor was the coolest room in summer—and while Marie was taking up the luggage, Oncle Charles told us of family matters.

"Mother thinks you've married a Maharaja, Mado," he said, looking at me, "else there were no reason why you should marry a man from Les Indes. *'Mon auteur dit,'* she would say, and then go on to tell me about the castes and the kings, and of the Vishnu, Brahma and Shiva that some schoolbooks of the fifties of the last century had taught her in her convent. But she cannot believe India is no more British India, nor you, Rama, dark as a Negro, and that you will not make Madeleine one of your concubines—for you must have a palace—and then make her mount your pyre and be burnt with your dead body. She's not so much worried about the marriage, but she's worried about burial and resurrection. Poor woman! Let her be what she is."

Oncle Charles was not a man to say things inconsequently: he was too much of a *notaire* to say the first thing that came to his tongue. There was much in his mind that Madeleine started guessing almost immediately.

In the afternoon, when the sun was already slanting towards the Pyrenees, we took our hats and our country canes and walked down the hill to the cool of the river. Oncle Charles, as he walked in front of me with Madeleine, talked of many things. He was anxious about her future: whether she would stay in France or in India. Now that my father was dead it seemed inevitable to him that she should go back with me. True, of course, now with the air services distances were abolished; ". . . but yet, a heart is a heart, and there's Grandmother at Arras. She's been asking strange questions too. Before she dies, she wishes for the peace of her soul to know many, many things. And she wants to make a gift to us all, Madeleine. The *curé* has been worrying us a great deal about the growth of the city. He says that since the cemetery of Saint-Médard is so near the city, the Government is bringing in all sorts of restrictions. Before the municipality brings the new law into action land must be bought. They are damn' socialists, you know, at Saint-Médard. The municipality is playing on speculation. Prices are going up. So far, there have been only seven places in the *caveau*," said Oncle Charles, and suddenly added, "Look at the swallows, I never saw such beautiful blue wings ever in my life."

There was a long silence. Then he added, "Mado, Grandmother is very old. To give pain to her is like giving pain to God."

Madeleine answered that she had nothing to say.

I said to her that evening, as she came to the room before going to wash, that I did not have anything to say either. To belong for ever to this Christian earth of this Christian land was no doubt a privilege and a mark of honour. But for some reason Madeleine put her face against my cheek, and a tear from her eye fell on my face. She wished I would say "No" for her. So I simply said, "Tell Oncle Charles we're soon going back to India." She replied, "No, that is not true."

"Yes, it is true. For me India is Freedom."

"And to me," said Madeleine, "India is Paradise."

Oncle Charles in the house was like an elder brother, and Tante Zoubie looked after us as though we were too young to look after the cruder things of life, such as washing and the market, and getting the house cleaned.

"There, Marie, on that staircase, there's a cigarette butt which must come from the time of Henry the Plantagenet," she would say, and Marie had never been so active.

Marie had grown somewhat sad since Lezo had left, for he must have made her many grand promises. She had grown lazy and rather irritable. But with the good humour of Zoubie she worked like a happy slave. Besides, Tante Zoubie made such nice *cassoulets* and *boeuf saignant,* it wasn't like being with us poor vegetarians—"*les herbivores,*" she called us. Servants like to obey those who really know what is right and what is wrong. I cannot make a *pankha*-boy obey, for I cannot understand why anyone should obey anyone. They should do their duty, their *dharma*. This is true obedience.

Oncle Charles loved to ride Blanche in the evening, and how

the mare neighed as soon as she saw him. Sometimes of an evening when we three were too lazy to go down to the river, and just walked down to the *clairière* behind the house to sit among the thyme and the marjoram, Tante Zoubeida would tell us fantastic stories of her travels with her first husband. He had been a professor, whom the other war, the war of 1914, had turned into a minor diplomat, and we rolled and rolled in laughter at the pomposity of the Germans, the stupidity of the Poles and the Ruthenians, the backwardness of the British. "They never wash their back," she said; "they wash their shirt fronts. So that if you want to smell le Comte de Saint-Simon you have only to sit next to an English diplomat!" And so on, and so on. When we returned home, and Marie brought the lantern and gave us homemade gin from the choicest of juniper, there would be Oncle Charles riding up the hill, his portly figure somewhat softened by the gentility of the moon. No, Oncle Charles could never look anything but a *notaire,* and he could only smell of hay and honeysuckle, and acrid French tobacco. He had given the horse a nice wash, and she seemed so much the wiser for it. She stood above us silent, as Oncle Charles, who loved to study birds, told us of the trees he had climbed to watch the nests of swallows and blackbirds.

Pierre, the peasant boy, came to take the horse away, and Oncle Charles of a sudden looked paternal. He was worried about my cough, and was happy I was going to Pau for three weeks. There was no better place for weak lungs than Pau.

"After all," he said, "we must be weak somewhere. I am weak in the liver, and that is why I go to Vichy once in three years. Yet I can eat a huge gigot, as you see, and can sleep like a barn."

It is difficult to say what it was that made me happy, whether it was the happiness of Madeleine or my own. But now and again when I was alone in the bathroom taking a shave, I would look at my eyes and see that there was something velveteen, something ringed, as though deeper down was sorrow.

Letters that came from India did not brighten me either. Saroja was not too happy at home. Now that father was dead, and with Little Mother not really so much older than herself, she felt she, too, was the mistress of the house. Little Mother never spoke to me of this, but Saroja's temper was revealed in her letters. "The forces at home are not meant for peace. I long for the day when I can follow Father," she wrote. On the other hand Sukumari was full of vitality. She had been elected secretary of the school debating society, and wanted to become a second Mrs. Pandit. Meanwhile she asked me to send her books on Marxism. "The poverty of our Motherland could only be eradicated with the abolition of every form of caste and distinction. I have read some Marx. But you, Brother, who know so much about all this, tell me what to read." It was strange for me to think that my sister was reading Karl Marx.

But life is so much more intelligent than we care to understand. Marxism, Hinduism, Christianity, Islam, Hitlerism, the British Commonwealth, the Republic of the United States of America: all are so many names for some unknown principle, which we feel but cannot name. For all the roads, as the *Gita* says, lead but to the Absolute.

I was also anguished, I think, for my Christian *becoming*.

In the recesses of our being there are great tracts of the unknown, pastures of the invisible, in which we the familiar, the sons of the family, go driving our cattle. The land knows it is us not from boundary-stone to boundary-stone, but as it were from bush and boulder and tree, so that even the evening birds know where to roost, and in which register of God their names be writ, for their nesting and for the birth of their young ones. Civilization is nothing but the familiarity with which we go into this inner property, cultivated and manured from age to age. The rivers have washed alluvial soil to it and the rains have poured and gone down to the sea, and brought back, as it were, the perfume of the same land; so that when our mangoes fall and we eat, we know it is the product of a thousand years. Wars may have come and famine, the Muslims may have conquered us and after them the British, but there is a common area, an acknowledged landholding, that is for ever ours, so that when we carry the harvest to our village temple, Kenchamma Herself knows we bring Her Herself—She Herself seen as the many, many. The gods that reside in us are of an ancient making; age after age our ancestors have copulated, and a bit more of each god grew in us as we grew up, as someone in France saying, "I'm a Montmorency," makes you think at once of Saint Louis and the Templars of Malta. It saves time and education to know what your kingdom is rather than measure the frontiers of another, however noble. To bring in a new god is like creating a new pine tree. The grafting of many an age could never give you the larch of the Alps. The Brahmin, the Brahmin, I said to myself—and to convince myself of familiarity with myself I chanted Sri Sankara again.

> *Mano-budhi Ahankara Chittani naham . . .*
> Not Mind, nor Insight, Mineness nor Substance . . .

I was almost in tears.

Perhaps I was growing weaker. My appetite had gone bad and my attempt to get fatter brought no visible results. I was no more than seventeen when the doctor killed the disease in its infancy, as he thought, by giving egg and port and making me go on long morning walks. I had recovered in due course, and the X-ray showed that there was nothing to fear. The sputum, too, seemed normal. But now I was seven years older, and the weight of the family was perhaps on me. Maybe the death of Pierre was something that no love could heal. Or perhaps it was only that I was tired. Oncle Charles was a fine person, but he had too much vitality.

I was happy to see how cheerful Madeleine looked. Madeleine herself found no difference in me. She was so close to me, she felt, when we lay side by side and heard the frogs that came in with the rains. Or when the cicadas sang through the whole night, she wondered if India was like that, warm and very full of countable sounds. She said for the first time she felt protected by me. Tante Zoubie remarked that never had she seen a couple so happy. "I never thought man could ever be so happy. Oh you Brahmin boy, who came to make this Charentaise happy," and she would press me to her enormous bust. Tante Zoubie was romantic, and she loved to ask Madeleine, awkwardly and gently, details that no woman would herself tell. "Be happy, my child, be happy. You are such a lucky girl. Rama reminds me of a giraffe, which has grown its neck through centuries, trying to feed on the tree of Paradise. You will now have a beautiful daughter, and what will you call her?" asked Tante Zoubie.

"Esclarmonde," said Madeleine.

"What a beautiful name."

"Why, Tante Zoubie, it's a name of these parts. Esclarmonde de Perelha is one of the famous figures of Albigensian history. She it was who protected the luminous Grail when the Roman armies were marching up Montségur."

"Anyway, what will you call the next one?"

"Why talk of that now, Tante Zoubie?"

"Well, you know what we say: Time in love goes quicker than the moon."

"Well, we'll call her Isobel. There was an Isobel, Countess of Montpalais."

Tante Zoubie did not carry the conversation any further, said Madeleine. She wanted to be the patron saint of our love, and maybe she thought she would have a right to perpetuate her own name. But my thoughts were elsewhere, and Madeleine knew me too well not to guess where I was.

"We'll call him Ranjit," she added, pushing my hair up and putting her hand deep into my pocket; "for he will look just like you, and though Ranjit is no Brahmin name, I know, let him be a hero, a Chevalier—a Rajput," she said. "You know, Rama, women must have names from their mother's side and sons from their father's side. It makes everything easier for marriage." And she laughed.

I was happy with Madeleine. I could be bent by the knowledge she had of me—the knowledge of my silences, the vigorous twists of my mental domain. But further down, where the mind lost itself in the deeper roots of life, she waited like an Indian servant at the door, for me to come out. Then would she know what was told.

The next day was Sunday. I took the whole family to Auch for the eleven o'clock Mass. The Cathedral of Auch is such a silly elucubration of black and Gothic flourishes—it looks awkward, unavowed, as though men had built it, so to say, between famine and sleep and plague, in the slow nightmare of living. How civilized, on the other hand, the beautiful building on the opposite side of the market looked. An eighteenth-century structure, no doubt, with the noble lines of the triangular pediment and four Italian windows, but altogether of such a light severity. There was a truth about it that made my morning rich. Madeleine said to me, "You know I knelt today for the first time in months. I never thought of cotton-wool or bacteria. Tell me I have improved. Haven't I?"

Tante Zoubie said, just to exasperate her husband, "Madeleine, I was admiring your profile. How beautiful you looked in that green hat of yours. You must teach Catherine to dress. She dresses like the *notaire's* clerk—like Madame Aufusson, in fact. And if she ever marries she should have a son and he should be called Titus Levitas, Master of Jurisprudence."

What could you do with Tante Zoubie's tongue—it was like that. "You can't stitch it with a gunnybag needle," I once said to Madeleine, quoting an Indian saying. "Nor with hellfire," she answered. "I think in fact Auntie would enjoy hell."

But she was a dear creature, and how early she rose in the morning, to see that Marie prepared the best of toast while she made coffee for *"les enfants."* While she was with us she made us many types of jam—one even a jam of figs—and she put half into my car and half into the "angel of resurrection." Eating sixteen pots of jam in twenty days, I said to myself, would need more than a hero. "What remains you can take back to Aix; I'm sure Madeleine would be happy to eat it. And you will remember your aunt, children, won't you? Good-bye, Rama, good-bye."

The "angel of resurrection" left first. Madeleine had such joy on her face, seated between her uncle and her aunt—they all sat in front. "Look after yourself," said Oncle Charles, "and we shall look after Madeleine, and send her back to you, a plump and healthy-looking thing. We'll make her eat a lot of beef."

"Oh, Uncle, just as I am leaving Rama!" protested Madeleine. She kissed me simply. She still looked very lovely in her black suit, the amber necklace falling just between her breasts, and her hair all turned into a big shining bun at the back. She looked true.

I wandered about a bit in the house, went to the chapel and

took leave of it with very real pain, and looked out once again at the fig tree and Blanche, who stood grazing in the fields. Blanche looked up and it was a pity I could not rub her with dry grass, nor take her to the stream for a drink of water. Marie filled the thermos with milk and coffee, and I wish I could somehow have consoled her. "When you want to marry, let me know," I said; "Madame and I will help you to complete your trousseau."

"Oh, Monsieur is very kind," said Marie. "But it will not be for a long time to come. We say here, to buy a vineyard or to slip on a wedding ring, you need more gold than the cross of Saint Catherine." And she added, "What is yours you cannot lose, and what is not yours even the Good God will take away!"

The day looked broad and very full of breath. Marie brought me a comb and a handkerchief that Madeleine had forgotten in her bed: her hair was so long, she needed a comb wherever she went, did Madeleine. I put them in my pocket, as a gift from Marie. What genuflexions of heart the simple, the true—who live with the trees, the fields and the animals—perform.

"Next year, sir. And I shall tell Monsieur Robert how well the house has been kept. If all his friends were so considerate . . ."

"*Au revoir*, Marie. And tell Pierre on my behalf that Monsieur Charles thinks Blanche has worms in her belly, the way she rubs her tail against the wall constantly, and sneezes on touching water. He must take her to a *vétérinaire*. Good-bye."

"*Au revoir, Monsieur.*"

Montpalais was behind me, and I did not want to see it again from the top of the road that twists round Biran. A year was a long way off, and how much the earth would have turned on her base, and how many birds would have gone from Gascony to Africa and the Arctic and back for nesting again by then. The Korean War was still going on, and who could say what the mad world might do. France, that country of peace and courtesy, had known so many wars of late that even as the Korean trouble started, the whole countryside was stock-piling, sugar and paraffin, potatoes, wine and motorcar tyres. As I drove through the villages the doors were not so widely open, nor were people so carefree as they watched the elders play bowls. But when I neared the Spanish frontier more richness and gaiety came into the life of the people, for they lived on two frontiers, and the noble Pyrenees gave one the assurance that war would never come as far as here. What Napoleon could not do, nor Hitler, the Russian could never do. And from Pau you could look at the Pyrenees and know that to be strong one must be pure as snow. Madeleine then seemed never to have left me.

I STAYED at the Hôtel d'Angleterre. It opened on to the north, and from my room the Pic du Midi seemed but a leap, a touchable stretch of murmuring, unsubsiding green. From the mornings the mist rose and floated about the sun, then hid itself like a serpent, and by afternoon great big trails of cloud coloured the sky. The evenings were intimate—and as September was cold, there were not too many people on the Promenade des Pyrénées. Life seemed as though reality had spread itself out with a pneumatic curve, and I and the mountain were points in some known awareness. The sun, when he did set, had a familiarity that I had never observed either in the Himalayas or in the Alps, as if he was a private planet that revolved at our command, for our benefit, and to our entire knowledge. The sun knew you and you knew the sun, and when he set it was just like a father, a friend leaving you, telling you you had just to call and he would come, if you needed him. No wonder that under this familiar sun Don Quixote thought the windmills were knights or that d'Artagnan was the valiant knight of France.

By day my lungs were filled with the sun's kindness, but when night came, and in the darkness the valley rose and filled the air, there was a sense of immensity, of a truth that was hid but too long; one felt that the sun indeed had cheated us, had made us characters of a *commedia dell'arte,* that night was a vacancy which

no sun could ever fill, no valley ever bear. There was an *absence*
that seemed familiar; known, seeable but not with these eyes,
knowable but not with the mind; something young, and of a
single elevated melody. The château of Henri IV might be Early
Renaissance, but there was a Rajput touch about Pau, something
of Chitor, and a queen that would sing of a Rathor. Dreams, too,
I had, wonderful muslin-like dreams, made of purest cotton white,
and beneath which shone breasts like the down of doves. I could
hear the whole night full of song, and sometimes I would wake
myself beating time with my hands, and feel warm with the coming sun of India.

> *Khelatha, nandā kumār,* —
> *Kumararé*
> He plays, does he, son of Nanda,
> He plays in Brindavan.

How very far seemed Madeleine at such moments. In fact, she
had said to me that if the X-ray were unsatisfactory and the
doctors had the slightest fear it was serious, I had just to send her
a wire and she would come down immediately. Otherwise, she
was going to be driven to Paris by Oncle Charles—for Catherine
was now to think of getting married. She had to be taught how to
dress, and even how to use lipstick, and how to make up; and
Madeleine was supposed to buy her the right dresses, take her to
the right hairdressers, and buy her the right handbags and earrings. There was to be a ball at the Hôtel de Ville, and Oncle
Charles wanted her to be beautiful for the occasion; he himself
had a special suit made. For nothing in the world would I have
liked Catherine to miss her ball—or not to be pretty enough,
for she was a lovely girl—and have her possible marriage put off
because one piece of my body, and a small portion of it, round
as a lamb's head, would not pump properly. Therefore when
Dr. Drager gave me the result of the X-ray I was so happy I almost sang with the sun, and wired Madeleine that the report gave
no need for alarm; good luck for Catherine's ball!

Two days later there came a beautiful letter from Madeleine.
She had had terrible dreams the first few days—of serpents and

elephants and of India, and she was saying to me, "Take me away from here, away to Grandmother!" And when she went to Arras, it was not the same house, nor was it Grandmother there but her father standing, dressed as an Indian soldier. The whole thing was terrible, and someone was cremated somewhere, and Madeleine left the cathedral a well-dressed Hindu bride with kunkum on her forehead and her ear-pendants touching her jaws. But my wire had put an end to her worries: she immediately started thinking of the ball, and she and Catherine drove down in Oncle Charles's car to Arras and paid a visit to Grandmother.

Grandmother had treated Madeleine as though she had never left Rouen and as if Madeleine had never been married. "When do you go back to Paris?" she had asked. She wanted to believe that nothing had changed. She gave Madeleine a chain that her father had had made when he was engaged, and which was to be given at Madeleine's engagement. "Take it, my child and be happy. I am old, and one never knows what can happen to an old thing of eighty-seven." After a moment's silence she had added: "And when you get married, there's that diamond brooch that your father brought when he came back from Turkey, after having constructed some railway there. It is Arabian, and they say it brings happiness to the wearer."

"Grandmother showed it to me," continued Madeleine. "Oh, it is so lovely, Rama, with black beads at the bottom, and a half-moon diamond and sapphire setting at the top. How I wished I could have worn it immediately for you. I will one day. The days are so long without you, my love, and during the nights for some reason I have wanted to howl, to cry. Maybe it was only an anxiety, a feminine anxiety about your state of health, for last night I had such wonderful sleep. All evening I had talked of you to Tante Zoubie and to Catherine. I spoke especially of the respect you show to me—for you, a woman is still the other, the strange, the miracle. You could never show the familiarity European men show towards their wives. You worship women even if you torture them. But I like to be tortured and to be your slave."

No, of course I did not want a slave. I wanted a companion of pilgrimage, for if you gaze long at the mountain, where after twist on twist of the bridle path the bells ring and the evening of worship has come, you want to lie at the feet of God together and unalone. Oh, to go to God and alone . . .

During the day I often worked on my Albigensians. Strange, so strange it seemed to me, that after Indian non-dualism had passed through different countries at different epochs of history, men came to affirm just the opposite—that instead of Advaita, where both duality and contradiction are abolished, men affirm that purity is not of the flesh, and so leap into the flame like Esclarmonde de Perelha. For in denying the flesh you affirm its existence. Just as thought cannot be transcended but has to be merged in that which is the *background* of thought, neither can evil be destroyed, but can only be merged into that from which it arose; the essence of evil, the root of evil, can only be the spring of life. Dostoevsky said that the tyranny of two and two making four was terrible—to think man could never escape it! But if Dostoevsky had studied the theory of numbers he would have known how all numbers merge into zero, from which they arose. There cannot be—how could there be?—a tyranny of zero. The absurd is the escape, the escape into phenomena of an urge for the noumenal. You cannot be happy and be a man. You can be Happiness or be Man. For Man and Happiness, these be One.

To be pure in the world is like being a human being when you are Man. It is like when India was under British rule and Indians carried British passports—Indians, I was told, had to say they were British at every European frontier. Sometimes an ignorant policeman would stop and say, "But you can't be British," and try to find the meaning of his statement in his book of rules. Finding nothing there, he would say, "You can't be *britannique,*" and yet he would let you go, for his rules never told him what to do. What is beyond logic must be the truth, thought Dostoevsky, like that frontier guard. But Truth may be simpler. You can never be a Cathar, a pure; you have to be purity. When there is purity there is no you. That is the paradox, and neither Christianity nor Islam has ever been able to transcend it.

The Cathars took this docetism from a mixture of Buddhist psychology and Zoroastrian dualism. Manichaeism had its origin not in Indian thought but when it repassed through Persia. (After all Mani was a Persian by birth though he had been to India and was profoundly influenced by Indian thought.) In fact the origin of dialectic might itself be the Ahuramazda. (For Plato, evil was about as true as it is to the Indian today—a thing to be expiated with a dove or a coconut.) But when Light and Darkness play against one another you have the hero, the saint. Strange that Nietzsche should have evoked Zarathustra, from which arose Hitlerism.

The Parsees sometimes remind one of the Zuni Indians—the best tribal society is also the most *moral* one. There, good and evil are distinct, known categories of phenomena like the night and the day, sun and moon, monsoon and summer. In the whole Parsee community for a century no man has been committed for murder, they say, but nor has any man been known to rise to the heights of many a Hindu sage. Parsee honesty has led them to banking, just as it led the Quakers to make chocolates. If the Cathars had remained they would have built a city of steel, in which virtue and vice would have been tested by electromagnetic oscillographs. And inside you would have seen beautiful men and women walk through well-heated corridors, almost naked; and they might have produced children in crucibles, and through chemical tests created the Cathar that would have no evil thought or bacilli. Only when he went out—when he crossed the iron wall—would he catch cold, and be sold to a prostitute. The Cathars created the noblest communist society of the Western world.

No wonder therefore, I argued, that early Buddhism was fought against by Hinduism, which ultimately defeated Buddhist moralism and integrated Buddhism into itself so that today one does not know in what way Mahayana differs essentially from Vedanta. Similarly Catholicism, with its virile tradition that came not only from the Church but a great deal from the pagans too, had such *truth* about it that had Catharism not been destroyed European humanity might have been. The war was not between Christianity and the Cathars, but between the living principle of Europe—from the time of Homer on to the present day—and this defeatism of life, against the *endura* and the slow death: Darwinism may not only be a biological principle, it may well be a spiritual one too. The *Bhagavad-Gita,* however Gandhiji might interpret it, is an affirmation not of the good but of Truth. Truth can take no sides —it is involved in both sides. Krishna is the hero of the battle, but seemingly a hero greater than he is Bhisma, the great warrior. Yet Bhisma's courage was Krishna's gift. Krishna fought himself against himself, through himself and in himself, and what remained is ever and ever himself—the Truth.

The Cathars were the Theosophists of the thirteenth century. If I had been a contemporary I would have joined Simon de Montfort, not for the love of money or of glory, not even for an indulgence—I would rather have fought against indulgences than against the Cathars—but I would have fought for the clear stream of truth that runs through Roman Catholicism. There's always a Karna and an Uttara in every battle, whether their names be changed to Innocent III or Hugues de Noyers, Bishop of Auxerre, *"ce prélat guerrier, âpre au gain . . . ce pourvoyeur de bûchers . . ."* It was the same battle between Pascal and the Jesuit Fathers.

Pau, with the purity of its air and the intimacy with oneself it gave—because one could see and participate of space—allowed me, strange as it may seem, an insight into Christianity as nothing else, so far, had done. It was from here that Henri IV, that noble prince, went over from the Protestant side to the Catholic, for he didn't want the French to become bankers, he wanted them to be saints and men of heroic thought. And Hitler's enemy was not Churchill alone, but verily, Saint Louis and Henri IV as well. France would one day have to become a monarchy: Georges, that strange Russian fanatic, was right. If you knew and loved France truly you could only be a Royalist, even if the Bourbons committed all the crimes of humanity, and poor Monsieur Vincent Auriol did not. Despite all the sins of Pope Innocent III, or later on of Pius XII with his pact with the Fascists, it is the papacy and not the British House of Commons, as people believe, that has saved Europe from destruction. The Resistance created a spiritual climate in which the abstract research of the Existentialists, those crypto-Catholics, was made possible. And the inspirer of the Resistance was not some Rousseau, it was Péguy —and Jeanne d'Arc. And so on . . .

France alone has universal history. Every battle of France is a battle for humanity. India is free today not because of Jeremy

Bentham but because of Napoleon. Napoleon was not, as historians think, a child of the Encyclopedists, but of those superstitious Catholics of the Maquis. He made himself an Emperor, by the grace of God, anointed by the Church of Saint Peter.

India has no history, for Truth cannot have history. If every battle of France has been fought for humanity, then it would be honest to say no battle in India was ever fought for humanity's sake. Or if fought, it was soon forgotten. Krishna fought against Bhisma by giving Bhisma courage. Mahatma Gandhi fought against the Muslims by fighting for them. He died a Hindu martyr for an Indian cause. He died for Truth.

Lezo was my constant companion in Pau. He had been to Biarritz to visit his friends, and heard I was in Pau—perhaps I had told him myself. I saw him walking along the Promenade des Pyrénées, with his bent and learned air, and no sooner did he see me than he ran to me as a schoolboy to his master. After that he made me visit several of his refugee friends, the Cathars who had left because of the new inquisitor. Little as I approved of the Cathar heresy, I would not join Franco or fight for this jackal Royalist. I was "corrupted" by noble socialist ideals, and my monarchy would be the ideal society of castes and functions equally distributed. I would have cooked for Enfantin and for Saint-Simon, but I would have shouted "Vive le Roi!" A stupid idea indeed.

Lezo and I discussed Buddhism a great deal. His learning was almost alarming: he could quote Chinese, Japanese and Indian texts with a facility that astonished me. He not only quoted, he seemed to understand. He also knew modern India and Mahatma Gandhi. I was always introduced to his Basque friends as "ce monsieur qui vient du pays de Gandhi." Lezo said to me one day, "You know, as a student in Germany I became a vegetarian for a trial period. I shall try it once again when I get back to Aix. I want to go to India, a Buddhist mendicant."

Of Madeleine we almost never talked. He mentioned her only once to ask if she would soon be in Aix. I told her yes, in two weeks.

I did not propose to Lezo, interesting as it might have been, that he should come along with me as I went visiting the various

Cathar sanctuaries, day after day, talking to the peasants and to heads of monasteries. The Albigensian traditions, I had heard, still remained alive everywhere. They even spoke of a mysterious cave where the Cathars had hidden their treasures, and on some nights one could see on that particular hill near Ornolac a bright star shine, of a blue that touched more the red than the yellow. Shepherds still saw it from their hills, and when you saw it you automatically said a *Pater Noster,* for it was some soul from beneath, some heretic, who must at last be going to heaven. I, who have a feel of presences in places historic, I should have liked to have looked on a pure, a Cathar. I am sure I would have loved him as I loved the Buddhists. But Lezo was too crude for my sensibilities. I did not want merely to write a thesis, but to write a thesis which would also be an Indian attempt at a philosophy of history. I wanted to absorb more than to know.

I felt splendid, and my weight had gone up so quickly that Dr. Drager laughed and called me *"le malade imaginaire."* Of course he did not believe it, it was only to give me good cheer. He gave me the new X-ray photographs and told me to have myself examined every three months.

"With modern medicine," he said, "phthisis is as much a superstition as sprue after the discovery of folic acid. Folic acid, as you know, was discovered recently, just about the beginning of the war. Actually it was one of your own countrymen, an Indian, who discovered it," he said, as though it were enough for me to know I had nothing to fear: I should be cured.

The plan to travel down to Languedoc was an old promise I had made myself, which Madeleine was eager that I should follow up before I started writing my thesis. On our first visit to the Basque country two years before, we had passed through the Cévennes, but she had been so unhappy that we did not stop anywhere to see anything. But this time I would see the scarred church of Béziers in which seven thousand men, women and children were put to flame, I would visit Narbonne and see the monasteries near by. I would, of course, visit Carcassonne and see the register of the heretics, in which they were named, and the day they went up the pyre shown. It was going to be interesting indeed.

I left Pau, not on a bright day, but when autumn was already showing signs of an early winter. Languedoc, however, was beautiful, with cypress and heather and hawthorn, and the Garrigues had a severe beauty that you could not get in soft Provence. I visited Sète, for Madeleine so loved the Cimetière Marin, and I could never forget that beautiful passage of his autobiography where Paul Valéry speaks of his native city:

> Je suis né dans un port de moyenne importance, établi au fond d'un golfe, au pied d'une colline, dont la masse de roc se détache de la ligne générale du rivage. . . . Tel est mon site originel, sur lequel je ferai cette réflexion naïve que je suis né dans un de ces lieux ou j'aurai aimé de naître.

Montpellier, as ever, was beautiful with its Arc de Triomphe and the panorama of the Peyrou. But I was anxious to get home: perhaps I could drive on and arrive that night and be able to keep Villa Sainte-Anne open for Madeleine. How happy she would be! I passed through Nîmes towards the evening, and it was so dark at the Pont du Gard I could only hear the deep roamings of the river. I was worried about not having brought my keys, then remembered Madame Jeanne always had a pair. By nine o'clock I was at Aix. Madame Jeanne was already in bed but she had been to Villa Sainte-Anne and had cleaned up everything for Madame. "I have left the mail on Monsieur's table," she told me, giving me the keys. I was happy to be back. I was going to be happy again.

The bull was almost roaring through his nostrils as I climbed up. I gave him grass and went in for more information. Villa Sainte-Anne was so familiar. As I undressed to wash, I saw my suitcases still in the corner. I shut them away in my cupboard. The past is past—and the past is history. Yes, I would be happy with Madeleine. I went over to my room to see the letters; there were five from India, and one from Paris. I made myself a hot chocolate, prepared a hot-water bottle and slipped in slowly to my bed. I was comfortable.

The letters from India intrigued me. Little Mother was full of hope. She had just heard that the University were expecting me the next summer. A formal resolution had been passed about the vacancy, which had to be kept open till my return. Obviously I had good friends in the Senate. She would be happy to welcome Madeleine to India. Of course we would have to stay in a more "European house, with butlers and a 'commode' and all that." She thought Saroja would be a good friend to Madeleine. Saroja always seemed lonely and sad. Sukumari, on the other hand, had such vitality! She would soon pass her matriculation—no doubt in the first class—and join the University. Little Mother imagined me already, I am sure, a Professor at the University, with Sukumari as my pupil. I would drive Little Mother back home from the College and she would come and speak to Madeleine in her childish broken English, which she would have learnt by then, for she proposed starting on her English lessons soon. Sukumari was to be her teacher. She hoped the toe-rings were of the right size; she did not know European feet, or she would have taken them to a goldsmith and had them all ready for Madeleine. "With affectionate blessings to my son Rama. Vishalakshi," she signed.

Saroja's letter was one of despair. She said she must come to Europe and continue her studies: she could not live another year in the house. Since Father's death it was a river of tears, and nothing else. Now even Grandfather Kittanna was dead. There were no elders left. I, I was very far away. I had only to make up my mind, and all would be well. She would be no burden on me, and she would be such a good sister-in-law to Madeleine. She knew Montpellier had one of the best medical schools in the world, and maybe I could get her a scholarship there . . . Saroja and Sukumari always thought there was nothing their brother could not accomplish.

There was an instinct in me—perhaps an instinct of self-preservation, something mysterious and unnameable—which was happy at the thought of Saroja at Villa Sainte-Anne; it might just add that steadiness of a sister's sensibility, which would give me a centre to radiate from. We all seek such an exterior point for ourselves—a party, a teacher, a father, a confessor—but in India, with our joint-family system, it has become a pyramid of many different shapes of a triangle, and we equalize each other's vagaries with our own steadiness. Especially a sister, she with the woman in her without the woman's demands, she in whom family pride and devotion made of you a god, she could make the un-understandable known, the mysterious simple and reverential. Besides, Saroja had a perfume that would fill my days and my nights— the perfume of the body breaking into the simple principle of womanhood.

I was happy, very happy at the thought, though I knew she would never come. In any case we could not afford it. Yet I almost saw her with her white sari and her large kunkum on her fore-head, her eyebrows meeting over her nose, and the bent gait of a deer. Her hand on my head would cure me; it would take the evil out of my lung.

The next letter was from Pratap. It spoke with such trust in my power to change his fiancée's heart. He said that from the re-ports he had heard my brief visit had been most promising. My affirmation of Indian values had found an echo in the young lady's heart. She who had never come down to the prayers in the sanctuary below was full of song and worship now. The Mother was surprised. The Mother had wondered if I could come again—but I had already gone to Hardwar.

"There is a further truth I could not tell you in Allahabad. Savithri seems to have found interest in a young Muslim boy in London. It may be absurd in the year 1951 to be shocked at this, but the Mother is very orthodox, and of course there could be no question of a marriage. The Father is a weak person—he goes wherever the family pulls. Besides, he can never say no to anything Savithri wants to do. The old rogue, I have reasons to believe, is not particularly enamoured of my attainments: how could a ruling prince (of however small a state) be satisfied with a petty Jagirdar, whatever his prospects? I think therefore your persuasions would be of immense help to a helpless fellow like me. I just do not know what to do.

"I told the Mother, or rather I sent word to her through my own mother, that if Savithri could be persuaded to see more of you it might help. She is only nineteen and she does not know France. It would be wonderful of you to invite her. If this does not inconvenience you in any way how very grateful I should be. You are like a brother to me. And forgive me.

"Yours affectionately,
PRATAP."

104

The next letter, too, was from him. It was a hurried note to say Savithri had left by boat this time, because the doctors thought her heart was not good enough yet for air travel. The S.S. *Maloja* would touch at Marseille on October the third. Could I meet her there, and perhaps she could spend a day or two with me and my wife? Gratefully yours, etc., etc.

The last letter was one from Savithri herself. It was posted from Port Said, and simply stated that her mother had given her my address, and that she would be happy to see me in Marseille if I had a moment to spare. She did not say whether she would stay with us or not.

"It was wonderful seeing you in our home. The vulgarity of the surroundings I hope did not hurt your sensibilities. We in the North are new to civilization. I want to see you. May I come to see you? I want to know France. I want to know India.

"Yours very sincerely,
Savithri."

I have kept that letter to this day. It was written on one of those white thick P & O notepapers, with the flag on the left, and not much space to write on elsewhere. But it was a good letter, I felt. It brought me *news*.

Somehow I felt Saroja herself was coming.

The last letter in my mail was from Oncle Charles. Madeleine and Catherine, he had himself driven down to Paris. He was happy to see them both so close to one another.

"What a beautiful couple you make," continued Oncle Charles, "and how Zoubie's heart and mine are filled with gratitude that our daughter—for Madeleine is like my own daughter—should have found such an asylum of peace and elevation in the home you have given her. If Christian prayers mean anything to you, I pray to God that he fulfil you in your life, and that your noble competence may find an adequate use in your own ancient and great land. Already India is playing a big role in international affairs. I am sure a person of your stature—I almost said, of so distinguished a family—will be called to places of eminence and of service. And I know how very devotedly and with what distinction you will serve your country. Thanks to Madeleine, I am sure Catherine will find a worthy husband. Already I have two or three young men in mind. But Catherine is difficult; like Madeleine, she's frightened of men. In fact we need another Ramaswamy in the household.

> *"Bien affectueusement,*
> Oncle Charles."

For a man who had been sick, such a flood of affection and regard could only be most consoling. What was more consoling still was that I would see Madeleine again in the morning. I would see her young, luminous face, as the train came into the Gare Saint-Charles. I would buy her a bouquet of azaleas, like the one Henri the taxi-driver bought her, and would bring her home like a new bride.

Suddenly my whole life seemed centred in Madeleine. There was no spot on earth or air which did not contain her presence and which, isolated in time, was not going to be ever and ever mine. I had not forgotten about Esclarmonde, but who could know the future? Astrologers did, and they had spoken of many children. My lung ached but I forgot it—I was thinking of Madeleine. The night would soon be over and morning would come.

I had to rise at four to meet her train. The cocks were still very active and the day was fresh as a pomegranate as I let go the brakes and was off to Marseille. The whole of the earth smelt of roses.

The next morning, I brought coffee to Madeleine. Collège was beginning. There was so much to fill a year with—and a life.

Georges came along in the afternoon. He had been spending his usual fortnight with Father Zenobias—his twisting hand, his flashing eyes, the way he threw back his head now and again, showed that Georges was like a good horse, champing for a ride and a leap. He had been discussing the theory of evil in the Church, and was sorry I had not been present during those remarkable talks at the monastery.

"You know, Ramaswamy," he said, "the evenings were full of light and silences. Father Zenobias and I spent hour after hour, he digging his grave with his long blunt spade, and I standing under the giant oak in the yard, talking away of the majesty of the Christian dogma. It is not often that you see the beauty of man when he has the means of existing in splendour—it is when a human being touches the cup of misery that you see the fine lines on his anguished face. The face of Christ on the Cross must have been more luminous than when He preached in Galilee. Evil is fascinating, for without it there would be no good, no world, no Christ. I can now understand the temptation of Lucifer. One can be drunk with evil as one cannot be drunk with good."

"Naturally," I retorted, "for in evil you seek good, but in the good you are goodness yourself. To be drunk you need the drunkard and he who sees himself drunk. You remember the saying in the Bible—the right hand must not know what the left hand has done? The good cannot know itself, any more than light can know itself."

"Then how does light know itself?"

I said, "It is like a man who is going to Paris, and who has been telling himself, 'Still four hundred and fifty kilometres, I am in Dijon; two hundred kilometres, I am in Auxerre; fifty-eight kilometres, I am at Fontainebleau.' And suddenly he reaches the Porte de Vanves, and says, 'Only seven kilometres.' Then when he enters the city, he asks someone, 'Monsieur, Monsieur, can you tell me where Paris is?' And if the person is a clever Parisian—and all Parisians are clever—he will say, 'It's still thirty-seven kilometres from here, Monsieur. You go straight down this boulevard, then you turn right. You see that road just where the sun shines? You go straight up it, past the aerodrome and the bridge, and the long cobbled streets, with poplars on both sides, and then a valley again, a cemetery, a station and the city.' But a few minutes later the visitor comes to a gendarme; asks him. 'Paris? Why this is Paris, Monsieur.' Paris is not there, Georges, because Auxerre is or Porte de Vanves is; Paris is there because it is Paris. You do not ask in Paris where Paris is—nor, once in Paris, do you know anything else but Paris. All distances, as you know, my friend, start from Notre-Dame, and Paris begins at zero."

"But Paris is made of the Étoile and the Buttes-Chaumont. Paris is made of the Louvre and the Usines Renault. Paris is not a whole. The whole exists because the parts exist."

"Now, now, let us be logical! The part implies the whole but in the mind of no man does the whole—the complete—imply the incomplete. 'When the whole is taken from the whole, what remains is the whole,' say the Upanishads. Resurrection is not because death is, resurrection is because life is. Nobody has died. Nobody will die. Death is just a negative thought."

"Oh, you are at it again—at your Vedanta. Maya is Maya to Maya—Maya cannot be where Brahmin is."

"But," interjected Madeleine, "was not Maya also the name of the mother of Gautama, the Buddha? Did it not mean, Truth was 'born' to illusion? And because Truth came into existence Maya died, the illusion died, and so the mother of the Buddha died."

"That is what Oldenberg or someone like him says. No, that is not how it is to be understood. Truth, which always is, and is therefore never born and can never manifest itself in any way, cannot have a mother or a father. Maya, on seeing the Truth born from herself—that is, man in seeing his own true nature as Truth—sees that illusion has never existed, will never exist. So Maya did not die; Maya recognized truth being truth; Maya was as such nothing but the Truth. Who has ever seen nothingness—Nirvana? The Void is only the I seen from within as the not-I. Evil is a moral, I almost said an optical, reality. Optics is no more real than gravitation is real. A certain distance beyond the earth there is no gravitation. A certain touch in the cerebral nerve can change your optics, and make you see long things short or short things long, as the surgeon wants. The relative cannot prove the absolute. The moral reflex is, after all, a biological reflex."

"And God?" whispered Georges, in exasperation. He had led me somewhere in Montpalais, and he had come prepared, after penitence and prayer, to finish off his work. "God after all is. And God is good."

"God *is*, and goodness is part of that is-ness. The good can only be the true, as the Greeks say."

"Then what makes the night?"

"Absence."

"And day?"

"Itself."

There was a long, unsteady silence, like some silence on a mountain. If one went to the east or to the south, in either direction the snow was deep, and one could see the avalanche go down on the other side of the valley. It was now not a question of the path, but of instinct—something in the silence, not in the geography of the mountain, that spoke. Truth is withdrawnness. God is affirmation. Georges, who saw the avalanche, stood fascinated. He only heard the stream murmur below, and the flight of birds.

"Cézanne, you know," I went on, "knew Baudelaire's *La Charogne* by heart. And Rainer Maria Rilke, who was deeply moved by the works of Cézanne—I don't understand painting, but I admire Rilke—well, Rilke said, 'The presence of *La Charogne* has added a new dimension to human understanding.' Indeed, the recognition of evil is the beginning of sainthood. Do you remember those terrible lines of Baudelaire?

> "Alors, ô ma Beauté, dites à la vermine
> Qui vous mangera de baisers,
> Que j'ai gardé la forme et l'essence divine
> De mes amours décomposés."

"There you are!" said Georges, happy.

"Yes, there I am, and that is why Rainer Rilke got lost amongst the angels, and gave his body such importance that when he fell mortally ill, he would not allow a doctor to touch him. The holiness of the body is like the duty of the *devadasi**—it functions within its own dimension. The body can no more be holy than the mind be pure."

"So?"

"So man must seek not purity of mind and body but to be purity itself. Man must not wish to taste the sweetness of sugar, as that old Bishop Madhavāchārya said in the thirteenth century—I always think of someone sucking a bonbon!—but one must become, as the Vedantins say, sweetness itself."

"Who is there to know it is sweet?"

---

* The temple dancers who are dedicated to the gods. They belong to the concubine class.

"Are you serious?" I asked.

"Serious? Why yes, of course."

"Then come," I said. I knew the path in the mountain. I had in my feet the knowledge of the avalanche, I had in my nose the identity of air currents. There was no fright, for in that silence you could hear your own feet move. Madeleine was in between us, and sometimes I could almost hear her prayers. "Where is the sweetness, when you feel it? In your tongue?"

"Yes, so it is."

"Because the bonbon, or call it sugar if you like, is on your tongue, does it make sweetness? If you put it on the tongue of a dead man or of a sleeping child, they would not wake up and say, 'Oh, what a wonderful bonbon!' No."

"No, they could not."

"And so the tongue must move, the saliva must rise, the chemical agglutinations must take place—and when it comes down the throat it becomes sweet. Just as it is not at the moment you drink coffee that you feel it is good—it is when you have a thrill at the back of your spine that you say to Madeleine, 'Wonderful, Madeleine, what wonderful coffee!' "

"That's true of Madeleine's coffee!"

"Or mine for that matter," I laughed. "Anyway, the bonbon is on your tongue—it has melted. Sweetness begins when sweetness is recognized. That is, in sweetness—wherever that may be—you taste sweetness. A rank absurdity."

"But a fact."

"As the Great Sage has said: In experience there is no object present. There is only *experience*."

"Well, how is that?"

"The sensation must finish its function before knowledge dawns. In Knowledge there is no object present—if so, who has knowledge of it? You might say, 'I.' And the I has the knowledge of the I through——?"

"Through Knowledge," said Madeleine.

"So Knowledge has knowledge of the I through Knowledge, which means Knowledge is the I."

"Yes, that is so."

"That is why sugar is not sweet but sweetness is sweet, or Georges is not a man but Man is Georges."

Madeleine sat fascinated. She wondered where I had gathered all this wisdom. She did not know I had felt the mountain and the mountain was in me and not I *on* the mountain.

"Georges knows all men in Georges," I continued.

"Yes. Go on," he said.

"Georgeshood is known only to Georges."

"Let us admit that."

"Georges sees men, many men, and says there is Man, an abstraction."

"So it is."

"But Georges has seen no Man. He has seen men."

"What is manhood then?" he asked.

"Manhood is the essence of all men—the truth of all men. And Georges?"

"He is a man."

"Is the Manhood of the man different from the Georgeshood of Georges?"

He thought for a long time and said, "Certainly not."

"Then what is Georges? Georges is Man. So Georges is not Georges—Georges is Man. And Man is simply Man: a principle, the Truth. So Georges is the Truth."

It was like a bathe in the Ganges for me—my sins were washed away. Georges looked so distant and elevated; he seemed to be in tears. I could almost hear him mumble a prayer. His hand was spread over his forehead, and he was looking into his own eyes. Evening was invading us from all sides—the birds were clamouring. Madeleine took my hand and pressed it against her cheek. This time I had wholly won her: I knelt before no alien God. The God of woman must be the God of her man. Pau, and the solitude of the mountains, had given me back to myself. Now I could go back with Madeleine to the cathedral in Auch, kneel beside her and be not afraid. When fear knows itself it is the truth itself.

I was not happy; I was simple. The world seemed a large and round place to live in. The evening was beautiful, and we went up the hill on a walk. September had come and gone, and yet winter had not set in. The leaves were lovely under the arch of evening. Far away, like a truth, I thought, the sea must stretch itself. You could smell the rough air, you could feel the salt in your nostrils. Standing on the elephant I sang, *"Shivoham, Shivoham"*; I sang it as never I had chanted, with the full breath in my lungs:

> *Natovyoma bhūmir natéjo navayur,*
> *Chidanānda rūpah, Shivoham, Shivoham.*
> Not hearing nor tasting nor smelling nor seeing,
> But Form of Consciousness and Bliss;
> Shiva I am, I am Shiva.

The noble periods rolled over the hills and to the valley with the assurances of Truth.

> *Aham nirvikalpi nirakara rupih*
> *Chidanānda rūpah, Shivoham, Shivoham.*
> I am beyond imagination, form of the formless,
> Form of Consciousness and Bliss;
> Shiva I am, I am Shiva.

Where was the evil hid that evening? Where at any moment of time is evil hid? Where at any point of time is there no sun? I ask you. It is your belief in the lack of light that makes the night. But the day always is. Evil is a superstition, the name of a shadow.

I felt such tenderness for Georges that evening. He seemed so childlike, so rested—he looked a saint.

I was a hero now, and all the indrawn compassion of Madeleine went to Georges. Madeleine was won and so I felt free. For days on end I went on chanting Sanscrit verses on my walks and all about the house, and I worked very well. My theory—my philosophy of history—explained many things about the Albigensian heresy that had seemed, it appeared, so abstruse to European historians. It was not the Pope, it was the orthodoxy, the *smartha,* that won.

Of an evening, when I was still busy at my work, Georges would drop in and I could hear him and Madeleine very fervent in discussion. Madeleine had by now completely abandoned her work on the Holy Grail. She said it was, as a matter of fact, part of the Albigensian tradition—she made herself sure of this—so she turned her attention more and more to Buddhism. The intellectual virility and the deep compassion of the Buddha often filled her evenings with joy and wonderment. She would tell me, lying on the bed next to me, story after story from the *Jatakas,* and she wondered that Buddhism had not conquered Europe but Christianity had.

I reminded her of the tradition that one of the sons of Asoka had indeed been sent to Alexandria to preach the Holy Law, and that some of the later Alexandrian school, especially Plotinus, must have owed much to Buddhistic thought. But our information, I went on, was still too meagre. The Greeks, like the Indians, were an intellectually curious people—perhaps even more open-minded than we were. So it mattered little whence the gymnosophists came, they were always welcome. There is a Greek tradition of an Indian Sage having visited Socrates himself, about the time when the Compassionate Master was still alive. Imagine, I concluded, how later Buddhist phenomenalism must have attracted the school of Aristotle . . . etc., etc.

Georges often went on long walks with Madeleine. He felt peaceful and protected in her presence. We saw a new Georges, more deeply humble, more truly elevated; sometimes, as one saw the drama on his face, one wondered if he had not spent the night in prayer. He was certainly deeply disturbed. For him Catholicism was still new, he could not feel his way through it, as he might the religion of his forefathers. Old Ivan Pavlovitch must have been writing to him on the subject, because once in a while Georges would open a letter from his father, and read out a paragraph or two. Evil could not be a proof of God, and yet evil was premonition of God. The paradox remained, and like Alyosha when he smelt the body of the Elder decaying, Georges looked gentle, intimate and forlorn.

Madeleine brought him that feminine presence which man seeks in pain—a hand, a look, the gesture to lift a coat or help across a difficult step. Madeleine's hand was ever there, and she seemed so sure of herself; it was now Georges that leaned on her.

Soon, however, we were all going to be pretty busy. Savithri was announced for October 13, and I was to go and meet her at the pier. She had sent me a wire, and I had told Madeleine about it. Madeleine was not sure how to deal with an Indian girl; she wondered whether Savithri would not be shocked with Madeleine and her ways. "After all, we Europeans have only been civilized for a thousand years. And what you pardon in me, Savithri may not." I assured Madeleine that Indians were a very tolerant people, and the "barbarities of Madeleine" might amuse Savithri more than hurt her. Besides, Savithri had spent two years in Europe already, and such fears on the part of Madeleine were silly.

"You are always right, Seigneur, and I am always wrong," she said, piqued and a little amused, and she went into the kitchen to put a béchamel sauce on the cauliflower. Since she had become a vegetarian she enjoyed cooking, for as she said, in winter when you only have potatoes and beetroot, tomatoes and spinach, it needed a lot of ingenuity to make food interesting. Whereas with meat, the dish was almost ready on the cow or on the pig.

"And as for 'vegetables of the sea,'" she continued, remembering Little Mother's story in Calcutta, "they may go straight into your mouth, and taste so wonderful. Look, look at oysters . . ."

Madeleine always needed a theory to convince herself. I used to tease her and say, "You are only called Madeleine because your *carte d'identité* says so. You are a nominalist."

Those October days were full of a rich, slanting sunshine. The winds began to blow, and Mont Sainte-Victoire was like oneself seen in a dreamless sleep, a point of nowhere against the blue. Waking up you could see the olives and feel Les Baux far away; you could almost eye the beauty of the Mediterranean and say, "Of course, I am here, I am Mont Sainte-Victoire." The world became real when others became true.

There were other truths too that filled our evenings with delight. Madeleine had not yet gone to the doctor; she said she would wait for a week more. In fact no doctor need have told her anything; the mystery on her own face, that inturned look as though she were looking down her navel rather than her nose, made one sense that there was something the matter. I told her teasingly that just as one can smell a good watermelon from a bad one I could smell her and tell her even the sex of the little creature.

"I have one more secret still," she said, as though to change the subject.

"What's that, Madeleine?"

"I have invited Catherine to Aix, as she hasn't had a holiday all the summer. She has just written to me that she will be here towards the end of the week."

"What a fine idea," I said.

"It is more than a fine idea. It is an inspiration." And she looked at me as though she wanted me to understand more.

"Well, it's an inspiration," I said. "And so what?"

"I don't want to lose Catherine. She is so serious. I don't want her to get caught in all that smelly nonsense, and end up in some Place de la Cathédrale. I want her to see sunshine."

"Well, and so?"

"She disliked the ball, and she disliked all men. She said she would never think of marrying any of the upstarts Father would like her to marry. Their very presence, she said, gave her the creeps."

"So?"

"She needs to love a man for his own good—not for her frills or her apartment in Paris and country house in Deauville. Oncle Charles can see nothing beyond a landowner's son, who has studied law, and is established in Paris, on the Rue de Rivoli. Catherine is a sweet creature—her dream is to have many children, and a good Catholic husband. She could not face modern life. She is already too frightened of existence—and it won't be Tante Zoubie who'll give her back confidence. She needs a man, a gentle pure soul."

I understood. "But," I laughed, "only evil can prove God, good cannot prove God."

"So you were the premonition," she added. "And Alyosha will have found his Madeleine."

A slight cold, one of those forerunners of our winter miseries, sent me to bed for a few days. I worked hard on my thesis, and once I was well I was happy to be able to go out again. The sky seemed young, and full of a big yearning. The swallows were already on the telegraph wires. The air was still. In the valley below, Monsieur Chévachaux's donkey was driving the flies away with his shortened tail. He seemed to know my thoughts, for he looked up at me, and then bent down and continued to graze. A gesture in silence seems a recall to truth.

I came down the hill almost with an adolescent heart. The next morning I said good-bye to Madeleine and went down to meet Savithri at the Quai Saint-Jacques. It was just like going to Naini Tal. The air was crisp, and you felt the snow beyond. I was going to meet the Himalayas. The Ganges flowed everywhere.

GRANDMOTHER Lakshamma used to tell us a sweet story: "Once upon a time, when Dharmaraja ruled Dharmapuri, he had a young son of sixteen, Satyakama, who had to be sent away on exile because his stepmother wanted her own son, Lokamitra, to be placed on the throne. Weak this Dharmaraja was, and the Minister one day took young Satyakama away, and left him at the white beginnings of a jungle path on the frontiers. And Satyakama, beautiful in his limbs ('As though moonbeams had been melted and made solid as silver for the hands and feet of this Prince,' said Grandmother), he walked down the path forlorn, now asking for advice from a butterfly, and now from a roaming elephant. Neither had anything to tell him but shed tears in compassion—which explains why the elephant has such poor sight, and the butterfly two additional eyes on its wings—and the trees, made hollow with the winds, rolled a lamentation that all the forest could hear. So much virtue had never walked that jungle path before; even the jackal went immediately to the rabbit to bring the gladsome tidings that a Prince was walking amongst them, shining with the disc of truth over his head.

"Then suddenly the whole forest fell into an act of silence, and just in front of Satyakama on the little footpath, round as a river pebble, big as a temple flower-basket, and with streaks like those on an antelope, black and white, was a *budumékaye*. Though there was neither wind nor sound, the little vegetable freed itself from its vine, and started rolling in front of the Prince. The Prince was too full of tears to see it. But suddenly he heard the lion roar from some distant mountain cave, and in that instant of fear he saw with his eyes this round and rolling vegetable. Fascinated with its movement he followed and followed it, till the day melted into the heat of the noon, and the noon sheltered itself under branch and root of banyan, and not a bird moved nor a squirrel nor a bee. Rapt in himself he followed the movement of the *budumékaye,* till the evening set in. And in the cool of the dusk, as the birds awakened to the waters, and the animals led out the little ones to their grazings and feasting, just as the night fell the round vegetable hit against a huge rock, big as a mansion, and burst apart. And from inside this *budumékaye* rose a young and auspicious Princess whose beauty could blind the eye, and illumine the night. 'Oh!' said the Prince in wonder. But before he knew where he stood, the huge rock rose as it were from inside, just as though someone had pushed the door of the loft, and golden steps appeared, and servants and eunuchs and maids, and in the world below there were halls and parlours and chambers of gold. Mirrors shone everywhere, and six white Princesses gathered together to pay homage to the Prince. And when they had bowed and stood aside, the *budumékaye* who had become a Princess came from the door opposite, a garland of flowers in her hand. She knelt before him and said, 'I am the eldest of seven sisters, and I be Princess of Avanti, banished by a cruel father,' and they wed each other. There was but one enemy in the palace, and that was a fat old monkey-chamberlain. He sat by a milk-cauldron, sleepy. The seven sisters gathered together and felled him into the cauldron, and the servants and the maids were happy and free, for he was a tyrant.

"Thus they lived for twice ten years, till the world became big, and overspread; for vast was the territory needed for the growing populace. And a huge capital rose just in the middle of the forest, with roads and parks and festoons, and pools for summer and shelters for the monsoon, and they watered the roads of evening mixed with the rich sandal of the forests. Dandakavathi the great capital rose, and one day, as Satyakama and Ramadevi ruled their small kingdom, they saw the elephants and the camels and the horses of another King enter the capital. It was an old King going to Benares on pilgrimage. Four were the Queens with him. They were made right welcome into the palace. Though Satyakama knew the moment he beheld them who the visitors were, Ramadevi, the Chief Queen, did not. A magnificent feast was offered to the visitors, and when Satyakama started serving Ganges water to his guests such a spurt of milk burst from the Chief Queen's breasts that all the world wondered. Satyakama fell at his mother's feet and told them the story of the seven Princesses. And with tears in their eyes the old King and his three Queens (for the fourth was the wicked one, young and ambitious) praised the young Prince for his obedience and beauty. They said that since his departure nothing but famine and penury had ruled the land, and as expiation they had started on a pilgrimage to Benares: maybe the Ganges would give them back their purity. Meanwhile the Chamberlain of the old King rushed horsemen to the capital, and while the citizens of Dharmapuri awaited the young Prince, with kunkum-water and silver censers, and with all the courtyards covered with rice-powder designs and mango leaves hung at every door, the old King and his four wives wended their way westwards to Benares, the holy city.

"And as soon as the very winds smelt of the Prince returning to the capital, golden grass grew on either side of the footpath, porcupines brushed away the thorns from the highways, and fledgelings put out their yellow bare necks to see the Prince and Princess ride on elephant and howdah to the capital. There was the music of the nine melodies in the air . . ."

"And you can hear it as you go to sleep, little children," said Grandmother.

I could hear such music in the air on that clear, cold day of Provence, as the mistral had removed all clouds from the sky like the porcupines the thorns of the jungle highway.

Savithri was a real princess by birth, but what must have brought the story back to me was that as I stood at the bottom of the gangway, this somewhat round and shy thing rolled down the steps as she ran, with her august and aloof and lone brother behind her. I had almost to catch her by the hand lest she fall against some trunk or cargo, as it lay on the pier.

She readily accepted to come with me to Aix and spend a few days with us, but her brother had to be rushed on to London. He had to go back to school at once—he was already late. We had a hurried lunch at the Cannebière, and even the Marseillais seemed astonished at so much laughter on a woman's face. She seemed, did Savithri, so innocent and true and free. Her brother, on the other hand, was shy, already learned-looking. He was to have gone to Eton, but the war had sent him to an Anglo-Indian school. He had suffered much from that atmosphere, and so to run away from the vulgarity of sons of Government Officers, and the fat, ugly bankers' creed, he read English poetry, wandering through the fields reciting Shelley, Wordsworth or Gerard Manley Hopkins to himself. He was, he had decided, going to become a professor and teach poetry.

All that he knew of France—he had read French at school—was her poetry. He admired most Victor Hugo and Lamartine, thought Gérard de Nerval involved, and Baudelaire he said he could not understand; for that matter, Paul Valéry too. I said to Anand, for that was his name, that Valéry's home was not far away—and before I knew where I was I heard Savithri start reciting,

> Midi le juste y compose de feu,
> La mer, la mer toujours recommencée,

in her gentle, intimate accent, as though French were better spoken like the *Braj* of Mira. It was Anand who had taught her this, for after the two lines her inspiration seemed to have stopped; Anand continued with a few more verses, and I could see it was not so much to show off his knowledge as to discover whether I found his accent improper. No, his accent was much better than his sister's. Whatever he did was done with thoroughness.

For Savithri life was a game, a song. She walked in the streets (she was a little shortsighted) like my sisters did, throwing four balls into the air and keeping them going with a puzzle rhyme and a beat of feet. She spoke rapidly, and in between her amusing chatter was a space of sorrow, large as her eyes; you could almost breathe and know that this came from no single act or thought, but from some previous *karma,* the sorrow of another age. She bore such sorrow, it seemed at moments, that she sang just to cover it up, or she would dramatize herself smoking or sit self-consciously as though to hide some unnameable disease that

120

others could see and smell but she could not know. I soon saw that her repertory of the frivolous—some light air from *La Traviata* or *Carmen,* or some Negro spiritual or jazz soprano "The sky is blue and I love you . . ."—was as rich as her deep knowledge of the Mira tradition.

We rushed Anand to his train and saw his Pullman move off, and hardly were we back in the car before Savithri started singing, *"Oh, mon cher, Oh mon amourrrr . . ."* I remembered Anand's last sentence to her: "Sister, I saw *La Traviata* on the posters in Marseille. Do not forget to go and see it—and ta-ta," he said, as the train moved away. Savithri continued to hum to herself: *"Oh, ma colombe, Oh mon amieeee,"* forgetful where she was—she never remembered, it seemed, she was at Marseille, Saint-Charles.

On the way home she started beating her feet to some ditty, and I felt I did not know what to do, for neither did I know this Tino Rossi nor did I think I should know him. I was a provincial Brahmin from Mysore, where everybody learns marriage songs of Rama and Krishna, or Sanscrit verses for banquet competitions. I had come with that background to France, where I fell among the group of Madeleine and her friends, almost all Catholics, or serious communists. But this world of, "The sky is blue and I love you," was completely irrelevant to me. I probably knew more of Bernard de Ventadour or of Marie de France and her

> Belle amie si est de nous
> Ni vous sans moi, ni moi sans vous,

than of the jazz masters.

Besides, I thought, amongst those olive trees which rolled like age after age before me, that had seen Roman consuls, bishops, Crusaders and princes, and perhaps Napoleon himself as he came back from Elba before his Hundred Days of Glory, I wondered whether before the antiquity, wisdom and majesty of Mont Sainte-Victoire, some Harlem feral piece were not a lack of piety. Maybe to a true Negro such jazz would have sounded like an adoration of the Invisible, but to an Indian it seemed a lack of respect to the earth, to those fervid hills—to France. We can only offer others what is ours, were it only a seed of tamarind, Grandfather used to say. Let us Indians then give France, if we would, Mira or the glory of Sankara, but let us not offer her, for her hierarchy of riches, for the generosity of her rivers, for the purity of her poets, such tam-tam. Does he who sets foot on the soil of France know he treads where Saint Louis trod, walks where Henri IV rode, goes where the great Mistral walked? Or that he looks at Mont Sainte-Victoire which Cézanne made famous, in violet and silver, in venetian green and in mud-red? Or that Péguy walked eighty-eight kilometres from Paris to Chartres, to carry the homage of the country of Beaune to the Queen of France?

> . . . Étoile du matin, inaccessible reine,
> Voici que nous marchons vers votre illustre cour
> Et voici le plateau de notre pauvre amour
> Et voici l'océan de notre immense peine. . . .

Much as I spoke these words to myself, Savithri must have felt it, for her jazz waned away into a more lovely lyric, and thence to an abrupt silence. Mont Sainte-Victoire rose before us with the familiarity of an acknowledged elder, not a father but a younger uncle; we were to be his wards. As the car tuned herself and ran uphill, I could see the lights of Villa Sainte-Anne, and by the time Savithri stepped out of the car, Madeleine had run down the steps to bid her welcome.

Months later, Madeleine said to me that Savithri was just as she had imagined an Indian woman should be, gentle, simple and very silent.

"You are thrice welcome to our little home," Madeleine said, standing near the bull, "the more welcome, because you are a woman and an Indian. Come in!"

As I laid the luggage on the floor, Savithri threw open the window and looked out and said, "Oh, it's so beautiful here, look at that Moon of Shiva!" And she added, "Just like in Naini Tal." As she went up the steps to the landing above, she felt it was a palace—and so did we. We make objects—objects do not make us. Madeleine could no more have made it a palace than I a home. For Madeleine it was a villa, and I always felt I was her guest. For me Villa Sainte-Anne should have been a sanctuary—

and like all sanctuaries it would then have belonged to the gods, and to my ancestors. The Brahmin is never contemporary—he goes backwards and forwards in time, and so has a Sage to begin the genealogical tree, and a Guru to end the cycle of birth and death. Where, I ask you, where was I to build a house, a home? By what river or tank or temple corridor?

The garden of Provence is like some Chinese fable-land, with bishops, prelates, Princes of the Church; snuffboxes, concubines and Châteauneuf-du-Pape, bastardy; the monster of Tarascon to keep treasure, the dungeons of Montmajour for prisoners; and some Faery Queen, that one may not win with a sword or a look, but by some subtle poem that she has to unweave and see the meaning of in a pool of clear mirrors. But where a Chinese queen would be young, full and ripe, the Provençal one would be lean, proud and virginal. There would be a donkey to have a jolly ride on, to go to a tavern and hear someone talk of the wisdom of birds, or of the knowledge of navigating stars; and when the moon shone, as in Sze-Chwan, would not the whole country look as though Wang-Chu or Chang-Yi had, while pounding rice (though in Provence, of course, it would be pressing the wine) with pestle and drink, sung up a kingdom to live in?

And Wang-Chu says to Chang-Yi, "The moon will fill the valley as on the night of the ninth dragon, and from the potion made of the four butterflies of the four valleys we can ride on moonbeams to the Castle of Changto. And there the Princess will receive us, with bamboo-wine and hemp-liquor, and the girls will come dancing round us, and we shall have a nice time, hé, Chang?" Just then, as in the good story of the Mule du Pape, some conceited servant of the Prince would lead the donkey to the top, to the very top of the castle, and when it has looked at the river, broad as a washerman's pool, it sees mounting chariots and busy merchant-men and horses that gallop; it sees sword and buckler and young sunshine, with ladies to the left who pay homage to a Duke, and ladies to the right who kiss the hand of yellow monk or Mandarin—till three white geese come flying from Mount Wu, and a dark, blue wind rises and sweeps the castle and the moon away. Then Wang-Chu will say to Chang-

Yi, "We have had a marvellous trip, haven't we—and the moon-beams were so nice to ride on," and Wang, laying the pestle against the wall, will say, "Chang, can't we make a cobweb, large as these four palms, thine and mine, and hold the Kingdoms in our waistband?" Chang thinks for a long time and says, "Maybe, maybe, but now take this pinch of snuff," and as he says so, the morning bells ring from tower to tower of the Temple, and Chang and Wang are found sleeping by their pestle. The bailiff of the house kicks them on the flank and says, "Hé, wake up, you! We do not give five pan-liangs for nothing—or do you think we grow pan-liangs on grass stalks?" and they wake up and see it is broad daylight.

It wasn't broad daylight for us, anyway, for the round full moon shone over us with the shadow of dark cypresses, now with the silver on the plane trees, now with pools and ruins of an abandoned Roman town or castle, now with vines and now with the long-going railway line—the whole night had a hum and a woof that seemed like a world built by fireflies. Some fairy tale had come true; some princess had indeed woven a world from her bonnet, and had spread it out for her own enjoyment, as if she were looking at her own face in the melody of the bamboo flute. And she awaited the coming of the Knight of Jerusalem.

> Del gran golfe de mar
> E del enois del portz
> E del perilhos far
> Soi, merce Dieu, estortz . . .

I knew I talked nonsense. I could not talk anything else. Savithri was made of such stuff that for her the real had to be clothed in terms of the illusory to make it concrete; truth was to be made the revelation of a puzzle, a riddle, a mathematic of wisdom. For her, I could see, everything was gesture and symbol, and time had been abolished, that the river might run through the night, the tree rise high, the mountains move as on themselves; that words be spoken as though left behind, and the body itself be a casket in which one sees oneself, not as limb and form, but as light cooled into space, as a gift, an object, a truth. All was secret to her but herself—so all was a legend, and every event a wonder.

Every man—the peasant on his horse, going back to his home at midnight, hay-rake on his arm, or the driver of a stopped lorry from whom I asked about some country road, his red light singing and chirruping—all, all were like a land seen from a palace, that some mysterious father had named but would not let you go anywhere near. The world was like the beggar at the palace gateway, and everything was fascination. And I was the father, the storyteller, the schoolmaster. What a job, I said to myself, and I was fascinated.

I was fascinated all the more as there was nothing that Savithri could not understand. If I said, "This is donkey-grass and is called *oenanthera* in Latin; and this the cypress of Barbary, for the Saracens brought it; and this is where Queen Jeanne was shut up for her father had gone mad; and this is the hell that Dante describes" (for we had now come to the plateau of Les Baux) it mattered little; all was an instant, an illumination. And it brought on her face a wonderment, a parted-lipped astonishment, that indeed grass should be called *oenanthera,* and that the Kings of Baux be descended from Balthazar, and Balthazar, the Mage, he came from India, as tradition spoke, and that Dante did say,

> Vergine madre, figlia del tuo figlio
> umile e alba piu che creatura
> termine fisso d'eterno consiglio

> tu sé colei che l'umana natura
> nobilibasti si che'l suo pattore
> non didegno di farsi sua fattura

and indeed that I was and she existed, that anything was not thus and that anything was thus; all seemed truths to her needing no proof. She was, herself, the proof that night did not imply the day or day the night, that France was this and so India was not this, that she was a girl, a woman, and I a man—all seemed a known mystery, an acknowledgement—and so to the next precipice, and then the moon that shone on to the distant sea. She could be filled with silence, and a steadiness filled the air then, as though the world was made real because one never saw it.

This explained why Savithri so often closed her eyes, and then when she spoke, it was as if she spoke to the me that I did not know, but the me indeed, the only one, which hearing did not hear, seeing did not see, and knowing did not know but was knowledge itself.

What could I not recite to her? She said gently, sitting on the grass, "Perhaps you know some Sanscrit verse that would befit this moment?" So I sang out those beautiful lines of Bharthrihari:

> *Mātar medini tāta māruta sakha jyoth sabhando-jala*
> O mother earth and father air,
> O friend fire, great kinsman water,
> O brother ether—to you all
> In final parting I make obeisance.
> Through your long association
> Have the right deeds been performed.
> Through you I have won pure shining wisdom,
> Unweaving the sweet delusions of the mind.
> Now I merge in the supreme Brahman.

We walked under the moon. On the ridge of Les Baux the dogs were barking in the village, some car was making a dreadful screeching noise as though the road were slipping underneath, and there was the shadowy flap of the night-wolves above us. I wondered if man could ever possess this earth, this moment; whether the world was not treading in me, and I walking into myself. Savithri gave one the sense that, do what you would, you could only *be,* and since you could only *be,* nothing could happen to you. Virtue for her was not a principle, a discipline; it was the acceptance that whether she married Pratap or "liked" that Muslim in London—she vaguely referred to both—they were both instants of an experience, always happening to itself. For her truth was not tomorrow or yesterday—that is why she scarcely ever referred to India; truth was wherever one is—for there is no anywhere or anywhen, but all *is,* for one is not.

I had never felt, no, not even in Saroja, a presence that made a gift of life to itself, and as such had a natural purity that showed up your vulgarities as the X-ray the bones. Madeleine had said to me that very morning, just before we had started for Les Baux, "But Rama, she is not real. She lives in a world of fantasy—a

126

dream. One cannot imagine her on the top of an English bus—and yet she walks, talks and laughs like everyone. She is strange, she just bewilders me."

"Is it long you've been married?" asked Savithri as we were going back towards the car. Not that it mattered what she asked or what I answered, whatever happened the moon alone shone—indeed, truth alone illumines.

"Some three and a half years," I said.

"Madeleine is such a truthful creature—she seems to say what she feels with a humility that moves me deeply. Tell me: is it possible always to speak the truth?"

"No," I answered. "At least I do not. Not that I lie a great deal, but it seems to me truth is a question of perspective. We're all like men and women and children at a wrestling match or a holy procession: the tall father sees the wrestler hit or the God bejewelled, and the son says, 'Papa, why is it you laugh, what did you see?' And he has to take the child on his shoulder and tell him the name of the Muslim wrestler from North India or of the Goddess whose Lord is awaiting Her at the temple door. But in either case the child, being higher than his father now, sees differently. Nobody can see at the level of your eye—and so nobody can speak the real truth. Not even the scientist."

"No, not even the scientist?" she asked.

"No, not even the scientist, for at best science is an equation within an equation, two symbols, first accepted by yourself, then compared in measurement, composition and action, to see whether they coincide with each other. It is just as if this moon, looking at the pool and seeing itself and knowing itself to be the moon, were to say "I am the moon." All science is only tautology. Do you know the famous story of Euler and God? My father used often to tell it to me. Euler and Diderot were both at the court of Catherine the Great. Someone said to Diderot, 'There is a man come, a great man, a German, and he can prove to you that God exists.' 'Excellent,' said Diderot, 'what a remarkable man!' So Euler was called in to prove God to Diderot. The court was all assembled. There was much powder, wig, garter and handkerchief about the place. Euler went straight to Diderot and said, and with a lifted finger,

'Monsieur, $\dfrac{a + b}{n} = X$. Hence God exists.'

A huge laugh shook the assembled court, and the humiliated Denis Diderot, says the story, asked permission of the Empress to return to France. Catherine the Great consented cordially, and Denis Diderot returned to his mansard in Paris and to his dictionary.

"We are all a set of Denis Diderots, for X explains away everything."

"A funny story," said Savithri.

"Well, it's the whole history of so-called 'progress.' To say electricity is such and such an equation, simply means electricity is electricity. It is just like saying I see a thing, or God is equal to X. When seeing goes into the make of form and form goes into the make of seeing, as the Great Sage says, 'what, pray, do you see?'"

"You see nothing or, if you will, yourself," answered Savithri, and I wondered at her instant recognition of her own experience.

"Therefore, what is Truth?" I asked. By now we were near Fort Sarrasine at the edge of the plateau of Les Baux, with the whole of La Camargue beneath us.

"Is-ness is the Truth," she answered.

"And is-ness is what?"

"Who asks that question?"

"Myself."

"Who?"

"I."

"Of whom?"

"No one."

"Then 'I am' is."

"Rather, I am am."

"Tautology!" she laughed.

"Savithri says Savithri is Savithri."

"And you say Savithri is what?" she begged.

"'I.'"

And the moon and the silence seemed to acknowledge that only the "I" shone.

"There is no Savithri," I continued after a while.

"No, there isn't. That I know."

"There is nothing," I persisted.

"Yes," she said. "Except that in the seeing of the seeing there's a seer."

"And the seer sees what?"

"Nothing," she answered.

"When the I is, and where the Nothing is, what is the Nothing but the 'I.' "

"So, when I see that tree, in that moonlight, that cypress, that pine tree, I see I—I see I—I see I."

"Yes."

"That is the Truth," she said, as we turned and walked back to the village.

She was silent all along the road, over the Rhône bridge, and by Montmajour, through Beaucaire, Arles, Vauvainargues, to the ruminant foothills of Mont Sainte-Victoire. Or if she spoke, it was just to say, "Sorry," when her foot touched mine, as we turned round a curve. Like all Indians she was sensitive to touch, and her foot shot back as though it had touched the *unreal*.

I told her then about the bull and the elephant and she enjoyed my stories.

"Could I take grass for your bull?" she asked, as we stood long above the hill of Cabasson, just before entering the sleeping city.

I said, "Of course." In the night she plucked some grass, and like a peasant woman she tied it in the hem of her sari. When we came to the Place de la République, she said, "How awake everything is! I cannot understand how anything could be dead."

"They say, here in Aix, that the dead live in cathedral towers—you can hear their echoes when the dogs sleep." And she remembered I had a memory that had not reached whiteness yet.

"I am sorry I am always kicking at your feet," she said, as though in answer to herself. "Father says I must once have been a lame horse. You can give me the most flat of flat floors, and I'll always find something to tumble against. I have fallen from an elephant while we were going shooting—and no sooner did Father realize I was under the elephant than he started sobbing; but like the *budumékaye* you spoke of in the fairy tale, I came up out of the jungle bush and nothing ever happened to me. There are people like that. I always fall off horses, stairways, trains— I once fell off a train from Allahabad to Ferozabad, and Father pulled the chain. Fortunately it was a metre-gauge line and we were going uphill; besides we were not far from the station. Yet how frightened everyone was. And I, like a confident child— but of course sobbing—came running behind the train. Since then there's always been a servant with me, wherever I have travelled, who has never to lose sight of me."

"But then how did they send you to Europe?"

"Well, between vanity and safety, they chose vanity. They wanted me to pass exams that no woman in the Rajput community ever had—so that my father could say, 'Here is Savithri; she's a Doctor of the University of Oxford or London.' Since the Princes have lost their titles, they must have other compensations. But I enjoy being in Europe. I love the activity, the singleness of purpose, the sense of freedom," she said and laughed. "But I am such an inveterate lazer that when I sleep I almost need a red-hot needle to awaken me. To me sleep is the most important of biological phenomena."

"I am sorry it is so late," I said.

"Nonsense, I meant that when I sleep I sleep. So, don't expect me before nine in the morning. I shall sleep like a buffalo."

We had by now got up the steps. She said, "Here is my bull, anyway," and she laid the grass at his mouth, like one does at the *ārathi* ceremony. Then I led her to her room and said, "Sleep well, sleep well, Savithri." I threw a last glance at that moon-coloured night, and as I went in, Madeleine was up and looking through the window at the back yard of Monsieur Ponchon.

"What a very beautiful night, Rama," she said, and led me to the window, and took me into her arms. I could feel the full joy of her presence in myself, and I suspected that there was another, an additional presence, that would grow, as this night, in the texture of being: a third presence, more real than our own, more lasting, and from that on to another, created through other presences, and thus more lasting again—like those olives which had been planted and made real to us by some Roman citizen of another age whose presence, unknown to himself, may have been felt that night—an embryo that had no eyes and no feet yet, but had lit the congress of circumstance in which two beings had known a truth, which had a beginning, a middle and an end, yet had been consecrated for an instant at the edge of the "I." Discovery is a whisper to oneself, and the night of love is an embalmment, a holiness that we place outside of time, in the knowledge that creation is truth.

When I woke to myself, I heard Madeleine crying, as if the womb bore a light that was too difficult to carry. I slipped her back to bed, and lay by her hour after hour, touching her forehead and wiping her perspiration, as though her pain was the first, the only one of mankind. There is no pain more acute than a pain unnameable, and all the shine of the world is only a prophecy, a shout that death is, that one loses another, that a tight breast has a pain no husband can take away, were he even within you. Who is within after all? No one. It is one's own pain that sobs to oneself. To be woman is to suffer, to bear the yoke of man. The rains will break before the door of the barn is reached. Night alone exists and the exhaustion of an empty day.

Madeleine's body had reached out to its full womanhood, and I was the lie.

When I came down the next morning, Savithri was out in the garden already, her fingers touching this rose and that, her nostrils smelling the air of pine and sea, and her eyes looking into themselves, as though something arbitrary had happened, as though somewhere the earth had slipped from its centre and a new equinox had commenced. Not that the polar ice would have melted, nor the bears run screaming round the world, nor the arctic palimpeds found it too hot for them to stand on the snow and preen themselves before the males in honoured delight, but something intimate, some geological substratum, had broken into bits, and space had emptied itself out of the depths. A new age had commenced, with new fauna and flora, with monkeys that spoke, with birds that walked, with men that were taller and understood each other in the instant of recognition. Time lay like sunshine over the earth, and when flowers grew it was not for adornment or for fruiting, but for the dew to gather itself into a round cognisance, and for woman to go touching herself in lit moments of the sun. There were not many women, there was but one woman—one form, one sound, one love. It was not something to say to another, or even to give or to take, but to see in oneself as a child discovers its navel; and once recognized it still had no name, no more than the navel for the child which saw it constantly.

The trouble with time is that it creates its own myth, and thinks we become with its becoming. Just as we can park motor-cars, we can park thoughts in time, and go away on our job, which is living. To forget time is to live in recognition, and whoever said love could be born? Love is never born, but all is premonition of love. You come upon it as you come upon—as you come upon a poppy, by the roadside. You drive past it and say, "Oh, the lovely poppy, how beautiful she looks in the sun!" In fact the poppy has nothing to say, not even that she is a poppy, but to you it has happened; to her nothing has happened, for what can happen to what *is?* The Is-ness cannot be added on to is-ness, love cannot be added on to love; for to know love is to love love and to love love is just to be.

To lie in the arms of a beloved, Savithri must have thought, is then just to take delight in one's self, to park the car in the village, go to the top of the mountain in the mist of night, and look out for the sound of the sea.

"What woke you up—and so early?" I asked.

"Nothing," she lied. "I had a rare and sound sleep. You know, they say round people like me sleep like a pumpkin," and she laughed at herself.

It was true she was rounder than she—or maybe even I—might have liked, but one forgot it; one knew she had some wisdom of herself that made her voice so intimate, so sustaining and so pure.

"What a country!" she continued. "I have marvelled at these dragon-flies. I played with one, all about the garden. It's a pity I must be going away so soon."

"Villa Sainte-Anne does not go anywhere," I answered. "Nor do Ramaswamy and Madeleine. Everything will be here when the Princess wants to be here." Covering my lie with a barbarous joke I bowed. Savithri no more felt the Princess than the poppy felt she was the poppy. Savithri just was; it was only me that had the Brahmin, with the Brahmin and the I as separate points of reference. Having only one point of reference, it seemed to me she had no problems, no equations. For her, marriage would be to wed anyone, for whatever happened would just happen, and the wedding too would be a happening. He alone acts who is a stranger to himself.

Innocence, I thought, was like her breaking into song. And seeing a jasmine in my garden—though she could scarcely believe that Europe could ever have jasmines—Savithri sat on the stone seat and said, "Shall I sing? I feel like singing," and like a seagull that leaves the waters and goes slowly upwards, she started,

> Asuwanajana seejá seejá,
> Préma bŏla bŏyi
> With the water of my tears I sprinkled it,
> And I reared the creeper of love,

with her eyes closed, and the swallows in the olives above us making quite a fuss about it all. I felt it was somehow improper for me to stay, and I slowly left her to her song, and went up to make coffee for Madeleine. Being a Thursday, she did not have to go to Collège, and so I went about my job quietly. Once the table was laid and the coffee ready, I went to wake Madeleine, but she was already lying with her eyes wide open. She said the song had woken her up.

"What a mélopée! And what sadness there is in your people. That is why, Rama, I always ask you when you laugh, why is there such an acute sorrow behind it?"

"Existence," I answered her, "is a passage between life and death, and birth and death again, and what an accumulation of pain man has to bear. Is it then a wonder the Buddha, with palaces and queens, with a kingdom and an heir, left his home to find that from which there is no returning? Suppose, Madeleine, you were always and always travelling: from hotel to hotel, from Hôtel du Midi to Hôtel de Venise, from Pension Mimosa to the Hôtel Baltimore, through mountain, sea and air you could travel —yet where would you *live?* You could only live in Life, and to find what that means is to know the whole of wisdom."

"Sometimes, Rama, I want to run away from you, run far away

from you, just to listen to stupid innocent laughter, like Tante Zoubie's, or go to a circus and see the clown make everyone laugh —this high seriousness reminds me of poor Werther. I am not serious, you know, Rama, and one day, perhaps, I shall run away." She laughed, but I knew she said it in no fun—I could see the curve of her thought. "Yesterday I felt lost without you," she continued. "You had left early in the morning, and I knew you would not come till late at night, and I felt utterly lonely, and so lost. I went to the hairdresser after Collège to have my hair done—I was a week too early, but I told them some lie. Then I went to buy some papers for you. It was only six o'clock. I saw the Grands Magasins open—so I went into one and wandered. And what do you think I bought myself? A *moulin à poivre,* just a wee little thing, that would serve no purpose; but it could be there all the same, and maybe one day it will yet come in handy. Then I bought the pepper for it. I must use it some day—you know, I am French, and nothing should be useless; everything must have a function, a right to exist. Thus instead of curry I will now and again grind you some pepper," she said, and rose to have a wash.

I laid the table on the veranda, so that we could all have breakfast together, and when I went down to call Savithri, I found her doing her hair.

"Come in," she said unself-consciously, but I did not go in.

"Breakfast ready!" I shouted. In a minute she was ready too, her braid in her hand, and she ran up with the hairpins between her fingers. She sat at the table while I brought the coffee, and when I returned I found Madeleine fixing up Savithri's hair. Women have intimacy with each other in the things of the body— in face powder, shoes, disease and underclothes—that men could never have with one another. That is why women have to speak of frocks and frills, of jewels, medicines and gynaecologists, as though it was their algebra of living, and men have no more to do with them than the hog with the lotus.

Life is made for woman—man is a stranger to this earth. We are all Bodhisattvas, and one night we, too, will leave the wife, lying by the newborn one with the lamp lit behind her, and the curve of her eye folding life itself into its depths. And while

Kanthaka wakens to this tiding, and sends the neigh that would awaken the citizens of Kapilavastu to the news of departure, the awaiting angels will close keyhole and tile-edge, that none be awakened, and Channa the appointed groom bring the horse to the door, while the sentries sleep. As door after door of the city opens, the sentries sleeping at their seats, the angels shutting the noise of hinge and lock, Kanthaka flies to the frontiers. Cutting his hair, the Buddha sends it to the very skies, for the gods to receive in homage and devotion. And when they reach the River Ganges, Kanthaka kneels to the Lord and says, "Lord, may this poor creature, too, be permitted to come?" And the Master says, "I go thither, Kanthaka, whence there is no returning," and then he departs on the journey from which there is no returning. Kanthaka goes back to Kapilavastu and dies immediately, to be reborn and return to the Compassionate One, a disciple, an Arhat. "For all that is created, Ananda, is composite. And the composite knows decay and death. There is a point in one, a centre, a knowledge, touching which there is no becoming; there is only the end of the quest, the desperation, the Truth." All men are but pilgrims of the Tree.

Savithri, like most Indians today, knew little of the Buddha. In fact, Madeleine was astonished at this strange ignorance of so great a wisdom. I explained that Buddhism had merged into Hinduism so that today we cannot distinguish one from the other —just as in South India you cannot distinguish the Dravidian tradition from the Aryan tradition, and truly speaking Aryan wisdom seems to have found a more permanent place in South India than in the Aryan North.

"India absorbs everything and makes it her own," I repeated a banality, and Madeleine looked at me with an almost desperate irritation.

"India makes everything and everywhere an India. But if anything does not achieve Indiahood, it is the untruth, the lie, the Maya, the British," she said and laughed.

"Why, the British are very much loved today," I said, knowing what she meant. "Isn't that so, Savithri?"

"So much so indeed, Sister," said Savithri, "that when Mountbatten left, we all wept. We are a set of sentimental fools," added

Savithri very wisely. That was not her phrase, I thought; it sounded like the adage of a politician.

"The French haven't left Pondicherry yet," said Madeleine. "The old French peasant does not leave anything. He also absorbs —in terms of dividends . . ."

It was a poor argument, and it showed how we were all trying to hide ourselves from each other. Meanwhile the postman brought the mail, and Savithri went down to have her bath. Madeleine said she would start cooking, for Savithri's train, the *Mistral,* left at two-thirty, and I sat looking at the letters, some from India and some from London and Paris, feeling I wish I were not, and were I, I should never be again.

There was also a letter from Oncle Charles, which spoke of Catherine's visit. He would put her on the Saturday morning train in Paris—they would have to leave Rouen early (at four or thereabouts) but she could always sleep sitting in the train. He did not like the idea of a night journey for a *jeune fille.* Of course he was being old-fashioned, but you could not cut away his years, even with a knife from Saint-Étienne. What was was, and he knew I would accept him as he was. I did—at least I tried to. He hoped Catherine would learn much from her contact with me. "Give her bright ideas so that she can build a happy and a solid home. For a woman her home is her paradise," he concluded. He was sure that the sight of me and Madeleine together would be an inspiration, an example for a whole life. "A father's hope is always that his children should be happy. I have done practically nothing for Madeleine's happiness—she almost grew up like a blackbird. But Catherine was different. Rama, she needs advice and help. Help her, and Zoubie and I will be ever grateful to you. *Je vous embrasse tous les deux et bien affectueusement,* Oncle Charles."

Catherine's impending visit brightened my horizon. It encouraged me to think of other things, more concrete. I liked Catherine too, her shy joviality, her suppressed *joie de vivre,* her maternity (for you could not think of Catherine without a brood of children), and her natural affection for all men and things. She was what the French call *"une bonne maîtresse de maison."* He who would wed her would not just wed an heiress—for her father had made considerable money—but a good housewife. And she was pleased with that, and when Father retired she would inherit the *notariat*. Like this the orchard would not change hands . . .

The lunch was rather a sad affair—everyone was merged in his or her own thoughts. Georges dropped in to say good-bye to Savithri. He was always so elegant in his thought, as though life were a series of genuflexions, said not in Latin but in French. God was the immediate ground of every gesture. He bent low, and lifted his hat to Savithri and to Madeleine, then waved his hand to me as he walked down the steps.

"He is one of the finest human beings I have met," Madeleine averred. "If only he didn't make a lifelong apology for not being in a soutane. A man left to himself," she went on, looking at me, "will end in a mathematical puzzle. He needs to clothe his thoughts with the cry of children—with the sobbing of a woman. If man wants to be a superman he has just to be a man." They both laughed.

"I may still be a Yogi, some day," I said. "I shall follow Sri Aurobindo, and abolish death."

"Oh, Rama, to think that you will have to be bored with me for eternity—a sad thought."

"Eternity is only for men," I remarked. "Women will die at the opportune time. I have always told you polygamy is man's nature. Both the Hindus and the Christians are wrong about these single-hearted devotions. Islam is the better religion, from that point of view—it treats life naturally."

"And leads you thus—straight to Pakistan," added Savithri, somewhat bitterly. This was the only time, I felt, she showed any personal feelings.

"We're in France," I reminded her, "and French trains don't have the euphoria and the fantasy of Indian railways. If we want to catch the *Mistral* let's get the cases out. And while the ladies drink coffee, the he-man will put the luggage into the car."

"There's no he-man in the world of God," said Madeleine, rising. "But the she-woman of France is just made to carry the burden for a Brahmin." She knew with my lungs I should not carry anything. When the coffee was finished we all came down, and with what absolute acceptance did Madeleine carry down Savithri's luggage. Savithri gave some grass to the bull, and she looked a long, long while at the two big eyes of Villa Sainte-Anne while Madeleine rested the cases against a rock, and then at one stretch we reached the car.

How incompetent we two Indians felt before *things*.

"I am a peasant woman, after all," said Madeleine, excusing us. "My great-grandmothers must have carried potatoes and eggs to the fair of Saint-Séver." And we all got into the car.

Madeleine was gentle, sad and understanding. Savithri's thoughts were already in London. Hussain Hamdani awaited her, with his violence and his devotion. "I dread going to London," she said. "I wish all the world were Provence."

"Then you'd have the farandole every evening, a big snore every afternoon, and in between you'd hear Mistral sing of Mireille. Never saw anything more lazy than this," was Madeleine's confirmed conclusion.

My silence was pitiful. Madeleine had her feet on the ground; Catherine, after all, was coming on Saturday, and Madeleine had such grand plans for everything. She even knew what gâteaux she would buy, and when she would invite Georges. Latterly, feeling Georges might be too shy in the beginning, she had begun to think Lezo might be of some use. So this evening there was going to be a comeback for Lezo, and the first Sanscrit lesson again. No, she was going to learn Pali direct. Lezo was even more happy, for thus he proved his importance. The more obscure a thing, the more familiar Lezo was with it. Georges was coming at five o'clock to have a chat with me. At six all of us would go on a walk, say hullo to the elephant, and if the mistral were not too severe, go up to Sainte-Ophalie, coming back through the olives under the moonlight.

Madeleine seemed almost lighthearted, happy. "Rama is either a thousand years old or three," she said to Savithri. "He cannot do anything wrong, for he's either so wise or so innocent. He drives a car well, but just let it purr a little and he jumps from his seat as if he'd heard a cobra hiss. He is very frightened of machines. But let him have silence to himself, and then he'll talk to you of trees as though he'd been a tree in his last life, and will become one in the next. He's been born a man by mistake—for my joy," she said, convinced she was convinced of her own happiness. "To think that a man born in Hariharapura should marry a girl from the Paroisse de Saint-Médard. Strange, very strange, isn't it? Rama says, when a Mysore peasant woman sees a rainbow, she exclaims, 'There, there! It must be the wedding of the dog and the jackal!' There must have been a rainbow somewhere," she finished, "on that dull, rainy sky of Rouen."

Madeleine spoke a great deal like this, almost to herself, when she knew what was not true should be true, and could be a truth, by repetition. She put her hand on her belly afterwards, as though some greater truth lay within her, and my eyes catching her gesture gave me confidence that life would continue; for men are born and men "die"—even women are born and marry and continue to live. Life was like a railway line: it went and went on almost as though by itself, slipped into a branch line, stopped at the small country *gare,* and whistled and ran off when the bell rang. Then the cypresses would come, and the marshes, and after Saint-Pujol and Saint-Trophime and Sainte-Madeleine would be Tarascon. And all who know Tarascon know the Rhône flows through her, and the Rhône, broadening out, flows all over the place and reaches Marseille.

Marseille, as you know, is a big port, and ships come there, come from all over the world, from America and even from India. And people come in them—and people take trains and go away to Paris and to London. People go to London, anyone could go to London. I often go to London myself and I work at the British Museum. I did not tell her—I mean Savithri—that. Madeleine alone knew. Savithri of course knew with the knowledge she had of what Savithri was and not what I was. For Savithri London was not a city, a place in geography—it was somewhere, a spot, maybe a red spot in herself. Like the London traffic lights, it might suddenly grow red, and then like a kunkum, a large one on the round face of a Bengali woman, would the green go up, the cool, round, auspicious green of London.

"What a strange noise these trams make," she said, "and how strange these road signs look. They look so primitive." Then remembering Madeleine was French, she added, "And as for India,

139

we have no road signs at all." That brought the car to a stop—for we were already at the Gare Saint-Charles. The train came in very simply and easily. Savithri got into the compartment as if she had always known Marseille and the train, but could always be forgotten by herself. I felt anxious for her, and so I said, "Please send us a wire as soon as you reach London. Will you?"

"That's just like my father or my great-uncle!" she exclaimed spontaneously. With Savithri truth and tact were but one instinctive experience. She could no more tell a real lie than grow taller —or even, maybe, leaner. The departure was normal and simple —I bought a dinner ticket for her, and waved a long and simple good-bye. Madeleine was happy to have met her and was sad at her departure.

"It's three thousand years of civilization that produces a thing like her," she said, as though paying a compliment to me.

"And five for me," I said, claiming my Upanishadic ancestor, as though my grandfather's grandfather had seen him, and we'd inherited land from his estate. My sadness was intellectual, abstract; it took refuge in history and metaphysics. What would I have done if there had been no Georges coming at five o'clock and no chance for us to go crazy over the Monophysites? We were now studying their texts, and not knowing Latin I was dependent on Madeleine and Georges to help me decipher Catholic, rather Christian, theology. Georges was the master there, and he was happy. Work is holy because it hides our love of love. The fig leaf, perhaps, was the first civilized act of art.

It was a jolly day, though, and Madeleine was singing. She was singing some old refrain from a Provençal *berceuse:*

> Soun enfant es mai blanc que la néou,
> E tréluisis coumo uno stello
> Ai! ai! ai! que la maire es bello,
> Ai! ai! qu'Enfant est béou.

She said, "I'll drive now," and with her at the wheel the car took on a new rhythm, felt familiar and happy, as horses feel when their real masters come, not their grooms; bending and lifting itself up the car carried us back, and I had fallen into myself. I knew that there, in that steadiness, man knew the only everlasting peace.

"Peace, Madeleine," I said, "is where the wife drives the car at eighty kilometres an hour, and the man falls into his abysm looking at his nose."

"I will put honey on your nose, one day," she said and kissed me on the top of my olfactory organ to prove that love lay in familiarity. You think you possess what you have known so well. Love at nineteen is as illusory as happiness at twenty-five. Marriage is a bond, and you live together because you can change hands at the wheel, and bring gâteaux for guests, as you pass *chez* Madame Tissier. I was lonely, and looked at the trees on the Place de la République. I counted them and they were twenty-three.

PAGES from my diary.

October 17. "Catherine came here the day before yesterday. It's no use pushing her and Georges into each other's arms. Of course she's shy—but she looks at men as she would a legal book, for reference and for dependence—not because she's a lawyer, but because she seeks permanence. All men and women (and they are, for some reason, contemptuously called 'bourgeois') who need permanence—that is, the majority of mankind—are dharmic, in the sense that if they did not know that these fat, huge, gilt-lettered tomes existed the governance of France would be impossible. No child would be born, and no man could keep a shop, and no prostitute a card, and no woman a husband. Birth and death need a law—the smaller law that flows from the greater Law, beyond birth and death. All rules are for liberty. To obey (the *dharma*) is to be free. (Nobody looks freer than a soldier or a police officer.) A true bourgeois then is a saint, an anointed being, to whom his home is a monastery, his *dharma* his citizenship.

"The saint of the monastery is the real bourgeois; he lives frugally, he stores up for Paradise. He who stores up for another age, another world, can only have a great imagination. It was a Provençal woman who said—and Madeleine heard it from a friend, who'd heard it—'Monsieur le Pasteur, are there any English people in Paradise?' 'Yes, *ma vieille,*' answered the good Pastor of Antibes. 'In that case,' the old lady answered, 'I do not wish to go there. They are so immoral, the English are. A second question, Monsieur le Pasteur. Do you think my granddaughter Marguerite could join me in Paradise?'—'Oh, yes, dear lady!'—'Marguerite makes such lovely fried aubergines.' The good Pastor could not say anything, so he smiled, lifted his hat in adieu, and went away muttering many a prayer."

October 23. "I am a tired man. I am of a tired race which for three (four or five?) thousand years has led such a studious, thin-fed, sedentary existence, that our nose and throat, our ears and tongue and eyes, have lost somewhat in native agility. We understand by other means, however . . . I suppose our sensibility—made more for talking to the gods than to man, made more for formulating the incalculable than the concrete—our mind slips round objects with the facility of water over pebbles. Yes, we Brahmins do make engineers, doctors and even military men today, but it's like one of those pillars in the inner courts of our old houses—though eaten by wood-lice it continues. Not that it supports the roof, no—it supports its roots, and the rest is held by air, by faith. Oh, this fight against the contingency of modern life, of modern civilization; the battle is lost before it's begun! We've the fibres to know, not the sinews to act: we, the real impotents of the earth."

October 26. "The biology of woman—and the cardinal part it plays in her activity—you see it best, not when she is in love (for that is a melodrama) but when she wants to get a man and a woman entangled for the continuance of the race. Just as a mother elephant when she senses an enemy lifts her trunk fiercely, whether the little one be hers or another's—for maternity is anonymous—how Madeleine fights (in mind and body) against sun and rain, as it were, against hunger and cold; her one preoccupation is, a poor meal or a strong mistral might upset her astrology of events. How relentlessly, and with what instinctive wisdom, she makes every move, now pushing Catherine forward for her stability (economic and otherwise, hence talks of the sad fate of notaries, so dependent on the goodwill of everyone, more like a confessor than a doctor, etc., etc. . . .), now for her education (for Catherine had done very well in her exams, especially in her Latin); but when it comes to Georges the maternal instinct gives way to something more unacknowledged, more shy. Madeleine, whom anyone could see has such insight into the human mind, knows Georges's dependence on her. She knows she has just to come and stand behind us, her hand on my shoulder, as we play chess together—like all Russians, he is excellent at this ancient Indian game—and Georges will suddenly grow so agile with his fingers, and stupid in his calculations. She is the angel against his demon, and now it is not he who bears her rags, but she bears her crown of his making, and resplendent it shines, though somewhat sadly, against my Brahminic autocracy.

"God, that invisible force in man, seems to have given the Brahmin a whip, a trident, with which invisibly he plays his chess. The elephant goes in and out of the jungle at the invisible magician's command. The king falls or moves according to a silent imprecation or a mantra. Words are made inwardly, and a pressure here or there makes the smile, the anger, the tear. No man should have so much power over a woman.

"But woman has no morality in this matter. For her the beauty of this earth, the splendour of houses and parliaments, the manufacture of sword and of brocade—be it even from Benares—the pearl necklace, the lovely cradle, the cinema, the circus, the Church—all, all is a device for copulation and fruition, of death made far, of famine made impossible, of the smile of child made luminescent on the lap of her, the Mother of God. Perhaps as civilization grows more and more terrestrial—and civilization, as against culture, is terrestrial—the feminine permanence will grow, as in America. Death will be abolished, through the funeral parlours, and love will be made into the passion of the bed. Man is a stranger to this earth—he must go."

October 29. "Today, how nearly I was on the verge of tears myself. We had gone up to Sainte-Ophalie with the young moon (Madeleine has her own astrology). Slowly and as though by accident she drew me into an olive orchard to seek, she said, some mushrooms. Georges, of course, could not follow us into this world of thickets and low branches, and Catherine and he were left to themselves. Evening fell, and Madeleine found a new path for us to make our way down.

" 'I found it the other day,' she lied. 'And Rama, I wanted to show it to you. You cannot imagine how beautiful our house looks from the bottom of this hill. Rama, I'm happy,' she said, and kissed me on the cheek. She knew I knew that her thoughts were elsewhere.

"The young moon slid over the olives as though he, too, were in connivance. But 'Mado, Mado!' Catherine started searching for us. Madeleine did not answer, and put her hand against my mouth. 'Sssh! Please do not answer.' Soon the moon would go down. And Georges had, in addition to his half-paralysed hand, very bad eyes. I always led him about on our walks.

"Madeleine and I sat on some rocks and talked of insipid things. She was not interested in what I was saying—something about my family and India, and a letter from Saroja. Madeleine talked to me of her Collège.

"It is always a subject of major importance to her, especially her headmistress, who is anything but a saint, and fears Madeleine for being the steadiest of all of them. They are mostly old maids, who not having enough money were not able to marry whom they wanted; the men who did not have much, mainly teachers or municipal clerks, had courted them, in the days when Madeleine's colleagues were still quite young—and a professor is a professor after all, and they thought of their education and their future family and children, so they married no one. How Madeleine shows off before them her matrimony and her joy! Sometimes, I almost said, joy is needed for official purposes: you do not go so far and marry an Indian, however clever and well-to-do—and in the eyes of many I must at least have been a minor prince, for all Aix believes it—unless you can prove on your face that joy is not a by-product, but the very stuff of your daily existence. For a woman her joy is a social quantum, a proof of her truth.

"Georges must have been unhappy, as the wind was still quite strong—not the mistral, but the wind from the sea. He must have limped down, almost like the donkeys, with ears laid back, as they carry the olive barrels from the mountains. Catherine cannot have been happy either—she must have been shy. This was perhaps the first time she had ever been with a man alone, and of an evening. She must have been frightened too—he might have done something. But as we came down both he and she were seated on the elephant, like two children who had quarrelled over dolls, waiting for their mother to come and settle the dispute. Thus no sooner did Catherine see us, than joy rose to her face—even her voice changed, and she started blubbering like a schoolgirl.

" 'We went in search of some *champignons du pays*—they're so delicious. I wanted you to taste them before you go,' Madeleine shouted. The last sentence was for Georges—better know Catherine is not going to be here always and for ever. Catherine and Madeleine both begged Georges to stay on for dinner, and he reluctantly agreed. We made rice and curry—at least, I and Catherine did—while Georges and Madeleine were in the drawing room, talking away about Buddhism. Georges is never so happy as when he is talking abstract things, and especially if Madeleine is about. To him somehow Madeleine is the proof of recognition, the touch on the shoulder that says, 'Yes, it's perfect,' and the world then looks not so much bright as right. For Georges purity is everything in its place, like the bell, the candle and the censer; the glory of God can thus be celebrated. Georges, in fact, is a holy bureaucrat.

"In this again, for law is but the continuance and the determination of the Law, Catherine and he have much in common. Only the hierarchies vary—Georges's dominion is the Heaven and Catherine's the earth. All that one needs is a ladder, a golden ladder.

"I am becoming a cynic—so I must stop. I am angry against someone. I must remove it in the seed, or like a cactus it will grow all over the place, and it then would need a superior intervention to clear *my* land. Oh, the ricefields, the yellowing green that flows from canal to the tank-bund, from the tank-bund to the jackfruit-tree fields across the Himavathy, and the coconut garden of Māda above; and Grandfather Ramanna reading the Upanishads to old fogeys, who come and listen, afternoon after afternoon, saying, 'Oh yes, Maya, it's like the son of a barren woman or the horn on the head of a hare,' and the shaven widows and the tufted heads say, 'So it is indeed, Rammanoré.' I should have been a Bhatta, and looked after my ricefields; should have read the *Mandukya* Upanishad with Gaudapada's *Karika*, and then Sankara's commentary on it; should have read the *Ramayana* and the *Uttara Khanda* especially for the villagers' benefit; carried my copper tumbler and spoon to funeral feasts, with the shawl on my shoulders, and with betel in my mouth (not to forget the fee, the silver tucked at the waist in the dhoti-fold); belching and spitting would I have come home to have a Kaumudi or a Rukmini press my legs and sit beside me waving the fan—'Ah! how cool the breeze is.' The Lord sleeps, come cattle for water, come peasant for astrology. They gave one rupee eight annas today, did Eight-Pillared House Nanjundiah. Ramappa is having his nap after the funeral feast.

"The peasant would leave his cucumbers and the snake-gourds at the door, 'Mother, tell the Learned One, Timma, the left-handed, will come tomorrow. We've to let down a new boat on the river.' Rukmini, or Kaumudi, would give warm coffee on waking, and once the evening prayers were over, and the betel leaves eaten, and the vessels in the kitchen washed, how wondrous it would be to have a cup of warm milk, and the beauty of Rukmini's young body beside one. It smells of musk and of the nests of birds . . .

"No, I shall never be a Brahmin—I should be such a poor eater at a funeral feast. I shall tear my clothes, and set off to the Himalayas. Something hypostatic calls me. Mother mine, I will go."

November 1. "I must talk less: talk less even to myself."

November 3. "Once again it happened last night—that same emptiness, that mango-seed-like kernel that lay within me, and I remembered what Grandmother had said of the mango seed: 'My child, if you swallow it, it will grow and grow within you, put out its branches, through your nostrils first, then through your ears, and then through the mouth, and it will become so big that it will grow out of you a tree.' The whole night I lay with it in me, and I could not go to sleep till the early hours of the morning. Madeleine, too, I could hear, rolled about in bed for a long time. Then she went to sleep and spoke in her dream. I could not make out what it was, but she was not happy either. There should be nothing in an act but the act itself. But if the mango seed

147

enters into it, then it becomes three acts: one before and one after, and in between is the space of no one, which no one wants. It is like a dead rat in plague-time—you throw it opposite your neighbour's door, and he throws it opposite his, and this one slings it on to the veranda of widow or concubine. These lift it up by the tail and with mosquitoes, fleas and all, throw it neatly into the right dustbin. Till the municipal cart comes and takes it away—it lies there, a reminder of our infection. And some, of course, may die of this too . . .

"The whole thing started, I think, on that Saturday night. The evening walks have been going on, of course. How truly the classical poets have sung of Phoebe and her influence on the lecherous humours of mankind. Georges, of course, has been coming every evening. Though he's such an innocent creature, it hasn't needed much time to realize what he had to know. And like a sincere and good *homo sapiens* he has been playing his game discreetly and correctly. He does not look back so often for Madeleine, and sometimes, too, we conveniently stay back or take a different route to return home, for we are skilful with our limbs and we can skip down goat-paths easily. 'Catherine,' Madeleine shouts, at the beginning of Sainte-Ophalie, 'Rama is cold, and you know he needs good exercise. So we're going to run,' and hooking her arm in mine, she drags me downhill. Though my lungs ache, I just do not interfere. 'Look after Georges, Cathy,' she shouts again, from the bottom of the olive grove, and we hear Georges shouting back, 'Enjoy yourself. We shall soon be back for the soup.'

"And in all honesty it could not be said Georges is unhappy. If his voice does not carry that spontaneous, almost innocent lilt, it is not without a human touch. For Georges, like all human beings, wants to care and to be cared for. Nobody knows if ever he has loved anyone in his life—he never mentions it. But one can see, somewhere, a scar on his mind and on his heart; his impotent arm seems but the external signum of an internal event. Catherine has one thing which Georges cannot but see: she has maidenhood, she has innocence—in the Church sense, for in my sense she knows all that she should know as female and future mother—and she is a good Catholic. That she is not so much

148

interested in metaphysical discourses might just as well be the one thing to be recommended in this case.

" 'Imagine Catherine with a brood of four children—she says she wants at least six—discussing the Monophysites and the Manicheans, and Georges learning Chinese in order to tell the difference between one monastic costume and the other. One particular order might wear camel-hair and the other yak-hair, but for Georges this made all the difference in their dogma. To Georges, tradition is like a dictionary—it gives the right meanings. Imagine Catherine concerned with the morphology of the word, *itsu* or *Ki-to*, which in Chinese, I've read somewhere, means "in-between-two" or "the indivisible." It applies as much to cloth that is woven or to the thought that is constructed. Being probably of Buddhist origin the Manichaeans applied it to thought, and Georges will make your Monophysites take it as "garment," "cloth made of a hard-stuff, the fibre of a hard-fruit or peel of tree, like the acacia cinna, etc. etc. . . ." '

"I heard Madeleine's discourse with conviction. I am convinced—and it needed little effort to convince me—that Catherine is the right wife, the perfect mate, the holy companion for Georges. If she had nothing in her, at least she would never be an emotional problem for Georges. And Georges above all needs calm and rest—for work and prayer.

"True, Madeleine fascinates him. She fascinates him by just that which he cannot have, must not have. It is, to use his own expression on another subject, *'la concupiscence de l'esprit.'* Georges loves the intricacies, the *sorties,* the *clairières,* the bogs and marshes and clear silences of Madeleine's mind. To be near her, he realizes, is to feel intelligent. He can no more have a sinful thought beside her than he could beside a running brook . . . No, not quite, but almost.

"Catherine on the other hand is such a safe, such a *known* creature. (Astrologically speaking, Catherine is a Capricorn and Madeleine a Scorpio—and that makes all the difference between the two cousins.) It did not take long before Catherine knew where Georges should rest, where stop to change the position of his paralysed hand—he put it sometimes at the left elbow, and sometimes he made the two hands clasp one another. And just as

I used to ask Grandfather Kittanna, 'Grandfather, shall I now give you the snuffbox?' and Grandfather Kittanna would say, 'How well you know when I want it, good boy,' and allow me to open his silver snuffbox—not knowing that when he stopped reading it was not because the page had ended but because he wanted to understand something, grasp a philosophical point, maybe even wait for an illumination, and then it was snuff just did the thing—so it is with Catherine, when some thought pursues Georges, and it goes round and round his head like a fly in a dark room, and she talking away of Rouen and the quays, of Zoubie's stories of her diplomatic career—brief though it was— or of Oncle Charles and his jokes about the Republic. ' "In my village," Oncle Charles tells proudly,' Catherine will begin, ' "they say when the Third Republic of 1870 was proclaimed there was but one man and a dog to salute the tricolour flag on the Mairie, and the name of the man was Léon Henri Portichaut, and his dog was called Zizi. So we always called it the Republic of Zizi Portichaut. And to speak the truth, this Fourth Republic could not even be given such a distinguished name; it should be called the Republic of Mimi Portichaut, in honour of a famous woman who played her part behind the scenes in the making of this great Republic." ' And Georges will remark, 'Ah, is that so, is that so—Catherine, you are full of such wonderful stories.'

"Catherine does not want much; she just likes to go about with this man, and when one comes to the corner by the Englishman's villa and the dog, to say, 'Shall we stay here for a while?' and see how grateful Georges looks for this kind suggestion, his glasses catching the rays of the evening sun and making him look every inch a professor. Or when they limp up higher, to say, 'Now, this is what schoolchildren do—*les enfants à quatre pattes en avant!*' and Georges will even try to laugh. Catherine is not silly or uneducated, but she has that awkward compassion which makes women think a man can be happy by being taken to a picture, or given the cake he usually says he relishes, or offered a packet of neat, nice handkerchiefs. Catherine's heart is in the right place, only it has to be metaphysically educated; if she be indeed the Catholic she says she is, then must she know the great saying of Saint John: 'For love is of God and he that loveth but loveth God.' And if only Catherine could understand her own face, I am sure she would see what beauty has come into it, what clarity, and what rounded hope. She knows with the simple faith people have, she knows like a local train always coming somehow to the right station, that her destiny is bound with this man's. When she kisses her cousin Mado so often, it is not merely affection but gratitude.

"The other day we found Catherine taking Georges's arm, no, not on the main roads, but when he, impatient, wanted to go down a mule-path with us and cut the distance by so much twist and gradation. But as soon as he reached the main road, he said, *'Merci, Mademoiselle!'* as though to a pupil of his. Madeleine's arm he rarely takes—he has too much respect for her, and maybe an unnameable fear.

"So evening after evening goes without a word being said, without a gesture of any consequence from anyone (for Madeleine waits, and with what anxiety, every evening to come home and cast a sly look at Catherine's lips, to see if the rouge has had any dents in it—I call it the examining of the wedding sheets, which eunuchs do in upper-class Muslim houses, to report that all is well to the mother-in-law) and yet there seems, like the quiet and simple flow of the Rhône after Lyon, through Valence, Montélimar and Tarascon, that there is nothing but the wide, the inevitable sea. On just a point of this watery expanse of the Middle-of-the-World is the thrice-sacred Saintes-Maries-de-la-Mer, and there the gipsies come once a year for the festival of their Saint, because it was there, on those sacred sands, that the early Christians brought the relics of Marie-Madeleine; and it was there that they hid them, in caves and cellars, till they could come out into the open, and raise a cathedral at Saint-Maximin, and praise her with:

Beatae Mariae Magdalenae, quaesumus, Domine, suffragiis adjuvemur: cujus precibus exoratus quatriduanum fratrem Lazarum vivum ab inferis resuscitasti.

If Georges marries, no doubt it will be in the Chapel of Mary Magdalene at Saint-Maximin. There is no question about it whatsoever. Father Zenobias will be one witness and I the other. How Oncle Charles will love it and thank us for a lifetime . . .

"Yes, everything is ready but a gesture—a symbol. It will not be, to put it crudely, the examining of the wedding sheets—and this by now Madeleine has fully realized—but some elevation, some communion; a revelation that will make the inevitable emerge, not as knowledge, but as a fact, a recognition, a binding on the altar of one's own being."

Reading through these pages, I can see how a certain vulgarity had entered me—me the great "purist"—and how it already indicated the meaning of those confused and sad predicaments which were to follow. The problem, alas, is not for the psychoanalyst to explain, but for the metaphysician to name.

The psychoanalyst, after all, is only like the Indian magician who can make the mango grow before you, but you cannot eat of it; he can make the whole riches of the District Treasury come and lie before you with label, seal and all, and yet you cannot take a copper piece out of it; or make the rope go high and the sun mount with the mounting rope, but you cannot go up to the sun; nor can you be like the boy bound in a basket and cut into bits before you with sword and knife, and when called, "Baloo, Baloo!" there he is coming down yon coconut palm; you could no more be a Baloo than I a village beadle. The psychoanalyst is concerned with illusory objects. Yet nobody is happy or unhappy with the mind; we are happy or unhappy with our hearts. And we no more know our hearts than Sigmund Freud knew the being of Leonardo because a feather in the painter's mouth proved, through the magic of psychoanalysis, that the great Italian painter was a homosexual, or rather "had ambivalent tendencies." Psychoanalysis does not prove why or how Leonardo painted the Saint Anne or that noble bust of Saint John the Baptist.

Vulgarity had entered from the backwash somehow, and my story will show how we drifted into the whirlpool of the river.

And as all that is true happens simply and undramatically, this happened, too, in the most natural manner.

One evening, Catherine seemed somewhat sad. We had all gone up to Sainte-Ophalie on our usual walk, and I stayed back a while to be near her, to feel her, to know her, and maybe to offer her any hope or advice that someone older, and like an elder brother, could give.

I acted, no doubt, from my Indian instinct, for in India every woman who is not your wife—or your concubine—is your sister. You feel the responsibility of a brother to every woman on this earth, whosoever she may be, and in whatever part of the world. Left to himself, the Indian would go tying *rakhi** to every woman he met, feel her elder brother, protect her love, and enjoy the pride of an uncle at marriage and at childbirth; and later he would feel the orphans as his wards, his nephews. Thus the danger has been circumvented, the pride of the hero kept firm; and when you die, if no one else will, your sister will weep for you!

So I joked with Catherine, for joking is part of binding a woman into safety, and told her she was my little daughter, my niece and my sister-in-law—Georges being my brother—and little by little Catherine opened herself up and spoke to me of herself, of the deep sorrow she felt, something unnameable, un-understandable.

"I should be so happy, my brother," she laughed, "but there is sorrow, such sorrow. It seems to come from the very depths. I want to weep, I want to call Madeleine at night, beg her to lie by me, weep with me, even protect me. Rama, I just do not know what it is; it simply aches." She became silent. What answer could I give her? Only a woman could have told her the truth.

"Catherine," I said, however, "the fact is this. When a girl would become woman, there's a whole universe that rebels in you, as though a kingdom, a sovereignty were to be lost, as though some demon were at your cavern door, and you would lose the all, in fear, in blood and in anguish. Catherine, it's just like the great frost that falls in March, before the spring comes. Death and life are not opposite things but alternate events, like spring and winter, heat and monsoon. There's anguish in India before the rains come, just as when people die in spring—you know most old people die at the end of winter, in the beginning of spring? That is why, Catherine," I concluded, "there is so much sorrow in

---

* A silken spangled string in yellow, tied round the wrist by brothers and friends of a woman towards whom they feel protective, for *rakhi* means "protection." The festival of Rakhi comes in the month of Srāvan, in autumn, on the day of the full moon.

spring. You want not to be born, for death, winter, looks like peace. For man, I mean for the male, the leap into spring is his death, but for women the leap into life is anguish, is pain, is rounded knowledge, is continuance. For woman pain and continuance are one, and for man death and joy are one. And that is the mystery of creation." I spoke as though I were telling of Madeleine, and not of Catherine.

We walked slowly, haltingly, as if knowledge were pain, mystery were joy. We lingered by the rocks and by the trees; we sat on a bridge and started throwing stones into the empty earth below; we were silent, even though we knew we were talking to one another. Then Catherine must have thought of Georges, for she said, "Come, let us go."

We entered through the kitchen door—for the goat-path, going upwards, went just by our back yard—stealthily like children, and knocked at the drawing-room door as if, when Madeleine opened, we would shout, "Tiger, Lion, Elephant!" But no answer came, and slowly the door opened—it was Georges who opened it—and when we walked in the room was filled with a wide silence. Catherine went almost on tiptoe and sat by Madeleine on the divan. Georges went back to his chair, and I put on more lights, and stood looking at the books.

After a moment Catherine said she had had such a wonderful walk with her brother-in-law, and I said, "I've tied *rakhi* to Catherine." When Georges asked, "What's that, Rama?" I said, "Why, that's what Rani Padmavathi tied—a silken, a yellow silken thread, with gold on it—to Emperor Akbar, says the legend, and thus becoming his sister she could not become his bride."

"What a beautiful story," said Georges.

"Oh," said Madeleine, "India does not lack beautiful stories," and while I went into my room, to search for some *rakhi*—I had kept the *rakhi* Saroja had given to me—Madeleine went into the kitchen; and when I came back to the drawing room, Georges and Catherine were in each other's arms and so very happy. Georges kissed her again in front of me, and she let him do it, and with such freedom that Georges had tears in his eyes. Something had happened to Georges; he seemed so elevated, so pure.

154

"Here, Catherine, is my wedding present," I said, and tied the *rakhi* to Catherine's wrist. She danced with joy, and ran into the kitchen and shouted:

"Look, Mado! Look what a wonderful wedding present for me!"

Meanwhile Georges said, "Come, Rama, haven't you got another?"

I said, "No." So when Catherine returned Georges untied it, and while Madeleine came with onion and kitchen knife in hand to see what was happening, Georges caught hold of her, tied the *rakhi* on her left hand and kissed her on the mouth; yes, did Georges, and in front of all of us. Even the lamps glowed a little brighter that sudden moment, and then we all felt we belonged to a magic circle, and we all laughed, as if to some mysterious cymbal and tambourine. We laughed and we laughed, we teased each other in the kitchen and in the corridor, laying the table we laughed, searching for the spoons and forks we laughed, talking of Lezo we laughed; of the headmistress we made fun and laughed. Then we fell into long silences, and we started laughing again.

Madeleine, however, went into the bathroom and stayed away so long that Catherine went knocking and banging at the door and said, "One can have diarrhoea laughing." Georges hung down his paralysed arm and went about moving the ladle in the saucepan. We were having tomato sauce, and the wheat flour must not become sticky. Catherine took the ladle from Georges and went back to tease Madeleine about the diarrhoea.

I went into my room for a while and drew the shutters. My work was not progressing too well, was it? So I laid the pencil beside some fresh paper, as though that were enough to make my work go forward more quickly. When Madeleine came out of the bathroom I went in to have a wash, and we had a wonderful dinner. Everything looked so perfect—except that there was a little too much salt in the tomato sauce—and we naturally fell into a large and meaningful silence. Afterwards Catherine went into her room and must have wept, for when she came out her voice seemed different.

Georges went away carrying some book. "Good night, Rama; good night, Madeleine; good night, my little wife," he said and kissed Catherine again in front of us both. Then the night fell back into the world, and when I went to our bedroom, Madeleine was busy at her Katherine Mansfield.

I went to say good night to Catherine, but before she came to her door I was already in our bedroom. "Good night, Brother. Good night, my knight protector," she shouted from the corridor.

"Good night, my sacred sister; sleep well."

How I waited for Madeleine to wash and return. I read this and that, but nothing went into my head. She had let down her lovely, her golden hair, as she came in—she had on a kashmir nightdress I had bought in London; and her limbs moved as to destiny. She came to me so gravely, elevatedly, and lifted me up into herself.

November 4. "I love Madeleine now with a new love. I love in bits and parts and all, like an antelope does its doe, the elephant does with the ichor dripping from his brows.

> *Kandula-dui-paganda-pinda-sanotkampena Sampathi bhir . . .*
> Elephants wild with ichor frenzy
> Shake the trees, rubbing trunk on trunk;
> Freed, the heat-loose flowers in worship
> Fall to the waters of Goddess Godaveri.
> Birds, leaf-canopied, twist forth the tunnelling grub;
> In the mirrored treetops hemming the river's edge
> Loudly murmurs the heat with languorous swans
> And the "coo, coo, tackularn, coolay" of the nesting doves.

I love the curved nape of her neck, so gentle, so like marble for me, almost saffron-coloured under the light of the moon, or when I call her to myself in the day, and take her in my arms, how her throat smells of some known musk.

"The body of woman is so like a wood, with herbs and marjoram and creepers that fall from the top; and bees that hum, while the tiger calls for his mate. The cubs are all about; and you lick the head first, and then the neck, and then the back, and when you slip over the breasts, you feel the navel shake as with oxyaphic anguish. You delay and you wander, you creep over the zone and you say sweet tinkling things to yourself. You know the still wonder is already within her, the wonder that makes the sun shine, or the moon speak; you know the world will be, for it is; you know the banana ripens on the stem and the coconut falls on the fertile earth—that rivers flow, that the parijata blossoms, white and pink between leaves. And as the wind blows, wave after wave of it, and mountains move, the wind stops and you settle into yourself; and you hear it again . . . And Madeleine is there, with her hips so wondrous blue and red, and she smells, God, she smells of me, of my elephant, of my suchness, and I ask of her, and she murmurs such ontological things that her very eyes seem fixed; and taking me into myself, I transpire as the truth, as though touched by itself, like the wave that sees itself to be sea, like the earth that was spread out and was called Madeleine. But when I want to call her Madeleine, I have to say Rama—her lips are mine turned outward, her flesh mine turned inward, and what a sound she makes, the sound of a jungle doe.

"And she calls me, does the doe, with sweet cries and painful cries, as though I were far; and I tell her, 'My love, my doe, I am drinking the waters of many fountains, for the evening be come and the tigers have not yet left their lairs,' and she saith, 'I am full and alone; I am the bearer of the day; I run with the waters, I leap with the skies, I murmur with the trees, the frogs; I become the serpent of sweetness, I am the song that leapeth; take me into the evening and fold me in Kashmir silk.' And I take her away to a world from which there is no returning—like those Tibetan *tanakas,* with cypresses and moons and waters below, and the dragon throne in the middle. You seat him and say, 'Son, sit here,' and he sits, does he, the Lama; you cover him in brocade and sound the horn outside, and wave after wave of it comes echoing back to Lhasa; across mountains and deserts it incarnates and comes, for the Lama is crowned and seated in the Potala. Then all the treasuries are opened and all the windows too, and the white horse waits with decoration, sash and fife, for the summer palace and the pools.

"Lord, it is full of scented grass, and the music has been piping a long while, and you have eyes in between the ears, you accept gifts in between the acts, you touch the heart between the breasts; and you lie on Madeleine as though on a great seashore. The night has ended, the dawn has not yet broken. It's the time for

157

ablutions, for the murmur of prayers and the road to the temple by the river. The God knows you and you know the God, and his jewels shine as if arisen from the earth but yesternight. For a moment you had gone beyond the body, and Oh, how sad it is to come back—to bear this heavy limb.

"The elephant has been lost in a dream by the winter pool: you feel a tear by his left eye. And he must rise and he must go. For you can never be free, son, but through yourself. You see those hills there? You would go beyond them, and beyond the hills, my son, my child, be the mountains and the rivers, bigger and full of maned lions. And beyond the lions, the country of man, where they build houses, factories, funeral grounds; where they buy and they sell, where they shout and they sing. And beyond that again be another forest and another lake, another tiger and another porcupine, and beyond again other towns and cities, other worlds and nights. But the dream is the same, you can no more catch it than you can speak to the elephant who is speaking to you, there in the waters; he is but you, seen on the other side. You cannot talk on the other side; the ichor flows on itself, and becomes the tear with which we've made the lakes, the fountains, the rains. The ichor made the rivers of the worlds, and the fruits and the perfumes, the cities and the zoological gardens have all been made; for man has been led by his own ichor.

"I give it to you, Madeleine, but you are where you are, and I am but nowhere. Madeleine, dear Madeleine, let us go on another voyage, on another excursus of the world. Let me smother you in muslin, let me take the lip to its ultimate twist and congression. Madeleine, let me touch you here by the waist from which rises birth, and Madeleine, let me touch you on this the right breast, that I lie there as on my deathbed, Madeleine, dear Madeleine. Oh, give it to me, give it, give it! Oh, give that! Madeleine, do not cry. Oh Madeleine, do not suffer. For God's sake, Madeleine, I'll hang all the *tanakas* about you; I'll call him Krishna again, Madeleine; let me squeeze the juice out of you, let me lick you like a dog, and let me see you in my spittle, on my tongue; and Madeleine, let me smell you, smell the you of me and the I in you; Madeleine, it's sweet to the taste, it's so wondrous bitter, it smells of peppermint and of gelatine, Madeleine, dear

Madeleine. Oh, give me back my saffron, my honey of woodbine, my *parajātā* of the temple yard. Why do you cry so, Madeleine, did I hurt you, did I awaken you, did you rise and did I fail? Oh, I would smother your sobs, Madeleine, I would die with your pain.

"The day is still bright outside, but I want Madeleine, I want Madeleine, and I say, 'Sweet love, shall we try again? For the peacocks are about the garden and I hear the first snows melt on the Himalay, I can hear the winds of the North arise. I'll take you to Alakananda, and we'll become clouds, Madeleine; we'll visit all the townlets of the Yakshas. I'll take you to bejewelled palaces and recite to you Kalidasa; I'll show you women whose breasts hang like this with love, and whose waistbands fall, for they cannot bear the love that rises in them.

> *Nīvibandhocehvasanacitalam yaha yakshāganānam*
> *rāsah Kāmād ambhitakaresv ākshipastu priyesu*
> *Arcitungān abhi mukham api prāpya ratuapradīpan*
> *hrōmūdhānām bhavaki riphalapreranac cūrnamushi.*

> The women of the Yakshas suddenly discover
> The knots of their girdles loosened.
> Their lovers, by passion made bold,
> Tear down the loose-hanging garments:
> Maddened with shame the women throw
> On the high-lit lamps—but studded gems—
> A handful of the powder of unguents;
> To no avail, even when consumed by the light.

I'll take you to Himalay and make love to you there. Come, come, Madeleine! The train is ready, and can you not hear the whistle go?'

"Madeleine chokes and I carry her on my back, she cries that she needs many medicines from all the hospitals of the world, but she has had a coma, and she's had an internal disorder. Call surgeon Bonnenfant, call Dr. Sugérau, call Nathan and Bernadine! You can sense white aprons all about and the smell of ether. There is wondrous music of the Yakshas in the Himalaya.

" 'Madeleine, did I hurt you, did I seek you too far, and too long?'

159

"Madeleine simply says, 'Lord, leave me alone. I do not belong to the man kingdom. I'm torn as by a porcupine inside. I am finished, I am aghast. O Tante Zoubie!' And Madeleine cries."

November 6. "She looked at her watch, this time, and it was already ten minutes to two, and Madeleine rushes to the bathroom, adjusts her hair a little, shouts '*Au revoir, chérie,*' to Catherine, who didn't need much intuition to see what had happened, and, '*Au revoir,* Rama,' she says, as though to herself, and goes to teach the Napoleonic wars to her students—she is teaching them about the Duke of Reichstadt, Roi de Rome—while I try to plunge into some magazine, and forget the elephant."

November 7. "How I waited yesterday for Georges to go home, how I hated him for staying on. He knew my knowledge. Oh, I wish Georges had never existed, for God has given eyes to Satanael. Awkward and unashamed, as soon as Madeleine and I came back to our room, while Catherine was having a wash, how I pressed Madeleine to myself, how I forced her to undress, and how without sweetness or word of murmur I took her; and she let me be in her, without joy, without sorrow. I just remembered Georges was not there.

"I seemed to have no shame either, for when Madeleine had washed and returned, I hurried through my own ablutions and went back to her, and said many silly and untrue things, and she said yes and no, as if it mattered not. Then I told her about Kalidasa and the Yakshas, and kissed her again with so great a demand that she said, 'Come.' I wandered through empty corridors, and alone. Madeleine caressed my head with compassion, and said, 'Be happy, my love, be happy.'

"But I was not happy. So I spoke to her long whiles about all sorts of things, of Mysore and of Grandfather Kittanna, of my father and of Little Mother. I gave Madeleine details I had never given—how Uncle Seetharamu used to go to his room four times, five times a day, and shout, 'Lakshmi! Lakshmi!' And his good, round wife would come, and the door would close. Auntie came back just as she went in, and we children never lost an occasion to know what had happened. 'Uncle Seetharamu has had ten children and eight are alive,' I said.

" 'I'll bear you eleven, if you like,' said Madeleine. And humiliated, I bathed and went back to bed.

In the middle of the night, I know not what took hold of Madeleine. She came into my bed and made such a big demand on me that I felt afterwards like a summer river—the sun sizzling on the Deccan plateau, and the stones burning; the cattle waiting with their tongues out; and the neem leaves on the tree, still. You can hear a crow cawing here and there, and maybe the oppressed hoot of an automobile.

"This morning I made no coffee for Madeleine. She went shyly into the kitchen herself, and when she came to say good morning I pretended I was asleep.

"I must stop this tufan of the deserts."

November 9. "Tonight, it's again Madeleine that came to me. She knew, as by an instinct, that I would not go to her.

"A woman hates a male when he withdraws. She cannot accept his defeat—his defeat is the defeat of her womanhood. She must be the juice of his love, she must give him again and again that which he asks for, till his asking itself becomes a disgust. Then the woman has contempt for him, she rubs her breast on his back, she whispers sweet things to his ears, her body speaks where no words could speak, and she lifts him up and takes him into herself, like a mother a child. Then you want to take a cactus branch and beat her and scratch her all over. You want to bite her lip and pull the breast away from her chest, and taste the good blood of her wounds. You want her to be young and new and never named. You want her to be your first love, your first woman, you want her to be the whole of the earth. She knows it—for every woman is a concubine, a mistress of passion, a dompter of man's condition—and she becomes virginal and simple and, Lord, so new, so perfumed, that the ichor rises in the elephant, and you are at it again.

"This time you've gone far, very far—the winds have arisen, though the summer heat be still there, and the neem leaves wave a little. You hear the cry of a child, and the washing of cloth by some well. The world will be purified. The world is pure. For the mistress has become the mother."

November 10. "Today I could have destroyed Madeleine, so richly, so perfumedly she hung to me. I could have spat into her mouth and called her the female of a dog.

"It is time I went away. The farther I go, the farther the truth seems. It cannot be good for that which is ripening in Madeleine. I must respect life. I must respect Madeleine. I must go to London."

November 13. "For these three days I have been much nicer to Georges. The elephant has destroyed the jungle, all the jungle, with the creepers, the anthills and the thorny branches. The monsoon winds have arisen. It will soon rain. And I will go."

November 15. "It's terrible to think of Georges and Catherine going through all this. Madeleine said to me last night, 'Rama, it's gone beyond the stage of powder and lipstick,' and I answered, 'Well, don't be a eunuch anyway, Madeleine, for God's sake.' Madeleine grew very silent at first, and then went to her room and started reading Katherine Mansfield. Nowadays, she reads Katherine Mansfield a great deal. 'No man can understand a woman, Rama, no, never,' she said, laying the book down. 'Only can a woman speak of a woman. We are not angels. But we are no beasts.' I said, 'The elephant dies where no one knows. You seek the true for you know the full falsehood. Maybe Georges is right.'

" 'No, Georges is not right,' Madeleine answered, 'but you may not be right either. For if truth is truth it must explain everything. Did you not say, Rama, it was Sri Sankara himself who, defeated in discussion by a woman when she questioned him on things essentially feminine, left his body in the hollow of a tree by the river Narbada, and incarnated in the body of a dead king? That he lived for ten years with the four queens and wrote those celebrated verses on love, which you say are among the most beautiful lyrics of India?' 'But that was Sankara,' I said. And after a while, I went on, 'I will still defeat you.'

" 'The Queen awaits you, my liege, my Lord,' she said. It was this time not Madeleine who spoke but someone else, superior, simple."

November 17. "Today I will just copy the following verse of Baudelaire:

> L'éphémère ébloui vole vers toi, chandelle,
> Crépite, flambe et dit: Bénissons ce flambeau!
> L'amoureux pantelant incliné sur sa belle
> A l'air d'un moribond caressant son tombeau.
>
> Que tu viennes du ciel ou de l'enfer, qu'importe,
> O beauté! monstre énorme, effrayant, ingénu!
> Si ton oeil, ton sourire, ton pied, m'ouvrent la porte
> D'un infini que j'aime et n'ai jamais connu?

November 20. "Again I copy from Baudelaire:

> Je te hais, Océan! tes bonds et tes tumultes,
> Mon esprit les retrouve en lui! Ce rire amer
> De l'homme vaincu, plein de sanglots et d'insultes,
> Je l'entends dans le rire énorme de la mer.
>
> Comme tu me plairais, O Nuit! sans ces étoiles,
> Dont la lumière parle un langage connu!
> Car je cherche le vide, et le noir, et le nu!

I could thus go on quoting from my endless diary. But I will stop here.

I shall only add I left for England at the end of the month and that Madeleine seemed not unhappy with herself.

I took Savithri back to Cambridge. At the station we jumped into a taxi and I left her at Girton College; then I went on to the Lion Hotel (in Petty Cury) where a room had been reserved for me. The short porter, called John, led me up the staircase to my little room under the roof. It was somewhat triangular, but with the Bible beside the bed and the cross above me I felt what I always know I am, a pilgrim. The night was not long, and dawn broke very early. I went to the Library and with some difficulty got a card to work there.

Libraries always speak to me; they reveal me to myself—with their high seriousness, their space, and the multiple knowledge that people have of themselves which goes to make a book. For all books are autobiographies, whether they be books on genetics or on the history (in twenty-two volumes) of the Anglican Church. The mechanics of a motorcar or of veterinary science all have a beginning in the man who wrote the book, have absorbed his nights and maybe the nerves of his wife or daughter. They all represent a bit of oneself, and for those who can read rightly, the whole of oneself. The style of a man—whether he writes on the Aztecs or on pelargonium—the way he weaves word against word, intricates the existence of sentences with the values of *sound*, makes a comma here, puts a dash there: all are signs of his inner movement, the speed of his life, his breath (*prana*), the nature of his thought, the ardour and age of his soul. Short sentences and long sentences, parentheses and points of interrogation, are not only curves in the architecture of thought, but have an intimate, a private relation with your navel, your genitals, the vibrance of your eyesight. Shakespeare, for aught we know, may have had hypertension, Goldsmith stones in the gallbladder; Dr. Johnson may have been oversexed like a horse, just as Maupassant was a hypochondriac and Proust had to lie in bed with asthma, and weave out long sentences like he eked out a long curve of breath. Breath is the solar herdsman of the living, says the Rig-Veda, and hence Yoga and all that.

Therefore the biography of Dr. Norman Coleman is not in the scientific "Who's Who," but in each rhythm of his heading: "Orbitoethmoidal Osteoma with Spartaneous Pneumocephalus."

So many men have lived and *breathed* and written books. What a breath it gives you! With my poor weak lungs a library is always a place of a broad, a propitious breath, and so books are not only my professional need, but also my respiratory, my spiritual need. And in between the tomes, in that blue of space—as though wisdom were hid; some mysterious, unwritten, unknowable knowledge—in that blank, that silent, wise blank between books and behind them, I felt the presence, the truth, the formula of Savithri. She was the source of which words were made, the Mother of Sound, Akshara-Lakshmi, divinity of the syllable; the night of which the day was the meaning, the knowledge of which the book was the token, the symbol—the prophecy.

I would meet her by the staircase of the University Library at five, and wander along over sluices and bridges, showing her the spots of silence as in between the two purrings of the Cam, or the broad sheet of space that the sun lit up from Clare Bridge to the tower of Saint John's. It was as if some swallow had curved out this space, for the game of its young ones. The Cam had flowers floating on it, and boats and the laughter of the very young. The Cam seemed never to have grown old, even though the buildings were so aged, for the Cam like us men and women flows right in herself, outside of history. Who, after all, could write the history of the Cam, for she was certainly there before man came to the British Isles, and she will be there even if the whole of England join the European continent, by geological upheaval, and the Thames flow again into the Rhine or Britain be frozen in because the Arctic regions began to get warmer for life, and this belt of the earth too cold for man to inhabit. The Cam is silent and self-reflective. It teaches you that history is made by others and not by oneself. I am history to you, not so to myself. You make my biography, I live my own autobiography. Trinity may have a bridge over the Cam, but the Cam has no bridge. I might call Savithri, but Savithri speaking to Savithri did not call herself Savithri. The sound is born of silence and the river is of space. Love has nothing to do with loving, for "I" itself is love.

Night has a great, a tender innocence. No one harms another in the night but with the convictions and irritations of the day. Those who speak of the dark night think of the dark day which precedes it. The night of Cambridge had an absolute silence, as though paths and roads had stopped suddenly, and time had passed by them, and into Hertfordshire. The trees, though, made time, for winter had covered the earth with a grey, remembered existence. Man has a fire within, a substance, a light, and he illumines his night not with the stuff electric, with a touch that is no touch, a lip that is no lip, but a smell, a curve of breath and silence, as if truth were a presence, an instant, an eye. Words are made of such stuff as breath is made on.

The impossible is the reality, the fervent is the intrepid, the passionate, the high. Fruits are made of space; grass is made of light; mankind makes paths and roadways; all, that night be measured in her own silence. King's Chapel was not made by workmen but by the prayer of pilgrims; colleges were built not by the donations of noblemen and kings but by the leap of light within, by the aura of substantialities within man's blood and becoming, in which God floats as a castle, builds a bridge and shapes a tower. And in between the archwayed walls are studious boys—and far away, the girls, that weave into life the space of thought, the substance of sight and movement of the moon, that a better England, a better India, a better world be circumscribed. The Cam is a river that lives on giving dreams.

Savithri was shy, very shy. Her touch was simple and had no name, she spoke as though she were covering her head with her sari, and throwing the *pallo* more amply over her breast. She was shy of no one, she was shy of herself. There were moments when one wondered if she were afraid to touch her own waist, or hear her own words. I think she liked best to hear her own heart, and you felt that was where you could meet her if you dared, but you dared not, for to do this you needed the humility of a saint. Saint I had to become if I would know Savithri, not a saint of ochre and bone-bowl, but one which had known the extinction of the ego. Just as reading poetry at the break of day is like remembering the feel of one's dream but not the acts of one's dream, to know Savithri was to wake into the truth of life, to be remembered—unto God. She never pushed you away, but you drew away from her, because there was no common knowledge, no language in which one had similar symbols to exchange. Her simplicity was her defence, and her laughter—for she laughed so widely but softly—was like the laughter of the clown in a circus, when his body ripples with merriment before the lion: Savithri was just afraid. My courage was a failure turned into strength, her laughter was fear turned into simplicity. There was no Clare Bridge to link us together, and we looked at each other from opposite banks, like the duck on one side and the cycle on the other, lamplit and churring on its gear, forlorn.

I walked Savithri back to Girton College, one evening, feeling we were laughing in a cinema. At the hotel John the porter gave me a letter. It was from Madeleine. It was a rigmarole of aches and anxieties. But it gave me self-assurance: man needs a woman to stand on his pedary bones. You must have a spot, a centre—to run away from.

People have asked me—Georges among them—what indeed it was that happened between Savithri and me in Cambridge. Nothing more had happened, in fact, than if you look deep and long at silence you perceive an orb of centripetal sound which explains why Parvathi is daughter of Himalay, and Sita born to the furrow of the field. I heard myself say I heard myself. Or I saw my eyes see that I saw. She became the awareness behind my awareness, the leap of my understanding. I lost the world and she became it.

For whatever I gave her she accepted, as the Ganges receives the waters of the Himalayas, that go on down to the sea and come again as white flakes of snow, then blue, then very green; and as, when the sun comes northward again, the ice melts and once more the Ganges takes the waters down to the sea—so we gave love to each other, as though it did not belong to us but to a principle, an other, an impersonal reality, from which we saw gifts emerge in each of us, and gave each other with ceremony. For us therefore all was celebration, festival . . .

Truth is the fact of existence. That is, truth is the essence of fact; and as such truth and existence are one and the same. Man sees himself in woman as essence, the fact of womanhood is the meaning of his life. If there were nothing other, you could not know that you are. If Parvathi had not sat and prayed that Shiva would open his eyes, Shiva would never have opened his eyes and there would never have been a world. Love is the honey of knowledge, knowing is sweet because woman is.

A man's world would have led all of us, one by one, to the top of Himalay; and like the Cathars, who hated mating and the making of children, we would have taken consolamentum and flung ourselves over the precipice, singing hymns on the Void: "No aias merce de la carn, mais aias merce del esperit pausat en carcer." Buddhism died in India because it became ascetic, and so denied womanhood its right to exist. Those who hate woman— who debase woman—must end themselves, as the Cathars did, fasting unto death. Mahatma Gandhi respected women as sisters, not as mates—he too disliked the process of loving and of having children—and so he made them into little men. The world of man is the denial of the earth, it is just like a country with a president and not a king.

All the world is spread for woman to be, and in making us know the world woman shows that the world is oneself seen as the other. Union is proof that the Truth is non-dual. "As one embraced by a darling bride," says the Brihadaranyaka Upanishad, "knows naught of 'I' and 'Thou,' so self embraced by the foreknowing (solar) self knows naught of 'myself' within or 'thyself' without." Not one is the Truth, yet not two is the Truth. Savithri proved that I could be I.

One cannot possess the world, one can become it: I could not possess Savithri—I became I. Hence the famous saying of Yagnyavalkya to his wife: "The husband does not love the wife for the wife's sake, the husband loves the wife for the sake of the Self in her."

Thus the King is masculine to his Kingdom, and feminine in relation to the Absolute, the Truth.

That ugly revolutionary word "capitalist" took on a new significance for me: clearly it was born of the man-proud nineteenth century, century of inventions, empires. Man, the hero of man: Clive more proud to be the obedient servant of company directors than of some Azalais des Baux. And after the death of the Prince Consort how much more Queen Victoria incarnated in him than as herself. Victorianism was born of her widowhood —in the contemplation of *him*. Gladstone and Disraeli were her alternative symbols. She the sovran of the Empire, to whom Gordon of Khartoum knelt as to a liege. How different the lovers of Queen Elizabeth I, and the world of Marlowe, Shakespeare and the Armada! The ascetic world of Queen Victoria disintegrated into many man-kingdoms, and the last was the one created by Mahatma Gandhi. Victorianism died not in London or Melbourne but in New Delhi, cremated there by a distinguished representative of the Germano-British royal family. Godse, who killed Mahatma Gandhi, was like Saint Dominic. But the Inquisition was born to justify life, not to kill life.

Strange, it seemed to me, on those days walking by the Cam, singing Sankara's hymns to myself, waiting for some bus or car that would deposit Savithri by my side, how my thoughts took corporeality, how I understood the rhythm and meaning of history through her. My thoughts turned to Christianity. How curious that it starts—even in the Catechism—with Eve and the Fall, and that Hinduism, too, glorifies the Mother. How beautiful are those hymns to the Mother, of Sankara:

> *Annapurné Sadapurné*
> *Sankara prānavallabhé*
> She, ever full and plenteous,
> Sankara's divine lady.

But alas, decadent Hinduism led pure Vedanta to end in the concretization of womanhood—the Tantriks.

I suddenly remembered Father saying that one of my ancestors in the sixteenth century or thereabouts was a great Tantrik, who had written some textbook on the Yogācāras. The story goes how he brought a virgin to the house, for adoration and worship, and when he had sat hour after hour in mantra and meditation, milk was brought and honey, camphor and kadamba flowers. Then the young lady—someone of the concubine class, called Radha—was made to stand naked, and sixteen men came in, who had all fasted for eleven days and prayed for eleven nights, white as muslin in their skin, bright-eyed as the sacrificial fire that burnt in front of them, with ashes on their foreheads, and with filigree at their waists and ankles. They poured the honey first, then the milk and the flowers, on the young head and breast and limbs of the girl, and how it flowed over her womanhood, as though the world was made of the true substance of woman, just as honey is made of the true stuff of flower. And the girl herself stepped forward, singing:

> I have no body, I have no mind,
> I am the essence of creation;
> Myself uncreate,
> The world my dwelling place;
> My Lord is he who dwells in Kailas,
> Lord of the Trident,
> He with the moon in his hair;
> My spouse, the origin of Sound.

Now she stepped towards the fire, went round and round it, seven noble times, smeared her body with ashes, and borrowing a cloth from one of the Brahmins walked out an ascetic, a nun fulfilled. The woman needs our worship for her fulfilment, for in worshipping her we know the world and annihilate it, absorbing it into ourself. We should be Shiva that woman be dissolved—and with her the world. For the world is meant not for denial but for dissolution.

The object, I said to myself, is woman. Hence the concupiscence of ascetics for their loincloth, their Kamandala, their stick or naked feet. And Georges, eating marmalade or chestnut jam, how he sucked it, rolled it over and over his tongue, then swallowed it, little by little, making glougloutinating sounds, and looking innocently at Madeleine. And the Abbé de Grefonville, when he came to visit us, rubbed his snuff as though it gave him a self-exciting sensation, a release of himself. When it went up his nose he closed his eyes, surely not in fear of burning his eyes, but because it was such joy to feel himself in. No sinner, no Don Juan can have come back to the world as ghost, but most cenobites must have. No wonder then that mostly women are possessed by ghosts and not men. Ghosts prefer—in India at least—girls of sixteen or widows.

One afternoon, how long the path between the main road and Clare Bridge seemed to me, waiting in the dark and cold for Savithri. Knowing she must be having some dubious and interminable discussion with her communist comrades—for she saw a great deal of them, liking their sincerity, their disinterestedness, their *cleanliness*, "not smelly like the bourgeois" was her definition—I began to think of bourgeois and capitalist.

Nazism, I said to myself, must have been born of the He-principle: Nietzsche, that great "prophet of Nazism," thought of Superman because Lou Andreas Salome, alas, had jilted him. Refuting the she-world Nietzsche took Zarathustra to the top of the mountain, whence he imprecated the world. The Jews belong to the world—they are great world-builders—hence the hate of the he-man for the Jew. More men marry Jewesses—Savithri's best friend was a Jewess, daughter of a German refugee, and an Englishman from one of the best families, the bluest of blue blood, was in love with her—than Jews marry gentile women—in Cambridge at least, where Betsy once heard a Jewish boy say, "At least let us have some Jewish girls for ourselves! We might have to take to evil ways, if all the Cambridge Jewish girls fall in love with the sons of dukes and lords."

That Marxism was born of a Jew seemed inevitable. That Marxism was succeeding in China also seemed inevitable—who but the Chinese accepted the reality of the world with such full authenticity? If the world is to be lived in, the world has to be accepted: woman has to be accepted. The quarrel between

Nazism and communism, between Hitler and Lenin, was one between the ascetic of Godsberg and the little, heavy Slav, with bicycle and book, returning from the British Museum to the warm fire and Krupaskaya. Who ever talks of the wife of Danton, the purist, but who does not know the Princess from Austria? Communism is the acceptance of life, the justification of life: Nazism the denial of life, its destroyer. I am sure more Nazis gloated at the thought of London on fire, than communists on the burning of Hamburg. When the Germans entered France, there were still officers who made the *Le Silence de la mer* possible; when the Russians entered Berlin they raped every woman they could. The one ran to the fulfilment of life, the other glorified himself by denial. Mephistopheles was a solipsist. Lenin was a Saint Francis turned inquisitor. If I were not a royalist, I should have become a communist. After all, Stalin was a usurper, a Césarévitch who *succeeded* Rasputin. Ivan Karamazov was a fine disciple of Christ—an enemy of the Inquisition. Alyosha was a true Christian. When the Mother of God replaced the Son of Man Catholicism became a universal religion.

How true, I thought, as still I walked backwards and forwards on the path—thinking of history was thinking of Savithri—how true that ascetic Protestantism, the Puritan spirit, was combatting feminine communism. Communism, I concluded, would be defeated not because of the atomic bomb or the heroes of the Korean War, but because the civilization of America was changing over from its Puritan background to the magnificence of women's clubs. The American man accepted woman more deeply than did the European. To worship woman is to redeem the world.

She would come to me then, perhaps, like she had the other day, under the bare trees and the yellow lamplight, with a gesture of sari and books, her voice lilting up with excuses, with implorations of forgiveness. "Did I make you wait very long?" she had asked, putting a warm hand through my overcoat arm, as when the sluices are lifted and the canal waters run back, gurgling and rolling, splashing their joy back to all the recurrent past, with a feeling of intimacy, a fervent churning prayer, saying man has no empty kingdom in himself, but all is true and reverential.

Yes, Savithri had such a sense of reverence for things—were she picking up a spoon, or holding your pen in hand to write an address (for she always forgot her pen and her glasses anywhere, in classes or digs or in a restaurant, and one of the most lovable things I could do for her was to go back to Lyons or to Witfolds, and ask the management for Savithri's glasses. "This Indian lady forgot them in the afternoon," I would plead, and more often than not, they were found). Sometimes, too, sitting by her on a bench behind Trinity we would be talking away at some abstruse metaphysical subject, and there would come some elegant young Indian or Englishman ("Your paramours," I called them, mostly out of fun, but not without a touch of other feelings) whom she had sent searching for her glasses, lost at Heffer's maybe, buying her Michael Drayton (for she was specializing in the early seventeenth century), or at the Copper Kettle (opposite King's) where girls gathered together in the afternoon to talk shop. Sometimes these girls themselves, whether it were Betsy (whom I had met by now) or Lakshmi or Sharifa, two Indians, one a Brahmin from Trichinopoly, and the other a Lucknow Muslim, both of them seeking her warmth and intelligence, but each of them detesting her for their own feminine reasons—well, some boy or girl therefore would bring Savithri's glasses or pen, or even her notebook, and say "Sorry to disturb you, Savithri," or sometimes even, "Sorry to disturb you, Princess, but we thought you might again get lost, and not find the doorway of Girton. You don't want that to happen again, do you?" "Oh, no," Savithri would smile, "oh, no, and thank you ever so much."

My looks would not encourage any disturbance; thus our conversations on the Bogomil dualism or on the good Revolution of '48 would go on. She was not, in fact, very much of a communist, but she once said, "You know, Ramaswamy, if you'd seen the misery I've seen in North India, say, amongst the Pasies, a tribe where a man would murder another for five rupees, or if you had ever visited, as I often did in stealth, some village or home, when my father was away shooting a tiger, or having a huge assembly of notables coming to pay homage to him with sword and *ashrafee;* or, worse still, if you had been with me on that atrocious day when my father tied a miserable son of a clerk, a *munshi*'s son, to the middle post of the palace hall and took a whip to him just because he'd dared, like a true Muslim youth, write poetry in my honour and sing it below my window—and in all innocence; if you'd seen such things, and the way when the floods came, Mother Goomtie's kindness brought such waters that in the middle of the monsoon, with blanket, cradle, and pot on their heads, man, woman and child had to mount up trees and live full fifteen days, as it were from moon to moon—for the river entered the huts and homes, and carried away cattle, boundary-stones and children; if you'd seen all that, you would know whence comes my communism. My communism is made of Mother India's tears."

"Oh, yes," I answered, "but that is because you cannot weep yourself."

"You are right there." She was always willing to agree. I was her schoolmaster, and she liked to learn from me.

"The fact is, for you, love is an abstraction."

"How right you are," she said, her eyes fervent as with a sudden illumination. "Lakshmi often says," she continued, "that Savithri can never love. All is given to her, money and adoration—those are her own words—so Savithri can never love."

"No," I protested, somewhat in selfish defence perhaps. "You can love. Or rather you can be love."

"Now, now, what's that?"

"For you love is not a system—a canalization of emotion, an idea. For you love is a fact, an immediate experience, like an intuition," I said.

"Wonderful, wonderful. Go on."

"I've seen you look at a flower or stand at the weir and hear the Cam purr till you are absorbed in yourself. You come out after a long, long silence and say, 'Have I made you wait too long?' And with what a melting voice!"

"Tell me then, wise man, what happens when I hear the Cam purr?"

"The wise man says: When the Cam purrs for a long time Savithri becomes Savithri. First Savithri listens to the river, then she listens to her own heart, then she listens to her own silence— and then she is lost."

"Where, sir?"

"Nowhere, young lady. You are lost to everything—and not to yourself. '*Ambo yatha salilam seva tu tat samagram*'—that is, 'it's always and for ever but water.' "

"I think I understand. Go on."

"I obey. As Proust says, after all we can only know ourselves."

"Does it mean, then, that one cannot love another?" She was in haste, as she wanted to hear it proven that Pratap could love her, but that she might not love him and yet marry him. Pratap was always on her mind.

"No, you can love another. But love can never be a movement, a feeling, an act. All that acts can only be of the body, or the mind, or the ego. Only the selfish can love."

"And the loveless?"

"They become love."

"Meanwhile?" she asked eagerly, apologetically, like a peasant asking an astrologer when the rains will fall.

"Meanwhile you sing the song of the Soviet land," I said, and we laughed so much that some kind professor's spouse, taking her pug for its walk, found that the Britannic canine sensibility had been hurt in this, the Kingdom of England, by such outrageous behaviour. The halls of Trinity must have heard our laughter and the dog, relentlessly, continued to bark.

"Pugs, madam," I said to Savithri, "are a bourgeois conception, and would not therefore be allowed in the fatherland of socialism. You can say '*psh-psh-psh*' (like our peasants call back dogs in India) to most people in the Soviet land—anyway, they carry labels, chains and municipal hygiene certificates, allow their tails to be cut or have muzzles put on their snouts—so dogs are not allowed."

"That's sheer American propaganda!" she protested.

"Don't you know I'm in the pay of America?" I laughed. "Except that the Americans are anti-George the Third, so they're confirmed anti-royalists, and they'd have nothing but laughter for my kingless royalism or for my Vedanta. I should have been born in the seventeenth century, should have called myself Rama Bhatta and written complicated panegyrics on some obscure prince, like the great Jagannatha Bhatta did."

"Not on a princess?" she asked.

"No, a Brahmin in those days could never have married a princess."

"But Jagannatha Bhatta did."

"Well, so they say . . ."

"He married Shah Jehan's own daughter," she continued, half in fun and half seriously. "Or rather, he took her to Benares, and the whole populace rose in anger that a Muslim, even a Mogul princess, should enter the great temple of Kalabhairava Himself. So the poet led her through lanes and by gutters to the ghats of the Ganges, and said, 'Mother Ganga, great Mother Ganga, I bring thee my bride, my princess . . .'

"The River Ganga rose, she rose wave after wave upwards, and washed the feet, did Mother Ganga, of the holy bride . . .

"And Jagannatha Bhatta thereupon composed those celebrated verses of the Gangalahari:

> Nidhānam dharmanām kimapi cha vidhānam
> Navasudām tīrthanām amala paridhānam trijiagatah
> Abode of all *dharma*,
> Sole giver of pleasure to the young;
> Centre of holy waters,
> Bright garland of the three worlds.

"He might at least have praised her too." she added.

"Well, I shall myself. And may I then write a Sanscrit verse in *Cardulā vikrīdita,** about you?" I asked. "Will you permit me?"

"Since my eighteenth-century ancestor perhaps no one has had a panegyric addressed to him in Sanscrit, so why not? My more recent ancestors employed Mogul poets to write of Alexander the Great or of Suhrab and Rustam, and at best some bulbul might drink teardrops from a princess's marble hand. If you went further you were tied to a pillar, and your skin peeled off your back. I didn't tell you the end of the story. My father wept the whole night with the father of the boy, and gave the young Muslim a scholarship and sent him to study in Aligarh. The verse wasn't bad; I can still remember it:

* The Tiger's Sportfulness: the name of a metre.

176

The dew waking asked the Sun, O thou all-seeing,
Give me the eye that sees, the red lamp that illumines
So that before the bulbul has begun to sing her lamentations
I will have looked on the curve of her eyebrows."

"True," I said, "your eyebrows are the most beautiful part of your face."

"A nasty thing to say, but go on."

"Your skin is perhaps even more wondrous. Five hundred years of being shut away in the zenana."

"Seven hundred, please, for it was Altamash that conquered us first."

"Well then, seven hundred years of zenana life has given your skin the texture of self-luminescence."

"And so?"

"And so when you fall into your silence, it's as though you contemplate a crystal from inside."

"And what a roundsome bowl too!" she added, hilarious.

"Roundsome, true, but a *jalatrang** on which a musician could play." Suddenly the hilarity stopped, the eyelashes fell on themselves, and any professor's pug, mesmerized into the orbit of Savithri's knowledge, might have sat as some dogs do, in the tapestry of Bayeux, their ears stretched back, their tail out, their hind quarters from which rises a conviction, a strength that illumines their eyes.

When Savithri went into this state I fell into myself, and forgot all but the feel that existence is I. I am, therefore the world is. I am, therefore Savithri is. How I would have loved to have taken Savithri into my arms; how natural, how true it would have been! But we were not one silence, we were two solitudes. What stood between Savithri and me was not Pratap, but Savithri herself. Meanwhile she had her gods and her holy land, and she was happy with the Comrades, and the Union of Soviet Socialist Republics. Mao was still unfamiliar, and too near the Indian frontiers: she had given him no official recognition in herself yet.

On this particular afternoon, however, she suddenly appeared, unusually late, her high heels making her look more unsettled

* A musical instrument consisting of jars filled with water.

on her feet than ever. As she came running up, with her two companions following almost behind her, and stood before me, I must have looked so lonely and angry that she just laid her hand on mine as it lay on the wall of the bridge. Nothing was said, nothing needed to be said: her sorrow just gurgled out of her, as she breathed a long and heavy sigh. Her companions stood on the opposite side of the bridge, looking down into the waters. She knew damp was no cure for my lungs and said suddenly, like a nanny might to a child, "I've not heard you cough for a long time, for such a long, long time. It's true, isn't it?" It was true indeed, and she knew it was she that made my breath regular and rested.

"I'm sorry," she said, as we all walked through Senate House Passage towards the Adelphi. "Come, Ramaswamy, let's have dinner together—all of us—and then you can go back to work. I'd completely forgotten I'd told Jack I would keep this Wednesday evening free for a dance. He'd bought the tickets, and I was starting out here when he suddenly appeared."

"Ah," said Jack Hollington as though apologetically coming towards us, "if I'd been a minute late I couldn't have known where Savithri was unless I'd gone round with a loud-speaker van." How heavy British humour looked after the niceties of French wit. "Yes," he continued, as though speaking of a rugby match, "and we'd hardly gone ten yards when Michael Swanston appeared at the gates of Girton, saying 'Hullo, Miss Rathor! I've a date with you. Don't you remember we promised to go to that Kingsley Martin lecture?' But Swanston hadn't bought his tickets yet, and as he's a Comrade he hadn't dressed, as I had." And Hollington looked himself up and down.

"And then," intruded Savithri, "what with dressing for the dance and meeting Michael I forgot whether we'd arranged to meet here or at the Library, so we went there first—and I with these terrible stilts, and we did everything to be on time. You know watches are always against me," she apologized, as she removed her coat.

We had come to the Adelphi, and the terrace was all that is gracious and sprightly in Cambridge, pink dresses, frills, magnolias, bow ties, whispers, laughter. Swanston and I were the only two who looked like boors: Swanston had abandoned his lecture—Savithri had a way of begging people to excuse her which made everyone follow wheresoever she went. As we all sat for dinner I saw for the first time that Savithri could be beautiful. She had put on some ancient Agra jewellery—her ear-pendants were very lovely—and she had blacked her eyebrows with collyrium; the smell of Lucknow attar made me feel I should like to be back in India. For Hollington, doing radio-engineering at Pembroke, Savithri was just another undergraduate. Her father and his father had shot tigers together, or some such thing, and so the old Raja Sahib had written to Sir Edmond who in his turn wrote to Jack and asked him to take care of her. This was the first time they were going out together.

Swanston they both knew from hearing him plead the communist cause at the Union. He was clever, a scholar, and ever so willing to be of service. You found him often at the Library or outside the Copper Kettle, talking of Molotov or Haldane. It was the time of the Soviet accusations against the United States about germ warfare in Korea, and Swanston had the names, qualifications and findings of everyone on the international committee of inquiry, from Joliot-Curie to some obscure professor in Australia. What continually surprised me was the obscurity of the great defenders of the Soviet land—if Lysenko were to be proved right you quoted a Melbourne newspaper; if Stalin was to be virtuous, you invariably quoted a Tokyo or Toronto source. Again, the Negro of America, whether he were called Jim, Harry or Peter Black, was always a great leader, and knew everything about the great Peoples' Democracies. This amused me a great deal, for it reminded me of Georges with his obscure authorities for the defence of the dogma: it only needed some patristic father or a Bishop of Nevers in the thirteenth century to prove to Georges that his theory was correct. It was incontrovertible when he said, "*L'Archevêque Henri d'Auxerre a dit . . .*" and I had to be silent. Haldane was the same for Swanston. It would have amused Henri d'Auxerre, Archevêque, to face history with Haldane. This eighteenth-century prelate being more trained in diplomacy and unction than the British biologist, the Archevêque would no doubt have opened some Burgundy—the best is grown near

Auxerre—and then, after a meal of *rognons à la brochette, une caisse de foie gras aux truffes, et enfin la fondue,* a pinch of strong snuff from the Levant would be passed on to Haldane; which would have proved that Bishops and Comrades, whatever their origin, never go wrong.

"Well, Dr. Ramaswamy, what have you been thinking?" started Savithri. "Ramaswamy has always such interesting things to say about everything. He relates things apparently so unrelated—for him history is a vast canvas, for the discovery of value, of metaphysical value. He's my Guru," she concluded, a little hesitant, a little shyly, as though it was such a big thing to say that it might not be named.

"What's that?" asked Jack.

"Well, it's such a difficult thing to explain. A Guru is a real teacher—the one who shows you the way to Truth."

"That's asking a great deal too much of anyone, isn't it?" said Swanston, not because he did not think Truth was possible, but because for him it had only one route, as it were, one system, the end of one dialectic. And in his own mind he named that one to himself—a man, a great man, far away and big, and gentle and kind to children; thrice married but virtuous, a Generalissimo, the Father, the creator of the past, the present and the future Socialist Republics. I could follow his thought, so I broke in:

"In fact, I've been thinking about the inevitability of communism—this new Catholicism—and why Nazism had to be defeated, had to die. Hitler," I went on, "was an extraordinary man, but he could no more succeed than Ravana did against Rama. Rama is the river of life, the movement towards self-liberation, the affirmation of one's true existence; Ravana is negation, is the earth, the fact. But the earth is made for dissolution, so he who holds the earth in bondage, he who *possesses* in the real sense, works *against* life. That if anything is the meaning of communism."

"There are too many incomprehensible factors in your statement, sir," said Swanston, removing his glasses. He wiped them carefully, respectfully, and put them back, as though the shine on his nose gave his intelligence acuity.

"Ah, that's just like Ramaswamy," explained Savithri, "he

works with symbols and equations. History for him is a vast algebra, and he draws in unknowns from everywhere to explain it."

"So do we," said Swanston. Jack Hollington was busy looking at the other tables; his red rose sat self-consciously in his button-hole.

"Well, there's a difference. Ramaswamy is like a scientist—his history, thank heavens, has no morality. In his history, there are no bourgeois or capitalists; to him the whole of history is one growing meaning. Or rather, it is instantaneous meaning." She turned to me. "Am I right? To think I am trying to explain you while you are here!" The jewel at her neck shone with such simple, intimate, unswerving splendour.

"Ravana, the King of Lanka, in our great epic the *Ramayana,* was compared by Mahatma Gandhi, who read the poem every day, to the British Government of his time." This brought about general laughter. "Your father," I said, turning to Swanston, "and your father, were henchmen of Ravana, and so, if I may be permitted to say it——"

"——was this young lady's father too," intervened Savithri, and we all laughed again.

"Well, Ravana wants to possess the world—he's taken Sita, daughter of the furrow, child of Himalay and wife of Rama, away; he's kidnapped her and taken her away and made her his prisoner."

"And so?" said Jack, joining the discussion.

"And so Rama has to fight his battle. He goes about in the forest and the animals of the wild and the birds of the air join him, for the cause of Sri Rama is dharmic, it's the righteous turn-ing of the Wheel of the Law. For right and wrong are questions of a personal perspective, but *dharma* is adherence to the im-personal. So when Rama goes to liberate Sita from the prison island of Ravana, the very monkeys and squirrels build roads and bridges, carry messages, set fire to fearful cities, because *dharma* must win."

"What's *dharma?*" asked Swanston.

"*Dharma* comes from the word *dhru,* to sustain, to uphold. It's as it were the metaphysical basis of the world—in so far as the world exists, of course—and it's the same *dharma*, to continue the story, that forced Sri Rama, after having burnt Lanka, killed Ravana and liberated Sita, and after returning to Ayodhya the capital, in the splendour of banners, victory-pillars, music and worship, to send Queen Sita away in exile. The fair, the pregnant Sita was sent away, for the *dharma* of Rama, the *dharma* of a king, demanded it."

"Why?" pursued Swanston.

"Because some suburban gossip between washerwoman and boat-builder's wife leapt from mouth to mouth, saying that Queen Sita could not have kept her integrity while prisoner of demon Ravana. And although the earth and sacrificial fire proclaimed the purity of Sita, yet the populace spoke of this and that, and Sita had to be sent away in exile, that the Kingdom of Ayodhya be perpetually righteous. The impersonal alone is right," I said.

"How do you explain that?" asked Savithri, thoughtful.

"The impersonal alone could be the Truth because he, Sri Rama, was the Truth."

"How can one be the Truth?" asked Swanston with a silly little laugh. The elementary minds which go to make the majority of communists are exasperating.

"How can one not be the Truth, sir?" I asked a little angrily. "Standing where do you judge falsehood?"

"In truth, naturally," Hollington said.

"And can truth judge truth?"

"No," said Savithri.

"Then when truth sees truth, as it were, what happens?" Everyone was introspective—they were trying to understand.

"One is truth," said Savithri, almost in a whisper, as though she feared others might hurt the Truth by saying things irreverent. And we fell into a large-eyed silence.

Meanwhile, the food came, and the drinks, and the function of masticating took a lot of our time. Savithri fiddled away with her bit of lamb or veal, for when she was thinking food did not go easily down her gullet.

"So you say communism is inevitable."

"Yes, like smallpox inoculation is inevitable."

"That's new."

"Between the normality of birth and the normality of continuous existence there's a difference," I continued. "In one you are given a chance to live, and in the other you are prevented from dying for a certain time, for the normal length of time; and so you take inoculations." Swanston looked at me, not knowing what I was driving at.

"History proves Darwinism," I went on. "Just as there is a biological Darwinism—the survival of the fittest, which Marx affirmed was one of the greatest truths in the history of humanity —so there is a psychical Darwinism. You survive because you want the race to continue? But why, may I ask, should continuance be so important?"

"That's not a question," spat Swanston, as though I were being childish. His system of logic had not foreseen such an argument.

"Yes, it is possible to explain. You do not only say light travels at such and such a speed, you also inquire if it goes in pulses or in waves, and why it does so."

"And so?" asked Savithri. She wanted me to go to the end of my argument. The fact however was, Savithri knew, as I knew, that I spoke from a knowledge, a conjoint discovery, that came of her.

"The *why* is the most important of all questions. If there were no why, there would be no dialectic, in fact there would be no Marxism. The only trouble with Marxism was it ended with itself. The dialectic, unlike the parallel, must meet somewhere. It had to end in some Spartacus of history, or in the Paris of 1871, or in Moscow 1917. And thus Paradise came into being; God, the Angel Gabriel and the Generalissimo."

Swanston, by now, had nothing but contempt for me, Jack was thinking of other things—it was soon going to be half past eight and they would have to get ready for the dance. But Savithri sat there as though time had been absorbed by her, as Shiva had absorbed his poison; as though she had made of it a jewel, to be hung at her neck. Her breath became deep, and her whole body had a quality, a tingling quality of crystal, which almost made sound unto itself inwardly. It had become a musical instrument, the *jalatrang*.

Thoughts intoxicated Savithri as nothing else did: men for her were just givers of thoughts. Her maidenhood had no physical basis. It existed, just as in fairy tales you cannot win a princess unless you solve a riddle. For her life was such a riddle, and she rejected man after man—not because she found them tall or lean or fat or too rich, or even learned or boring—but because she fed, as it were, on life itself; meaning consisted of food, breath, sensation. She was restless because nothing, no, nothing at all, could fill her—save a steady, self-sounding but unrippled silence. Who gave her silence gave her life. Sometimes I did, I think, so she liked to be with me. I once teased her, saying, "You function according to the endocrinology of semantics!" And she laughed approvingly, letting fall the flower from her hair.

Communism she understood that evening. She understood it for she acted rightly, if often for stupid reasons. She might say, "I like being a communist because Swanston is so nice," or "I like to dance with Jack because his father is a great friend of my father," not seeing that both reasons were false. She just fell on the right thing—she took the English Tripos only because somebody had said, "It's a nice discipline; take it." But actually she spoke an English, albeit with an Indian accent, of a beauty that was gentle, unobtrusive, indrawn, as though it was her most intimate breath; each word seemed created, as it were, at the moment—coming from the depths of sound and meaning at once. That was why, when I had quoted to her Kalidasa's first verse of *Raghuvamsa*,

> *Vāk arthah vyava çampruktho,*
> Just as word and meaning are binomial
> Indeed be Parvathi and Siva himself,

she had stood there that day in Avignon with wonderment, that someone, even such a great poet as Kalidasa, could have formulated her own intimate apperception so completely, explaining Savithri Rathor to herself.

Communism for her was also an explanation, a fact of history, with a meaning. What was irrelevant turned itself away from her by some power of simple negation—like water on a swan or on a lotus leaf. Not that ugly smearing things did not come near her —they just did not reach her. There was no one to receive, at the other end. So passions fell with a gesture, vulgarity swallowed itself, and the aftermath of silence cleansed everyone, gave purity back to every decadent undergraduate.

I remembered how one evening, when Savithri had had to go back early to College to see her tutor about something, Lakshmi had come to dine with me at the hotel. No different from other girls of her age, Lakshmi, who swore such undying affection for Savithri ("She's here, in my belly, like my own child," she used to say)—well, Lakshmi had said, "I cannot understand how Savithri can go about with so many men at the same time. You'll hate me for saying it, but she's a flirt." I had looked at Lakshmi with the look of a Brahmin at a bird-catcher or barber. Brahmins don't need words to say anything.

"I don't mean she does things," Lakshmi had continued. "But whether they are socialists, communists, conservatives, or anything else they all have to dance round her. Indians are shocked at this freedom. It comes from going straight to liberty after centuries of zenana life."

"It's like young puppies or birds—when they open their eyes and try to walk they fall anywhere. Isn't it such joy, Lakshmi, to have so much innocence before one? You and I, who come from the South, we know too much: we shall never have such innocence. Savithri is a saint," I had said, and closed the discussion. After that Lakshmi had not been so free with me. She was just jealous. Jealousy with women is a greater biological quantum. We go to another woman—but they eat their own feelings out. Pity that a male prostitute is so anti-natural. For women possession is knowledge. To hold is to be: to love is to submit. Bondage is her destiny.

Not so with Savithri. Having accepted bondage she was free. To be a woman, she knew, was to be absorbed by a man. If such a man did not exist, then the masculine principle in all men—and in women when they were intelligent, for she had many women friends—could give food for her intelligence. She wanted to surrender to Truth—and be *free*. Life was too much sorrow: not joy was its meaning, but *liberation*. That is why when I taught her the *Nirvana Shataka* of Sri Sankara she was so happy—and she could sing it with deep emotion. *"Mano-budhi Ahankara,"* she would start and, closing her eyes, enter into herself. It led her to her own silence.

She must have followed my thoughts, for she said, "Do me a favour?"

"What is it?"

"Lakshmi and Sharifa have gone out to the cinema. Poor girls, they are alone. Will you take them out and give them a meal, for my sake? Now, let us come back to communism."

She lit a cigarette, and though she knew how offensive it was for me, the South Indian Brahmin, to see an Indian girl smoke, yet she continued to puff at it, not to convince me that she smoked, but to convince others she was just like most undergraduates. Her humility was to accept the common denominator of all. This explained, too, why she was never un-at-home anywhere. She slipped into events—and from event to event she slipped, as a fish slips from space to space of water. I looked on at life.

"Communism is a positive movement. It is a spiritual movement. It moves in the direction of life. When the Americans wonder why communism succeeds, they might just as well ask why ammonites and belemnites vanished in the Mesozoic but lamellibranchs, members of the oyster family, continued to exist. Death is a left-over of existence. Nothing really dies: even death does not die. All continues. Ultimately nothing continues. For that which is itself cannot continue in itself. As the Great Sage has said: It needs space and time to make water into a wave. And what is it that can make life into a wave? It cannot make itself, and nothing else can."

"Then what happens?" she asked. By now Swanston had lost all hope of intelligence. He thought we talked nonsense.

"Nothing happens," I answered. "The question itself, as it were, becomes the answer."

"And communism . . . ?"

". . . dies," I said.

"And what remains?"

"Truth," I answered, as though she knew what I knew.

186

She was doodling on the table with a spoon. Then she lifted her head and said, "So what, then, is history?"

"History is like saying one's name to oneself. It convinces you that you exist. *C'est la carte d'identité de l'homme,*" I said, not to prove my knowledge of French, but to give my statement the aphoristic value which the French language offers.

"And communism?"

"It's the stamp of *renouvellement.*"

"And Nazism?"

"A wrong declaration crossed out. *Annulée.*"

"And after communism, what next?"

"The King," I said.

"The King?" she pleaded.

"The principle of man as ruler, as regulator of the kingdom; just as woman is mistress and doctor of the household. Kingship is a catalytic principle. It dissolves terrestrial contradictions, for us all to live."

"What a job!" muttered Swanston.

"The pyramid is a pyramid, whether it be in the deserts of Africa or in Red Square. Mummification is what ends the feminine principle made masculine."

"Now, what's that?"

"Materialism—the importance given to *yin,* or *prakriti.* It can only lead to the acknowledgement of the object as real."

"The object *is* real," protested Swanston, as though to himself. He was getting exasperated and bored.

"Nobody has yet known an object—in the whole history of humanity," I added. "If they had known, there would be no Royal College or Institut Curie."

"What nonsense!" he cried.

"Try to understand please, Michael. India still has the most ancient civilization on earth."

"Yes, with the whip, and five-rupee murders," he said, obviously quoting Savithri back to herself.

"And Mahatma Gandhi!" said Savithri, indignant.

"And more than Mahatma Gandhi," I added, without further explanation. "Unless the masculine principle absorb the feminine, the world cannot be annihilated, and so there can be no

187

joy. Joy is not in the thought, but as it were in the thought of the thought, in the *'ma pensée s'est pensée'* of Mallarmé. In fact it is only in the stuff of thought, that is, where there is no thought."

"Wonderful!" exclaimed Savithri.

"I am the only Indian royalist," I said, as though to give conclusion to my argument.

"Well, when you are King, I shall be Queen," added Savithri, not, as it seemed, as a joke, but as a dedication, a prophecy.

> *Cāntam idam ācramapadam sphurati ca bāhuh kutah phalam*
> *ihasya atha va bhavitavyānihām dvārāni bhavanthi sarvatra*
> Calm this retreat, this hermitage:
> Yet my arm throbs—what presage can it be?
> For from this, from all that lies about us,
> Gateways open to future events.

It must be very late, I thought. I looked at my watch. It was twenty-five minutes past eight. I had to rush to meet Sharifa and Lakshmi at the cinema.

I think Savithri was sorry she had given me a job to do—was sorry I was going. I think she almost said, "Don't go." But acceptance was so natural to her. For a moment only I think I saw a struggle in her, as if she wished there were no Governors of Indian Provinces with sons at Cambridge, no horrible jazz which had already begun to syncopate from the next room; no communism and no Swanston, with his red tie and his shining, gold-rimmed glasses, which made him look like a tailor or a quartermaster; as if she wished only the Cam ran through the world, past Trinity with its square tower and many birds, and gargoyles —and night would fall, and the darkness would be filled with one's unthinking thought, one's breath.

But as I left her she had regained her positive existence: her feet almost started tapping on the floor—I had become a stranger already. Swanston stayed behind, saying, "May I join your party?"

Outside it was cold, and as I went along those rich and surprising alleyways of Cambridge, with churches, crosses, bookshops, bicycles, I recognized I had a strange feeling of which I could not be too proud: I wished I were alone and with Savithri.

If I felt thus with Swanston, why should not Lakshmi feel whatever she felt about Savithri and me? My masculine exclusivity thus made me kinder to Lakshmi. To possess seems so simple, so inevitable. Truth only dawns when you know you can possess nothing. We can at best possess ourself—and life is one long pilgrimage, one long technique of such a possession. I felt sorrowful and kind, I laughed a lot with Lakshmi and Sharifa. I took them to an Indian restaurant: the Taj Mahal.

My own countrymen, outside my country, terrify me. They somehow seem to come from nowhere—from no particular province, caste or profession. They all look like Brahminee-kine left at some funeral, so that when the ancestors make the voyage on to the other side—as the Brahmin in Benares explains—they catch hold of a cow's or bull's tail to go to their lunar destination. Meanwhile the cow steals from this shop and from that, is fed with grass by a passer-by, is decorated with kunkum by a shaven widow; children touch her with fear and beg for jewels, clothes or husbands; until some passing policeman beats her on the back, and drives her to a lane. There she lies, and chews her cud, till the sun sets and the evening pilgrims come whispering mantras as if to themselves, caressing her with great worship and tenderness: "Gauri, Ganga, Maheswari," and so on. Sometimes, too, the cow or bull has a great feast, when some late funeral meal is at last over. There are Brahmins, imagine, that do three funerals a day, so sometimes one has to wait a long time for them to come. Of course it is always an illness or a new arrival that has stopped them coming sooner, for they can only come on an empty stomach . . . but you know from their belchings and rounded bellies much food has already gone into them. Ah, brother, Benares is Benares, Kashi the Holy, and whatever sins you commit in Kashi—well, there even a dog, or a bull, or a four-shoulder Brahmin attains liberation.

I told Lakshmi and Sharifa all about Benares and made them laugh. "All of us, that way, are Brahminee-kine, and someone who's lost his dear ancestor searches for a cow or bull to offer it the *pinda,* and the bull suddenly remembers the strength in its feet, and rises, comes slowly, condescendingly; and not only eats away all the rice, but even the darbha grass. We, the Indians, abroad, therefore, I repeat, are the Brahminee-bulls. Nobody strikes us because we are so virtuous. Nobody washes us because we are so clean. We get the worship of others, and we have nothing to do. We ferry the dead to the opposite shore . . ."

The other Indians were not at all amused at the ripples of laughter that came from us: the Punjabees thought it did not sound Punjabee, the Dakhsinees found it irregular—women do not permit themselves to laugh in Maharastra!—the South Indians thought it was a sign of easy widowhood. Only a Muslim here and there enjoyed himself. We were grateful to Islam, that evening, for respecting human freedom.

"India today," I continued, "to change the metaphor, is like the Second Empire. Every Indian in Cambridge is the son of a minister, or the daughter of an advocate-general (Sharifa's father was an advocate-general), and you find sitting opposite the nephew of the Prime Minister, the son of the Minister of Finance from Jodhpur, the grandson of Sardar Patel, Rafi Ahmad Kidwai's cousin, or the chief Minister of Travancore's brother-in-law. You have new Maharajas and a new Emperor. The first Emperor —the Eagle—must die in exile or be shot. I, Napoleon Bonaparte, Emperor of the French, etc., etc. Then you have a revolution, and there's his son the gentle Duke of Reichstadt, Roi de Rome, l'Aiglon, who dies at Schoenbrunn or anywhere else, for that matter. The Revolution of 1848 can come through an economic evolution—history is not concerned with fact-sequence but with a pattern-sequence—and you have a Napoleon again, the Prince-Président. There's a Victor Hugo in exile and but now in Moscow—Bipin Chatterjee would be his name. There's a Balzac, and today his name might be Jainenendrakumar Jain. There's even a Princess Eugénie. She's not a wife—she's a Sister."

Sharifa roared with laughter. "When, pray, is the Third Republic?" she said.

"This time, madam, there will be no Third Republic, no Monsieur Thiers. History has changed its mind. We will have a King this time."

"Who?" asked Lakshmi, amused.

"Some Rathor, of the dynasty of Sri Rama, with a Sage Vasistha behind him. Vedanta must become real again before

India can be truly free. You know what Mahatma Gandhi said: 'My freedom is not when the British leave India, for that is inevitable and will be soon, but when we become true *satyagrahis* —when we seek the Truth humbly, fervently, and with non-violence in our hearts.' That for me is India, not a country, not a historical presence among nations, but a hypostatic presence. Someone before the war wrote a book, *Forward from Liberalism*. Now someone must write, *Forward from Marxism*."

"Forward to what?" asked Sharifa.

"To Vedanta," I said, as though I'd murmured to myself "Savithri."

"You are going back in time?" remarked Lakshmi.

"In Vedanta there is no going back or forward—just as in Indian music there can be nothing new, for all that is musical has been included in Indian *rāgas*. You can only sing and create, hour after hour, day after day, as our musicians do—like Fayyaz Khan did when he sang *Khelatha nandā kumār* for four nights on end. In the same way Indian history plays a melody to itself, creating and re-creating itself, standing not against sound but in silence. India is apart, that is why she has no history. India is everybody's: India is in everybody. It is in that sense, I think, that Mahatma Gandhi said, 'When we are free, all will be free.' Let us truly be *satyagrahis*—graspers of the Truth—and that humbly is my India," I said, with almost a failing voice.

I was paying homage not to my country—not to the land of great mountains and big rivers, for these too I love; not to the country of Asoka or Akbar, however great and universal these may be—but to some nameless magnanimity, a mystery that has eyes, a sense of existence, beautiful, beautiful Mother, my land . . .

I went home and wrote a sweet letter to Madeleine. I told her what to me was a truth. I loved her more than ever, not because of what she was—for that was, as it were, her affair—but because I had changed, had enlarged into myself, I felt thinner, lighter, and with a greater curve of being. I loved her, I told her, because she had borne Pierre, I loved her again for the reality that was shaping itself in her, I loved her for the woman that she was—that was mine, and that I had, for an instant, for a series of instants, seen and was merged in light. I had grown to respect her more, knowing that human love as I knew it then was imperfect, as language is imperfect, but that love was possible, was real: the more real and possible because I was far away—I would go farther away still. Space is the need of love, I had once read somewhere, and she who gives space to one, gives one the permission to love.

I realized by now that I was not in fact writing to Madeleine but to Savithri, and I abruptly brought the letter to an end. "I shall be back in Aix, within a week or ten days, and meanwhile grow into beauty, my love, my wife," I begged her, as though I had come to a conclusion. The toe-rings remained in my trunk and I knew no peace. All was an absence, like the space over the bare trees and the Cam. Some bell rang the hour, and silence journeyed back among the streets: the proctors had gone to sleep. And one dim, rainy Sunday I left Cambridge for London.

IN LONDON I could not say whether I was happy or unhappy. I walked back and forth in my room in Kensington—it was on the third floor of an old building, and looked out on a lovely square beyond which one felt the river—I walked up and down the room, stopping sometimes to put a shilling into the gas meter or to warm myself. Or I would snatch a book and read a quarter of a page, or jump on my bed and go to sleep for a blank quarter of an hour. And I tried thus to formulate myself to myself. I like these equations about myself or others, or about ideas: I feed on them.

I could see in myself a vastness, as it were a change of psychic dimension, an awareness of a more ancient me. There was no joy in this knowledge, no, no exaltation. There was just a re-discovery, as though having lost a brother in famine or on pil-grimage I had wandered hundreds of miles, had asked policeman and mistress of household for him, had asked barbers, tradesmen and Sadhus for him; as though walking back through time I had asked men with a more antique form of tuft on their heads, with voices more grave, with lips more lecherous; as though from Muslims as they consolidated their ramparts, sentry-chambers, palaces, "Brother, have you seen my brother?" I had asked; from Kings, and going beyond, by the Ganges or the Cauvery, from Saints and Sages I had asked, backwards in history to the times of the Upanishads, even unto Yagnyavalkya and Maitreyi; and as though at each epoch, with each person, I had left a knowledge of myself, a remembered affirmation of myself; and in this affirma-tion had been the awareness of the Presence that I am, that I am my brother. Thus it was as I walked about in my Kensington room, feeling the cold of London, the dampness of the river, and my own lung twist a little here and there, as though it also was a recognition, a memory.

How much of the time we live in our past: in a Florentine bridge or a kneeling Madonna of Santa Maria Novella; in a breath of thyme and rosemary from the Pyrenees, the face of a child seen at an Easter Service at the Montagne Sainte-Geneviève; in the name of a book, the look of a bishop; and far away, in all India, with its little railway stations, with turbaned, *beedi*-smoking stationmasters—Dhumath Khed, Bhumath Khed, Parusram, Alviya, Medhi Mogharpur—all sounding like some names one has known, one has lived, just as one remembers the names of battles at school in a history book. Then you like cucumber and not the bitter gourd, like the honey of the Vindhyas and not that of the Kuruvai Hills; you like Subramanya at first sight and you do not bother so much about Subbu, your brother-in-law from Bangalore; you like Little Mother and hate your grandmother; you like Saroja, your sister, not because she is your sister but for something else; you marry Madeleine. Where, I ask you, does history stop, and where do you begin? You can go back through biological constructs and though it be difficult to know yourself you can think yourself a dinosaur, an orang-outang, a bison, heifer or nightingale. You might feel yourself a peacock or a porcupine, then feel the more ancient tall deodhar of the Himalaya. Sitting under the deodhar you may feel memories that have no age, filling you with continuity. You cannot escape time. But you can escape yourself. And in such an escape, in the dim periphery of yourself you meet with fear, with biological fear. But if like a boar or a dog you dig deeper with your muzzle, you will see with wonder the *budu-mékaye* break open on the jungle path—and you enter, the huge rock lifting like a gate, you enter the Kingdom of the Seven Sisters; a Cathar, *un Pur*, you enter the Grotte d'Orolac, the *Mani*, with the Holy Grail in your hand.

There never was time, there never was history, there never was anything but *Shivoham, Shivoham:* I am Shiva, I am the Absolute.

Walking back and forth in my Kensington room that day—it was a Thursday, I clearly remember, the day of Jupiter—I thought of the letter I should write to Pratap. For how could I have gone to Cambridge and seen so much of Savithri without dropping him a line, some concatenation of words (and images) that might give him hope? For hope he certainly could have. Savithri always talked of Pratap as one talks of one's secretary—it must have come from the atmosphere of palaces—as an inevitable support in all contingencies, a certainty in a world of uncertainty. If she talked of him with a touch of condescension it was not because of social differences; it was just because she liked being kind to something, something inevitable, unknown, such as a lame horse in the stable or it might be an old bull, fed in the palace yard till it die; but meanwhile being treated as an elder, a palace bull, given the best of Bengal gram and the choicest of green grass. And when it died, for it would "die," it would be given a music-and-flower funeral and have orange trees planted over its grave. And one day some virgin would light a lamp and consecrate it, and every day from that time on the sanctuary would be lit with an oil lamp, as dusk fell over the palace grove . . .

To speak the truth, I hated this attitude of Savithri's. I felt she was so truly indifferent, so completely resigned to her fate—like all Hindu women—that for her, life was like a bullock-cart wheel: it was round, and so it had to move on night after night, and day after day, smelling chilli or tamarind, rice or coconut, over rut and through monsoon waters purring at the sides to the fairs in the plains; or to the mountains, high up there, on a known pilgrimage. What did it matter, she would ask, whether the sun scorched or the rain poured, or you carried tamarind or saffron? Life's wheel is its own internal law. Nobody could marry Savithri, nobody could marry a soul, so why not marry anyone? And why should not that anyone be stump Pratap? It certainly could not be Hussain Hamdani; and thank heavens his vanity and self-interest took him to Pakistan and a good job—and Pratap was, anyway, so very clean, so gentle, so sincere. If one should have a husband at all, said Savithri, Pratap was the very best.

"What do you think?" she had asked me one evening, a day or two before my departure from Cambridge. We were not by the river, which was reserved for *us*, for our conjoint intuitions of poetry and history—of a song of Mira's, and again maybe of some historical character from Avignon, Nîmes, Carcassonne, Albi or Montpellier. But when we came out into the open street-light we could talk of anything, of Nehru's Government, of Father's despair at having three elephants instead of eight, a tradition which had come down from Rajendra Simha III, in the sixteenth century. Finally, in the heart of this extrovert world one can always dig a hollow, make oneself comfortable in a bus shelter, an A.B.C., or with hot coffee at the Copper Kettle one can sit and talk of Pratap.

"There's such goodness in him. I have never seen anyone so good in life. Not even you," she had said, in mock severity.

"I never said I was good."

"Of course not," she teased, "but you want to be called a saint."

"You say so," I laughed, "and that is your responsibility." I could hear the bells ring the hour on Trinity Tower, so gathering her notes we had jumped into a taxi at the Market Square and rushed off to deposit her safely at the gate of Girton.

"It's me," she said, with that enchanting voice, and even the gatekeeper did not seem to mind very much. "Am I very late?"

He had looked at the clock first, and then at me. "Well, Miss Rathor, the world does not always function by the clock, does it?" he said, with a wink.

She laid the red rose I had bought her on his table, saying, "This is for Catherine," and turning to me she had added, "She's such a nice girl, seven years old; we're great friends. Good night, Ramaswamy, good night, Mr. Scott. Good night."

Back in the taxi I said to myself, "Catherine or Pratap, for Savithri it makes no difference. Both are dear because both are familiar, innocent, and inevitable in her daily existence."

Thinking over all this, my letter to Pratap never got written. It was a damp day and I did not go to the British Museum for my work, but as it was already long past three, I took a stroll by the river.

What an imperial river the Thames is—her colour may be dark or brown, but she flows with a majesty, with a maturity of her own

196

knowledge of herself, as though she grew the tall towers beside her, and buildings rose in her image, that men walked by her and spoke inconsequent things—as two horses do on a cold day while the wine merchant delivers his goods at some pub, whispering and frothing to one another—for the Londoner is eminently good. He is so warm, he is indeed the first citizen of the world. The mist on the Thames is pearly, as if Queen Elizabeth the First had squandered her riches and femininity on ships of gold, and Oberon had played on his pipe, so worlds, gardens, fairies and grottoes were created, empires were built and lost, men shouted heroic things to one another and died, but somewhere one woman, golden, round, imperial, always lay by her young man, his hand over her left breast, his lip touching hers in rich recompense. There's holiness in happiness, and Shakespeare was holy because Elizabeth was happy. Would England not see an old holiness again?

For me, as I have said already, the past was necessary to understand the present. Standing on a bridge near Chelsea, and seeing the pink and yellow lights of the evening, the barges floating down to some light, the city feeling her girth in herself, how I felt England in my bones and breath; how I reverenced her. The buses going high and lit; the taxis that rolled about, green and gentlemanly; the men and women who seemed responsible, not for this Island alone, but for whole areas of humanity all over the globe; strollers—some workman, who had stolen a moment on his way to a job, some father who was showing London to his little daughter, two lovers arm hooked to arm—how with the trees behind and the water flowing they seemed to make history stop and look back at itself.

London was esoteric and preparing for the crowning of another Queen; and Englishmen felt it would be a momentous insight of man into himself. The white man, I felt, did not bear his burden, but the Englishman did. For, after all, it was the English who founded the New World, yet now it was America that naïvely, boastfully, was proclaiming what every English man and woman really felt—that the dominion of man, the regulation of habeas corpus or the right delivery of some jute bales on Guadalcanal Island in the Pacific, was the business of these noble towers, clocks, balances, stock-books, churring ships, and aeroplanes above, and that there would be good government on earth, and decency and a certain nobility of human behaviour, and all because England was. That I, an Indian who disliked British rule, should feel this only revealed how England was recovering her spiritual destiny, how in anointing her Queen she would anoint herself.

It was nearing six by now and knowing that about this hour Julietta would be at the Stag, I dropped in, took an orangeade and sat waiting for her. Julietta was a great friend of Savithri's. She had left Girton the year before, and though I had met her only once I felt I could talk to her about anything.

Julietta and the whole generation of young English people who had either fought in the war or matured during it—Julietta was eighteen in 1945—were fascinating to me. That is why for an outsider pub life seemed so valuable—he saw the new England, even when the English men and women he met were not particularly young. But England herself had become young—and sovran. Young Englishmen looked so open, so intellectually keen, and the girls seemed so feminine, so uninhibited. It was all so far from the world of Jane Austen or Thackeray, or even from the world of Virginia Woolf. Boys and girls met and mated and helped each other through life with, as one girl remarked to Savithri, the facility of eating an apple. "In fact I was eating an apple," said Marguerite Hoffner, "when he did it to me. What is there in it, anyway, to talk about so much?" Indeed it was explained to me that the coupling of male and female had gone on more and more normally, and that a modern Lady Chatterley would not have to go so far as a gamekeeper, but would find her man beside her in a theatre, on Chelsea Bridge, or in a pub. I only knew the foul-smelling bistros in France, and almost never went to any—could you imagine Madeleine at the Café des Marroniers or in the Rencontre des Pêcheurs?—but the pub, the Stag, was so civilized.

Julietta came in, accompanied by Stephen, a Logical Positivist with a curve of sparse golden hair, a high forehead and lilting green eyes. In his opinion Aristotle had proved that the world was very real: he could not understand how one could doubt one's self.

"And who doubts the doubter?" I asked.

"The doubter."

"Who sees the doubter?"

"My mind," he answered.

"Can my mind see itself?" I pressed.

"Of course. Why not?"

"Can you have two thoughts at a time?" I continued.

"Come, come," he said, waving his glass and feeling very happy, "you don't want me to grow mystical, do you?"

"No," I said, "I am talking to Aristotle."

"Well, Aristotle has decided on the nature of syllogisms."

"Why, have you never heard of the Nyaya system of Indian logic?"

"Nyaya fiddlesticks," said Stephen good-humouredly.

"Come, come," said Julietta, with womanly tenderness, pushing back Stephen's golden hair. Her hands, I noticed, were not as elegant as the sensitivity on her face.

"Can light see itself?" I asked.

"Obviously not," said Stephen.

"Then how can the mind see itself?"

"I told you," shouted Stephen, "not to talk mysticism to me!"

"He's talking sense—and you, non-sense," said Julietta, chivalrously.

"And you, my love," he said, kissing her richly before everyone, "you own the castle of intelligence, and I am the Lord." He was obviously getting drunk. I stopped, bought them each a drink and sat down. There was by now a gay crowd of artists in patched elbows, old stockbrokers with indecipherable females, landlords with their dogs, writers who talked, their noses in the air, as though publishers belonged to the tanners' or the drummers' caste—writers, of course, being Brahmins—and there were silent, somnolent painters carrying the tools of their trade, with canvases hidden under some cover, chatting with the bartender. "Half of bitter, please," came the refrain, gentle and gruff, elegant and cockney, and the whole place filled with smoke, silence and talk. The smell of perfumes mingled with other smells of females and men, making one feel that the natural man is indeed a good man—*lo naturale è sempre senza errore*—that logic had nothing to do with life. Life was but lovely, and loveliness had golden hair and feminine intimacy, while the Thames flowed.

"One last question," I said, bringing more beer to Julietta and Stephen. "The brain is made of matter . . ."

"That is so, my inquisitor," said Stephen, laughing.

" . . . so the brain is made of the same stuff as the earth?"

"That is so, my Indian Philosopher."

"Then how can the earth be objective to the earth—understand the earth?"

"It's just like asking—I beg pardon, Julietta—if I copulate with Julietta, as I often and joyfully do—and the nicer, the better when there's a drink—then how do I understand Julietta? The fact is I don't understand Julietta. I never will understand Julietta. I don't know that I love her—even when I tell her sweet and lovely things. I'm happy and that's all that matters. I'm a solipsist," he concluded laughing.

Julietta was pursuing her own thoughts, seemingly undisturbed by his statements. "I'm reviewing a book on the subject," she broke in, "which says God is because evil is. Is that what you mean?"

"I don't know what you mean by God. But it needs a pair of opposites to make a world. Only two things of different texture and substance can be objective to one another. Otherwise it's like two drops of mercury in your hand, or like linking the Red Sea and the Arabian Sea—they are both water and the same. I ask you, how can the mind, made of the same stuff as the earth, be *positive* about the earth? Water is not positive to water—water is positive to nothing. Water is. So something is. And since isness is the very stuff of that something, all you can say is, 'Is is.' "

"I knew Indians were mad, that Gandhi was mad. And now, now I have the proof," said Stephen. "I'm an old anarchist. I believe that matter is true, that Julietta is true, that I am true, and you also my friend, who stands me drinks, and spends ninepence each time on me and ninepence on Julietta. Now, go and get me another. This time I don't want a half. I want the whole damn' thing, and long live Pandit Nehru."

People from the counter turned to look and lifted their glasses to India, to me. How wonderful to be in an English pub, I thought. Such humanity you would get in France only amongst the working classes, never among the dark-faced, heaving, fingering bourgeois. The sensuality of the bourgeois is studied, it is a vice, because he was defeated before he went to it: Baudelaire was already defeated by his stepfather and his smelly mother before he went to his Negress. You see the dark because you want to prove yourself the light; dialectic is on the lip of the rake. But in this young England, which I knew so little, I felt man was more primary and innocent, more inexhaustible. He did not have a "judas" on his door— he did not cultivate the concierge yet. Flowers grew in his gardens, red fluorescent lights lit the top of the buildings, and beneath them, the Thames flowed. White cliffs of chalk begirt the isle at the estuary, and you could see seagulls rising with the ferry lights and returning to the night. Soon I'd have to be back in France, and I shivered to the bottom of my spine. Lord, would that I could make the moment stay, and make the world England.

Walking beside Savithri the next day, towards the evening— we were on the Embankment—I told her of my premonition of England, of this new island, knowing she was going to have a Queen: the King was already a little not there, he was so ill, and the leaves and the water in Hyde Park, the very sparrows and doves and dogs seemed to feel that there was something new happening to England, that the Regency was going soon to end.

"What Regency?" asked Savithri, with the air of a pupil to her teacher.

"Why, don't you see, ever since the death of King George the Fifth. Ever since the abdication of Edward the Eighth—that new King Hal who would have created his own Falstaff, and which a fat and foolish bank-clerk civilization drove into exile—this country, which chose her own church because her King preferred to choose his own wives—having become big, with an Empire and all that involves; and she became so afraid of the Stock Exchange, and of what Mrs. Petworth would say in Perth or Mr. Kennedy would say in Edmonton, Alberta—for remember it's all a question of wool shares or the London-Electric—this mercantile country drove away what might have been her best King, or at least the best loved, since Henry the Fifth. Do you remember those broken French sentences addressed to his Kate: '*Donc vostre est France, et vous estes miennes*'? And England put in his place a noble Bharatha who apologized every time he spoke, saying, 'You think I am your King, but I am only Brother to the King; I tremble, I hesitate, I wish my brother were here.' And he ruled the land with the devotion of a Bharatha, worshipping the sandal of his loved brother placed on the throne.

"Kingship is an impersonal principle; it is like life and death, it knows no limitations. It is history made carnate, just as this Thames is the principle of water made real. And when a king apologizes for being a king he is no king; he establishes a duality in himself, so he can have no authority. 'The King can do no wrong,' comes from the idea that the Principle can do no wrong, just as communists say, 'the Party can do no wrong.' Talking of the communists the other day in Cambridge, I forgot to say that communism must succeed; happily for us, to be followed by kingship. Look at the difference between Hitler and Stalin. Stalin, the man of iron, the mystery behind the Kremlin, the impersonal being; to whom torture, growth or death are essentials of an abstract arithmetic. As the Catholics looked for omens in the Bible, Stalin looked to impersonal history for guidance. Stalin lives and dies, in history as history, not outside history. Hitler, on the other hand, lived in his dramatic Nuremberg rallies, visible, concrete, his voice the most real of real; his plans personal, demoniac, his whims astrological, his history Hitlerian —Germanic, if you will—dying a hero, a Superman: Zarathustra. Duality must lead to heroism, to personality development, to glory. The dualist must become saintly, must cultivate humility, because he knows he could be big, great, heroic and personal, an emperor with a statue and a pediment."

Here, silently Savithri led me on to Chelsea Bridge, and looking down at the river, I continued:

"But the impersonal is neither humble nor proud—who could say whether Stalin was humble or proud? But one can say so easily and so eminently of another Cathar, another purist, Trotsky —that noble revolutionary of perfect integrity—that he was vain. He would gladly have jumped into the fire, down the *campo di crémats,* smiling and singing 'I am incorruptible, I am pure, I am the flame.' Stalin would have the Kremlin guarded with a thousand sentries, a few thousand spies, killing each one when he knew too much, first a Yagoda, then a Yezhov. For him history killed them, just as an Inca chief believed his god, not himself, wanted a sacrifice. Stalin bore no personal enmity to Trotsky, for this was real history. Even if Stalin the man was jealous of Trotsky 'the flame of pure Revolution' (and Stalin might have admitted this), Stalin, who is history, had to kill Trotsky the anti-history. The pure, the human, the vainglorious leader's personal magic was an unholy impediment to the movement of history. In the same way Marshal Toukhachesvsky had to die—the impersonal cannot allow that any man be a hero. Stalin was no hero: he was a king, a god."

"How well you hold forth," teased Savithri, tugging my arm. She wanted me to look at the barges as they floated down, or at the clear moon that played between the clouds and delighted Savithri as it might have a child.

"Moon, moon, Uncle Moon," I chanted a Kanarese nursery rhyme, *"Mama, Chanda-mama,"* and then we went back to history.

"The Superman is our enemy. Look what happened in India. Sri Aurobindo wanted, if you please, to improve on the Advaita of Sri Sankara—which was just like trying to improve on the numerical status of zero. Zero makes all numbers, so zero begins everything. All numbers are possible when they are in and of zero. Similarly all philosophies are possible in and around Vedanta. But you can no more improve on Vedanta than improve on zero. The zero, you see, the *sunya,* is impersonal; whereas one, two, three and so on are all dualistic. One always implies many. But zero implies *nothing.* I am not one, I am not two, I am neither one, nor two: *'Ahām nirvikalpi nirākara rūpih.'* I am the 'I.' So, to come back to Sri Aurobindo, he shut himself in Pondicherry and started building a new world. If you can build a house of three stories, you can build one of five, eight, ten or twelve stories—and go as high as the Empire State Building or any other structure, higher and yet higher. And just as aeroplanes at first went fifty miles an hour, then eighty, then a hundred, two hundred, three, and now go far beyond the speed of sound, similarly you can build any number of worlds, can make the mind, the psyche so athletic that you can build world after world, but you cannot go beyond your self, your impersonal principle. And just as the materialism of Stalin and not his impersonal sense of history, but his material interpretation of history made him end up like the Egyptians in being embalmed and made immortal as history, Sri Aurobindo tried to make this perishable, this chemical, this historical body, this body of eighteen aggregates, as Nagarjuna called it, *permanent*. Moralism and materialism must go together. The undying is a moral concept—for death is a biological phenomenon, an anti-life phenomenon, against the nature of the species. Not to die, to drink the elixir of life, is moral—it is to transcend the phenomenal as celibacy is the transcending of nature. The moral must end in mummification and the pyramid."

"I am breathless," said Savithri; "you take me too far and too quickly."

"Just a moment," I begged, "I'll soon finish. The Superman is the enemy of man—whether you call him Zarathustra, Sri Aurobindo, Stalin, or Father Zossima."

"That's a new gentleman in history," laughed Savithri.

"Oh," I remarked, a little irritated by her disturbance, "it's a saintly character in Dostoevsky: he smells—he decomposes—when he dies, and thus disturbs the odour of sanctity his miracles had brought to him. When Sri Aurobindo died his disciples must have felt the same: the deathless master, who wanted to consecrate his body, consign it to immortality, died like any other. His breath must have stopped, his eyes must have become fixed in their sockets, but being a Yogi he may have been sitting in a lotus posture, and that would have given him beauty and great dignity."

"And now?" begged Savithri. The damp of the river was rising. "I am a biological phenomenon, and food and warmth are necessary. Besides," she added, pulling her sari over her breast as though it was she who would suffer, "besides, I am terrified of your lungs." So I obeyed and we slowly strolled along the Embankment.

"You know," I said, "Julietta is probably at the Stag."

"Ah," she burst out laughing, "so you remember geography and biography, do you? Come, let us go."

"Oh, never, never!" I shouted. "You, Savithri, in a pub?"

"Pub or no pub, take me anywhere, my love," she said, so gently, so dedicatedly and with such a pressure of her fingers on my arm that the whole world rose up into my awareness renewed; "take me anywhere, and keep me warm." Was it I, the foolish schoolteacher, this miserable five foot eleven of Brahmin feebleness, this ungainly, myopic over-bent creature, to whom she had said those two tender, commonplace but perfect words? It was the first time she ever said them to me, and perhaps she had never said them to anyone else. History and my mind vanished somewhere, and I put my arms round that little creature—she hardly came to my shoulder—and led her along alleyways and parkways, past bus stop, bridge and mews—to a taxi.

"Let's go to Soho," I said, and as I held her in my arms, how true it seemed we were to each other, a lit space between us, a presence—God. *"Dieu est logé dans l'intervalle entre les hommes,"* I recited Henri Frank to her.

"Yes, it is God," she whispered, and we fell into the silence of busy streets. After a long moment, she whispered again, "Take me with you, my love."

"Will you come, Savithri?"

"Take me with you my love, anywhere."

"Come," I said; "this minute, now . . ."

"No, I cannot. I must go back. I must go back to Pratap."

I pressed her against me ever more tenderly. "Come, I'll take you," I persisted.

"To God," she said and fell into my lap. I touched her lips as though they were made with light, with honey, with the space between words of poetry, of song. London was no longer a city for me, it was myself: the world was no longer space for me, it was a moment of time, it was now.

At Barbirolli's I ordered a Chianti, and said, as though it had some meaning, "And now you must learn Italian."

> "Io ritornai dalla santissima onda
> rifatto si come piante novelle
> renovellate di novella fronda
> Puro e disposto a salire alle stelle,"

I recited. "You must learn Italian, for God has texture in that language. God is rich and Tuscan, and the Arno has a bridge made for marriage processions."

"So has Allahabad," she added, somewhat sadly. "And appropriately it is called the Hunter Bridge."

"May I go on with my Superman?" I begged.

"The biological sense of warmth having come back to me—and how nice this Chianti is"—she raised her glass—"I can now follow any intricacy of thought. I like to play chess with you in history."

"The Minister is the Superman," I started.

"And the King?"

"The Sage. The Vedantin, himself beyond duality, is in himself, through duality and non-duality."

"That's too difficult with Chianti. I wish, Rama—shall I call you that from now?—I wish you could sing me a song, and I would lie on your lap, far away where there is no land or road, no river or people, no father, fiancé, filigree, palace or elephants—perhaps just a mother—and on some mountain . . ."

"In Kailas . . ." I said.

"You would sit in meditation."

"And you?"

"Pray, that you might awaken, and not burn the world with that third eye—that eye which plays with history," she laughed.

"And parrots would sing, and the mango leaf be tender, be like copper with morning sunshine."

"And I would go round you three times, once, twice, thrice, and fall at your ash-coloured feet, begging that the Lord might absorb me unto himself . . . I am a woman," she added hesitantly, "a Hindu woman.

> "Mérétho Giridhara Gopāla . . .
> Mine the mountain-bearing Krishna,
> My lord none else than He."

History, Stalin and the Superman had vanished. Trying to solve the puzzle of history, like some hero in a fable, I had won a bride. A princess had come out of the *budumékaye*, but the moment I had entered the world of the seven sisters the Prime

Minister's son had led a revolution in the palace, had imprisoned the other six, and put us two under arrest. King Mark of Tintagel awaited his Iseult. I would have to give her to him, but having drunk the potion of Granval I would meet her by brooks and forests; I would be torn by dragons, but someday we would lie in the forest, the sword between us. Some day love would be strong enough to shatter the rock to fragments, and we should be free to wander where we would, build an empire if we cared.

"And we shall have a bambino," she said, and laughed as though she had caught my thought.

"Two," I added. "One is Ganesha and the other Kumara."

"And we shall throw colours on each other at Holi under the mountain moon. Our Indian Eros shoots with a flower, so why burn him?"

"Why not?" I asked. "The third eye opens when the attraction has ended. I hope you are not attracted by me?"

"Oh, no," she said. "If I were attracted by attraction, there would be no one like Hussain. He looks like someone from a Moghul painting, lovely with a long curve of eyebrow, a thin waist, very long gentle hands—and inside here," she pointed to her head, "all empty. His heart is filled with popped rice, curly and white and isolated. Muslims know how to please a woman," she finished, rather sadly.

"And a Hindu?"

"A Hindu woman knows how to worship her Krishna, her lord. When the moon shines over the Jumna and lights are lit in the households, and the cows are milked, then it is Janaki's son plays on the banks of the Yamuna in Brindavan. The cattle tear their ropes away, the deer leave the forests and come leaping to the groves, and with the peacocks seated on the branches of the asoka, Krishna dances on the red earth. What Gopi, my Lord, would not go to this festival of love? Women lose their shame and men lose their anger, for in Brindavan Krishna the Lord dances. We women are bidden to that feast. Come," she said, as though it was too much emotion to bear.

As we wandered down the streets, Piccadilly with its many-coloured lights, the Tube entrances and the bus queues gave us a sense of reality. Finally I took her to some women's hostel off Gower Street—where she always had rooms reserved for her and where she was looked after by her friend Gauri from Hyderabad, round as Savithri herself, but loquacious, big and protective. I was always so afraid of Savithri getting lost. It was not only a matter of bringing back her glasses or pen, but one always felt one had to bring Savithri back to Savithri.

"Ah, I am very real," she protested. "And tomorrow you will see how clever I am at taking buses. I'll jump into a 14 at Tottenham Court Road and be in Kensington at ten precise," she promised as I left her. I knew that at ten she would still be talking away to Gauri about some blouse pattern or somebody's marriage in Delhi. I knew I would have to telephone and ask her if she knew the time. "I promise you, you need not telephone. Tomorrow I will be punctual as Big Ben." With Savithri the profound and the banal lived so easily side by side.

I touched her hand at the door, to know I could touch her, and carried the feel of it home. It was like touching a thought, not just a thought of jug or water, or a pillow or a horse, but a thought as it leaps, as it were, in that instant where the thought lights itself, as the meteor its own tail. I felt it was of the substance of milk, of truth, of joy seen as myself.

Next day, when I was washed and dressed and had meditated and rested—I was in a muslin dhoti and kudtha—there was still no sign of Savithri at ten or at ten past ten. Not long after, she entered in a South Indian sari of a colour we in Mysore call "colour of the sky," with a peacock-gold choli, and a large kunkum on her forehead. She looked awed with herself, and full of reverence. As I went to touch her I refrained—something in her walk was strange.

"I have been praying."

"To whom?"

"To Shiva," she whispered. Then she opened her bag and took out a sandal-stick. Her movements were made of erudite silences. "Please light this for me," she begged.

By the time I had lit the sandal-stick in the bathroom and come out she had spread her articles of worship about her. There was a small silver censer, with the camphor. There was a silver kunkum-box. She had a few roses, too, fresh and dripping with water.

"Bring me some Ganges water in this."

I put some plain water in her silver plate. She put kunkum into the water.

"Will you permit me?" she asked. "Permit this, a woman's business?"

"Oh, no!" I protested.

"But it was you who told me—at home a man obeys a woman, that it's Hindu *dharma*."

"I obey," I said.

Then she knelt before me, removed one by one my slippers and my stockings and put them aside gently—distantly. She took flower and kunkum, and mumbling some song to herself, anointed my feet with them. Now she lit a camphor and placing the censer in the middle of the kunkum-water she waved the flame before my face, once, twice and three times in *ārathi*. After this she touched my feet with the water, and made aspersions of it over her head. Kneeling again and placing her head on my feet, she stayed there long, very long, with her breath breaking into gentle sobs. Then she gently held herself up. Taking the kunkum from the box I placed it on her brow, at the parting of her hair, and there where her bosom heaved, the abode of love. I could not touch her any more, nor could she touch me, and we stood for an isolate while. Then suddenly I remembered my mother's toe-rings.

"Stop where you are for a moment," I begged.

"I can go nowhere," she answered, "I belong to you."

Gently, as if lost in the aisles of a large temple, I walked about my room, opened my trunk and slowly removed the newspaper cover, then the coconut, the betel nuts, the kunkum that Little Mother had destined for her daughter-in-law. "I, too, had come prepared for this morning," I said.

"Really?" she smiled, for in me nothing astonished her.

"Yes, but it was a preparation made a very long time ago—a long, long time, Savithri. Not a life, not ten lives, but life upon life . . ."

"Yes," she said. "This Cambridge undergraduate, who smokes

like a chimney and dances to barbarian jazz, she says unto you, I've known my Lord for a thousand lives, from *Janam* to *Janam* have I known my Krishna . . ."

"And the Lord knows himself because Radha is, else he would have gone into penance and sat on Himalay. The Jumna flows and peacock feathers are on his diadem, because Radha's smiles enchant the creepers and the birds. Radha is the music of dusk, the red earth, the meaning of night. And this, my love, my spouse," I whispered, "is from my home. This is coconut, this is betel nut, this is kunkum and these the toe-rings my Mother wore, and left for my bridal." Slowly I anointed her with kunkum from my home, offered her the coconut and the betel nuts—there were eight, round and auspicious ones. "And now I shall place the toe-rings on your feet."

"Never," she said angrily. "You may be a Brahmin for all I know. But do you know of a Hindu woman who'd let her Lord touch her feet?"

"What a foolish woman you are!" I said, laughing. "And just by this you show why a Brahmin is necessary to educate you all, kings, queens, peasants and merchants. Don't you know that in marriage both the spouse and the espoused become anointed unto godhead? That explains why in Hindu marriages the married couple can only fall at the feet of the Guru and the Guru alone—for the Guru is higher than any god. Thus, I can now place them on your feet."

So much theology disturbed and convinced her, and she let me push the toe-rings on to her second toes, one on the left and the other on the right. The little bells on them whisked and sang: I was happy to have touched Savithri's feet.

The toe-rings were the precise size for her. Little Mother was right: for Madeleine they would have been too big.

Savithri sat on my bed, and the sun who had made himself such an auspicious presence fell upon her clear Rajput face as she sang Mira.

> *Sadhū matha jā . . . Sadhū matha jā . . .*
> O cenobite, O cenobite, do not go.
> Make a pyre for me, and when I burn,

Put the ashes on your brow,
O cenobite, do not go . . .

We were at Victoria by nine o'clock. We were so happy and so sad altogether, as though no one could take us away from each other and nobody marry us again. We were not married that morning, we discovered, we had ever been married—else how understand that silent, whole knowledge of one another?

"My love, my love, my love," she repeated, as though it were a mantra, "my love, and my Lord."

"And when will Italy be, and the bridge on the Arno, and the bambino?" I asked.

She put her head out of the window of the train, and for the first time I noticed the collyrium that tears had spread over her cheeks and face.

"I promise you one thing," she said.

"And what, Princess, may that be?" I replied, laughing.

"Parvathi says she will come to Shiva, when Shiva is so lost in meditation that were he to open his eyes the three worlds would burn."

"Meaning?" I was so frightened that my voice went awry and hollow.

"I'll come when you don't need me, when you can live without me, O cenobite." I knew the absolute meaning of it, the exactitude, for Savithri could never whisper, never utter but the whole of truth, even in a joke. But it was always like a sacred text, a cryptogram, with different meanings at different hierarchies of awareness.

"I understand and accept," I answered, with a clear and definite navel-deep voice. I can hear myself saying that to this day.

"Italy is," she continued, relentless, "when *Shivoham, Shivoham* is true."

"Meanwhile?"

"Meanwhile I go back to Allahabad and become Mrs. Pratap Singh."

"And run the household of the new Governor," I added, to hide my knowledgement and pain. For by now Pratap had become

Personal Secretary to His Excellency the Governor of some Indian Province. "Palace or Government House, they're equal and opposite," I laughed.

"And what will the learned historian do?" she asked.

"Finish the history of the Cathars, and well-wed and twice-wed, become Professor of Medieval European History at some Indian University. India is large and very diverse," I pleaded.

"I shall always be a good pupil," she joked. The train whistled, and took her away.

I took a taxi, went back to the Stag—or the Bunch of Grapes, for I do not remember exactly—and stood a drink to some bearded painter who talked abstract art and had a beautiful face. Holy is a pub when one is holy oneself.

DESTINY is, I think, nothing but a series of psychic knots that we tie with our own fears. The stars are but efforts made indeterminate. To act, then, is to be proscribed to yourself. Freedom is to leave nothing of yourself outside. The whole of event is the eye of life, and eternity the "I." Never can you escape eternity, for never can you escape that "I." Even when you say you can, it is the "I" saying it. Can the "I" say anything? No, it cannot, no more than eternity can be seen in time. But time seeing itself is eternity, just as wave seeing itself is water. Meanwhile the winds lift and the monsoon blows, and white flakes of wavelets curve and rise, dash and demonstrate, and from crest to crest they cavalcade processioning to the shore. Not wavelet or crest, however breathless with foam, is life: water is the meaning of life, or rather the meaning of life is *līla*, play.

Not achievement but self-recognition is pure significance. The extrovert confederates of action must stop, then we leap back to our own safety, our own desperation. The knots are thus undone, and calm as the Mediterranean is the effortless sea.

For the going inward is the true birth. He indeed the Brahmin who turns the crest inward; even if you are a pandit great as Jagannatha Bhatta or learned in logic as Kapilā-Chārya, the true life, the true Brahminhood commences when you recognize yourself in your eternity. At some moment you must stop life and look into it. Marriage or maternity, pain or the intimacy of success—love—may dip you into yourself. And as you go on dipping and rising in your inner Ganges murmuring,

> Kashi Kshetram Shāriram
> Tribhuvana jananim vayapim gyana Ganga
> My body, the holy site, is Benares,
> Spreading within me as knowledge, the Ganges,
> Mother of the three worlds,

you undo your knots. It is thus Benares is sacred, and Mother Ganga the absolver of sins. Sin is to think that in acting you are the actor: freedom, that you never could be the doer or enjoyer of an act. In the Ganges of such a life destiny dissolves—and you sail down to your own ocean . . .

As the ferryboat chugged and chattered through the English Channel, the blue of sky covering from crest of wave to shore, I thought there was the isolate, the holy realm of England, and on the other side, beyond the green water and waves, the wide sea of concussing humanity: France of the Revolution, France of *les Droits de l'Homme;* the romantic burst against slavery, the confusion of caste and confession; France, where "God sits at the crossroads" warming his hands at the fire.

> Je suis fier d'être admis à vos cérémonies
> O Dieu du peuple élu.

Sitting on the deck, with seagulls flying over me and the saline smell of air giving my breath depth, I slowly and deliberately opened my letters one by one. I had not been to Cook's in Berkeley Street, where I used to receive my mail, for at least six days, and had gathered it all just as I was coming to catch the train. Green Park was so beautiful on that morning as my taxi went up Piccadilly, she seemed lost in her own imaginative agreement with herself, creating space, streams, palaces; and almost as though there was always a palm-wide stretch of England that was mine—my own, named, railed off, consecrated. He who cannot possess a habitation and grove in England has never been admitted to her circle, her ceremony. The Druids have left something of their silent circumambience in the living trees of England.

The letters were four. I was so free within myself, I felt I could walk down to the sea and leap over the waters, or fly across the curve of sky, or be transparent and sheer as a musical note. Happen what might elsewhere in the world, what triple-heat be it to me! I was confirmed and true in my centripetal being.

The first letter I opened was Saroja's. It was sad and very clear-spoken. She wrote of the frustrations she had had to face, day after day: the refusal by the medical college because at the last moment the University discovered she was a Brahmin; some of the million little indelicacies which life with a mother who is not one's own can bring, to disturb, distort and ultimately obsess a feminine existence. "I lie in bed, morning and evening, thinking of the father that is not, and the beloved brother, so far away. I cannot fight life's battle alone, dear Brother, and I am not a saint like you are. I have decided to get married. The man I have chosen for myself is not one you would have chosen for me. Such a good man—so generous, sincere and competent—but he's just not made for me. It's as though if I talked Kanarese he would talk Nepali, or if he played golf I would play chess. But he earns well, he will be loyal and devoted, for he's been wanting to marry me, he says, since I was a girl of five. Brother, bless me."

So that was how I'd functioned after the promises I had made to Little Mother by the sea of Bombay.

The other two letters from India were just business papers needing my signature, concerning my father's insurance money, some property title-deeds I was transferring to Little Mother, the sale of father's car and the change of house ownership. I also received, being Sukumari's guardian, the quarterly report on her progress at school. Wish as I might to possess the whole sky that afternoon and feel the freedom of the sea in my nostrils, I was reminded that I was a brother, a son, and the single head of the household.

But Madeleine's—the last I opened, for the fear in me had tied such knots—was very sad and free. Something had happened to her too; the elephant always communicated everything to her, she said, when I was away. There was about her a sense of calm desperation: nothing could be as it was. Such a chunk of sorrow entered my throat: O Madeleine, Madeleine . . . "I cannot ask anything of you," she wrote, "for as you say, asking is at a level where receiving can never be. Who asks and who receives? *La vie est une mélopée du néant.* You are, and I know you are there. You are not, and yet I know you are. I lose you—I know I will lose you. And yet where can I go but to you?"

Boulogne seemed ugly, with chimneys, unwashed houses, bistros and ungainly rain. In the train I warmed myself with some good coffee, and night covered me up with movement and singleness. Nothing helps sorrow so much as a rhythm—a steady prayer-wheel turn, or the sound of an engine. Peace comes with the annihilation of acquired positions. You can slip into sleep and wake to a Paris that is dull, vacant, and elongated with the Eiffel Tower.

My hotel was in the Avenue Mac-Mahon, and its *meubles anciens,* its boudoirs, panelled cupboards and Louis XV chairs, all seemed to come from another world: if I touched them, I thought, I would touch awake death. I undressed, however, and washed; then, being sleepless, I dressed again and wandered down the Champs-Élysées, wishing the bookshops were open. But I was in the wrong area for books. Here the holiness of womanhood seemed torn asunder, when you saw bits of elegant flesh, in all its length, roundedness or thinness, and sorrow filled me—I wished I could have smiled back at that girl outside Fouquet's, have laid her beside me and told her sweet and enveloping things. My purity was intact, but my sorrow tore holes in it, and gathered me into demands.

Man in his flesh is unutterably weak and the sorrow of a Paris prostitute seems somehow to give meaning to one's own sorrow, to show one's intimacy to oneself, and perhaps even reveal the nature of poetry. For all women have the womb of poetry, and it is we that seek back our integrity of flesh and so lose our freedom. In the City of Shiva, Benares, concubines powdered the Ganges with yellow turmeric and gold, and dipped into the river and arose, their breasts firm for the taking, their bodies tender as the vine. They made you leap into yourself, with the feeling that knowledge is of oneself made, that the knowledge of knowledge is fathomless, unnameable, but with the smell of green camphor on the lip: "My moon, my jewel, my pride."

No, these were not the riches, I told myself, of this so different a civilization, where virginity was lost by too much knowledge, and womanhood had lost its rights by forsaking that involved slipping secrecy, that mendicant shyness, with which a woman hides her truth. You should know a woman and not understand her—for if you understand her, then you can never be a pilgrim to knowledge. Women, all women, speak poetry: whether they are talking of houses or aluminium vessels, of a sick child's diaper or a reception *chez* la Duchesse d'Uzès, it is all *naming*. It is because a woman, even a prostitute, can name things that we seek woman and lay her by our side; perhaps love her for a minute, an intuition, a totalness, a luminescence—when we die unto it, and so to ourselves.

I walked back to my hotel alone. My demands were ancient, primal, inevitable. Yet was I Brahmin. The prostitute of Paris could be a woman gone astray, a bourgeois, like the girl I once met in a café in Clichy. After I had given her drinks and made her feel at home, she told me she was an Italian, the honourable wife of an honourable man, who had gone away with a bad woman and left her stranded. So she had wandered faithfully from one respectable man to another, till age had overtaken her unawares. "I can keep a house, wash clothes, mend stockings. All I need is an apartment and an ironing machine. You will see how fresh your clothes will be. I am not extravagant—I will look after *les économies*. . . ." I gave her some money, took her address to show how very serious I was—and, of course, never went to see her. I needed the smell of camphor, and the yellow of turmeric on the limbs.

No, all this was vague and silly: wandering thoughts that come to a traveller on a cold night, in the Paris of the Champs-Élysées. I wished I had taken an hotel in the Latin Quarter, where I could have gone to the Deux Magots and spoken to Henri Baudouin, the art critic. He wrote his books or articles in the Rue Jacob, and came out exactly at midnight to go to the Deux Magots; there the lean waiter called Jean would say, "*Bonsoir, Monsieur Henri, quel temps tout de même, et on est en Février encore,*" and the small-moustached *patron* would come and say, "*Bonjour, Monsieur Henri; alors, la commande est prise?*" "*Eh, oui, c'est le chocolat, avec un peu d'eau chaude et une brioche,"* would retort Jean. Of course he knew! Pray, who would, if he did not?

Yes, I should have taken my room at the Hôtel Atlantide, Rue de Seine, and it would have been lovely. I suddenly realized it was beyond midnight and Savithri must have gone to bed; or maybe she had her eyes open, and her collyrium was still flowing down her cheeks—with the tears. "Let them stay," she would say, "for when I see them, I know I have wept for you." "I'll tell you something terrible," she said to me on the telephone, the morning I was leaving, "could I tell you, Rama, I've not washed my mouth since Sunday, I've refused to gargle or wash, as is my Hindu habit, after eating. I may smell bad, but till you left England I wanted your smell to perfume my mouth. I'm a Hindu woman after all, my Lord."

Yes, it was that very morning she had said this to me. And yet what distances of land and sea and of gathered time had built themselves between us. Even the look of a streetwalker in the Champs-Élysées was like the touch of Savithri's presence, her sound, her gait, her gesture, her womanhood. For man, woman is anonymous. Clean or messy, I offered all my thoughts to Savithri, cleaned my mouth and went to bed. I slept very well.

For the next few days I kept myself busy between the Rue de Richelieu and the Sorbonne, collating my notes, looking up a reference here or there—something about Pierre de Beauville, of Avignnonet (in the Fonds Doat at the Bibliothèque Nationale); or some obscure episode in the ghastly burning of the Cathedral of Béziers, for example the woman who begged that she be allowed to escape because she was with child, and the Abbé de Citeaux saying, "Like this, my dear, there will be one more heretic killed," and pushing her back down the steep pathway.

I also went to the Sorbonne to see my Professor, one of those very shy, very dirty, learned, inexorable, breathless, subtle, universal men. I was always happy with Professor Robin-Bessaignac, if only for the deep sense he possessed of the poetry of history. For him metaphysics was a game of civilization, and the philosophy of history the more wonderful the greater the paradoxes it cultivated. One of his ideas was that the Buddhist *Mani* (jewel), become Manichaeism, had travelled through Persia gathering strength, and had penetrated Bulgaria to make itself European and establish the sense of the dual-in-history. "It is a particularity unique to Europe," he averred, "for Europe is feminine. Nobody goes to fight for a Helen in India; rather does Rama send his devoted wife Sita to exile, to protect his impersonal Kingship from any shadow falling on it. For if the whispered concoction that a washerman had broadcast were true—that because Lady Sita had been prisoner of the demon Ravana there was a shadow on the purity of Ayodhya's Queen, an absurd, an illogical formula, and yet a believable one—then must Rama the Kshatriya send his Queen away into exile. The masculine, the impersonal principle is affirmed," went on Professor Robin-Bessaignac, "and here you must read Michelet's beautiful pages on the *Ramayana,* in his *Bible de l'humanité.* What power, what mastery of style, what childishness! But that was the nineteenth century—Victor Hugo, Lamartine and all that—all so feminine, you see, concepts created and spread by the romanticism of the Revolution, with gun and sword in the name of humanity. For, as a clever colleague of mine says: *'Tout humanisme est une mutilation.'* Childish, perfectly silly that humanity could be bettered by the sword or the lance, any more than Monsieur Benda's intellectual paternoster had brought about a revolution of 'clerks,' or Monsieur Sartre's jejune lubricity will make us more philosophical. Did Sully Prudhomme make us more poetic?

"Europe, I tell you, is a market place of ideas," he continued; "we sell our wares, not as in India or China where you can trace your artisan ancestor or your Brahmin Guru for two or three or five thousand years—we were still in the Iron Age then, and not long before that our men were drawing those bisons in the Dordogne caves—we sell our wares, I tell you, because they are newest, because they are of the *temps modernes,* the freshest, the most *original.* Europe is made, my friend, of Fath and Dior, of Leibnitz showing his backside and calling it a monad, and of Renan and Taine calling in the chemistry of the apple to prove their theory of history."

"You are, I fear, too harsh on Europe," I tried to intercede on behalf of *my* Europe, but he would not listen to anyone when he made one of those Gangetic escapades into history.

"You, coming from India, were the first person to bring to my notice," he went on, "the fact that it was not because there was a change in the building material, or because suddenly after a thousand years of Christianity we wanted to have more light in our cathedrals, that the Romanesque went up and shaped itself into the Gothic ogive—that it was Abelard, Peter Abelard, that castrate prince of thought, who like some Yagnyavalkya or Nagarjuna opened the windows of our smelly Oecumenical Councils, established scholastics (maybe—why not?—because of Heloise) and cried for light and for yet more light. You could perhaps go further, and prove anthropologically that the dead and buried illegitimate *rejeton* of Heloise and Abelard, becoming a taboo, a crypt in space, made Abelard long for light, for space, for generosity, a hope for truth.

"If you asked me what was the difference between Vézelay and Notre-Dame, I would say one is narrow, earthly, circumscribed, the other is pure gift, the outer adoring the inner, the hiding of the Holy Grail that light may transmigrate into space. 'Happy is the people,' as you so rightly quote the Nestorian Martyrs' Anthem, 'happy is the country where are laid up your bones as treasures. For when the light of the sun sets, the light from your bones will shine forth.' Yes, you are right there.

"But our humpty-dumpty historians would prove that on such and such a date some old municipal clerk made an entry in his accounts book: 'Sieur Morothor gave two pieces of gold to the Cathedral of Sens, because his father had gone to the Crusades and had not returned.' And so his grandson Guillaume de Morothor joined the Second Crusade, and brought back the new style from Constantinople or Syria (only you must add *'peut-être'* and probably end with a question mark, or your theory will have no academic distinction). Ha, ha, ha, ha . . .

"You are right too, *mon ami*, when you say that that ecclesiastic of Saint Denis, hero of the Crusades and enemy of Abelard, Saint Bernard, condemned the Gothic—its gargoyles, and so on—for he was a realist. Conceptualism in giving essence to objects destroyed the reality of the object, and thus gave lightness to stone and man, and built the apse of the Cathedral of Notre-Dame. The real heretic, as the Church knew well, and that is why they castrated him, was Abelard, *le Socrate de Gaul*, as he was called—not some ascetic Cathar of Montségur. But just as Catharism spread and has become an actual part of our culture—through the troubadours, through Saint Dominic and the purity of a Simon de Montfort—so did the Gothic idea spread and give light to our lives, so that when Constantinople fell we did not have to sit in smelly, bat-infested Romanesque dens, but in the Cluny there," said Professor Robin-Bessaignac, pointing in the direction of the Rue des Écoles.

"Modernism, you might say, started with Abelard, and perhaps Abelard was in no way ignorant of the Manichaeans. We know definitely that he had read a great deal of Nestorian dogmatics. But our poor scholars think that because we have the wireless and the aeroplane not only do we know more of history—but we actually make it. No, we no more make history than the swallow makes the spring. Students and merchants brought ideas from all over the world, and since in the past people were more earnest for wisdom—they did not have the newspaper or the dull speeches of Monsieur Vincent Auriol—they understood more quickly and deeply what they *heard* and not what they read. Did you not say the definition of a teacher in India is 'he from whom one hears'? That is real teaching, that is the real cultivation of intelligence, and not this rushing to the Librairie Gibert to get the latest book of Jaspers. We are poisoned by words, we French," he concluded, signed my scholarship papers and started to send me home with a feeling that I had brought light to him and not he to me.

"What do you want?" he added, as he turned towards the Salle Guizot. "You have the wisdom of ages—you're not barbarian like us." He had a class, and he begged me not to come. "I am going to speak on Henri IV, for soon it will be his fourth centenary and our University thinks every decent Frenchman should know something about him. Well, compare Henri IV, crude, brave, confused, to, say, Akbar. Good-bye, *mon ami*, work well, and lots of greetings to your wife. Good-bye . . . and remember me and say a prayer for me when the sun shines in Aix!" he laughed; turning round on himself, he was gone.

I felt bewildered with so much generosity. If generosity of thought built cathedrals, no wonder, I said to myself, Rodin was right when he said: We have no Shakespeare, we have no Dante, perhaps, but we the French have cathedrals.

> Nous te bâtissons de nos mains tremblantes
> nous entassons atome sur atome,
> mais qui peut t'achever
> toi, Cathédrale.
>
> Au crépuscule seulement nous te laissons seul:
> et tes contours futurs paraissent comme une aube.
> Dieu, tu es grand!

Oncle Charles came from Rouen to see me. *"Ah, je suis si content de voir mon neveu,"* he said, as though to himself. He always stayed in one of those large and well-established hotels near the Gare Montparnasse, and this time he had come in his car so that we could move about more easily. He looked so happy, so childishly happy to be in Paris with me, as though I being the younger would reveal something new and surprising to him. But what did I know of Paris?

"Au Périgourdine pour le dîner," he decided; *"Montmartre pour la nuit—et les Halles pour le petit matin,"* he concluded, and I agreed with him. He chuckled constantly and was enormously amused with everything.

"Coming to Paris with you is like the times we came to the city when we were doing military service; *nous venions chercher les filles. Ce n'est pas des choses à dire, Rama, mais la vie était belle avant l'autre guerre.* My father gave me a lot of money—my mother was dead—and those were the days when we were very sentimental all over France. An only child had the whole world at his feet—the good parents just gave it to you, saying, 'Take it, take it! You will grow old one day and there will be time then for other more serious things.' You are too young to know the France of Monsieur Poincaré, of Déroulède and of Maurice Barrès. Life was simple, gay and rich. There was always a war, but far away somewhere—not like the Russians sitting at our doors here. Yet a cough or a sneeze from the Kaiser brought all of us back to the barracks.

"We liked barracks life—it made us patriots and comrades. We spoke of our mothers or sisters feelingly, and in nine cases out of ten it was some comrade's sister we married: a fellow went to the country house of a friend, had champagne, and knew so much about the girl opposite that he felt nobody could make him a better wife—so he proposed to the father. The father always accepted, for no one ever proposed without knowing it would be a 'yes'—and usually we wore our uniforms; it made us look more distinguished. Then we went about from *boîte-de-nuit* to *boîte-de-nuit faisant la noce*—for marriage is a very serious affair—and then the wedding came: the smell of new clothes and of perfumes, hats, invitations, the ball, and the honeymoon in Corsica. That's how I married my first wife—Catherine's mother. She was a good woman. I was constantly unfaithful to her, and she knew it, she smelt it as it were, but never said a word. Sad and almost without a word, she died in her second childbirth. In those days people still died in childbirth: it was not as it is today—going to have a baby as though you're going to Biarritz . . . But one thing I will tell you, as I always tell Zoubie, the younger generation is more honest, more true, and stands less nonsense. We were the sacrificed."

He laughed to himself and suddenly looked silent and lost.

"This France," he started, gazing at the moving crowds of the Boulevard Saint-Michel and the Luxembourg, for we were at La Capoulade, "this France is a healthier, a much better France. *Mais qu'est-ce que vous voulez*, one does not become younger by wishing! At best one can cut one's hair or colour it as I do. I hate to look like a grandfather: I hate the thought that Catherine may soon have a child . . . By the way, tell me, Rama, what sort of a fellow is your friend, Georges Khuschbertieff?—*oh, là, là*, what a difficult name to pronounce! But you know, I'll tell you before you say anything: I like him—I trust him because he is your friend—otherwise I don't trust foreigners," he said, and laughed again. "After all, you're not a foreigner, you're Madeleine's husband; '*notre Rama*,' as Zoubie always says. I feel I have always known you—always."

"Georges," I replied, "is a considerate, clever, devoted and pious man. Outside a monastery you rarely see a man loving the Church or God as he does. Georges is something of a saint," I said, with no great conviction. But to make up for it I added, "He will make a wonderful husband for Catherine. To see them together is to believe in happiness."

"Oh, that's all your making. You and Madeleine are so happy, it reflects on all around. When we are with you even Zoubie and I are so loving and sensitive to one another. She's a romantic, you know, Zoubie is, and she did not care so much for Madeleine before—though she was fonder of her than she ever will be of Catherine. Zoubie has not a particularly loving nature, she's more like a man, fond of ideas, of poetry, of music—more like you in fact—well, she just loves and respects you. She says you are either an idiot or quite admirable to treat any woman like you do Madeleine."

"Oh, nonsense!" I protested. "Besides, Oncle Charles," I said, looking at my watch, "if you do want to go to Montmartre, and as we have no tickets, don't you think we'd better get in early?"

"Grand, *magnifique*. It's so nice to think you like going to such places: I thought you were an ascetic. You know we can never be true to each other—we men, I mean—when we are with women. Something in the woman is so complicated, so tortuous. I think a woman is just good enough to have babies and nothing else, don't you?"

He was not interested in what I said. As we came down from the first floor of La Périgourdine, he tried to adjust his tie and rubbed some dust off his black evening hat. Downstairs he looked at all the tables and at the bar, wondering if there was anyone he knew, or who would recognize him. It is nice to meet fellow countrymen in Paris—it makes you feel younger. Maître Lefort is twenty years younger in Paris than in the Rue Saint-Dominique at Rouen, and Charles Hublot the advocate's belly looks less ridiculous in Paris than in the Rouen Palais de Justice.

"The Seine is greener here than in Rouen," he concluded as we got into the car.

Later that evening, as we came down from Montmartre, he

winked at me several times and I did not know whether it was the songs—the ribald ones—or the cognac, or the champagne, or just the atmosphere of women half or completely naked, but like a tired horse turning to familiar alleys he went round and round the Place Clichy. He looked up one or two addresses and said *"Ah! la vie, la vie!"*—the houses had changed hands, he said. He seemed tired of living or of driving the car, so he deposited me near the Pont Sainte-Michel and I took a taxi and went to my hotel.

The next morning he rang me up at ten to say he had a bad headache. But we could still meet *chez* Weber at one o'clock upstairs. "We can have a light lunch—after the *escargots de Bourgogne* and the *coq au vin* of last night, anything would be good, even a simple salad. And at Weber the vegetables are excellent."

As I usually went to collect my mail from Cooks in the Place de la Madeleine it was very helpful to me to eat near by. There was always the Rue de Richelieu in the morning, dull and warm, with the dust making my breathing somewhat difficult. But it was joy to think of all the great men—Victor Hugo, Lamartine, Baudelaire, Sainte-Beuve, Guizot, Taine, Renan, Rainer Maria Rilke—all had worked at those tables. The past, as I said, must always speak to me for the present to become knowledgeable.

The lunch was a dull affair, except that Oncle Charles rang up home from the telephone booth and I talked to Catherine, whose voice was rich and singing, and full of joy. She would soon be married and life would have some meaning. "You are my godfather of happiness," she said, "and you have to be there when the right time comes."

"My sister is getting married too, Catherine, and things at home are not going too well. After all, I'm the eldest son. I may have to go home—fly—for a few months, perhaps."

"Would you take Mado, then?" she asked. "For unless one of you at least is there, I will not marry till you return."

"Well, we won't put off your happiness even by a day," I promised. "I only hope by then Madeleine will still be able to move about."

"Of course, that's true. I never thought of it. Fancy being a woman and not remembering things like that. You know, Rama, one grows to be such an egoist in love."

"To whom do you say that?" I replied, as though she would know what I meant.

"I hope my marriage will turn out to be even a little like yours. Tante Zoubie says I have not gone far enough geographically in my choice. I've gone eastward all right, towards Russia, but I haven't gone far enough. She would have liked me to have married an Indian."

"Who would become a *notaire* at Rouen?" I laughed, remembering the Cimetière Saint-Médard and the Caveau Roussellin.

"No, I suppose not. I shall be happy to be a *professeuse*, as our maid Jeannine says. Yes, *Madame la professeuse*, I shall be."

"*Au revoir, petite Catherine*," I shouted, as Oncle Charles was scratching his thighs distractedly and paying the telephone bill. He joked about something, and how he made the telephone girl laugh.

"*Au revoir, patron*," she smiled. "*Et à la prochaine*."

Oncle Charles left that very afternoon—he embraced me when he was saying good-bye—and though my work was over, I wandered about Paris doing nothing, feeling foetid and forlorn. It is at such moments one feels the loss of a father or mother, something steady whose affection is assured, as it were biologically, like the sap to the tree in spring. Walking about aimlessly on the quayside I dipped into this old book and that—some history of the Cistercian Order, or the *Qualité intellectuelle des Indiens corbeaux*, published by some Reverend Father in the hope of converting them to good Christianity. It was the time of Chateaubriand and *Atala*, and the conquest of empires—"*Les écrivains impériaux*," as Thibaudet called the whole group of Chateaubriand, Hugo, Lamartine and Balzac. The books on naked women revolted me; who on earth, I wondered, could look at such vulgarity, even if it were real? Was the body so important, so consistently in demand, that man forgot Peter Abelard who had preached Conceptualism just on the other side of the river? How often Heloise and Abelard must have wandered together over the bridges, looking like those young couples into the Seine, to see their still faces side by side.

Love is ever so young, so elevating—like the flying buttresses of Notre-Dame, pure, leaping, coloured by the stained-glass windows of the apse. I could love, yes, I could. I was in love, yes, I loved, I knew love now, I spoke Savithri. Round as the rose of Notre-Dame was love. Colourful and violet as the *rosace* was love. There had been days in Cambridge when I felt I could not say "You" to her, only "I"—but what a strange thing to feel, and how foolish it all seemed. Rilke was right: you discover the nature of love as you grow older. What does one know of love at nineteen? The fresh scent of eau-de-Cologne on the hair of Madeleine, or maybe the shy, as yet unformed curve of her breast. Can one really love lips or limbs?—no, that could never, never be complete, and a sin it would be. Love demands nothing, it *says* nothing, it knows nothing; it lives for itself, like the Seine does, for whom the buildings rising on either side and the parks and the Renault factory farther downstream make no difference. Who can take away love, who give it, who receive? I could not even say that I loved Savithri. It is just like saying "I love myself" or "Love loves Love." "Tautology! Absurdity!" I cried, and looked more courageously at the naked women in the books. Finally, as though it would make me reverence Savithri the more, I bought a copy—almost a Montmartre copy—of Baudelaire, with big breasts and twisted limbs about the waist: the dark sensuality which seemed so attractive to Oncle Charles.

For I was sure Oncle Charles's headache had other reasons than the champagne and the cognac. Trying to recapture his youth, he must have looked up old addresses. He probably wanted only to be recognized by some former *patronne,* some girl who would still hold herself bravely—and he must have received a shock. Age is true, very true; especially when one is past fifty. After that age you might choose other, rarer perversities—and Paris could supply you with anything you wanted—but this barracks mentality was the bane of Europe. No wonder Monsieur Sartre became famous during the phoney war—the Devil becomes interesting when you have no devil to face. In the Middle Ages, the devils went up high and on to the roofs and became monster gargoyles against whom the virtuous Saint Bernard fulminated so. And Baudelaire, he could never have become a Conceptualist. He would have been with the good Saint Bernard, for having gone as far as Italy on the Crusades, he might have bought himself his liberty, and died contrite, a devout monk. Verlaine fulfilled the secret destiny of Baudelaire, as Ronsard's inversely might have been by Villon.

> Frères humains qui après nous vivez
> N'ayez les cuers contre nous endurcis
> Car, se pitié de nous povres avez
> Dieu en aura plus tost de vous mercis.

The train to Aix swung with a rhythm that seemed to give intelligence and feeling back to me. Esclarmonde would of course be born, and how beautiful she would be, with Madeleine's gold in her hair, and perhaps my eyes; I already saw her big and tall, ready for the change into lovely womanhood and the pang of the first ache for love. She would combine the shyness, the natural intelligence and the deep gravity of, say, Saroja—yes, she could be like Saroja! Why not? And perhaps I would touch her, and feel in my fingers that I was touching something very real, something far and personal: the Truth.

We seek in our progeny the incarnation of lost hopes. We fornicate on our wives the gifts we would give our loves. We breed bastards, because we lack courage. We lie by each other, clasped in each other's arms, breathing each other, sucking each other, as though Truth was in the instant of that conjointhood. We speak tenderly to one another, year after year and life after life we may go on, but the ultimate may be on the bank of a river, a green patch of wide-awake grass, a Norman archway, bicycles, and the bridge of Clare. There is only one Woman, not for one life, but for all lives; indeed, the earth was created—with trees, rivers, seas, boats, buildings, books, towers, aeroplanes—that we might seek her, and remove the tortor act of Saint Bernard. Poor Charles Baudelaire.

At the station Madeleine looked so beautiful in her big womanhood, so sad, that I kissed her with warmth, certitude and devotion. She was the tabernacle of my habitation. I would build a paraclete yet.

THE REST OF THE STORY is easily told. In a classical novel it might have ended in palace and palanquin and howdah, or in the high Himalayas, but I am not telling a story here, I am writing the sad and uneven chronicle of a life, my life, with no art or decoration, but with the "objectivity," the discipline of the "historical sciences," for by taste and tradition I am only a historian.

Yet even in history Catherine de Braganza marries Charles the Second, and so Bombay comes into being; or Marie de Médicis marries Henri IV, becomes a widow, and, stupid and resolute, fights against Cardinal Richelieu, dies in exile and in Cologne; or India de Travalcen marries someone, is taken prisoner by the Turks and becomes first the wife of Noureddin and then of Suldan. Or look at the marriages and widowhood of Eleanor of Aquitaine, but for whom there would never have been the troubadours, nor, perhaps, modern love ("L'amour?" said the famous French historian Charles Seignobos. "Une invention du XIIᵉ siécle"), which means I might never have met Madeleine or married her—like a good Brahmin of the older generation I would have sat in meditation morning and evening and changed annually my sacred thread, for even in Aix-en-Provence, though you cannot make pipal-fire, you can always make an olive-wood fire, draw the swastika on the wall, decorate the sanctuary with mandalas, light the sacrificial hearth and walk round Agni. You can get Ganges water by air every week for aspersions and mouth ablutions. And going back home, I would have gone seven times round fire again, and safely married some Venkatalakshamma or Subbamma, who would have borne me my heir and my funeral fire-lighter; and at the end I would certainly have held the tail of some bull or cow that my son had bequeathed for my further journey, and thus my story would have ended. Madeleine might have married some doctor from Rouen or naval cadet from Toulon, would have borne him two children and possibly even a third—it did not depend as in India on the stars, but on arithmetical figures at the Bank and the Caisse d'Épargne, and certainly this Roger Marbillon or Claude Carillon would have accepted a safe and historical place at Saint-Médard—but Madeleine married me, and this is the sad part of the story. For life is sad, whether you look at it from the bottom or from a backward-turning look, or from any side, in fact; and we roll our lives with events, and cover ourselves with history and position, till the last moment arrives. For whether we drive a carriage and four—or are like that famous *lakpathi* of Lahore, who came to visit Guru Arjun with nine pinions to his carriage, because he owned nine lakhs in silver; and who was mischievously given by the saint the needle he was stitching with, and asked that this instrument of sewing be brought over to the next life—or whether we wear ribbons, medals, sacred threads, or tufts on the head, or like the Yorubas mark our faces with lines each time our heroism has shone by cutting off the head of another; or whether we get the Stalin Peace Prize and have a photograph printed in all the Soviet papers—for they all print the same things, simultaneously, say I the historian, and in every language of the eighteen or more Republics, including Tamlouk, Uzbec or High Azerbaijan—be it any of these, but when we have to catch the bull's tail we all catch it the same way, whether our heir has left one for us in Benares or not. Marriages are because death must be: the end implies a beginning. The fear of extinction is the source of copulation: we make love that the heir be born—the son who will light our funeral pyre. Even Stalin has a son, and he will do his job, don't you worry, when the bell tolls . . . For the bell will toll even for Stalin, say I the historian.

So marriages are and marriages must be. For otherwise what would happen to the wife and children (or mistress and children) of Pierre Boissier or Jean Carrefour, *greffier* at the Mairie of the VIIIth Arrondissement, in charge of improving the national demography? To him you go and say, "Monsieur, here are my

papers—here my *papiers de coutume* given by the Embassy, here
my birth certificate (however bogus, for in India we do not yet
have this municipal proof of having come to be), and here my
bride's; and here, may I permit myself to offer you most humbly,
most courteously, three thousand francs, for your great, for your
charming kindness; for without your assistance Madeleine Roussellin will never become my bride, my wife, the bearer of my
heir"— and so Pierre Boissier or Jean Carrefour prepares a book
of heirs, the three thousand francs having warmed his gullet and
his bed. But what would become of him if all became Cathars, and
talked of the corruption of the body, the sin of fornication and
the horror of birth? There would be no funeral fees to pay either,
if everyone went to another Pure, took *consolamentum* and
fasted in some Caverne d'Orolac till sweet death, dovelike, benign messenger of the happy world, came and took them away.
For in that other world you do not need any bulls or cows: it is
full of the loveliest firebirds, pigeons, nightingales . . . No, you
should not starve Pierre Boissier or Jean Carrefour.

Nor must any poor Brahmin of Benares be allowed to take his
own child to the Ganges banks—for there he would pay nothing,
not even the hire of four shoulders; being just a child, his own
arms would do. Because whatever happens, the Ganges is always pure, and he has no money to buy firewood from all those
clamouring scoundrels on the pathways to the ghats. "Oh, Panditji, I've received such fresh, dry consignments from the Tarai—
and I'll sell it to you for two annas a maund less than that ras-
cal, that robber, across the road." "Oh, Panditji, you know me,
and your father knows me," says the other, "and did I ever sell
you bad firewood? No, never. Whereas—ask the street-cleaner
Panhan—yesterday the body would not burn with that fellow's
firewood, so they came running to me. And look at this deodhar,
heavy as gold . . ." But he needs neither, for he can afford
neither; so he takes the child, wraps him in the white of his
shoulder-cloth, and muttering some mantra goes into the water,
and lets the little one float down. "Float down, float down, little
one, and we could not even give you a shawl and a pyre. Son,
we could do so little for your short existence . . ." It rains on
the Ganges, a gentle murmuring rain, creating little circles like

some flowers, and there is not even a tear in his eye, for who can weep? Why weep and for so many dead? What would happen to this poor Brahma Bhatta if our fathers did not die, and we did not have to take their ashes to Benares? Death and birth are meteorological happenings: we reap and we sow, we plant and we put manure; we smile when the sky shows rain, we suffer when it rains hail—and all ends in our stomach. There must be a way out, Lord; a way out of this circle of life: rain, sunshine, autumn, snow, heat, and the rain once more, in gentle flower-like ripples on the Ganges . . .

Little Mother wrote to me that Saroja had made up her mind to marry Subramanya Sastri. "He's a very nice man, Rama, and one can have nothing but esteem for his purity, gravity and deferential ways, but he's not made for Saroja—so lovely, so sensitive, so sad . . . What can a woman do, Rama? You alone could have done something, were you here. Now it's foolish to say anything—to do anything. Already the Other-People treat her as one of their own. What invitations, gold, chains, diamond earrings, evening drives . . . But it gives me such pain in the heart, I know not why. Saroja somehow thinks, and it is a natural thing to think for a girl of her age, a girl and a stepdaughter, that I am her enemy. Rama, I have tried my best to treat everyone alike— after all, are you my own son? Yet what confidence I have in you. Rama, I wish Saroja would marry someone like our Rama . . . Come soon, we need you. And blessing to you, and to my daughter-in-law."

What sweetness flowed from Little Mother to me. She, it seemed, was my inmost centre, the mirror of my life. With no word, or sometimes with just a word, she understood the curvatures of my silences and thoughts. She seemed to have borne me without bearing me, and somewhere, I knew, she suffered for me, felt the sorrow that filled my nights with such breathlessness.

Often I would lie with the moonlight entering my window— my bed was at the farther end of the room, almost by the window, and that of Madeleine against the wall, for light disturbed her—and feel the wakefulness of the olives, the figs ripening on their branches, the nests waiting for the blue swallows to come;

I could see the long, white highway to Marseille, on which yellow-lit cars must still be moving, and beyond Saint-Charles and the Vieux Port, you could almost go step by step to the top of Notre-Dame-de-la-Garde, turn round the cathedral and look at the stretch of the Mediterranean—*"la mer, la mer toujours recommencée."* After a lapse of long silence, I would look towards Madeleine. The secret of inner formulations and growth had widened her cheeks, given poise and sadness and a certain pride to her lonesome face. I could have knelt by her and taken her hand and pressed my lips against it, and whispered many irrelevant, untrue things.

Sometimes, on an afternoon, breaking her clear quiet she would say, "Rama, talk to me, say something to me," and she would look at herself as though she carried some holy sin, some loved impurity, and I would remove my heavy glasses and tell her, "Oh, Madeleine, I'm sure Little Mother would be so happy to see you," or "She will be so lovely, Esclarmonde, just like Saroja." She would say, stopping her knitting (for knitting, like nest-making, is an instinct, a biological function), "Rama, say something about yourself." And I, speechless, for one cannot tell an untruth before a child-bearing mother, she is holy, a symbol of some certitude: like breath, like a mountain, or the silence of a river. I would take her head in my arms, play in the gold of her hair and kiss her on the crown of her head. She was not mine, maternity had given her an otherness—she seemed secretive, whole, incommunicable. Words had no great meaning for her; she spoke, it seemed, always to herself, and alone. I wished I could have bought her a garland of thousand-petalled jasmines and tied them round her hair. And all the night I could smell them. But Madeleine, unlike other women, never seemed to have pregnancy-desires, no sudden intolerable wish for malagoa-mango or for red grapefruit—not even for good strong eau-de-Cologne. Her passion had turned elsewhere. She read and read a great deal, though doctors told her to be very careful; she continued her Pali lessons, and studied every book she could find on Buddhism. She went to the library and brought back Renan, Senart and Alexandra David Neel. She ordered books from England, from the Sacred Books of the East series. She loved the Psalms of the

Sisters so much she started translating them herself. One story particularly upset her for, coming home that evening from one of my long walks alone, I found her bathed in tears. I could not understand what had upset her—I always thought the chief, the single origin of all sorrow could only be me. I wondered what I had done. Then she slowly put her head on my lap, and told me the story of Vassita and the Lord.

"Go, mother, go, bereft mother, go and find a household where they have mustard seed, and bring it to me quickly. I shall awaken thy child, Vassita. So shall he be the Buddha-become. Only this, Vassita, must thou remember, ask whilst thou crossest the threshold, sister, 'Brother, has there been anyone dead in this house ever?' And if they say, 'None, none, sister Vassita,' then bring thou a seed of mustard to me . . ." Vassita, whose child had lain dead on her arm, said at each door, "Has there been anyone dead in this house ever?" And they all said, "Yes, yes, sister, yes, mother." Then did she come back to the Lord and say, "Lord, be this not the name and nature of Motherhood, that that which we bear must always perish, as we ourselves shall, of eighteen aggregates compounded?" And to her then, with the child, the dead child before her, did the Buddha, the Lord of Compassion, speak and say, "Thou speakest the Truth indeed, little mother, for all that has birth must perforce have death. The complex must dissolve, the becoming end in being." Then she said, did Vassita, "Lord take me unto thy fold."

"Lord," muttered Madeleine to me, "Lord, take me unto thy fold."

The sorrow of woman be indeed the barrenness of man.

Every evening Georges came as usual to the house. He became freer and more simple and jolly, making puns, laughing and making us laugh; and thanks to his new certitude and happiness —for he really was beginning to be happy—he brought a release from the sorrow of our household. Sometimes he carried his papers to correct; I gave him a little table in my room, and as I worked on my history he would correct his papers, and from time to time make humorous remarks.

"Look, look, what humanity is coming to!" he said one day.

"A sixth-form student, when I asked what duty was, said: 'Duty is what one does the soonest'—and forgets all about afterwards, I suppose! And another bright young lad puts it: 'If duty be anything universal, then it seems strange that in Tibet, they say, the same woman has five husbands, and in Islam four wives at least are *de règle* (for example, the Sultan of Morocco). August Comte was probably right in saying that duty is the law of the Great Being, who is nothing but growing humanity itself. Your duty is to the narrow world around you—the serf of the Middle Ages had his duty to his lord, the bourgeois to his city council, and in Soviet Russia duty is to the Party. Duty could be defined as that system of personal behaviour which gives man the maximum of happiness and incurs the least pain to others . . .' How well defined," continued Georges, "and to think this bright lad is a communist. *C'est triste.*" And he went on to his next paper.

Meanwhile three times a week, on Thursdays, Saturdays and Tuesdays, Madeleine continued her lessons with Lezo. There was such a change in Lezo since I had seen him in Pau. Either because he realized the sorrow of Madeleine, for I think he did care for her a great deal, or because Georges had given him a nice talking-to, or possibly just because he had learnt more of life—he had changed considerably!

Later I was to know that one day while I was still in London Georges did not come—he had one of his usual "malarial" fevers that shook him all over and made him take to his bed, an aftermath of some infection caught during his Resistance days—well, Georges had not come, and Madeleine was taking her Pali lessons. As usual, after the work was over Madeleine went into the kitchen to make some fresh, good coffee for Lezo—"Poor man, he's so lonely—think what it must be like to have so little money and live in a pension"—and when she came back, with a cup in each hand, and entered the drawing room, she saw no Lezo. Before she could know what had happened he had come from the back, having hidden behind the door like a schoolboy, put his hands over her eyes, and tried to bring his hands farther down, when Madeleine, with her Charentaise ire, dashed the cups against his face, and slapped him angrily and kicked him in the belly.

"I was a fury—a wild fury," she explained. "He fell on the floor, and begged me, begged me humbly and simply to forgive him. '*Je ne suis qu'une bête sauvage,*' he pleaded; 'my ancestors were probably Berbers. Forgive me.'

"What does one do to such a fool but forgive?" said Madeleine. "And after that, he's become obedient as a dog. Sometimes I tell him: 'Don't behave like a rat,' and he smiles. Now, Rama, there's no fear. You could go to Quimper-Corentin, and Lezo would behave like a faithful dog."

"What can you expect?" said Georges one day. "He lives with that seamstress."

"Does he?" I asked.

"Yes, I never told you. But one day he was boasting of his bucolic adventures, bucolic I tell you, like some schoolboy's: 'You are a born puritan! and as they said about somebody: You were born middle-aged and will never grow younger. You, Georges, are made for the inquisitor and hellfire,' he said. 'I, I am, I, of the warm country of Spain; not one of those *Bogoroditza, Bogoroditza*-crying Slavs, weeping over the sleeves of the Virgin. You should see me with Rose. She's a seamstress all right, but she's warm and round and wonderful to *mettre dessous*'—I quote his words. Humiliation," continued Georges, "is a terrible thing. When you've been a Professor of a University, and you have drawn a decent salary, and you are forced to emigrate for some brave speech you made, defending your language, your mother tongue, be it Catalan or Serb or Malgache, and you have to live on giving lessons, far away from father and mother, sisters and brothers—and far away from your church . . ." said Georges. He became silent for a moment, then continued ". . . what else could happen to you? But Madeleine is having a very good influence on him. Perhaps even Buddhism is good for one!" he declared, and laughed.

I enjoyed Georges's new, open laughter. No, Catherine was not going to be just an appendage, she was going to bring some strain of happiness into the sad soul of this Slav. Alyosha Karamazov would still be happy . . .

So Madeleine continued her Pali, and her own gravity increased, partly because of her maternity, I think—for a woman feels very serious and responsible and even ponderous when she bears a baby inside her—and partly because of her natural sadness. Our lives were now grown more intimate, it seemed, for we spoke less in words and gestures than with silences. She *knew* something, she knew not what herself. Maybe the elephant had told her, or the bull. He often did tell something, with a peculiar telluric vibration, some sort of telegraph code, which seemed to hum on all the time inside; and the moment you touched him, caressed him and left your hand long enough to feel itself, the cthonic message came through and you knew. The bull gave Madeleine these messages too, as to when my letter would come— for I wrote so seldom—or when her inspector-general would visit her Collège. And sometimes the bull gave her happy news: for example, that she would have a son—and that was about Pierre —or a daughter—and that was Esclarmonde. And it gave sadder news too, sometimes. It seemed more communicative and friendly, this Nandi, to Madeleine than it ever was to me. But, after all, Nandi was Parvathi's companion and only Shiva's vehicle.

I remember, as though it was told me but yesterday, how the landowner of the plot opposite, who wanted to get rich and so let the plot lie there till the *crise économique* was over—the Korean War had brought the price of land down—one day decided to make some money. He was a retired Italian fruit merchant, without children, and he thought it better to do things while he still could, so probably Monsieur Scarlatti said to himself, "Let me hew some of this stone, and maybe I could sell it to that Englishwoman who's just bought the Villa Malherbe opposite." Madeleine described how when he put his chisel against the stone and started hammering, two birds, two sparrows "with stripes as big and dark as your fingers on them" came twittering and clamouring to the window, and would not leave till she rose, and when she went to the window there he was, one could see, Monsieur Scarlatti, and he hammering away. "My heart bled," said Madeleine, "as though something terrible was going to happen." And without a moment's thought she ran down to Monsieur Scarlatti and said, "You know, we like this huge, bulging stone at our door. Couldn't you let it stay? Look what a kind shape it has." "Madame Ramaswamy," he replied, "I am a man without work; so I thought, why not make some money selling stone to that *Anglaise*? But I'll leave it, since you ask, *en bon voisinage*. I'm too old, in any case, to hew such stone. Look, look at what I have performed, after half an hour of sweat! And please look at these hands—*ah là là!*"

"Your husband is back home, Madame Ramaswamy?" he had asked after that.

"No, not yet," Madeleine said. "You know his father died?"

"Yes, that is what the postman told me. And such a nice husband you have. Always saying '*Bonjour, bonjour,*' to all the neighbours. You never hear him make a sound in the house."

"Ah," Madeleine protested, "you haven't heard him singing! When he sings in his bath, it's as though the roof would fly to his own country."

"He has every reason to be happy. My wife says, 'That couple there, they're nice people—and so learned. They have such interesting-looking visitors too.' And, being Italian, she likes to hear a foreign language. It makes her feel at home when you pass our windows speaking in English."

"Thank you, Monsieur Scarlatti."

"Thank you, thank you, Madame. And if ever Madame has something to dig or carry, a bulb to be planted, the jasmines to be trimmed, 'There he is,' you should say to yourself, 'there's neighbour Scarlatti.' By the way, Madame Ramaswamy, I was telling Madame Jeanne you should cut that jasmine a little now, that it may grow big by spring and make you a nice bower by summer. Anyway, it's good to have spoken to you, Madame, and say *bonjour* on our behalf to Monsieur your husband when you write to him . . ."

Madame Scarlatti, seeing them from the window, had shouted, "*Bonjour, Madame; comme il fait beau! Les hirondelles sont déjà là . . .*"

And Madeleine looked at the sky and found the world glorious. The bull was saved. He had only a knock on the head, and Madeleine said she had filled the hole with olive oil that night so that the stone would absorb it and grow black. When I came back from India the hole remained, but like some caste-mark on a basavanna bull it gave him a look auspicious. I must have gazed so many, many times at Nandi in Shiva's temples and he must have liked to look like his Indian counterpart. And why not, I ask you? Is there a difference between an Indian bull and a Provençal one? Our bull nodded his head like a basavanna bull and said no.

So, news of sorrow or joy came to Madeleine through the good bull's messages. She read them like a gipsy reads her cards. In some past life Madeleine must have been an Indian woman, no doubt. She believed it firmly, and so believed even more firmly in the truth, the everlastingness of our marriage. Otherwise she could not explain, she said, how a man from Hariharapura, Mysore State, could come and marry a girl from Rouen, Saint-Ouen—orphan of an engineer, niece of a *notaire et conseiller municipal de la ville de Sainte-Jeanne.* I myself, of course, believed in reincarnation—how could I not?—but it did not always explain everything. Some time, in England, I would be an elm.

I shall be very honest: there is no need to be otherwise. On those early spring days—it was just a year since my father had died—when the birds were coming back and I could almost feel the swell of the earth as it rose to greet the revival of sap and returning great sunshine, I thought once again of the large spaces of atmosphere before me and the journey back to India, and there was a sorrow that filled me and which had no name. The whole sky and jubilant earth were one dominion of sorrow, as though somewhere the earth was seen as a drama, enacted in an isolate, an unuplifted, a non-happening apocalypse. What you loved most, the closest, the nearest, that which spoke its breath to you, that which was the balsam, the burthen-bearer, the hearer, the carrier of your sorrow—was impotent, dead. I pressed Madeleine, on those nights, with the warmth and tenderness of a mother for her child—I would have suckled her if I could, and thought how well I now understood why pregnant wives at home are sent to their mothers. Just as bottled champagne remembers its own springtime, the grandmother-to-be goes through a new motherhood, and absolves the pain of her own child. She offers her big, round daughter cashew nuts and paprika, Bengal-gram paysam and hot tamarind chutney; she makes brinjal curry for the evening, with Maratha-buds, coriander and cardamom; and once in three days there is onion curry, smelling from the kitchen to the mat on the floor. The pregnant daughter eats almost where she lies, and when she is taken into the lying-in room, how wonderful to hear the child cry—a long, broken-glass sound, but happy, new, reviving—the limbs become renewed, fresh, whole; the stomach feels vacant, and the nostrils are filled with the smell of garlic and betel nut. I wished I were the one who would press Madeleine's legs—I wished I might have cared for her as I should.

And yet love and sorrow create such an intimacy in one—at a certain level they seem so alike—that if Madeleine had asked, as she often seemed to ask me, with her deep-set eyes, "Rama, tell me—tell me, that you love me?" I should have said to her, "Beloved, my beloved, don't you see, I am near you? That which is within you is mine; I am mine and you, Madeleine, are—a chunk of truth, a reality—as the sun, the moon and the space of the stars . . ." It would have been exact, and I would have betrayed no one.

For, lying by Madeleine, I was overtaken by no remorse, no inhibitions, no eating back my own sorrow on thinking of Savithri. Savithri was there, not in me but as me; not as someone far, unreal, relegated to a country in rounded space, but as light which seemed never to fade, never to know where to go—like that constant sound the texts say which in the silence of things, the first vibration, the primary sound, the *pranavam OM* propounds itself, and from which all that is World is created. Savithri, as it were, was the meaning of meaning, *Sabdharta;* and everything read from her, because she was—she is—she will be.

But the texture of our lives, that of Madeleine and me, was woven with such respect for one another, that a false gesture, a sentimental note would have laid us aghast. If I wanted to kill Madeleine I had only to breathe an untruth. We seemed to have entered some magic being, made of thin, pure glass—and breath. We breathed to each other as though in this respiratory movement we became united as never in flesh we could be. And in breathing with Madeleine I felt sometimes I was breathing to her the breath of another, a known presence; the tender, compassionate hand of Savithri was perhaps there, and I was the outsider. Gently, and carefully, when I tried to remove my hand and slip back to my own bed, there would be a tender pressure from Savithri, as if to say, "Love, my love, do not go."

One day, I sat and wrote to Catherine: I asked her to come. After all, it would be nice to have her there, I thought, and she would be so happy, I was sure, to see Georges again: in love, days and space pass so painfully. I did not tell Madeleine about the letter, and Catherine seemed to find some difficulty in convincing Oncle Charles about her coming.

"We are not Indians," explained Catherine, when she did arrive a week later, "and Oncle Charles said, 'You cannot be all the time living in your cousin's house. Remember you have spent almost a month there. And they're no millionaires, my daughter.' "

This attitude towards hospitality I understood, but I suffered a great deal from it. As Father said, "They who come will eat rice and dhal-water if we can give them nothing better; and sleep on a mat if I cannot spread them a bed in velveteen." Catherine was young, and she knew my real feelings; besides, it was natural that she should be back with Georges. They were going to get married in the spring soon after Easter, it was tentatively decided, so that Georges's old father could come from Munich.

Catherine said, "And you, Rama, will not be there, as my godfather and Georges's only brother."

"Oh, Catherine!" I replied. "You know that after Father's death this, my sister's marriage, is the first marriage in the household. Besides, I have a vague hope that I may still stop Saroja making a mistake . . ." But as I said it I knew that what was was, and Saroja would never go back on a mistake—it would be inauspicious.

Catherine drove all of us to Marignane Airfield, Madeleine sat behind, with her enormous, real and sad presence, and Georges sat beside her, smoking away. Lezo, good Lezo, looked even more like a schoolboy than ever before. "Ah," he exclaimed, "I wish I could go to North India, and learn Bhutanese. There's very little work done on that language, except for a small grammar by the Reverend Father Templeston, published in 1882." Georges seemed truly sad to leave me. Madeleine looked like someone drugged, or a pious woman telling her beads. Buddhism had given her a certain insight into her own nature, a protection from something smelly, foreign and other—it gave her a step, a conscious foothold in India.

Georges, and all that she meant to Georges, only affirmed my own presence in her. "She will be under my care," said Georges, at the aerodrome, while we were going through the formalities. *"N'est-ce pas, chérie?"* he asked Catherine, like an afterthought. "Madeleine will just be ready for the good news, as we shall also be thinking of good things," whispered Catherine, and kissed Madeleine on her bulging cheek. However holy maternity may be, "civilization" has made it ugly: peasant women do not grow so fat. Little Mother had washed the vessels and was spreading wet, washed saris on the bamboos when the pains started; and in an hour the child was there, Sridhara was there. That is how it should be.

"I'll be back soon, Madeleine," I said, making her a long *namaskar*. I had never learnt to kiss good-byes in public. Even to take Madeleine's arm in public seemed a desecration to me. But with Savithri it was different. Why, I wondered, why indeed, as I left the barrier and went towards the waiting plane.

Once the door of the plane had closed behind me, I knew it would never be the same again. Something colossal and complete had happened to Madeleine, to me—to the world. Beautiful was the Mediterranean, green as a silken sari, and the world was covered with noble filigree sunshine.

Man cannot and should not be petty. The magnitude of Marcus Aurelius and his natural wisdom was permanent and universal; the discourses of Socrates everlasting. I thought how Alexandria had taught man medicine, geography and Oriental wisdom, and Eretasthenes, Alexandria's famous librarian, had written an encyclopedic book on India. Ptolemy Philadelphus himself sent an Ambassador Dionysius to Pataliputra, for the fame of Indian wisdom had spread far and deep, and Dionysius was "to put truth to the test by personal inspection." Forget

Cleopatra and her rage and think now of Carthage, I said to my-self. Baal was cruel and so was Semiramis, but how sacred, how luminous the sky became, beyond the Persian Sea. Darkness had grown, a mountainous, sky-reaching darkness; a hot darkness between India and Greece. But the Mediterranean is an Indian sea, a Brahminic ocean; somewhere the Rhône must know the mysteries of Mother Ganga. India, my land, for me is ever, ever holy. "If only to be born in a land with so beautiful a shape, should make you feel proud and wise and ancient," Madeleine had once said to me. And I agreed with her.

> The continent north of the Ocean
> And south of the great snows
> Is the holy land of Bharatha.
> It's there they live, the descendants of Bharatha,
> Nine yojanas long,
> And where all acts have their fruits
> For those that seek liberation.

I FOUND MYSELF saying the Gayathri mantra as we landed at Santa Cruz. I had said it day after day, almost for twenty years; I must have said it a million million times: *"OM*, O face of Truth with a disk of gold, remove the mist (of ignorance) that I may see you face to face." But this time I said it quietly, tenderly, as one speaks to something near, breathful, intimate. It was India I wanted to see, the India of my inner being. Just as I could now see *antara-Kasi,* the "inner Benares," India for me became no land—not these trees, this sun, this earth; not those ladle hands and skeletal legs of bourgeois and coolie; not even the new pride of the uniformed Indian official, who seemed almost to say, "Don't you see, I am Indian now, and I represent the Republic of India"—but something other, more centred, widespread, humble; as though the gods had peopled the land with themselves, as the trees had forested the country, rivers flowed and named themselves, birds winged themselves higher and yet higher, touched the clouds and soared beyond, calling to each other over the valleys by their names. The India of Brahma and Prajapathi; of Varuna, Mithra and Aryaman; of Indra, of Krishna, Shiva and Parvathi; of Rama, Harishchandra and Yagnyavalkya; this India was a continuity I felt, not in time but in space; as a cloud that stands over a plain might say, "Here I am and I pour"—and goes on pouring. The waters of that rain have fertilized our minds and hearts, and being without time they are ever present. It is perhaps in this sense that India is outside history. A patch of triangular earth, surrounded by the three seas, somehow caught the spirit without time, and established it in such a way that you can see the disk of gold shine miles above the earth. And as the plane cuts through the night of the Persian Gulf, you feel a streak of gold, a benevolent cerulean green, that you want to touch, to taste, to rememorate unto yourself. You feel it belongs to you, be you Indian, Chinese, French, Alaskan or Honduran. It is something that history has reserved for herself, just as humans reserve an area of their own being, known but hardly used; it exists, as it were, for one's rarer moments: in the simplicity of dusk, in the breath after poetry; in the silence after death, in the space of love; in the affirmation of deep sleep; an area all known but atemporal, where you see yourself face to face.

That is the India I glimpsed—and lost again, as the customs officials called and the coolies clamoured. The hideousness of Bombay hurt me as only an impersonal falsehood can hurt. But I quickly took a bath at the Taj, and drove back to Santa Cruz, where once again on the green of the airfield I was back in the intuition of India. All the way to Hyderabad I looked down on hills, trains, plains and villages, on rivers and roads—Oh those endless white lines, between streaks of yellow, maroon and green! Soon I would be at Hyderabad.

I remembered how the city was founded. The King of Golconda, so the story goes, was ill and impoverished, despite his celebrated diamonds. His Prime Minister, a Brahmin, was deeply concerned over the finances of the State. There were enemies abroad—the Moghuls on the one side and the Marathas on the other. But one night, as the Prime Minister lay in anxiety, restless and concerned over the fate of his Sovereign, he saw a great spread of unearthly green and peacock-blue light, and he saw the bejewelled form of Devi, processioning in the sky. "Where mayst thou be going, and who mayst thou be, Goddess, Auspicious Lady?" he asked. "I am Lakshmi," she said, "and I go to the Himalayas, to Brahma my Lord." "Couldst thou not, Lady, stay a while, just a moment, just a trice, the time a man takes to open his eyes and shut, and I shall call my King, my Liege, that he behold thy beautiful form." "Earnest thou art, and thus the prayers be answered," she said. So our Brahmin, with turban, cummerbund and tight trousers, ran up the hill and stood before his King. The night was vast and very luminous. "There She stands, over across the river. She awaits us. Come, my Liege, my Sire." Hassan Qutub Shah went in, and soon came out dressed, sword and buckler in hand. He looked from his high, round citadel towards the luminous sky, and across the river. As the Brahmin bent low showing his Liege the way, the King cut him in two, that the Goddess of Wealth, Lakshmi, might reside in his Kingdom. So he rode down to the Goddess on his white charger, and said, "My Prime Minister, Great Lady of the Lotus, will never return. I have killed him that thou mightst remain here for ever and ever." And Hassan Qutub Shah built her a temple with four spires, as though it were a mosque, and she resides with us, the Goddess does, to this very day . . . She shines on our coins, does Lakshmi, as Bhagyavathi and that is why we call our city Bhagyanagar—city of beautiful wealth, for Hyderabad is but a vulgar homonym.

I hadn't told Little Mother the day and the hour of my arrival. I wanted so much to surprise them all—I thought it would remove from them the sense of distance, of unfamiliarity, of otherness. It was about the middle of the day when I arrived home. The gate was closed, and when I opened the door, Tiger, the dog, made a lot of angry manifestations against me, till he fell flat before me, helpless, and begged for forgiveness: "The Master of the House had come." I could see that the water-tap in the garden still needed mending, and as I went up the steps and peeped in, the house was one knit silence. I knocked, and Little Mother said, "Who's there?" from the sanctum. From her voice I knew she must be at prayer. "The son is come home," I shouted back. And you could have heard Little Mother's sobbing voice even from the door.

"You've come," she said, and being in sacred clothes she would not touch me. I brought the luggage in—the servants had gone for their siesta and noonday meal—sent the taxi away, and went for my bath towards the familiar, warm, soot-covered bathroom. I saw the ever-active wall lizards over the stores, and peeped out to see if the papaya and the moon-guavas were in fruit in the back yard. I took the huge ladle-jug of the bathroom and saying "Ganga, Jumna, Saraswathi," poured water over myself; then, dressed in a dhoti, I went into the sanctum. Little Mother was still praying—the gods were covered with flowers—the casket of the gods was the same that Grandfather Kittanna had brought from Benares, and it was thence that Little Mother had taken the family toe-rings to give to me. Drawing Father's wooden seat before the gods I sat with Little Mother, thinking of Grandfather Ramanna, who had given me the love of Shiva and Parvathi, the worship of incarnations; who had first whispered unto my ear the Gayathri "OM, O face of Truth . . ."

Sridhara woke up, and I told Little Mother to continue her prayers while I went to swing the cradle. I remembered a beautiful *berceuse,* the one with which I used to send Saroja to sleep, and I sang it to Sridhara.

> The Swan is swinging the cradle, baby,
> Saying "I am That," "That I am," quietly;
> She swings it beautifully, baby,
> Abandoning actions and hours.

Sridhara had no illusions as to who was at the cradle—it was not his mother. He cried and cried, till Little Mother came and talked to him and the noon silence fell on the house again. "It's Saturday today, and you've come just in time for the Story of Rama," said Little Mother, and seating me beside her, she told me once again the Story of Rama . . .

"Once upon a time there was a Brahmin, and he said to himself, 'Oh, I am growing old; I want to go to Benares.' And so he called his Son and said, 'Son, Brahma Bhatta, I am growing old, I've grey hairs on my skull, and my body is parched like a banana skin. I must now go to Benares. Keep Mother and the cattle in good state, and I leave you this House of Nine Pillars, and the wet-fields and my good name. Look after them then, Son, for a twelve-year.'

" 'As the Father ordains, so it shall be,' said Brahma Bhatta.

And the Father said, turning to his sacral-wife Bhagirathi, 'And so, Wife, I go and come.' And she wept and made many holy requests, and she said, 'Yes, but what about this Daughter?' The Father said, 'O give her to me, and I'll have her wed on the way.' And he took his female child on his shoulder—she was but seven years old—and with music in front and fife and elders he came to the village gate. The villagers wept and made ceremonies of departure, and the wife fell at the feet of her Lord and said, 'Well, he goes, my Lord, to Benares; to bring light on the manes.' And she asked, 'What may we do meanwhile?' And he said, 'Wife, my sweet-half, keep the house clear and auspicious; the Son will look after the home and cattle. And when Saturday comes—just tell the Story of Rama.' And the Son fell at the feet of Ishwara Bhatta, and said, 'Yes, indeed, Father.' They all stood at the village gate, where the road bent by the Chapel-of-Swinging-the-Swing-in-Spring, and the giant mango tree, and then he was gone, was Ishwara Bhatta, beyond the folds of the hills, across the river —to Benares.

"So while Ishwara Bhatta wended his way upwards to Benares, Brahma Bhatta said to his Mother Bhagirathi, 'When Saturday comes, Mother, we'll tell the Story of Rama,' and he looked round, and the house was very bright with vessels and decorations and with cattle that lowed in the cattleyard. Peasants came and peasants went, some measuring rice, others cutting shoots and vines; some drawing water, others sharpening the shares; while the maidservants plastered and washed the floors with cow dung, and Bhagirathi covered the threshold with red lead and drew sacred designs before the main portals: pentagons of lotuses and mandalas many and sumptuous.

"Now the traveller had gone away, and when he had gone but a few leagues he rested. He cooked, said his prayers, ate, gave food to his daughter; and when evening came he meditated, and spreading his bedding said, 'Lord!' and went to sleep. In the morning, shivering, he went to the river, bathed and took the bathed girl to the temple; and before the sun had said, 'I am there,' he had started again on his pilgrimage.

"Now league after league had gone, and day after day, and days turned into weeks, and weeks into many moon-months; and when he came to the banks of the Nerbuda, he saw an ascetic seated in firm meditation. And when he had approached the ascetic and offered many courtesies, Ishwara Bhatta said, 'Venerable Sir, you are lonely. I have a daughter to marry. Please become my son-in-law.' And the venerable ascetic said, 'What may I do with a wife? I have all my five austerities to perform.' To this Ishwara Bhatta made answer, 'No, Venerable Sir, it is meet for a man to marry and found family and hearth, that sacrifice be made. Aye, Sir, fulfil the duties of a householder.' And the venerable man said, 'So be it, so be it,' whereupon Ishwara Bhatta took tulasi leaf and water and gave the daughter unto the venerable ascetic. Then he said, 'I go. Be happy, Daughter and Son-in-law,' and running towards the setting sun, he went. He went and he went, he went very far.

"As he journeyed thus he came to a lonesome house, and knocked and said, 'A pilgrim, Lady, a pilgrim.' And the inmate said, 'Oh, what an auspicious thing! The Master of the House has gone on pilgrimage, and has not returned this twelve-year or more, and I weep.' And she wept. 'Oh, do not weep, Lady,' said Ishwara Bhatta, and when he was fed and had feasted and rested, he called her and told her the Story of Rama. Then he went, just where the sun sets—there he went, did Ishwara Bhatta.

"When he had gone on leagues and leagues, the day turned into the heat of summer, and the nights turned into the chill of winter, still he went, he went towards Benares.

"And when he had gone far, very far, he came on a lonely wheatfield; and a voice said, 'Traveller, stay.' And he stayed. The old man, the owner of the field, was blind; his son had gone on a journey, and no one had news of him for many round moons and suns. His wife and father waited for him to return, while the fields became full of weeds and parrots. Oh, the parrots, they were too many. 'The Old Father sits on the perch-hut and shouts at them,' explained the daughter-in-law, 'but they are so clever: they come from all sides, and he is blind. What can we do?' Then Ishwara Bhatta sat then and there, and told them the Story of Rama. 'Rama, Rama, give us wealth and give us splendour; give us the eight riches auspicious, give us an heir, give us a home and sanctuary, give us earth and gardens; those who go to towns distant, may they return, may the body be firm and innocent; give eyes to the blind, legs to the lame, give speech to the dumb. Rama, Sri Rama, give us Thy presence and Thy blessings. And daughter,' said Ishwara Bhatta to the daughter-in-law of the house, 'tell the Story of Rama every Saturday—it will bring you things auspicious.' And with many and varied polite compliments he went.

"When he had gone far, very far, he came upon an open sward in the forest. And as he stood there, They appeared amidst lightning and peals of thunder; there They stood, Rama and Sita, Lakshmana, Bharatha and Satrugnya, with the faithful Hanuman behind Them. There was such music, and so holy a look on the face of the Lord, and flowers, petals upon petals sailing and raining on the earth, that Ishwara Bhatta fell on his eight-parts and arose. And when he stood, the Lord of Compassion vouchsafed him many a blessing, and said, 'The pilgrimage is fulfilled; let the pilgrim return to hearth and home.' Then having contemplated the face of the Lord, Ishwara Bhatta turned southwards, with benediction in his heart. And the world looked holy and full of light and gentility.

"Now when he returned, he came to the blind man and his fields. 'O Brahmin, Sir, O Brahmin, Sir, how wondrous to behold your sacred looks again. No sooner had you told the Story of Rama and left than my father-in-law, blind these two-score years and more, had his eyes given back. "There, there, the parrots," he said; and now he flings his catapult at them, and they fly away. Sir, we kept guards at the north and the west that the returning pilgrim be brought home; and Guest, Sir,' said the daughter-in-law, 'please be seated.' And she laid leaf and silver vessels before him and gave him the meats of the pilgrim. Ishwara Bhatta said, 'Wonderful, wonderful.' And when he had risen and had washed his hands, he sat on the veranda and told them the Story of Rama again. He had hardly told them the Story when the son, staff and satchel in hand, bare and bedraggled, so long gone a-travelling, returned. And as he entered he said, 'Father, you can see!' and the Father said, 'Yes, I can see now, for I have heard the Story of Rama.' After telling them the Story again, Ishwara Bhatta wended his way homewards.

"Going and still going along Ishwara Bhatta came—after nights and jungles, rivers and many wild spaces awesome to behold that make the hairs stand on end—to the country where the lonely woman was. 'Now, sir, learned and auspicious Brahmin, hardly had you turned to the north, when my husband returned from the west.' And they both stood by Ishwara Bhatta, she serving many meats and sweet dishes, while the husband waved a peacock-feather fan to the pilgrim. Then when he had eaten and washed, and had partaken of the betel nuts and presents, as he started to go he told the Story of Rama to the united couple. 'Rama, Rama . . .'

"And then he went, and the rains came, and he saw the new creepers of the autumnal woods, and the birds with fresh-washed plumage, and the fields rich with rippling harvests. He came nearer home, and when he entered the hermitage of his son-in-law, bright was the home with grandchildren and daughter. And having partaken of all the offerings of the daughter and son-in-law, and blessing the children as he rose to go, the daughter said, 'Tell the cruel Mother, I am happy.' And he said, 'Nay, nay, not thus. After all, it was she who bore thee, Daughter, and one does not speak ill of that which bears one.' The daughter said, 'So be it, Father'; and he sat himself down by the pool of the hermitage and told them the Story of Rama. 'Rama, Rama . . .' Soon, very soon he would be home again, and would see with these God-seen eyes the son, Brahma Bhatta, and the wife and the cattle and the bright Nine-Pillared House.

"But here after the traveller had first gone forth, Monday, Tuesday and Wednesday came, and then Thursday, and auspicious Friday of the woman. And on Saturday Brahma Bhatta said, 'Mother, come; it's Saturday and we'll tell the Story of Rama.' But his Mother said, 'Son, wait; I will go and give rice-water to the cattle. Measure the grain for pounding.' And with this and that the morning went by, and the evening fell and the Story of Rama was not said. The next day was Sunday and then came Monday, then Tuesday, and Wednesday, and Thursday . . . And on Saturday the Mother said, 'Come, Son, it's Saturday, and we must tell the Story of Rama.' And the Son said, 'Mother, I've to go to the fields, and look after the sowing and the manuring, and the repairing of canals.' And the day went and evening came and the Son did not return. When he returned, he was so tired he had no breath, and his face was all covered with sweat and dust. Brahma Bhatta washed and came to the kitchen. 'Poor child, he's so tired,' said the Mother; and the Story of Rama was not told.

"The Saturday went, and Sunday and Monday, and when Saturday came again the Story was not said. Week after week went by, and there were always the cattle to look after, and the sowing to be done. The byre roof started falling and the pillars of the house, and cracks appeared on the walls; the fields became fallow, and yet the Story of Rama was not told. Sickness came and old age, and the house fell and the lands were all sold; the cattle had died of this pest and that, and stubble beard had appeared on the face of the Son—and the Father did not return.

"One day, however, passing travellers brought the news, that the pilgrim was returning to the village—and all with fife and turban, garland, scents and umbrella, they went to the village gate. There he was, the returning pilgrim, who had seen the face of Sri Rama. Bright was Ishwara Bhatta's face like a million suns effulgent, and he had grown neither old nor young, so steady his looks, so kind his eyes. And when Bhagirathi fell at his feet and rose, he said, 'Who mayst thou be, Lady?' for so dishevelled was she. And when Brahma Bhatta fell at his Father's feet prostrate and arose, the returning pilgrim said, 'Who mayst thou be, Sir?' for he had such a stubble beard, and many a tooth had gone, and he was so fibrous. 'Father, I'm your son,' said Brahma Bhatta. Ishwara Bhatta was so moved, he wept and said, 'Son, how has this become?' And they told him, 'This is so, Master of the House; thus it was and thus it is.' And the Master of the House said, 'I am so sorrowful. Have you told the Story of Rama on Saturday?' Then Brahma Bhatta said, 'No, Father, when I went to Mother, Mother was busy with the kitchen; and when she came to say, "Son, it's Saturday, the day of the Story of Rama," I had to go to the collection in the fields. What with this person and that, week after week went by.' And the Mother said, 'The Nine-Pillared House is falling, and the cattle all dead. Oh! Oh!' she cried. So Ishwara Bhatta said, 'Tchi, tchi, sinners,' and told them then and there the Story of Rama. 'Rama, Rama . . .'

"And no sooner did he start telling them the Story of Rama, than the house rose on its pillars and the granary stood on its four walls; the cattle began to low from the bright red byre, and there were servants and bailiffs, and the carriage house full of carriages and chariots. A chariot of four white horses stood at the village gate, and with music and procession the villagers brought back the returning pilgrim. The Son had grown so young to look at, and the Wife with marks auspicious of venerable splendour. Then she said, 'How is she, my Daughter?' And he said, 'Oh, they are happy together. I married her off to a worthy ascetic. And they have many children, and a shining house.' The music and four white horses now stood at the door. And thus with many mantras and aspersion ceremonies Ishwara Bhatta, who had seen the face of Sri Rama, returned to his noble Nine-Pillared House.

"Rama, Rama, Sri Rama, give us wealth and give us splendour; give us the eight riches auspicious, give us an heir, give us a home and sanctuary, give us earth and gardens; those who go to lands distant, may they return, may the body be firm and innocent; give eyes to the blind, give legs to the lame, give speech to the dumb. Rama, Sri Rama, Rama, give us Thy Holy Presence."

Little Mother had hardly finished the Story of Rama when a car stopped at the door. "That must be Saroja," whispered Little Mother. She went to open the door, and said, "Saroja, I'll offer you now the best jewel you could ever have at your wedding—the only diamond that's true." When Saroja came in and saw me, tears began to roll down her cheeks, for she thought of Father and not of me. "You've come to bless me, my brother," she said. "It's so large-minded of you to have come." And like a child, like a doe in fear, she curled herself and sat against my knee, protected. Little Mother distributed the sugar and Bengal gram and we sat for a silent meal.

Those were days of pain, of such a luminous, nameless pain, but there was no cruelty about it.

Men and women came in and out to decide whether this sari was good or the other, peacock-blue one; whether the opposite party should be given Dharmawaram saris or only cotton Kanchi ones—"And the gold sovereign will do the rest." The cooks, fat-bellied, belching, bejewelled, snuff in their palms and money tucked away at their waists, came in to ask if one needed a thousand laddus or a thousand two hundred, and whether the laddus would be for the second day or the third, and whether milk had been ordered for the khir, and saffron, almond and sugar. The house began to fill increasingly with neighbours making pappadams, the Brahmins came and showed their thirty-two teeth, knowing that now the Master of the House was come—"And from London too," they said between themselves—there would be nothing lacking in honour and silver. The bamboos for the pandal began to arrive too. "Where shall they lay the bamboos, Mother?" asked Baliga, the servant. "Not here, you silly fool. Is there place here to erect a pandal, say? You have them taken to Engineer Shivaram's house. There you'll find everybody you need."

Of course Uncle Seetharamu was there, and my cousins Seetha, Parvathi, Papa, Lakshimdevi, Nanja, Sita, Cauvery, Anandi, Ventalakshmi, Bhagirathi and Savithri. (This Savithri was a lean and haggard thing, having borne four children in succession, year after year; her belly was round and her breasts indeterminate.) Father's cousins Ramachandra and Lakshminarayna were there too, gay with laughter and spontaneous pun. Sanscrit, Kannada, Urdu, Telugu, English, were full of contradictory significances, so a word in this language meant something to me and something quite different to you, and so you laughed. Smutty stories, too, there must have been and many, as the coolies were laying the palm leaves on the roof, and the string was being tied to hold the pillar decorations. Green cloth with white lilies covered the bamboos, and someone, in patriotism, hung a huge, crude picture of Mahatma Gandhi, paper garland and all, to show our devotion to the Father of the Nation. Nobody had the courage to remove the picture, so we were protected from every form of criticism. Ladies now came in and out of the place, with more and more silk on them, and their gaiety and their fussations were always amusing. The men were good for nothing in these affairs. They would go straight to the kitchen and talk to Little Mother, whether she was praying or feeding, or shut up in the bathroom having a bath, or away in the garden and in some unmentionable place. Fortunately Little Mother had her "month" this time quite early, and as she could not go into the kitchen, she was available to anybody at any time, so the work went on the quicker.

People began to arrive by train. My cousins, Raghu or Chandu (he who worked in All-India Radio), went to receive them, and the visitors were put up with the Sanjivayya or Finance-Office Sankarnarayan Iyer. Now that the examinations were over, it was a splendid time for the young. Saroja's joy was golden, you would have thought, if you had not known her. But she used to sit by me, as I lay in my room, and I spoke to her of Madeleine and myself, or of Georges and his forthcoming marriage with Catherine, for I talked a great deal. She wished she had been a European woman; it would have given her so much freedom, so much brightness.

"What freedom?" I exclaimed. "The freedom of foolishness. In what way, Saroja, do you think Catherine or Madeleine is better off than you?"

"They know how to love."

"And you?"

"And we know how to bear children. We are just like a motor-car or a bank account. Or, better still, we are like a comfortable salary paid by a benign and eternal British Government. Our joy is a treasury receipt."

"Oh, it'll be all right, Saroja. Time and experience soften all things."

"But a mother-in-law is a mother-in-law, and she can bring tears to your eyes. And the sisters-in-law, and the brothers-in-law . . ."

"Times have changed, Saroja."

"Not in India yet—and certainly not among Brahmins. You had better wait till you see my in-laws. They already think I'm a cloth in their washbasket: they'll know when to beat me against the stone, to make me white as milk. We girls are thrown to other families as the most intimate, the most private of our clothes are thrown to the dhobi on Saturday morning. Like cotton, we women must have grown on trees . . ."

There was no answer to give. But just then a jeweller butted

255

in to take a wax impression of Saroja's palm or finger or wrist, and some flower-seller asked whether she wanted jasmines in the morning and roses in the evening, on the second day.

"Throw your flowers to the Musa River, and drink a warm cup of milk afterwards," Saroja spat back.

"Don't say inauspicious things," Little Mother admonished from the inner courtyard.

The lizards on the wall were merry. There were lots of flies, for there were piles of rice and jaggery, and bananas, *bésan* for laddus, and pappadams lay drying all over the terrace. Our maid Muthakka's child, a boy of five, sat noiselessly somewhere saying "Hoy-hoy" against the crows and the flies. And when the flies went back to their walls to feed on their discoveries, the lizards slowly, without effort, discovered them. Everybody must have their share of marriage.

The guavas became red on the trees—and never was the jasmine so profuse with flowers. "A marriage at home," quoted Little Mother, "maketh well-water rise to lip of earth."

"Between a funeral and a marriage," said Saroja, "there isn't much to choose. In both you have Brahmins with mantras—whether it is in Benares or here, it makes no difference—and in both you have the pandal first, and then music in front, flowers, bright shawls, fire. The only difference is that in one you are two, and in the other you are alone . . ." Saroja was thinking of Father. "There, you see," she went on, "they're bringing the mango leaves, and they'll erect the pandal now . . ." Little Mother listened to all this and said nothing. She looked towards me for help.

"God knows," she said, when Saroja had gone somewhere, fooling about in her restlessness, "God knows, Rama, he's such a nice person, is Subramanya. Not because he's my own cousin's son do I praise him; not because he's Audit Officer with the Government of India do I praise him; but he's so deferential, so clean. True, he's not refined like you people are, but then all sorts must live in the world to make it a world. If your grandfather had looked at me and my great learning, would he have chosen me for your father, even for a third marriage? A woman has to marry, whether she be blind, deaf, mute or tuberculous.

256

Her womb is her life, and we cannot choose our men. True, in your part of the globe, in Europe, they say they choose their own husbands, and I've seen all this in the cinemas. But we are not Europeans. We are of this country—we are Brahmins. Well, yours was a destiny, strange, magnificent; you were always a favourite of the gods. How like a prince, a god, you looked as you came and stood in the sanctuary, Rama. You are not of this, our earth."

"From where am I then, Little Mother?" I laughed.

"Well, I do not know. You are made differently. There you are, a boy bright as you, going to Europe, winning big University degrees—and you do not drink, eat meat or smoke; nor take on those vulgar ways Belur Krishnappa's third son or Modi Venktaramayyas's son-in-law had when they came back—with ugly pipes in their mouths and talking to their mothers as if they were charwomen of the household. And they would soon have to eat at tables and wear European clothes even at home. It must have been your mother, that holy lady," she said, pointing to my mother's big picture on the wall, "that made you thus." There was a desperate little silence, and then Little Mother continued: "This time, Rama, you won't abandon us, will you? Even the fire knows you are here—from the day you came it has purred and purred . . . A man at home is like a god in the temple." To Little Mother a proverb always meant an incontrovertible truth. "You will like Subramanya," she added after a moment. "He's just the man to keep under yoke a betwixt-left-and-right girl like Saroja . . ."

I lay on my bed in the afternoons, aloof and silent; waiting for something to happen—anything.

One afternoon—it must have been some two or three days before the marriage—the postman dropped a letter in through the window. It was from Madeleine, and this is what it said:

"Rama, *mon ami*,

"In the width of vast and varied spaces, I feel there is always a spot for happiness. Our unhappiness comes from the fact that we do not know what to choose, and when to choose. Life could be filled with pepper mills—the whole of the equator could be lined up with the silly wooden and iron contraptions, for triturating black pepper over salad or baked potatoes. But one can also stop before a jasmine or a rose (like the one you planted last autumn, which has such lovely red, claret-red roses) and see the pattern of existence—know that all is everywhere, joy is in the instant; that what Georges calls God must be somewhere hereabouts, in the garden, perhaps, between the rows of *petits pois*. When I leave the water-hose on near the cypress by the gate, the water gurgles and subsides, flowing evenly to the *petits pois*, the jasmine and the roses.

"This is just to tell you, sad though I am, that I think of you a great deal, and know you in many small things. For example, I miss you when the bathroom is not splashed about with water, or the pencil is not broken as it lies on your table. Women may grumble at their husband's lack of consideration for them and for things, but our grumbling itself is a form of our love. Look at the letters of Heloise to Abelard, full of grumbles to her Lord in bed and her Lord in Christ. A woman must grumble—it's her biological defence against the strength of man. I put flowers before your books, and light sandal-sticks at your table.

"I wonder how you feel back in India, back in your family. We who are brought up in Europe—and especially of late singing Gide's *'Famille, je vous hais'* like an incantation, like a mantra—for us any person other than a brother or sister is an outsider, an enemy. Sartre's *'L'ennemi, c'est l'autre,'* is the continuance of Gide's dictum. I know your father did not mean much to you, but your family does, I think. I've seen such joy on your face when I said, 'A letter from India—from Saroja.' Love them for me—for I can love no one but you.

"I often ask, lying in my bed, and reaching out in my feeling and touch to that which you have created in me, and which I continue to feed and to fulfil, what it is that brought us together, and what it is that will keep us together. Love is something so indefinable—though we glib Europeans use the word frequently —one cannot possibly love a body (made of the eighteen *dhatus*, elements, as the Buddhist Nagasena told the Greek King Menander). One cannot love that mirror with a thousand false facets called the mind, which hates what it once adored and fears what

258

it once cared for so dearly. Beyond the body and the mind there may be the heart, but what does it mean? Is it that pumping machine, which feeds our veins with red blood? Can haemoglobules be a proof of love? We are such ignorant people. Every word seems a neologism or a tautology. I often laugh at Georges, who seriously talks of the monads of Leibnitz or the intellectual love of Spinoza as if they were eternal entities, just as Lavoisier thought of oxygen and hydrogen as chemical fundamenta that were pre-ordained in some timeless textbook of God. But as Einstein came and upset the orderly, solid, Monsieur Hommais universe of our ancestors, India may still upset the Saint-Sulpice of Georges Khuschbertieff. Then hurrah to the Himalay!

"Do I love you, I often ask myself? When I say that I mean, do I love you as Buddha loved Ananda . . . ? 'Ananda, dear Ananda, do not grieve that the Enlightened One, the one who was like a father unto thee, has gone. Say, rather, "I shall be like a flame unto myself," and shine.' To help others *be*—to let the flower flower, let the water flow; to accept that birth and death are cycles, the affirmation of something: that is what love should be. Love should not be different from Truth. But could love be where Truth alone is? Could the sun be tender or the sound gentle? *We* make tenderness and gentleness. Shine on me, my Rama; as you see I am becoming a good wife.

"MADO."

"P.S. I should not worry you with medical things, but Dr. Contreaux says, though he is not anxious, really speaking—my reactions are very normal—that the X-ray is a little blurred in places. I am so fat, Rama, and pink as a Charentaise. I am glad you are not here to see me: I prefer it this way. I have to go again to see Dr. Contreaux next week, and I shall write to you. You know how wonderful it is to have happy Catherine about in the house. But I miss you much. Come back quickly, and do not go out in the sun too much: I don't like a dark husband. And cut your hair, so that it is not like a medical student's. After all, I am a teacher at the local Collège, and such things do count. *'C'est le mari de Madame la Professeuse . . .* etc.' And forgive the bourgeoise that I am. My affection to Saroja. M."

For some reason I was angry, but I could not name the name of my anger. Maybe it was for Saroja.

Two days later, I made my first visit to the bridegroom and his uncles, aunts and elder brothers—they had at last arrived—and my indignation became heavy, silent, firm. I came home and there was a cable waiting for me. This time it was from Savithri. It was from Cambridge, and said: "Be happy for me. In your joy is my freedom. And greetings to Saroja."

I understood it. I must make this marriage a success. I must strive and pray, work myself into a state of happiness and bring joy and rainshine to others. My happiness was forfeit, but who could prevent me from the gift of joy? Who could stop me making Little Mother and Saroja happy, and Saroja's ugly, big lieutenant-looking husband—for he did look so military: governments must make people responsible, heavy and authoritative. Yes, I would make Subramanya happy. I would make the whole world happy.

I was going to be happy myself. I found joy in the notes of the serpent-clarionet—for the music had already begun—and I went about the invitation-rounds, shouted at the Brahmins, saw to the cars being duly sent to the station for the right trains and the right people, had a look at the horse, a fine white Arab, that was to carry the bridegroom to the pandal. I sang hymns in the house and at seven—the bridegroom-procession was to be at nine in the evening—I took Saroja on a walk to the temple. "What a thing to be done on such an auspicious evening!" grumbled Little Mother. But I wanted to give myself and Saroja a last chance in space, for some understanding, some statement of the truth. I walked heavily but quickly; Saroja was like a filly dancing about the mother elephant. "Brother, what shall I do, what shall I do?"

"Do about what, Saroja?"

"Oh, Brother, I want to run away, run away, anywhere. I cannot marry him. I must not marry him. It is selfish of me to marry a man whom I detest, I look down upon. I think I only like his car, his position, and the feeling that he's like Father.

Since you came I have understood better, Brother. Brother, take me away."

It was no moment for cowardice. I, the head of the family, could not be a coward; I could not, should not, let down anyone in the world. That was my *dharma*. We came to the Hanuman temple. I bought a coconut and betel leaves, I bought camphor and sandal-sticks, and we gave them for worship. The God seemed so happy, so serene and confirmed in his devotion to his Lord, his Master, Sri Rama. We circumambulated, and sat on the rocks for a moment. Of course, Saroja will be happy. We make our own happiness. Yes, Madeleine, haemoglobules make for happiness. Madeleine, I shall make you happy. "Saroja, when you're married you'll come and live with us in Aix. And you'll look after my little daughter." Saroja did not answer. I had betrayed her. Then rising, she said, "After all, the dead body, when it goes to the crematorium, must feel happy. It does not say, 'No, I'll go back, I'll go back and be a ghost.' How could it? I have flowers and music, lots of people around me—and I shall be married . . ."

We came down the hill in silence. Already at the bridegroom's house the pipers had started their music. Cars were rushing up and down the street and the Hudson lights had come; they came one by one, as if they wished to be counted. I slipped round to see if everything was in order. The horse, bejewelled with necklace and gold anklets and yellow scarf at his neck, stood behind the gate, while the groom was chewing his betel away.

Inside the house there was the terrific noise of man believing he could create happiness. If Yogis could will and raise themselves above the earth, I thought, happiness, too, could be created. What was wrong with haemoglobules anyway? They were beautiful to look at—like rubies. And man, after all, takes a woman to his bed and makes her happy. I felt I could have taken a coconut—one of those hanging in the pandal tied to bamboo pillars—and sent it straight at Subramanya's head. Murder, too, could be joy: haemoglobules have no ethical standards. For them joy is when they can enter the heart at a certain rhythm. I wished I could have gone to the Stag and talked to Julietta about anything. Did the Thames still flow? Had Aristotle said anything interesting? Was there a British Museum with a cupola on its head like a chapel? I suddenly remembered a passage I had read in some huge history of Cambridge, which I had accidentally stumbled upon in the British Museum. A bridge across the Cam was permitted by the authorities because the monks from Clare Hall had wished to take their horses to graze across the river.

Your petitioners doe humblie begg of your most sacred Matie that they be suffered at their owne chardge to land a bridge over ye river and enjoy a passadge through ye. But-close into ye field, which would be of great benefitt to your petitioners, especially in times of infecion, having no passadge into ye fields but through ye chappel yard of your said Kings Colledge, ye gates whereof are shutt up in those tymes of danger . . .

Saroja went into her room on the top floor and shut herself in. I knocked and knocked, and she called out, "Brother, leave me to myself for a moment." Little Mother came and said, "Rama, it's already half past eight, and at nine the procession will pass before our house. I must tell you what to do. Come, son." So I washed quickly, and clothed myself in white Aurangabad satin, with chudidar pyjamas, and I combed my hair, remembering Madeleine's admonitions. All the women were gathered under the pandal, and there was a smell of camphor, Lucknow perfumes and betel leaves; the shine of white teeth, the splendour of black and gold saris, the magnificence of earrings, neckbands, nose-drops, diamond-marks on the forehead—an innocent joy which showed that man was made for natural happiness. The women grew silent as I came down the steps, carrying the silks and muslin in my silver plate, with attar-bottles, sandal-sticks, flowers. Then everybody burst out laughing. "What a hoary Head of the Family!" Aunt Sita said, "He looks more the bridegroom than the other." Little Mother gave her such a look.

The music started; on the other street gunfire went off; the vulgar brass band started playing some military march, with Indian-style music being piped amidst, in between and behind it all; and when the procession turned into our street and I stood under the pandal, awaiting to honour the bridegroom, I looked up at the house. It was absolutely silent: Saroja's window was closed. By now the Brahmins had raised their voices; they were powerful and magical, the hymns. It was such a long time since I had heard them. I threw flowers to the bridegroom, spread sweet-scented perfumes on his clothes, gave him honey and milk and melted butter to taste—I dipped my jasmine in silver cups and placed it on his outstretched tongue—sprinkled him with rose-water, and anointed him with kunkum and turmeric; I begged him in melodious Sanscrit, repeating syllable by syllable what the Brahmins enunciated, to marry my sister and found a hearth and household. He agreed nobly on his horse, and the women sang hymns of victory, of joy:

> Why, O Lord of Brindavan, O Krishna,
> O why, but in compassion, didst thou stray amidst us,
> O Son of Janaki?
> O thou beloved of Radha, beautiful.

The horse was splendid—it seemed to understand songs in Kannada and hymns in Sanscrit. The music moved on. I led the procession, and it went through the dust of the evening, the beauty of cooled summer streets, round the Hyder Ali Road, Mohammed Bagh, Residency Corner, Mahatma Gandhi Main-Road, and round about the clock tower to the Hanuman temple. I was not feeling well. I did not go up to the temple. "Uncle Seetharamu," I said, "my chest is giving me some trouble. Do you mind if I slip out? Don't frighten anyone. Say I have gone home to get something."

"Oh, one can't say that! It's too inauspicious a thing to do."

"Then, Uncle Seetharamu, I'll sit in one of the waiting cars."

I slipped into Dr. Sunadarm's car; the old ladies and pregnant women were all huddled together, but they made space for me, and I sat there breathing with some difficulty. Haemoglobules after all have their own laws. I was choking, but I was the head of the family. Little Mother looked so happy: Sukumari was bright and full of fun.

It seemed an epoch before the procession came down the hill. "Here is some coffee for you." Uncle Seetharamu slipped in to warm me up. "I cannot give you anything stronger in front of everyone." I did not want anything stronger; the coffee revived me. The procession started moving again. People, common people, gathered on both sides of the street to see us pass by. How many women looked enviously at us! They had also known this, and their daughters would soon know it too. The bridegroom in his grey-green achkan, a necklace of diamonds on his chest, looked a prince. He threw two-anna pieces and four-anna pieces that his elder brother gave him—for the bridegroom's father was dead—and the streets were smelling of flowers. When the procession turned into the bridegroom's street, Uncle Seetharamu said, "Now, you can give us the slip. But come back quickly." A car was waiting for me on a side street; I jumped into it and went home. The whole garden was brightly lit, and was still smelling of flowers and sandal-stick. The servants and Tiger were all at the door, trying to see the procession come back. I bade them stand where they were and went in. But Tiger followed me into the veranda. The house seemed so lonely, so full of its own laral presence. For the first time I wept for Father. And Tiger went back to see the procession.

After a wash and a rest I went up the staircase slowly. "Saroja," I whispered, "Saroja, open the door."

"Is it you, Ramanna?" she cried, as though something untoward had happened.

"Yes, open the door," I begged. She was in the same sari as when I had left her, but there was no flower in her hair. She seemed to have had a wash lately, for her side locks were combed down and wet.

"Brother, what has happened to you? You look so pale."

"Oh, nothing; it's just that I am a little unwell."

"Lie down, Brother," she said, so very tenderly, and made me stretch myself on her bed. She took a fan and began fanning me. It was cool as I lay.

"What is it you are reading?" I asked, seeing a book half-open by my face on the pillow.

"Oh, it's nothing. I was reading *The Magic Mountain*."

To this day I know not whether it was *The Magic Mountain* that did it, or just that the haemoglobules wanted their own release, their own joy, but I sat up and burst my blood all over Saroja's sari and on the floor. She seemed so courageous, wiping my mouth, rubbing the floor, and gently removing the sheets from the bed; then she went to Father's cupboard—for this was Father's room—and gave me some old brandy which nobody had ever touched. It revived me, and when Uncle Seetharamu came, he had only to look and he understood.

"Poor boy—should the sins of mothers pursue their sons?" he said, patting me on my forehead. "I said you had a mild attack of asthma, when they asked me. Take your time; I shall say the attack is subsiding. The music is growing strong, and it can go on for a long time. One can stretch a *rāga* for hours: I'll ask Anandi Bai to end her 'Bharath Milan' at four in the morning. Good girl you are, Saroja," said Uncle Seetharamu, as though he understood everything, "to have such a brother."

I must have gone to sleep for a very long time, because when I opened my eyes I saw Little Mother sitting beside me, fanning. "We have no luck, in the family, no luck. To have a beautiful and bright son like you, and to have this. Ah, after that last illness of yours, your father said, 'He looks just like his mother, Sanna, just like her! He's frail as an acacia flower.' "

Death did not disturb me. But Saroja burst into tears. She said, "Brother, promise to come and stay with me. I will look after you."

I said, "I promise." It made everybody happy. I think it made me happy, for my breathing became just a little kinder.

Uncle Seetharamu rushed in and said, "Don't you worry, Rama, I've arranged it all. I said your air travel had upset you, that you have diarrhoea. That settles everything. Don't you have diarrhoea tomorrow," he added crudely, "or I'll have to produce a commode before everybody, and that's a damn' difficult thing." He spoke in English and Little Mother did not understand, but the three of us laughed.

"What a grand person to have about in the marriage-house," I said, turning to Saroja.

"All time-servers," spat Saroja. "When they see you here it's all milk and sugar-candy, but once you're out of sight they look at the sky, although we're standing at eye-level. There's no love lost between all of us since Father went," she added, and we were silent.

Saroja brought bedding from the other room, and laid it on

the floor. "They say, Brother, I should pray the whole of to-night. What better prayer for me than to look after you? Let us sleep now, and wake me up when you want me. Please do. And to the world, Little Mother, you could say I am in fervent prayer."

Little Mother was very sad, but she left us. She could not understand this new, university-created world, as she called it. "To learn English is easy, it may take only a few years. But to say 'Rama-Sita Krishna-Govinda' it takes many lives. The young will never understand," she muttered to herself, and left us.

Once or twice when I opened my eyes, Saroja was still at her Thomas Mann. She had washed the blood off the cover, and with the light low she was reading, it seemed to me with interest. I was defeated. I slept.

In the broad morning, as I woke, the house was full of auspicious noises: the musicians were busy with *mangalācharanam*, and in the bathroom the women were singing away. Saroja was having the lustration of the nine waters, and her young body was being prepared for its ultimate destiny. The fire and incense for drying must have been lit, for I could smell the acridity of incense even upstairs.

"Baliga," I cried, and the servant came running.

"How is the Master?" he asked. "So often has the Lady of the House come up and gone down, to see if the Master was awake. There is hot water in the bathroom next door. By the time the Master washes his teeth, I will bring up some hot coffee."

"Tell Little Mother I am awake and better," I said, and went as far as the door to look over the inner courtyard. What blues and greens of saris, what diamonds, rubies and sapphires were seen to glint. And by the tulasi Saroja was drying her spread hair on the fire-basket while the women were busy anointing her with henna and turmeric. Mango leaves and silver pots were to be seen all over the veranda, and how happy the women looked as they sang:

> Laving in the waters of the young stream,
> Donning the garments sacramental,
> Slowly, ever so silently, adoring Shiva the Lord
> She became a spouse, sister.
> O, to happy Parvathi,

Raise the censer, wave the kunkum-water,
O holy happiness, for ever and ever,
Auspicious happiness be.
The white hibiscus, the garland of round jasmines—
To the parting of the Moon's hair, Sister,
Pour pearls.

Not my heart but somehow my belly seemed empty—and I wanted to throw out something again. Children were crying loudly outside and the crows from the coconut tree did not stop their festival. Soon the sun would be hot—and at eleven o'clock the wedding was to be.

When I went in to wash I could see how much blood I had thrown out the night before. I must have thrown much even on Saroja, for her sari stowed away behind the bathtub showed deep red blots. I washed myself with some difficulty, and when I went back to my bed Little Mother was there with the coffee.

"Oh, I am glad you're up, Rama," she began. "You cannot imagine how difficult your sister is. To make her sit or stand you needed a hundred women, to plead, sing paeans and cajole. At last we'd had enough. I sent word to Uncle Seetharamu, and he came and stood there, his tongue like a temple bell; since he's come, everything has been moving well. It makes all the difference whether there is a man in the house or not."

Before I had taken two sips of coffee Uncle Seetharamu was there, with his gold-lace upper-cloth round his waist and diamond rings on his fingers; he was clearly feeling very breathless.

"Wake up and come and help me, Brother," he said. "We all know you are a delicate, tiptoeing family, but this cajoling and begging—I can't do it any more. A woman is a woman and she must obey, even if she's got a first-class University degree. I've done my job with Saroja. Now, you take charge of her," he begged.

I rose with some difficulty. Baliga brought me my shaving things and hot water for the bath. The music sounded; cars, horse-carriages, bicycles and bicycle-rickshaws came in and went out of the gate; women raised their voices, singing:

And eight are her virtues in which she's clad, Gauri,
Much the prayer that's gone, that the Lord open the Eye.

I could hear someone come in and say, "It's already half past nine, and nobody is ready. The *mohurtham** is at eleven seventeen." I rose and looked at my watch: it was only about nine o'clock. So I washed quickly, had my case sent up, and put on my new dhoti with a red-gold border, my Lucknow waistcoat and the beautiful shawl Saroja had bought for me, with lacquer-coloured *rudrākshi* band against a line of fine gold. Sukumari, who came to fetch me, combed my hair and cried, "Ramanna, you look so pale—but what a prince!" And proudly she put her hand in mine, and gently led me down the stairway. She wanted the entire world to see and absorb me.

But the whole house seemed empty by now. The women had all gone to the Other-House. Carpets were deranged, flower garlands were withering in corners, children were asleep on half-open beds, and smells of incense and children's urine wandered everywhere, with no one to smell them. Even Tiger seemed to have decided to go and smell the marriage-pandal and have a look at the holy Brahmins. I sat in my room and Sukumari said, "You cannot imagine how full of auspicious looks Saroja is, Brother. She is beautiful. What a bride! And to think those wretched people will have her." And she left me suddenly, as though her words sat in the throat like a gunnybag needle. Soon I could hear her whispering away downstairs—perhaps it was to Saroja, for I knew Saroja must be doing her Gauri-puja at the sanctuary. I was afraid someone would come and say, "They are all waiting for you. Come, Rama, come." But no one came, and that tumultuous silence was too much for me to bear. I was the younger brother of the world. I tried to tell myself I was the head of the household, and I must be strong. But to give away Saroja—she seemed more like me at moments than my own self. I gathered myself into myself, forced my thoughts out of their orbits, and withdrew into my own inner recesses where peace is like a river in the night, ever present, with fishes, shoals and reefs if you would venture out under the round stars—awake. My illness gave my thoughts strength, no doubt, and I must have gone

* The exact astrological time fixed for tying the *tāli* round the neck of the bride. This is the most important part of the wedding ceremonies.

268

far deep into myself, for when I awoke I found Saroja's hand on my head.

"Do you suffer much, Brother?" she asked. "But your breathing seems more normal today." Her voice was light, clear and like a child's—simple. She stood a long while, playing with my hair. Then suddenly, as though she had taken courage in her heart, she came in front of me; her peacock-blue sari, her gold-serpent belt, her diamond earrings, the turmeric on her face, the mango-gold necklace, gave her a sense of the important, of the inevitable. Her eyes were long and dark, but she closed them, folded her hands, knelt and touched my feet and begged, "Brother, bless me. I need only your tender hands, your firm protective hands over my head."

She lay long thus, without a sob, a movement. Then she rose and stood in front of me. What deep maturity had come into her young face. She smiled as though I was the one she was sorry for. "Brother, I shall bring but a fair name to the household. Do not worry." Slowly and respectfully, she slipped out of the room to the sanctuary.

I had hardly time to wipe my tears when Uncle Seetharamu came shouting from the gate, "Rama, Rama," and I gladly went to the Other-House with him. Sukumari stayed back with her sister. What a magnificent assembly it was, with elders, lawyers, ministers, the wives of the Secretaries and Under-Secretaries of State, of Professors and Raja Sahibs—it was a grand marriage. I was given the seat opposite the fire, a little to one side. How I longed for the golden, the venerable visage of Grandfather Kittanna; but he was no more. Lord, how men live and how men "die" . . .

The Brahmins were happy to see me. No sooner had I come than their voices went higher and yet higher. Old friends of my father came to greet me, to ask news of me. I could see some of my father's old servants too, who bowed low to me, turban, uniform and all. The sacrificial fire burnt, and there—the ghee was poured, and then the milk, the curd, the honey. *"Agneya namohoam . . . Svaha . . ."* and how much sacredness it brought to my heart. I, too, had become sacred with this sacredness. Meanwhile Sukumari brought kunkum and put a large tilak

269

on my forehead. The bridegroom looked virtuous and obedient, and there was a lustre on his somewhat commonplace features. His family was happy—he was their best-educated brother and nephew, and it was, they were sure, a very good match. The hymns rose higher and more anguished. Uncle Seetharamu disappeared, and returned from the back door. "She's come," he said, whispering in my ear. The bridegroom stood up this time, and Saroja appeared from behind me, serious, auspicious and firm. The wedding curtain-cloth went up, and Uncle Seetharamu held Saroja by the back of her waist. Her black bangles broke under their own pressure. The kunkum-rice got warmed in our hands. Flowers were being distributed.

> A thousand eyes hath man (Purusha)
> A thousand eyes, a thousand feet.
> On every side pervading earth
> He fills a space ten fingers wide.
> This Purusha is all that hath been
> And all that is to be, the Law of Immortality.

> When the gods prepared
> The sacrifice
> With Purusha as their offspring
> Its oil was spring,
> The holy gift was autumn,
> Summer was the wood.

Saroja put the garland round Subramanya's neck. Little Mother was sobbing away in the corner. Sukumari joined her. Then the aunts and the great-aunts wiped their tears. I just closed my eyes. Saroja was gone from our household.

> I am He,
> Thou art She,
> I am the Harmony,
> Thou the Words.
> I am the Sky,
> Thou art Earth,
> Let us twain become One,
> Let us bring forth offspring.

270

Even I threw flowers and kunkum-rice on the bridal couple. Happiness is a question of determination. You can be happy when you want to be happy; it is a question of haemoglobules, maybe. Happiness is in a husband, a home, children. After all, where would Saroja go?

Seven times she went round the fire making *saptapadi,* seven times taking the names of my ancestors Ramakrishnayya, and Ranganna, Madhavaswamy, Somasundarayya, Sanjeevayya and Ramachandrayya, and seven times she changed her name, that she might belong where she was going. The fire burnt, the ghee went in, the flames purred and rose and asked for more. Perfume was distributed to the guests. The *tāli* was touched by the elders first, then by the great, and then by all of us. The bridegroom tied it round Saroja's neck. "She looked a Lakshmi," said Aunt Subbakka to me.

Music went up, and it was wonderful, for piper Siddayya had come from Madras especially for the marriage. The women sang songs of blessing while coconuts were being distributed. Little Mother gathered the gold jewels, saris, silver plates and silver vessels, as the name of each donor went up and came down according to Sanscrit rhythm. There was joy in the atmosphere. People in the pandal started smoking. They came, the visitors, one by one to press my hands, and tell me what a wonderful son I was of my father. "You will soon be our colleague," added some professors. "How long do you stay on in India?" others asked.

Cars came to take them away, guest after guest—turbans, sashes, upper-cloths, wrist-watches, canes, pumps, coloured handkerchiefs, garlands—they all disappeared. The bicycle-rickshaws clamoured with their unholy bells and somewhere a horse neighed. Tiger stood at the door, as if he were counting the guests, and would go and tell Father in the other world. Meanwhile the musicians had to be paid, and the taxis were asking higher rates for over-work. The milk for the khir had been spoilt. The procession this evening had to change its route—nobody had realized you should never go south first. "Some ignorant females must have advised such an inauspicious thing," Uncle Seetharamu concluded. I was exhausted. Slowly I rose up and went in. There was a divan

meant for the bridegroom to recline on in between the ceremonies: Uncle Seetharamu took me to it and asked me to lie
down. Sukumari stood by me, fanning me with a large, decorated
palm-leaf fan. It was cool. I could smell sandal paste all over
the house. Jasmine garlands were hanging just behind me. "It's
too strong a smell for me. Could you put them away somewhere,
please?" I asked. The flowers were removed, and from the kitchen
came the noise of cooking laddus. They smelt delightful.

I must have gone to sleep, for I woke up, perspiring. Sukumari was not there, but Baliga stood fanning me. Uncle Seetharamu came in, followed by the Brahmins. The coconut and
betel leaf and dhoti and gold coin were ready. I placed one
silver plate before each and touched their feet. "May the householder, the giver of kine and gold, be blessed," they muttered,
with wrong Sanscrit accents. How very painful Sanscrit wrongly
pronounced can be, I was trying to say to myself, when I rolled
over and fell on a Brahmin, kicking the coconut and the betel nut
right across the room. They lifted me up, and Uncle Seetharamu
said, "Oh, it's nothing. Air journeys can be so tiring." The
Brahmins agreed with Uncle Seetharamu.

The bridegroom came and sat by me. He was full of respect
and affection for his new brother-in-law. He felt proud of Saroja,
and showed how honoured he felt to be a member of our family.
"I have a boss who knows France very well," he explained. "He
knows Monte Carlo, Paris and the South of France. You will
meet him when you come to Delhi." His brother, younger than
he, dropped in to say he had taken French for his degree. He
was reading *Lettres de mon moulin* and Molière's *Malade imaginaire*. He was going to be a diplomat, he had decided. Cousin
Vishweshwara's son Lakshmana came to say how delighted he was
to see me. He had just returned from Cornell. He had a degree
in radio engineering. The world was large and prosperous. There
was no reason why I should be suffocating in this room.

"You idiots," shouted Uncle Seetharamu, "here is a man who's
tired and wants air, and you are surrounding him as though he
were on the point of digging out sacred gold." Everybody left.
Only the bridegroom remained, with his crown, perspiration, and
gold on his fingers. As I closed my eyes he went, and returned

with Saroja. Saroja sat at my feet, pressing my legs. I went back to sleep.

It is no use giving you details of the procession, the laddu and pheni dinner at night, and the way in which the other party came to take Saroja away. Long after midnight, as Saroja sat near my bed, saying nothing but fanning me, the bridal car came and the ladies invaded the house. "The bride, the bride!" they demanded, and Saroja said, "It is time for me to go, Brother." She laid the fan beside me and started to go. "I'll come back soon. Get well quickly, Brother. Meanwhile I will look after the household," she said, smiling, and went down the steps. So much gravity, decision and responsibility had come into her that already she looked a woman.

Ladies sang songs of welcome as she came down, and laughed and asked her to name her husband, as she crossed the threshold of the house. Saroja did not need much persuading. "Mr. Subramanya Sastri," she said, as if it was the name of her Professor.

All the night Little Mother sat up fanning me. I spat blood once again, but it was not too serious. I pressed her to go to the Other-House and see the dancing and hear the music. "Baliga will do," I said. She went. Late in the night I could hear them come back.

"Low untouchables, they be," said Little Mother. "To think we gave such a flower of our courtyard to them."

"Ah," rejoined Sukumari, "till the *tāli* is tied all is sweetness; afterwards it's the festival of the bitter neem leaf."

In the morning, as I sat drinking my coffee, who should drop in to see me but Uncle Seetharamu. "Oh, Rama, to have given such a slip of a girl away to these cadaver-eating pariahs. They will sell their tongue for position, and the rest I cannot say before women. The whole night," he whispered into my ears, "the sisters and aunts went round and round the bridal room singing ribald songs, and in the morning hardly was the cock crowing before they entered the bridal chamber, those widow-born did. Are we Muslim, I ask you, Muslim? What? Saroja sat in a corner and wept. Ah, the butchers—did I give them a talking-to! 'We

273

don't sell meat in our houses. Sir, we marry our girls,' I told them."

Little Mother heard half of what was said: "Shiva, Shiva," she cried, and went into the kitchen to bring us more coffee.

Two nights later Saroja and Subramanya came to take leave of us. Little Mother had prepared all there was to give her—dolls, sheets, vessels, gods, saris, photographs of Father and myself—and Saroja seemed full of smiles. She left home looking bright and fulfilled, as though she liked marriage. "Come and spend at least a week with us in Delhi," she begged, and looked up to her husband for support.

"The climate of Delhi is wonderful—it's a tonic," said Subramanya. Saroja was really married.

"She looks happy. After all, Rama, what more happiness does a woman need than a home, and a husband? The temple needs a bell," Little Mother quoted some proverb, "and the girl a husband, to make the four walls shine."

The same afternoon Dr. Pai came to examine me. He was not too alarming, but there was no question of an air journey for the moment—nor the cold air of Europe. No, not even the South of France, he persisted: he knew that part of the world very well. "Later in the summer, perhaps," he said.

"But I have a wife, and she's going to have a baby," I argued.

"Your wife would no doubt prefer you alive here than dead there," he laughed.

Little Mother was shocked at his crude remark. She beat her knuckles on her temples: what an inauspicious thing to say!

"Today medical science is so well advanced that there is no danger for a patient like you; I don't think you're such a serious case. The X-rays will tell me, once I have them. For the moment take rest. And don't you let people come and worry him," he said, turning to Little Mother. "In Europe, people are so understanding about patients and diseases. Here we treat disease as though it were a terminal examination—whether you pass or fail it makes no difference. Look after yourself, old boy. After all, now that your father is no more you are the pillar of the family. You must get better."

I GOT BETTER. Dr. Pai ordered three months in Bangalore, so Little Mother, Sukumari, Sridhara and I, with the cook and Baliga, all went up to Bangalore. I hired a house in upper Basavangudi and with cauldron and drying-bamboo we established ourselves. Living in the intimacy of my own family—where every gesture, idiosyncrasy or mole-mark was traced back to some cousin, aunt or grandfather; where there were such subtle understandings of half-said things, of acts that were respected or condemned according to the degree of stature, age or sex of one another—gave a feeling of a complex oneness, from which one could never get out save by death, and even after that one would get into it again in the next life, and so on till the wheel of existence was ended. "Father scratched his leg just there, at the arch of his foot, with the second finger, just like you," Sukumari remarked one evening. "Look, Rama, look!" Little Mother said; "Sridhara has a mole under his right arm, just where you have . . ." One night, when Little Mother was telling me a story, I went to sleep saying, "Yes, yes. Hūm-hūm," and everybody laughed, for I was snoring. "Just like his grandmother," said Aunt Sata, who had joined us.

Later, when the rains had started, we visited our lands in the Malnad with Aunt Sata and walked by the Himavathy again. Little Mother had not been to Hariharapura for six or seven years. The peasants were trying to play false with us, complained Aunt Sata; "I am only a helpless widow, and I cannot look after my own twenty-five acres of wet-land. For what with the hay and the false measures, the pickaxe broken and the manure washed away, Lord, it is beyond a woman's ken to control these black-blanket peasants, especially in these evil mountain lands.

I tell you, forget your seventy-six acres of wet-lands, spread over Kanchenahalli and Siddapura, Hobli and Himaganga, Kanthapura and those dry-lands in Seethapura Taluka; forget your coffee and cardamoms. And as for your bright Sundarayya, he knows when to write charming letters to you saying, 'The Himavathy has run into the land at Sivganga corner, divine sir, and she's washed away canal-bund and all; during these floods she ate away fifteen man-lengths of land.' Or, 'The manure this year was bad, and Whitey, Pushpa, Mādhuri, Kāla, Nandi and Sankri have died of the new cattle-dysentery,' while actually he's sent them to Balapura Saturday fair for sale. Remember what he did to your father during the war? He sold your cattle to those Europeans—and for butchery, you understand. He who'll sell cows for butchery will sell you one day," continued Aunt Sata. "Ah, you do not know the people hereabouts, and you do not know the peasants either. For every yea and nay, for every sneeze or scratch, they'll tell you such a huge Ramayana; and if you question them too much or say this or that: 'The weeds have grown here,' 'The cattle look lean,' or 'When will you give us the spring rice? It's already three months due and the rains are here,' you never know when their scythes will be at the touch of your neck, never, never. Remember Posthouse Venkatanayana," concluded Aunt Sata, and became ominously silent.

But as soon as they saw me—they were in the middle of the rice-planting, water up to their knees and rice shoots in hand—Linge Gowda stopped his plough and came rushing towards us, blanket and folded hands and all. "The Learned-One has come! The Learned-One! The Krishnappa family has come!" And the women came rushing too; they looked at me and said, "Oh, he looks just like he looked when young, lovely as the son of a king," and they knocked their knuckles against their temples (that no evil eye should fall on my princely face!).

"Well, when you have drunk the Himavathy waters you can't ever look different," remarked Sakamma, fat, long-eared, deaf as a hen; she put her finger on her lip and proclaimed, "He looks just like his grandfather, when he started building that rice mill there, that never did function."

The Linge Gowda said, "Hé, Rangi, is this the way to receive

elders and big people? Go and get some milk, you she-buffalo!"
Meanwhile the villagers all came—Ramayya, Sundarappa, Bod-
hayya, Cart-Wheel Sivaramanna, Timma, Putta, Kitta, Nanjanna,
boatman Kalappa—they came with their silver bangles, their
whips and black-blankets, and fell at my feet. The milk arrived
and the bananas, and as we sat under the Buxom-mango—we were
near my Aruni-field—the blue Himavathy flowing below me, with
the fair-carts wading through the waters and the smell of rotten
mango and cow dung coming to us, I wondered at the gentleness,
the fertility and greenness of the earth that had shapen me.

We went home, and after my bath, meditation and meal I
went up the loft to see what had become of the manuscripts.
Grandfather had such a lot of palm-leaf manuscripts that had
come generation on generation down to us. And once in a
while when he found a child lighting the evening lamps one after
the other with one of those palm leaves, how Grandfather gave
him a nice marriage ceremony! And you burst your lamentation
the louder, that Aunt Sata or Grandmother Rangamma might
take you on her waist, and went to bed with a nice song and
many a restful pat. Night would come. And Grandfather
Ramanna, who got angry so quickly and forgot equally quickly,
would say, coming back from the morning river with his wet
clothes and wet vessels in hand, "Give that orphan his breakfast,
Sata. You know he's just like his father. He will never ask."

Some of the manuscripts were still there. I wiped them gently
and tried to read here and there. Some were on medicine, some
on Vedanta (mostly commentaries, on the Upanishads by
Gaudapada and Sankara, the *Rig-Veda Samhita,* or the *Ramayana*) and others on sundry things, such as a strange book on
lizard-wisdom, which interpreted the clucking of house-lizards on
the wall (unlike most of the others, this was in Kannada): one
cluck meant bad, two meant success, and four and five meant different things during different parts of the day. There were also
Sanscrit manuscripts on house-building, describing with extraordinary precision what to build for a merchant and what to
build for a Brahmin householder. There was a sixteenth-century
book on music, and a small palm-leaf manuscript on snuffs, which
read, "On the eighteen ways of autumn trituration of snuff, for

277

maladies, delights, cosmetic and erotic purposes; with the eleven ways of perfuming it, in the Northern, Southern, Southeastern and Malabar Ways, and with multiple fashions of making it a means for attaining peace and prosperity. Written by the Great-jewel of medical and other sciences, Linga Sastry." I also took out the copper-plate inscription, carefully tied in cotton cloth, and with many auspicious marks of kunkum, turmeric and flower-spots on it. How proud I was to read it again! I brought it in front of the still-turning sanctuary lights, and read it out to Little Mother.

"Be it prosperous. Adored be He of the Three Eyes, with Ganges in his Hair, etc., etc. . . .

"This day, in the year 1615* of the Victorious increasing Salivahana era, the year named Sri Mukha, on the twelfth of the bright fortnight of Pushya, when King Virabhadra the Great, he who hath killed his enemies with weapons of the very Pandavas, valorous, young, splendid as the new sun of the northern-turning Equinox, of the Race of the Yadavas, King of the sacred lands south of the ever-blue Krishna and north of the Cauvery, master of the eighteen sciences, learned, inexorable, kind, protector of the family Gods, He in his infinite Ocean of kindness whose foam is like the new moon; to the Venerable Three-Veda-Knowing, bright, auspicious, like the very Himalayas in learning, as if the Goddess of learning sat in his throat, who beams wisdom like the sun beams light, Vishweshwara Ramakrishna Bhatta; to him hath His Gracious Majesty this village of Hastinapura given, at the auspicious time of Makara-Sankramana, with presentation of a coin and pouring of water; that acquiring the eight rights of full possession belonging to this village, namely, present profit, future profit, hidden treasure, underground stores, springs, minerals, actualities and possibilities, yea, his offspring and descendants, as long as the sun and moon endure, that he fulfil the four duties of the Brahmin, keep learning aflame like the face of Brahma, that the said learned Brahmin and his sons and grandsons, in undivided property, and for generations to come, keep from every foe

* A.D. 1693.

and Turk; and may the Himavathy flow with noble abundance, for when the sacrificial fire be, plenty and righteousness also be. With horses, elephants and chariots did the great King, roaring like a lion in speech, whose very shadow frightens the demons in the underworld, He, His Majesty Virabhadra, made holy ablutions in the waters, the gentle, the soft, the fruitful Himavathy, daughter of the Srigiri Mountains, that rise like the very Himalayas on the Western Sea . . ."

Sridhara listened to it all as if he understood every word, and when Aunt Sata poured ghee to sanctuary lamps, how Sridhara fell before the gods. The lizards knowingly clucked, and the cows came to ask for rice-water. The temple elephant gave a shout somewhere: I was back in Hariharapura.

In the afternoon Alur Sri Kantha Sastri came and took me down to the river. Grave she looked, Mother Himavathy, but what a rich vesture of gracious peacock-blue she wore. We washed, and since I could not bathe I wandered about thinking of where Grandfather Ramanna had taught me this or that, of *Amara, Nirukta,* the *Isa* and *Kena* Upanishads. Sri Kantha Sastri came to remind me where Grandfather had been cremated: Mother Himavathy had just waited for the fire to die down and then she had risen suddenly and washed away his sacred ashes.

Timma and Ranga brought us vegetables, and the cook gave us a magnificent meal that evening.

I gave priest Ranganatha three hundred rupees for the repairs of the Kenchamma temple. "And here's a sari for the Goddess," said Little Mother, producing a small worship-sari from her box. I was happy to see the cattle when they came home; Gauri was still alive, and so strong for her age—she was eleven years old. "She gave this calf but a year ago," protested Nanja, "and she still gives us three measures." Lāli and Sethu had died of foot-and-mouth disease the year before.

When dusk fell the village elders came to invite us for the evening worship. How very splendid the Goddess looked, round, with her green eyes, and the serpent-belt that Grandfather, so they said, had given her after my birth. And when we went home after the circumambulations Mango-tope Siddanna came to discuss some boundary questions: the corner-house people had encroached on our elephant-fruit field, and they were not people to listen to kind words. "For just a question they'll throw you into the Himavathy, but we know how to deal with their grandfathers," said Siddanna. Little Mother knew all the details about the lands, though she had been here but once; Uncle Seetharamu had given her detailed instructions.

Everybody asked about Saroja's marriage. "What a wonderful family—a son in London, and a daughter in Delhi," said bailiff Subbayya. "Now that the youngest has drunk of Mother Himavathy's green waters, this child, too, will come back to us, for initiation and marriage," proclaimed Pattadur Patel Siddalingayya. In the night, as I lay thinking on my lands—this long stretch of Himavathy valley that had given us rice and sugar cane year after year, and the hills beyond that had fed us on coffee and jackfruit, cardamom and honey, for decades, for hundreds of years—it seemed to me that they were a presence, a more continuous, inexorable presence than Little Mother, Sukumari, Sridhara or me.

We went back to Bangalore happy and refreshed after Hariharapura.

Saroja came to join us the week after. Her husband had been sent on a mission to London, and she was going to spend a few months with us. Never in my life have I been happier than during those six weeks in Bangalore. We took walks in the Lal Bagh, we went to hear music at the City Hall, we visited relations—Little Mother knew every one of them, and like Father she loved visiting all of them, morning, noonday, afternoon and dusk-fall—and we played country chess at home and laughed all the time. Saroja came to understand Little Mother better, and often as I entered they changed their talk, as if they did not wish to worry me. "Brother, you get better first—and the rest is my affair," Saroja pleaded. Sukumari was happy too, for here she could go about with boys without people talking scandal.

"In Bangalore," remarked Little Mother, "it is not as in Muslim Hyderabad. Here girls can go about with boys and nobody thinks anything of it. After all it's Brahmin-land," declared

Little Mother, forgetting that the benign Congress regime had abolished caste distinctions.

The air in the evening of Bangalore is cool, and in Basavangudi how enchanting the dusk hours, with the bells of the Bull temple ringing, rich and long. We often walked up there when my breathing was not too hard—and let the evening fall on us across the rocks and the momentous hollows of the hills. Lights would suddenly shine out everywhere, and while the bats settled on the trees Little Mother and Saroja would go into the temple and bring back *prasadam*. Then with the smell of camphor mingling with the smell of champaks, we would go home, our nostrils rich and our breath sacred. *"Sambho-Sankara, Sambho-Sankara,"* repeated Little Mother, as though we were in Benares again.

Saroja had brought her cook from Delhi, for our own cook was no good at all. Appoo Nair made wonderful sambar and idlies. I was happy.

The doctors began to be more optimistic. They said it was my vegetarian habits that must have caused all this trouble.

"In Rome do as Romans do, is a good adage," said Dr. Bhimsen Rao to me. "It's because Grandfather wouldn't allow your father to die like the great Ramanujan* that your own father was never allowed to go to Cambridge. But times have changed and you have gone to Europe. You must eat meat and drink wine," he advised. "If not, why marry a European wife?"

What was there for me to say? I laughed and said, "I am a European Brahmin," and he seemed satisfied with my answer. Since that day he always introduced me to the nurses and X-ray assistants as "this European Brahmin, this French Vedantin." It made everybody laugh. In India we always laugh, at everything, auspicious or indifferent. It must do our lungs a lot of good.

Noble is the game of life and pentathlic the works of civilization. Birth and death, sowing and reaping, the communication

---

* It is believed the great Indian mathematician, Ramanujan, died in Cambridge of undernourishment, being a vegetarian.

of joys and sufferings; the subtleties of statistics, the names of loves; diplomatic determinations, subterfuges, losses, conquests; the crowning of queens (death of kings), the killing of dictators or of their fist-faced henchmen; all these follow one another, as if the magnificent line of ants at my feet in the Lal Bagh had any knowledge of other things than that the sun shines in between two gusts of monsoon winds, and have no premonition of the trees that wave their tops in jubilant youth, that aeroplanes hover above the earth, bearing people back and forth, and from all the lands and from round the roundsome globe, or that the telegraph wires which pass by me, have carried the destiny of men for decades: "Shamoo died"; "Subbu, succeeded exams"; "Lakshmana transferred to Dehra Dun, Military Depot"; and they will carry it for several decades more, unless more simple means dispense with wires and conglomerate absurdities, so that important news does not reach us on a bicycle, with a blue coat and khaki trousers, and brick-coloured envelopes do not contain the amalgam of destiny.

Through the kindness of the authorities telegrams from abroad were marked, "Cable Indian Overseas Services," so a cable generally meant a cable to me from Madeleine. The cable I received that morning after returning home, of which I had perhaps a premonition, from having sat looking at the telegraph wires so long, came therefore as no real surprise, especially as Little Mother had just said on seeing me, "How well you look, Rama! What clarity and blood has come to your eyes." It was just then, when Little Mother had hardly gone in, that the telegraph peon handed the cable to me. I sat on the stone bench near the pomegranate bush and opened it, letting my cane fall beside me. The cable was from Tante Zoubie. It said that Madeleine had had to be taken to hospital suddenly for a caesarean to be performed. The boy died soon after. "Madeleine well," it went on to say. "Don't worry we will look after your wife. Get better soon. Charlot sends love . . ." I could hear Saroja count the clothes inside the veranda—the washerman was there—three jubbas, four saris, ten handkerchiefs, four towels—and I put the telegram into my pocket: it was addressed to the ants.

In the bathroom, later, when I stepped on the wash-slab I laughed. I was neither in pain, nor was I relieved; I felt above both, like a child looking at a kite in the sky; I thought of Georges, and laughed at Leibnitz and the monad and all that. I saw the yellow and white of the kite and the snakelike tail that the wind swept curling, whirling on itself and leaping up back against the sun. The winds blew cool and fresh. I laughed as a child laughs, playing with the subtleties of the breeze. I was happy. The world is a happy place for anyone to live in: look at the ants in the Lal Bagh. Vassita found peace with the Lord.

I laughed hilariously the whole afternoon, playing country chess, first with Little Mother, and then with Saroja when she woke from her siesta. In the evening I took them all to the cinema.

News from Savithri was scarce. When letters came they were brief and full of humility: "This fat and foolish thing"—"I am unworthy—so uneducated a creature as I," and so on. It was just fear, I concluded, turned to nobler purposes.

Haemoglobules do perhaps have something to do with happiness, for my health improved steadily, so the doctors said. The monsoon abated, and the flavoursome Srāvan winds began to blow. The earth was covered with wide yellow patches of rice and sugar cane, and the tanks were red with new waters. The cattle seemed lovely in their washed skins, and young betel leaves appeared at the market.

Sukumari had long ago been sent away, in the care of the cook, to Hyderabad, for colleges do not open according to our convenience, do they? Saroja's husband wrote enthusiastic letters about Europe. It was his first trip abroad. "My sacred wife," he wrote, "you bring me good luck. Since you entered my house what a miracle it has all been: first I was transferred from the Refugee and Rehabilitation Ministry to the Financial Secretariat, and a month later I'm invited to go to Europe. Next time we will come here together. I long for you. I'll tell you everything when I come." Saroja showed it to me as a proof that happiness can be.

Just as the cattle know when the rains will burst and fall, and

Gangi and Gauri rush homeward, their ears pressed against their necks, so did I know the nimbed future of things. Savithri had not written to us for a month, but I knew she was back in India. "Some cloud must have told me," I wrote to her:

> samtaptānām tvam asi caraham tat payoda priyāyāḥ
> samdeçam me hara dhanapatikrodhaviçlesitasya
> gantavyā te vasatir alakā nama yakṣeçvarānām
> bāhyodyānasthitaharaçiraçcandrikādhautaharmyā
> You are the solace of those who are burnt
> With anguish, O Giver of the rains!
> Take then a message to my beloved,
> Far distant through the wrath of Lord Dhanapathi.
> You will go to the city of Alaka,
> Abode of the Princes of the Yakshas;
> In the parkland around resides Shiva Himself,
> And the palaces are brightly lit with the Moon
> Which shines from the head of the great God.

She was in Delhi, she wrote, with her father. They had taken a house in Mani Bagh, and the Raja of Surajpur was going to flatter the new gods in the same way as he had managed the British. Formerly it was a question of tiger-shooting and drink-parties; now it was nautch-parties and no tigers, please. Savithri seemed tired and sick of the world. "I may yet decide on the inevitable," she wrote. "Do not be angry with me. I am but a frail creature—like in the poem by W. B. Yeats you used to read to me. Woman is of the earth earthy, and if only you knew what an earthy creature I am. Pratap visits us regularly. He treats me like one does a deer at the Zoo, offering me peanuts and green grass. I am not a gazelle, Rama, for I cannot leap beyond my nose. But—shall I tell you?—I love you, I love you. Protect me."

The winds rose over the asoka trees as I read it a second time, at the Lal Bagh. On the other side of the lake five or six men were taking a bath. It was just before dusk; they must have come after some cremation. Beyond the crematorium was the mad-house; Dr. Appaswamy, who was a friend of mine, once told me that some of the inmates were quite extraordinary in moments of lucidity—there was one, a professor of mathematics, who solved many problems there that he could not in his native town of

Trichinopoly. Death, madness; Pratap, marriage; haemoglobules, telegraph wires above and stars beyond. Benares is everywhere you are, says a famous Vedantic text; Kapilavastu is the true home of mankind; each one of us has a Kanthaka at his door. Dare we leave the child by the mother, with his head under her curved hand, the light "lingering like moonbeams" on her young, seventeen-year-old face? Would angels shut the fissures in our being, that the world know not when we take the leap?

I became so tender, so understanding with Little Mother. She was the fifth of seven children, and her father, a court clerk, came home for ever angry, snuff in his palm and maybe eight annas in his pocket: "This is all, Sata, that wretched ryot gave for three hours of scribbling. Money does not grow on mango trees in the back yard." The children were scared by their father, especially the younger ones. He didn't want them: *she* had them. So the coconut branch and the bicycle pump were Little Mother's real teachers. "When you're married off I shall drink a *seer* of frothing warm milk, you widow!" he would shout, if the water was not hot in the bathroom, or the clothes not dry on the bamboo.

"Life to me, Rama, was like that municipal tap at the door, purring the whole night through. But at least, when women came in early in the morning, the tap heard someone sing, whereas I—I knew kicks and tears . . ." Little Mother had never gone back to her father's house again. "They are stranger to me than you are—whom I have known but these five or six years. People talk of the heart: the heart of some is made of cow dung or old buttermilk. Worms rise out of it. *Ashappā!*" And Sridhara was being patted into sleep. Saroja woke later in the night and said, "Little Mother, was I speaking in my dream?"

"No, my child, I've been recounting my Ramayana to Rama. Sleep and dream of your new home and of your wonderful husband. He's such a nice man, Rama, isn't he?"

The doctors suggested that I could now go up to a hill station, perhaps to Ooty or to Kodaikanal. "Crisp dry air will do you a lot of good."

"Come with me to Delhi, Brother, and then we'll go to Mussoorie," said Saroja. But I was bent on going to Kodaikanal. I did not know it; besides, it would be very dry. I could work there, I was sure; I had to finish my thesis soon. I had to return to India.

When Saroja and Little Mother had left—Saroja spending a few days in Hyderabad on her way north—I went back to those lovely Kodai Hills, rich with new verdure, ancient, alone and with a rocking, sealike solitude. I walked up and down the Observatory Ridge like a goat, and the doctors were very pleased with the result. "It is not always that heights are helpful," said old Dr. Ruppärt. He was a German, and had settled there forty years earlier, before the 1914–18 war. He was sure that in a few weeks I could return to Europe. "Lucky man," he said, "to have a French wife and live in Provence, and to be writing a thesis on the Minnesingers and *Parsifal.*" Frau Ruppärt played—oh, how badly!—that famous beginning of the Prelude. Strange, with the sound of servants speaking Tamil and the scent of thousand-petalled jasmines at the door, in that lucid moonlight to hear:

Then I remembered that the story of Mani was of Indian origin; so why not? But Dr. Ruppärt was sure it came from the Central Asian steppes, and was an original Aryan myth. "Why, if you read Frazer, you'll find that perhaps it's not only an Aryan myth, but is to be found among the people of the Toboogan Islands too!"

I was very serene at Kodai. It seemed as though happiness was just there, over the lake; some lotus would rise from the depths, and Lakshmi arise with it, and the elephant would stand beside her in those *"taralata-rangé"* waters, a garland in its trunk.

> *Shvretambara dharé Devi nānalankāra bhūshité.*
> *Jagasthithe Jaganmātha Mahālakshmi namosthuthé,*
> O Devi robed in white,
> Shining with many and varied jewels;

O bearer of the universe, mother of Creation,
Great Goddess of Wealth, to thee I bow.

I repeated to myself.

Sorrow was, of course, like a shadow behind one, yet one could look out at the silver of the lake and know that light dwells in between one's eyes. To be centred in oneself is to know joy.

Madeleine was full of concern and advice for me. "Don't come back too soon," she begged. "I have grown so fat I will look like your Frau Ruppärt, round and very red. Tante Zoubie threatens to send me to India if you cough once in her presence. What a kind, clever—devilishly clever—and charmingly inconsequent creature she is. For her joy is a biological need, as you would say. 'If I do not laugh half an hour a day, I shall eat the head of Charlot away,' she says, laughing. And when she has nothing to do she composes humorous verse, that is recited at table—towards gastronomical ends, she proclaims. They are not at all bad and have a touch of Prévert: *'Un jour le bois me dit, petit-frère, je te montrerai l'enfer, et puis tu verras l'oignon gros comme le poivre, car le Paradis est circonscrit.'* I shall now be a good Vassita."

Letters from Madeleine rested me. They seemed to contain a hidden wisdom, some touch of sorrow that was lit, as it were, with a great, round, impersonal love. She seemed to have touched a point of awareness where she could press herself unto existence as such and have perhaps the assuredness that this identity nobody could remove or corrupt. I felt ashamed of myself, and tried to grow more self-reliant, indrawn and earnest.

Savithri wrote more often now. Her letters varied with her moods, now chirruping away like a bird about some tour in the Tarai where they had been guests of the Raja Sahib of Tehri-Garnwal, or about some sickening news of governmental intrigue.

That is the beauty of Savithri. She is whole and simple where-ever she is; for her there is only one world, one spot, one person even—and that is he who is before her. From her distant perch of the impersonal she offers him a spoon of sugar or a glass of whisky, as though her only concern were his joy. No one can be near her—except perhaps me, I told myself—for she is everywhere, and you had to be her to be by her.

Pratap could be her husband, if he so liked, but he stayed in the Audience Chamber and talked with her father. He could, if he so wished, go out on the terrace and see the changing of the guards at the palace—for by now they had gone back to Surajpur —or hear the seventh-hour music play on the Main Gate. The Royal Elephant might just be coming in, with Mohammed Ali piercing its ears, *"Hettata-Het-ta . . ."* while Savithri would sit on a divan reading Bertrand Russell, or smoking a cigarette and throwing it away, trying to draw the evening into herself. She would go back into her silence and await there, for like some princess in the fables she would wed but he who could solve the riddle. The riddle was not in Sanscrit or in Hindi, it was in any plain language, and it said, "I want It, It, It. Pray, Prince, pray, learned man, what is the It I seek? The garland is there and the elephant, with howdah and the Nine Musics. Solve me the riddle, Prince and I'll wed thee." She walked through life as though she were not looking at the world at all, but at the kunkum on her clear, bump forehead.

She wrote from Surajpur:

"There was a young diplomat in Delhi who pursued me as though I were the Queen of God. He was convinced I would bring lustre to his job and do good, in addition, to my country. Father himself was not averse to it, kind though he is to Pratap. A Delhi diplomat today is worth two private secretaries to an Indian Governor. I laughed at Father, at his childish selfishness, his enormous vanity and his spacious goodness. Left to himself he would think of nothing less than the moon to marry me to. I keep him in good humour. I act the Cambridge lady, and that's a great success. You'll laugh if I tell you that at the Delhi Gymkhana my brother and I danced the boogie-woogie. You wouldn't know what that is, but this is just to tease you. I even won a prize.

"Rama, my love, as I write this to you, I lie by a lake in northern Surajpur. Father and others are away having a picnic on the lake. I stayed back at this rest-lodge, excusing myself with a headache. I think I wanted to think of you. The maid has just brought me one of those ancient palace lamps, with castor oil, cloth wick, and opening like a flower with five petals. 'It's not electricity for the memsahib,' she apologized. They think that now I've been to Cambridge I can only see with electric light. They do not know, poor foolish women, that I can see more splendidly now than ever before, for I have a light on my forehead, a hood of some noble serpent, whose seven-headed protection brings my breath down and establishes me in silence. 'My daughter,' said Father to me the other day, 'there's a strange beauty about you now, as there was on the face of your mother when I first married her. She was seventeen and had never left the zenana. But, dear child, you seem so sad, as though you had gathered all the sorrow of dusk and had tied it at your sari-fringe. We are not of the servant class that you should sorrow in life.' That is Father all over—why, when there is the elephant, and cannon at our door, and his own big, protective self, why is there anything to sorrow for? True, his friends the British have gone, but that sorrow was of short duration. Father is a pragmatist. 'We, the Rathors, dealt with the Moghuls first,' he declared, 'and then came the Lord Sahib. Now we can deal with a Brahmin or a Banya with equal ease. They may be the cleverest of all the world, but they are our own. We know their tricks—and they being new to the game we still have a chance.' Scheming and building imaginary empires is for Father like playing chess in the evening or going on a picnic—always there is an ulterior motive. He will never do anything for anyone without being sure of a return—except perhaps for his daughter.

"Rama, the evening has now fallen. Will you stand with me as the *ārathi* is being performed in the temple across the lake? I can see the torches being lit, I can hear the music sound, and then there is the vast ingurgitating silence of the weir-waters. If you stood by me there is a grave question I would ask of you: If I asked you, would you really marry me? Will you? Father may object and say you are just a professor. But Mother, whose values are more right, would say, 'Oh, a Brahmin!' She would think your presence amidst us august, holy. But I am too poor, too wretched a creature. No woman who's a woman can choose her destiny. Men make her destiny. For a woman to choose is to betray her biology. Tell me, Rama, tell me truly and as before God, 'Come,' and I'll come. The night is so auspicious, and tomorrow is Gokulashthami, when Lord Krishna will be born. We shall fast, and we shall worship, and I shall think of you, my Lord.

"Did I tell you that in Surajpur the whole palace rings with the little bells on my toes? I said to Mother it was the gift of a South Indian Brahmin. Mother was so pleased. She said, 'We don't make such lovely things any more here. How beautiful they'll be, when you marry, my child.'

"When the Muslims came, Rama, shouting and leaping on horseback across the deserts, and vowing vengeance on the Rajput; when they encircled our fortresses, bribed Brahmin ministers and tried to get in; when they cut off supplies of water and made us shout to the very skies with thirst; the men jumped on their horses and bid adieu to their wives, their daughters, the tilak of our blood on their foreheads; the gates were suddenly thrown open and the men charged the enemy, while the women read the *Mahabharatha* and leapt into the flames inside. No Hindu woman would wed a Turk. I feel besieged—the Turk is at the door. Help me to jump into the pyre, Lord my Master, of this life and of all the lives to come. Help me."

"S"

And beneath her name she had blackened the paper with the collyrium of her eyes, and stuck a kunkum mark from her forehead. What sentimental people we Indians are!

Of course, there was a charger waiting for me. It would not take me to the Turks. Its name would be Kanthaka, and I would change my royal garments by the Ganges, admonish him to return and let the people of Kapilavastu know that he, Kanthaka, was a noble steed that had led Gautama the Sakyan to the banks of the Ganges, and thus started him on the pilgrimage from which there is no returning. There was no need to go to the banks of the Nirvanjana for the Bodhi tree; there were many by the lake in Kodai. They seemed so ancient, ocelous and protective. But I was not ripe yet—I, the real betrayer. Savithri's letter, so true and limpid, luminous like the ancient castor-oil lamp with five petals she was writing by, needed the wisdom and the courage of evening. In between day and night is the space of dusk, that beat of an eyelash which is the light of Brahman. *"Jyothir méka Parabrahman,"* Little Mother always chanted at home, as soon as the lights were lit. "Light alone is the Supreme Brahman."

You can marry when you are One. That is, you can marry when there is no one to marry another. The real marriage is like oo, not like o1o. When the ego is dead is marriage true. Who would remove my ego? "Lord, my Guru!" I cried in the rift of the night. And looking at the town of Kodai reflected in the lake, with what breath and earnestness I chanted Sankara:

> *Vishwam in darpanadrishya mānanagarī*
> Like a city seen in a mirror is the universe,
> Seen within oneself but seemingly of Maya born,
> As in sleep;
> Yet is it really in the inner Self
> Of Him who sees at the Point of Light
> Within Himself, unique, immutable—
> To Him incarnate as the holy Guru,
> To Sri Dakshinamurthi be my salutation.

I composed several letters to Savithri. What could I tell her? "To him," says the Upanishads, "who is earnest, to the Atman comes the Atman." It was not land and rivers that separated us, it was Time itself. It was myself. When the becoming was stopped I would wed Savithri. If the becoming stopped would there be a wedding? Where would the pandal be, where Uncle Seetharamu and the elephant?

"All brides be Benares born, my love, my Lakshmi," I wrote. I knew she would understand.

Dr. Ruppärt was satisfied with my X-ray. "You are an ideal patient. You are so obedient," he remarked, patting me on the back.

"You must be so easy to live with—an ideal husband," Frau Ruppärt added, looking at her husband.

"All husbands are ideal when they are not yours," chuckled Dr. Ruppärt in Saxon gaiety.

I visited Madurai, worshipping She-of-the-Fish-Eyes, beautiful, bejewelled, compassionate and serene—I paid three rupees for a puja in the name of Savithri—then I went to Hyderabad. Little Mother was very happy to see me looking round and healthy again. "There's been no blood since Bangalore," I told her. I visited the new Minister of Education—an old student of Father's—and promised to finish my thesis in a year. I would come back.

"Come back by the time Sukumari gets married," remarked Little Mother.

"Oh, Little Mother," cried Sukumari, "you want to tie me to a quern-handle and get rid of me too. Let me study my medicine—oh, please, Brother?"

"For a Shiva's lip* of the courtyard," quoted Little Mother—another of her proverbs—"Shiva's head is the Kailas. And for a woman the sacred feet of her husband be Paradise." You cannot argue against a proverb.

I spent a week in Bombay. Not that there was anything important to do. But I smelt something, as it were, among the stars. I wanted to be far from home—far from Madeleine, far from everyone. Captain Sham Sunder offered me hospitality. I had met him in London: "When you come to Bombay, do not forget me," he had said. His Colaba flat was just by the sea. He had two very clever children and his wife, Lakshmi, was a fine-looking woman—somewhat round, but kind, sad and entertaining. Captain Sham Sunder, I think, had other interests; he came home from his club late at night, and every day of the week it was so. Once he said to me, laughing, "Since my return from Europe I prefer white skin to brown." What a very clever remark to make!

I took the children and his wife to visit the Gateway of India, or the Malabar Hill. Lakshmi had such a heavy sadness, like a sari she had wetted and pressed under her feet, and forgotten in the corner of the courtyard to rot. She was indeed not particularly clean in her habits, but she was a good Hindu wife. She despised man, however, and there was no reason why she should think any better of me.

"You like white skin perhaps, as my husband does," she said.

"That is why I married one," I replied.

But she cooked nice meals for me and begged me to take her to

* A small white wild flower, considered very sacred.

cinemas. Once or twice she came near me, but I moved away, almost afraid of her physical importance. One felt she had the power to pluck the manhood out of anyone and throw it into the sea, murmuring maledictions after it. But I was tired of the struggle, the endless roads, hotels, aircraft, sisters, marriages, X-rays; besides, I had never really known an Indian woman. I was perhaps eaten by my haemoglobules as well, and did not wish my manhood to turn dehydrate. There was not going to be Savithri anyway. I slipped slowly and deliberately into Lakshmi's bed.

She was happy with me, I think. Her children were happy to see their mother happy with me. Nothing very much happened, in fact. She did not want me; she just wanted to feel that I was like all men. She made me speak of Savithri. I gladly did, for there was no one else I could speak to. She felt prouder after that. "Men are worthless," she remarked often. "They are simpler than children. Any patch of flesh will do for them—the fairer the better."

Rumour of Savithri's marriage reached my ears through people coming from the North: there was Captain Sham Sunder himself, to whom the news of my "flame," as Lakshmi called her, was duly carried; and there were anyway so many people at the Cricket Club who came and went between Bombay and Delhi and always had something to say about the great gods up in the capital. So that when the news really came—first in the papers— I was not surprised, and then there was a line from Savithri herself. It ran: "Surajpur Palace. This evening, at four forty-seven, I entered into the state of matrimony. I married Pratap at last. I shall be a good wife to him. Bless me."

In a day or two Lakshmi yielded to me. I thought to myself it was like eating a pickle. My days and nights would be spent in luxurious enjoyment. I put off my trip by another week. Captain Sunder himself seemed happy—for he knew what it was all about! How splendid Lakshmi looked now! When once in a while I coughed, she was ever so tender to me, sitting by my side and fanning me, pressing my legs, my arms. She began to have some respect for me. She found me straightforward and simple, and not like those manly men—unclean, she said, so unclean—

who were about the place. "I would not touch them with my left foot, those fat, moustached fools, those friends of Sham's. They prefer fair skins. Let them." She asked me questions on Hindu sacred texts, started reading the *Mahabharatha* and the *Gita* regularly. She wished to visit Europe with me. She discussed the education of her children. Often lying by her I wondered whether I was Rama, Saroja's loved brother, Little Mother's stepson.

Then one day I remembered the damsels with wide-open mouths, lying naked and full in Kapilavastu. "There were Palaces of silver for Summer," ran the story, "and Palaces of sandal for Winter, and Palaces of gold when the Young Spring came. Musicians, too, there were and diverse. So that when the Raja Sudhodhana saw the Bodhisattva playing among them, he thought, Gautama will be crowned my heir, the King. And never shall he leave the palace, nor know the cry of sickness, the sorrow of death, the totter of old age, the misery of want. The Palaces were well guarded, and not a girl of the Kingdom was there that could not accomplish the joy of youth."

I booked my seat on the plane, somewhat secretly, for I had become a great coward. The night before I was to leave, I told Lakshmi. She made such a scene I thought the whole building would know.

"You eunuch," she cried. "You lecherous coward!" I thought she would beat me, but she was still very handsome. I took her in my arms and calmed her.

"Don't leave me. What will happen to me?" she sobbed. "Come to me again," she begged, and as I covered her she seemed lost in her sorrow and firm passion. "I'll thank you always," she cried, laying my small head on her swelling bosom, "for you at least treated me with respect. I know you will always be there when I want you. And you know, if ever you need me, I will come and look after you. Sham would be happy if I could make you happy. He thinks you are a helpless fellow and a good friend."

Strange to say, it was this Lakshmi who saw me off at Santa Cruz. My Indian pilgrimage was ended.

MADELEINE HAD MOVED to a new house. "I could never again live in Villa Sainte-Anne," she had written to me. The new one was called Villa Les Rochers, for the sloping garden was strewn with brown and white rocks. It was a little farther away from the town, and the house itself was smaller, but the olive trees that went from step to step, up to the gateway, gave the villa a sense of isolation and of abandon. Far away you saw only the Alpilles and the sun somewhere on the Camargue. Madeleine had decided on the house as though she had decided on her own life. "There's no question now of my going to India," she had written, and I never asked her why.

How true the unsaid *sounds* against the formulated, the uttered. Words should only be used by the perfect, by the gods, and speech indeed be made incantatory. For speech is sound, and sound is vibration, and vibration creation. To create would be to know what the creator is, and to claim creatorhood for ourselves is indeed to commit a noumenal sin. Silence is golden, say the Europeans. No, silence is the Truth. *"Maunavyakya Prakatitha parabrahma Tatvam,"* said Sri Sankara. "The publishing of Truth is the vocable of silence."

The day I arrived was a sad day. I remember it was the seventeenth of October, and a *raz-de-marée* had risen in the sea, and had dragged a horse and its rider and two bathers on the beach of Cassis away. Our plane was three hours late—what with the changes in the Mediterranean air currents—and Henri was not there at the aerodrome. Life had changed everywhere. I took the bus to Marseille, and took a taxi from there on to Aix. The afternoon was clear as prayer, with a touch of autumnal gold on the hills. Madeleine was writing a letter when I entered. She seemed calm, fresh and big; it was true, she had become very large. She carried my bags up the garden steps. It was a nice house she had taken, I thought, as she led me to my new room. My books were all arranged neatly, my large table laid against the window. She had burnt sandal-sticks, for I could smell them the moment I came in. My mother's portrait was hung on the wall above my divan.

"Have a bath quickly, Rama, and I'll give you dinner at once." Her voice was gentle, deliberate and strange. This time I undid my trunks quickly, hung my clothes and went into the bathroom. "This is a funny geyser; he's so temperamental," she explained, and let the water flow. "Just remember to turn off the gas when you get in. Otherwise it escapes, and you'd have to crawl out of the bath, like I did one night. We must get a plumber," she added, and went back to the kitchen.

I was too tired to think, so I slipped into the bath. When I got out I felt surprisingly fresh. The evening was cool, and I felt young and whole. My breathing seemed less heavy. I was back home.

There was a dining room in this house. It was downstairs and opened on to the garden, so that you could hear the crickets in summer, and see the fireflies among the olives. The kitchen was to one side, and I could smell rice and tomato again. It was to be risotto as usual, but with a difference: this time she had added curry powder to it.

"I thought you would like your wretched spices for some time," she said. "I never know how to cook for you—I never shall."

The table was laid and she brought the food. There was the same familiar saucepan with the burnt wooden handle, the same squares-and-triangles kitchen oilcloth, the same bent fork, with a broken recalcitrant tip. I suddenly realized there was but one plate. I stood up and took another out. Meanwhile Madeleine placed the food on the table saying:

"Rama, will you forgive me if I do not eat? It's the eighth moon today, and I've taken to fasting. I'm going to be a good Buddhist." She spoke quietly, undramatically. "Poor child," she went on, "you must be hungry after such a long journey. Rama, serve yourself, and I'll just go down to the post office and back. I must catch the last mail: it's for Tante Zoubie."

She went up to her room, then ran down the staircase and into the garden. It was such a lovely, large evening, with a bunch of stars above me, and the olives shaking with the sea breeze from the southwest. The big cypress at the door stood straight like a redemptor, and the evening was full of birds, sheep and cries of children. Far away on the other side was the silence of the hills.

I sat at the table and I ate. I concentrated on my food and I was convinced I had to eat. Food is meant for eating; of course it is: "*OM adāma, OM pibama, OM devo varunah Prajapatihi savihannam iharat, anna-pate, annam i hara, ahara, OM iti,*" says the *Chandogya* Upanishad. But lungs have temperament. My breathing became suddenly difficult. I stopped, however, any exhibition of the extraordinary. I was just the normal Ramaswamy, husband of the Madeleine who taught history at the Lycée de Jeunes Filles, at Aix. There was nothing strange about anything. I had come home from India, and it made no difference to the earth or the air or the olives, or the stars for that matter, that I came from India rather than, say, from Paris or London. True, time exists in clock-hours, in days that you can count, even on the postal calendar in the kitchen—March, April, etc. . . . up to October. The lungs can be very bad, you know, and so you stayed on in India. But Madeleine is Madeleine, the same Madeleine.

"Ah, I hope you were not so silly as to have forgotten I'd leave the grated cheese in the kitchen. Oh, Rama!" she exclaimed, like a child. "Oh, you are still the same old fool." She pushed the *entremets* towards me, and the nuts. "You must get stronger. Now let me have a good look at you. It must be your stay at Kodaikanal: you look less dark than when you returned from India last time." I spoke of the X-rays and the blood-test. She went up and found my medicines. "We won't go to the elephant today," she decided. "It's already a bit cold this year. Let us go up to my room."

Her room was a smaller one than mine, but opened on to the garden, as mine did. A cypress almost touched her window, and you could, as it were, caress it while counting the stars.

"This house has no central heating like Villa Sainte-Anne, but look what a wonderful fireplace. It is more economical this way, and besides, you will be so much away this year in Paris and London. For me, coming from La Charente, this is enough."

I looked at the room. The walls were of a yellow-grey and on the table by her bed stood the huge head of a Khmer Buddha.

"I had this sent from the Musée Guimet. Isn't it beautiful?" She had other, more lovely Buddhas on the walls, especially the one from the Hadda, the Greco-Buddhist one. She had a *tanaka* too, with ferocious heads, monsters with arms of lions and feet of buffaloes, *dhyāna*-Buddhas, and nimbus lotuses, with a serene Bodhisattva seated in the blue middle.

"Oncle Charles bought it for me in Paris," she explained; "now I meditate and sleep here. You won't mind your room, will you? Besides, you can work so much better."

We talked of Saroja's marriage, of Hyderabad and my job.

"This cold country of ours is no good. I am glad the job there awaits you. You must finish your thesis this year. I'll help you, now that the house is small and we are far away from anyone."

I asked news of Catherine.

"She's splendid as a rose, and to see her is to know that happiness is possible. Georges just adores her, and you cannot imagine how like a schoolboy he has become. They've got a nice apartment near the Bois, Rue Michel-Ange, *'deux pièces, cuisine, salle de bains.'* It's some distance for poor Georges to get to Louis-le-Grand, but Oncle Charles has bought them a small Morris—he got it through a client who has business in England—and it's Catherine who takes her husband to the Lycée. I'm glad we don't have the car any more. It's not good for your lung, and I am too exhausted to drive a car. Anyway, where's the need? So much income tax the less.

"You look tired. I'll bring you a hot-water bottle—'*la sainte bouillotte*,'" she laughed, "and you had better go to bed now.

There's an electric heater in your room, and I've put it on the whole afternoon. Go, get undressed, Rama," she begged.

I went to my room. Looking at my mother's picture I was filled with such pain that I was on the point of sobbing my heart hollow. But I rubbed my eyes carefully, undressed, and like a schoolboy I went to bed. Madeleine brought me my hot-water bottle, drew the light nearer me so that I could read, laid all the recent *Revues d'histoire des religions* on the table—she had even marked the articles useful for my work—and then sat at my feet playing with the tassels of the bedspread.

"I'm learning Chinese now, and Tibetan, from Lezo. Tibetan is only a form of Sanscrit, but Chinese is really difficult. I want to get to know more of Chinese Buddhism. Besides, some of the best Buddhist texts, as you know, no longer exist in Pali—destroyed by the Muslims when they burnt Nalanda and Vikramasila. The intellectual brilliance of Buddhism has no equal in the world: it's the religion of the modern age. Some Buddhist texts read like a novel by Aldous Huxley—so curiously intellectual, almost perverse. For the European, Truth can only be attractive when it is perverse. Your Dr. Robin-Bessaignac is right: since we could not accept God, we had to invent a Mother of God, make her into a Virgin, and then accept her Son and find out how he was born. How simple and beautiful is the birth of the Buddha, in comparison. Maya Devi has been pregnant for nine months. She is going to her mother's house. She has birth-pains, and she stops, holds to the branch of a mango tree in blossom, and the great Buddha is born, like any other, in the normal physiological way. To be normal is to be whole," she said, and stopped.

I, too, was playing, with the paper cutter—an ivory one I had had for many years—and my *Revue d'histoire des religions*.

"You probably want to look at your magazines," she said, rising. "Tomorrow there's a slight change in the programme. Nowadays I rise like a good Buddhist at dawn, wash and say my mantras. My Buddhas are kind: the early-morning meditations are wonderful. I shall speak of it all to you tomorrow."

She came near me, and as she tried to tuck in my bed, I slipped my hands over the smoothness of her hair. It was still golden and true, and mine own. But it did not smell of eau-de-Cologne.

And there was no powder on her face, I observed for the first time, and not even the slightest tinge of rouge. I felt helpless—and moved my legs to the other side, towards the hot-water bottle.

"Good night, Rama," she said at the door, "and sleep well. 'Worry is of the mind,' says the Buddhist text. Do not worry, *mon ami.*"

I fiddled with my paper cutter, went to the window and breathed a little fresh air, and went back to my bed. All night I dreamt of Little Mother and a puppy-dog, playing with her in our Bangalore courtyard. I smelt the monsoon and they put me to bed and gave me some brandy. The doctor came a little later, a fat and angry man, and gave me an injection. The X-ray had something written on it, maybe in Chinese. Georges stood on the table, explaining Prospero to his class. All the students laughed. They were all Indians and they wore black or coloured glasses. They smelt bad and they all seemed sons of princes.

With the wake of dawn I heard such a grave and long-drawn mantra, *"OM DHIH—OM GIH—OM JRIH,"* that I thought I was in Hardwar, and the Ganges flowing by me. It is beautiful to live, beautiful and sacred to live and be an Indian in India.

The next few months were spent in peace and hard work. We worked together, Madeleine and I, on a task which ultimately, I thought, would destroy her theogony: the anthropocentric civilization, whether it be the Purist (or Protestant) or the Buddhist (or Jain), must be self-destructive. The abhuman civilizations—the Greece of Socrates, the India of the Upanishads and of Sankara, Catholicism (and not Christianity), Stalinism (and not Leninism, Trotskyism or Anarcho-Syndicalism) had permanence, because they were concurrent with the Law. Man is isolate—and in his singleness is the unanimity of the whole: "When you take away the whole from the whole—*purnam*—what remains is the whole." The job is to build bridges—not of stone or of girders, for that would prove the permanence of the objective, but like the rope bridges in the Himalayas, you build temporary suspensions over green and gurgling space. You must feel the mountain in your nostrils, and know ultimately you are alone with silence. Death is our friend in that sense—life after life it faces us with the meaning of the ultimate. To be is to recognize integrity. The moral universe insists—whether it be according to Newton or Pascal—on the reality of the external world. That *dhira* (hero) of whom the Upanishads speak, enters into himself and knows he has never gone anywhere. There is nowhere to go, where there is no whereness. Alas, that is the beautiful Truth and man must learn it—beautiful it is, because you see yourself true.

Thus heresy proves the truth—as the world proves me. Buddhism proves Vedanta, the Cathars the Church of Christ.

Ours was a sort of anonymous collaboration. We spoke in symbols to prove our point. We would often rise in high indignation over some abstruse text of heresiatic commentary. Knowing little Latin as I did, Madeleine always had the upper hand. Whether Father the Heresiarch de Rodol's *"obumbrare"* meant simply the shadow in the etymological sense, as Jean Guiraud explained, or the same as the *"obumbraverat"* in: *"Deus non venerat in beata Virgine sed obumbraverat se ibi tantum,"* in the canon, would lead us into many hours of ardent discussion. Not only did we consult dictionaries and patristic commentaries, but also the *Corpus Scriptorum Ecclesiasticorum Latinorum*—and Lezo was always there for any interpretation we needed. The right would naturally be on the side of Madeleine. Sometimes too, and of late, Madeleine would easily and quickly lose her temper. On one such occasion she broke out:

"You haven't our academic discipline! How bad your universities must be to lead an intelligent man like you into such confusions. A child of nine in one of our schools would be less muddled."

I pleaded that neither French nor English were my mother tongue and that I might feel Sanscrit a little more than I did Latin.

"Then you should not have started writing a thesis on a subject so specifically French, and based on Latin."

"But I thought you were writing a thesis on the *Prajnaparā-mātīta Pindārtha* of Dinnaya," I hit back.

"I am not writing a thesis. I am studying Buddhism for my own spiritual benefit."

"And I Catharism to prove that I am metaphysically right."

There would be one end to such discussions, especially as Lezo was usually waiting downstairs for one of our evening walks. Sometimes it would be the shelling of *petits pois* that would retain Madeleine, or the buying of Gruyère cheese—"I forgot it this morning, coming back from Collège. You both go on your walk. I shall be a good housewife, and make you nice macaroni with black olives."

On the whole I think Lezo rather liked these quarrels on dogma, as his linguistic help was more often in demand. We used to beg him to stay—especially Madeleine—on rainy, dismal Saturdays when the discussion would have gone on the whole afternoon, and we wished to have some refreshment and repose. His presence made the discussion more superficial, so that we never got anywhere, and that is what we ultimately needed. After dinner I would return to my Church Fathers—good, serious men, who burnt people singing hymns, but who nevertheless loved their Church well, even if they sometimes loved their callings more. Madeleine would go back to her *Prajnaparāmā-tīta*. She always had questions to ask on some Pali or Sanscrit word, and Lezo would demonstrate his knowledge of Pali, Sanscrit and Chinese with the dexterity of an Indian pandit. ("The book has been translated into Chinese by She Hu, and in Tibetan it was included in *mDo agrel: a P'ags pa ses rab kyi pa rol tu p'yin pai ts'ig le'vr bya pa*, which in Sanscrit means, *Prajna, parāmātīta-sangraha—karika*.") "Lakshmana Bhatta," I often called Lezo in fun and he liked it, because there were not so many Bhattas in the Indian texts.

"But there are so many in our Brahmin streets," I once consoled him, "and Benares is filled with Bhattas."

"Ah, Benares," he said, "near Sarnath, where the Sakyamuni turned the Wheel of Law." And he recited with his strange European intonation the whole of the Sermon of Fire. "Foucher translates *Chakra* as 'wheel,' but it means in the original Sanscrit the support, the point of being, the withdrawn centre, which comes from the Buddhist idea of the Void. The hole is in the middle of the Wheel—even so is the Void in man. Oh, these European Orientalists!" he exclaimed. "I must go to India and wander as a Buddhist monk. Then I would understand Buddhism, but not till then. No, not till then."

"I prefer to go to Tibet," Madeleine put in.

"A country of devil-worshippers and devil-dancers," Lezo teasingly protested.

"Women like devils!" spat back Madeleine. "They are better than *homo sapiens* any day." Then, feeling she had said too much, she retired to the kitchen and to her macaroni or *petits pois*. She came back after a moment and added: "Cooking is a biological function of woman: it gives respite to her already small brain. If all the phosphorus in our brains were used up in discussion, woman would easily be fooled by man. So she must retire—cook macaroni or wash men's clothes—and thus she recuperates her strength. If you want to rule women just let them talk: they will fall into a coma."

"Franco's police know that very well," said Lezo. "A woman *détenue* is just made to laugh and talk, and she quickly exhausts herself. They did that with my sister. When they had allowed her to talk herself out they asked discreet questions, and my sister very discreetly said everything about me. Now she's married to a Franquist. He's *sous-préfet* at Burgos, the old university town. Do you know it?" he asked, suddenly turning to me.

"Women," interrupted Madeleine, "like to hear their own voices and not those of men, however learned." And she went back to her *petits pois*.

I took only one meal a day, despite the doctor's advice. The business of masticating and digesting was, I thought, such a waste of the human element. I had even considered, once when I was younger, eating those herbs that Yogis eat, and do not need to eat anything again, they say, for six months. The performances of man seem always so much nobler when his belly sticks to his spine, than when like a Brahmin of Benares—or like Oncle Charles—rotundity protrudes from his vertical system. The syphon should be a necessary apparatus for such enormous combustion.

I always wondered what it would be like to die with a big belly. It must make you feel less certain of the other world. Gluttony must indeed, as Dante says, lead one to the Inferno.

> Cerbero, fiera crudela e diversa
> con tre gole canina—mente latra
> Sopra la gente che quivi e sommersa

li occhi ha vermigli, la verba unta e atra
e'l ventro largo . . .

Lezo was, in fact, growing in girth. The way he was constantly
adjusting his trousers round about the waist began to look somewhat indecent, to speak the truth. There is, of course, every
reason for a poor man to make the best use of the clothes he has,
but lechery must be bad for the human form. Madeleine heard
through a nun who came to collect subscriptions for an orphanage and never stopped talking, that the seamstress was going to
have a baby. "It will no doubt have the fat lips of the mother,
allez," said the *bonne soeur* as she took the twenty francs. "It's no
use being learned if one does not know right from wrong."

"Strange, this world!" exclaimed Madeleine one evening to me.
"You can never predict human behaviour, no more than you can
predict the virtue of a cat. When you were away," she continued,
in almost the first personal conversation we had had since my
return, "when you were away, and Catherine came, I was so
happy she was going to be here. We were almost brought up
together, and though she's just five years younger than me, we
have always been like twins; besides, she's a clever girl and was
only two classes behind me—I could almost say 'This is Catherine' from the smell of her clothes. And yet how little I knew
her." She became silent for a while, as though taking courage
before going any further.

"Doesn't matter," she went on, "I will tell you all about it.
Georges came every evening as usual, and we went out on walks.
Georges will always make a perfect husband, except perhaps for
his moments of dull humour. All Slavs have that self-absorbing
sorrow, something that we Europeans—I mean we of Western
Europe—will never know." Madeleine again stopped and looked
at me, as though asking if she should go on.

"Yes, I listen," I said.

"Well, what devotion little Catherine had for Georges—still has
for Georges. It was 'Georges, will you eat this?' 'You have a
bad cold, you must do that.' 'Georges, you mustn't stay out in
the cold too long—you yourself said that arm of yours gives you
pain night after night.' And what fine dishes she prepared—she
is a good cook—*cèpes provençals, les olives farcies aux anchois, la*

pissaladière, le chevreau roti et les aubergines sautées. God knows
where she'd learnt all these Southern dishes. I was glad of all this,
for as you know, I hate cooking. And Georges this and Georges
that, and '*Chéri,* you are beginning to cough,' and '*Mon chéri,
demain, on fera cette randonnée en Camargue,* etc., etc. . . .' In
fact you never saw such lovers in your life, I thought. I longed for
their happiness—for myself to be happy at their coming happiness.

"Then Catherine went to her Mass every morning before
dawn, and sometimes dragged poor Georges from his attic bed—
she wanted them to be the perfect Catholic couple. Georges
found all this a little *encombrant,* but I understood Catherine:
the more she made Georges a good Catholic—although you would
think you could never make a better one, yet, you could in a way
—the better her life was going to be. Georges seemed to look
forward to a long and fruitful life of work and children. He
would now become a Frenchman not only by conviction, but as it
were also by right. His children would become French citizens and
there would always be a war somewhere or other, and they would
fight for France as he had fought for her. Even so, whenever he
said '*Nous autres Français*' it always sounded a little ridiculous,
don't you think, and he knew it." She suddenly stopped and said,
"Are you listening? I don't know why I want to tell you all this."

"Go on," I said, nodding my head. "Of course I am listening."

"Lezo, too, came every evening as usual. His behavior towards me was impeccable: I have been too long among young
boys in the Resistance, not to know how to deal with this curious
type. Besides, after that one wildness on his part—and the fault
was mine, for I should have known men better—I can deal with
him as any simple toreador with a bull from our Camargue.
But . . ."

"But?"

". . . with Catherine it was a different matter. He knew just
how to play with her sentiments, as a cat plays with her kittens.
He was full of attention for her, but being a close friend of
Georges's, and knowing Spanish extravagance, we took no notice
of their hide-and-seek. They played together like children, often
in front of Georges, so that being the elder I sometimes had to call
them to order, and tell them not to make fools of themselves

before Georges. Georges I think somewhat loved this exhibition of childishness, feeling all his tiredness come back to him. He must have thought, well, let her play like this while she could—very soon, this middle-aged professor would sit on her like a grinding machine. There is about the Slavic mind something angelic, simple, exalted and whole. For Georges a man, or for that matter a woman, is either a saint or the very devil. There is no in-between, no nuances of temperament and character."

"After all, they are a young people," I said.

"From India all must look young. If the French are so immature for you, what about the Russians?"

"And so, Lezo . . . ?" I interrupted, trying to bring the conversation back on to the impersonal level.

"The hide-and-seek among the olives in moonlight does not always end in innocence." Madeleine stopped for a moment and then continued, as though in fact she was talking of herself unknowingly. "One day—I could not move about much by then, and Georges was busy with some committee meeting at the Collège—Lezo and Catherine were as usual in the garden, laughing and playing about. The fault was mine, probably. I said, 'Cathy, you've been doing so much work at home; washing, cooking, sweeping. Don't you think you should take a walk together—say, as far as the elephant?' 'You think so?' she asked, perhaps sincerely, for women may have a deeper defensive mechanism than men possess. I said, 'Of course, Cathy, and I'm sure Georges would be very unhappy if you didn't go for a walk just because he isn't here. In fact I am sure he would positively be angry with me for not saying this to you.' Well, they left innocently, throwing grass-stalks at each other, and behaving like children out on a Thursday with their *curé*. I waited and waited for a long time. They came back very late: it must have been past nine o'clock when they returned. Catherine immediately went to her room on some excuse, while Lezo spoke of a footpath they had taken in Val Sainte-Anne and how they got lost. They had to ask someone and they had to wander far, very far, before they came to a hut —and so on. Rama, I was alone, and what experience did I have to warn me of anything? I convinced myself they were speaking the truth—I saw how silent Catherine was, how utterly devoted and almost like an Indian wife with Georges. I should have been more careful. I am such a fool. A week later I found them in each other's arms.

"I happened to come home unexpectedly in the afternoon, as my lesson had been cancelled because of the death of a pupil. It must have been half past two. I entered quietly so as not to disturb Catherine, for she usually had a siesta, and what should I find but Catherine's hair undone, rouge all over her face; Lezo's cravat was pulled to one side, and his belt as usual opened up. 'Oh, it's so hot here,' he said, as soon as he saw me. 'I was passing by and thought I would say hullo to Catherine. She was having her siesta. I said, "Come and lie in the drawing room, and we will talk." She made me coffee, and it made me hotter still. You can be born in Spain, you can have an Andalusian mother, and yet sweat like a bull in summer when the sun shines—even in midwinter. I must have too much sun in me,' he finished. Catherine did not say anything. She kicked her legs and muttered, 'I think I need a wash. Oh, this house is so hot.' And she went to the bathroom.

"I did not know how to face Georges that evening. But women have their protective sensibility. Catherine understood what Georges was to her. Nothing was said by anybody. The kitten games of Catherine and Lezo came to a sudden stop. Even Georges remarked one day, 'Why have the children become so well-behaved of late?' 'Oh,' I answered, 'there is a time for play and there is a time for work.' Catherine was so grateful to me. One morning she left the broom with which she was cleaning the corridor and came and kissed me on the cheek. Fortunately I fell ill the week after, so the story was over. 'What a perfect bride she looks!' said Tante Zoubie at the wedding. They are so happy now, she says, it would make the angels weep. Happy, happy, happy. It's now Georges who plays with her. They will soon have a baby and they will both play with it. That is what the world is: só évam samsārah."

"Why did you tell me the story anyway, Madeleine?"

"I wanted the Brahmin, with the clever inversions of his cerebral system, to explain to me why these things happen."

"L'homme moyen sensuel," I started, using the banal expression to hide myself from any untoward discussion.

"I cannot understand how Catherine could even touch that

307

bulging red flesh. When Lezo touches me to say '*Bonjour*,' I have to go and wash myself."

"You must have glandular deficiency," I laughed.

"Thank you," she said, and kept very silent.

"The fact is," I started again, after a moment, feeling I should not give up the challenge so easily, "we're not biologically so far from the animal. Love is a game; even peacocks have to play to their mates, and the *gēējaga* bird has to make extraordinary involutions in the air to prove his manliness. A hero is the perfect mate for a tender-hearted woman. The sweeter the woman, the more she needs extravaganza. I know one of the most serious and lovely girls in Paris, who now always reads books on philosophy, and refuses parties and balls. She once fell in love with a racing driver, who ultimately killed himself, very nobly, in an accident. He had many lovers, and yet she was the girl he chose, she was so feminine, simple and virtuous. When he died many women publicly shed tears, but this girl continues to live in her widow's weeds, reading Bergson, Maritain or Indian philosophy. That is how I met her, *chez* Dr. Robin-Bessaignac. She was a very good student of his at the Sorbonne."

"That is not love," protested Madeleine.

"What is it then? To be a lovely girl and at twenty-six to mourn the loss of an automobile-hero husband so much—and read philosophy to understand what it is all about."

"I suppose it is."

"Anyway, Georges is thirty-two years old, but he's ill, he has only one arm, and though he may have been heroic and his lost arm was the gift of a young Russian to France, he feels very old. Catherine did not want a confessor or a father—she wanted a mate."

"And so?"

"And so, when it came so damn' near of its own accord, she took what she could. However fat his waist may be, Lezo looks like all Spaniards, a hero, a chevalier, with a buckler and a sword; not like a smelly old priest with one arm. That is why the Hindus are right: no man can love a woman for her personal self."

"Then how does one love?"

"For the Self within her, as Yagnyavalkya said to Maitreyi."

308

And I continued, "All women are perfect women, for they have the feminine principle in them, the *yin,* the *prakriti* . . ."

"And all men . . . ?"

". . . are perfect when they turn inward, and know that the ultimate is man's destiny. No man is bad that knows 'Lord, we be not of this kingdom.' "

"And when he does not?"

"He forfeits manhood, as Lezo has, and lives with a seamstress."

"And what about the womanhood of a seamstress?"

"For her, Lezo is a hero. She's probably a communist, and for her all enemies of France are heroes. She will call her child Vladimir Ilyitch, or Pasionaria if she be a girl, and Lezo will dandle the child with a revolutionary song."

"Yes, you are right; I think she is a communist—anyway she's red all right. The nun said so."

"You see how wise I am," I said.

"Yes, Rama Bhatta." And she laughed as before, with a simple, carefree laugh.

"Some show physical prowess—and with some, their ancestors, generation after generation, have so sharpened the febrility of their cerebral fins that thoughts go involuting and leaping like whales in the Pacific."

"And some virtuous female professor admires this involved masculinity, and marries one of them."

"Oh——"

"And then?"

"The whale goes back to the sea," I remarked, and became silent.

"They found a Pacific whale off the coast of Brittany just the other day," said Madeleine.

"And what happened?"

"It lay dead on the shore."

"I told you so. What did they do with it?"

"They placed it at the Esplanade des Invalides, so that all the Parisiens and Parisiennes could see it."

"I wonder what his Antarctic ancestors would have said. I hope it teaches the Pacific whales a good lesson."

We had dinner soon after that, and we went back to our work.

There was a clear, a pure space between us. Something had happened to Madeleine; I knew it, but I could not name it. In Aix who was there to ask? When I went to Paris maybe Tante Zoubie would tell me. Tante Zoubie had lately been struck with a mild attack of paralysis, but I would be bound to visit her in Rouen. Meanwhile life at the Villa Les Rochers moved on in a civilized, almost limpid way.

I rarely, if ever, went to Madeleine's room. Whenever I went I could smell incense. Often when I had something urgent to ask her—a signature for the postman, or the electricity bill to pay—Madeleine did not answer me at once; and she would take some time before coming out. Later I hardly ever knocked at her door when anyone came and I needed her help. I kept a small notebook in which I made entries, and she saw them and did what was to be done. I went to the library often, and I wrote down in the blue book the time I would return. She generally went on walks alone, and when she came back she had real peace on her face. I often heard her in the night, saying some mantra or doing *japā*, and I wondered where she had gathered so much ritualist wisdom. She spoke with greater and greater authority on Buddhism. Her insight into Buddhism was more psychic, I should say, than religious. She read Sri Aurobindo, too, and found a great deal to approve of in the philosophy of this great philosopher and saint. "This is what the world needs," she said once, "but I, I prefer mysteries and things ancient. I shall stick to my bonzes," she concluded, laughing.

ONE DAY MONTHS LATER I took courage and went into Madeleine's room. She had influenza, and was coughing a great deal. She seemed almost shocked that I should have come in—so much indeed that having opened the door and gone forward, I stopped halfway to her bed, apologetically.

"Oh, why did you have to worry?" she said. "This vestment of the eighteen aggregates must have fevers and suffer. It is in the very nature of things composite that they should disintegrate. Brother," she said, almost begging me, "do not worry over this sorry mass of flesh."

I could have wept. I stood by her. And wanted to rub camphor oil on her chest. She gently put my hand away, as though I were not *sātwic* enough. The room had an intimacy with her now which made me a cognate outsider. But Buddha, by whom an oil lamp shone, seemed pleased with her adorations. Lovely hyacinths floated before him in a clear copper plate of simple water. Her books were carefully arranged on one side, all covered with yellow and brick-red cloth. I guessed they were the *Tripathikas*.

"I can read Pali easily now," she explained, as I looked at her treasures. There was a small mat on the floor, an Indian mat made of wattle. I wondered where she had got that from. There was even an Indian temple bell with Nandi mount and all, a censer and a folding bookrack, such as only Brahmins have in their sanctuaries.

"You are more of a Brahmin than I." I remarked. She seemed to agree, for she said nothing. "Let me make you a hot-water bottle, *la sainte bouillotte*," I begged her.

"No," she said, "my body should find its own psychic heat:

311

'*santampayathi svam deha mapadatalamastaka,*' as your *Taitreya Aranyaka* says. Then why feed this foolish thing?" She seemed so uncomfortable to see me there that I was on the point of going. She stopped me and said, "Beloved," as though she spoke to someone not there. "Beloved, it's you who have brought me all this." I looked at the Buddha from the Musée Guimet and begged forgiveness, for so much betrayal. I could see her bed was made of boards, and her mattress was thin as my palm. She understood my thoughts. "You know, whatever I do, I do completely. I'm a *Sādhaka* now; my Buddhism is very serious. Be a good Brahmin, Rama," she said, as if it were a prayer.

I went back to my room a desperate little creature, my breath broken within me. So this was the Madeleine I had cherished and made! The next day some of my own "irregularities" disappeared, I reduced my food, bed and clothes to real needs. Madeleine was sore distressed with this transformation of me. "You are not of this country. Besides you must think of your lungs," she protested. But the next time I went to her room she did not treat me as though I were an outsider, an intruder to her sanctuary. I started taking her soup, her medicines. Sometimes when I knocked she would whisper, "Come in.' And I would see her with a rosary in her hands, which she never hid from me any more. I did not go back to my rosaries, but I started on my meditations more seriously. In fact my health improved a great deal with them.

Lezo came less and less. He must be having difficulty with his fat communist and her baby, I thought. Or was it that the atmosphere of Villa Les Rochers was becoming too oppressive for him?

"We are so happy—are we not, Rama?" asked Madeleine one day, when I was sitting in her room. Her health though was not too good the whole winter. Even so she would not allow me to make up a fire in her room: she said, "Why this luxury?" I begged her to accept it as corruption brought in by a Brahmin. She could still be persuaded by humour, and she accepted that I should prepare her fire every evening. "After all, the Brahmin's first job is to make fire," I said, quoting a Rig-Vedic text.

Now and again when I went to her room she would be seated by her narrow bed reading away at some text, her legs crossed in lotus posture. She would sometimes ask me for the meaning of a Pali word, but I did not know Pali at all, and my Sanscrit was not always a help.

Her face shone as if she had come nearer death, and there was a glow of truth between her eyes. She reduced her food to considered proportions—she took the right vegetables according to the eight seasons of the round long year. She observed every festival, decorated the house with lamps and mandalas, burning incense everywhere. She even observed an eclipse and fasted the night before; she bathed both as the eclipse started and as it ended, though it was in the early hours of the morning. On the whole she grew gentler, but when she did become angry at times she spat the five fires.

She decided, after reading a Tibetan text, that three hundred words a day were enough to cover all our daily needs, so once a week, on Saturdays, she took what she called the vow of moderate silence. "But just as I need a little more cloth here than in India, the French language may need a little more statistical elongation," I teased her. "In French you have more prepositions like *en, à, de,* etc. . . ." So I sought Lezo's help, and we added one hundred and fifty words to her restricted vocabulary.

I should say Madeleine was happy, if simplicity and truthfulness are the attributes of happiness. Her colleagues, so Lezo told me, almost revered her, and she was elected President of the College Syndicate. When the inspectors came, they always made the best report on her work. The headmistress laughed and said: "This is the sister-soul of Simone Weil. Simone Weil always regretted never having gone to India. So here is her hope fulfilled." Even I received a little of this veneration; they thought I was the noble cause of this transformation of Madeleine.

Sometimes Madeleine would start off in the early morning, with just a bare pair of sandals, on an expedition to her various sanctuaries. She had discovered one on the way to Sainte-Ophalie, that she called the "Black Madonna," which answered her all her questions. There was the poor woman whose husband was fighting in Indochina; she had had no letters from him for six or seven weeks. The "Black Madonna" gave Madeleine the answer. "He's all right, and he'll soon be back in Saigon from the front.

You'll receive a letter in ten days." Nine days passed and nothing had happened. On the tenth day there was nothing in the morning either. Madeleine went to visit the woman after morning classes, to verify that nothing had come, and to console if need be. She said, "The mistake must be mine, though I can still see it clear in my mind, as if on the classroom blackboard—ten days." That evening Madeleine and I went on a walk together and as we were returning, there was the young woman waiting for us at the door. She had her youngest, a child three years old, in her arms, and she beamed such gratitude. The letter had come, of course, and Jean felt fresh as a carp. She had bought us some oranges. Madeleine would not touch them. She said, "I am not a priest, I am a miserable woman. It is your prayers, Madame, that have helped; yours and not mine." We took the woman in and gave her coffee, for the day was very cold.

There were days when Madeleine took her haversack and left a note for me to say she had gone away to the mountains—and Provence is full of mountains and sanctuaries. She would return late at night, having trudged for kilometres on end. On such expeditions she found grottoes and forgotten sanctuaries, and she was sure that most of the Virgins were old Roman gods and goddesses. Often she tried to scratch some plinth to discover the name of Mithras, Jupiter or Mercury, but I do not think she ever had luck in that direction. She laid flowers at their feet and probably sang a Buddhist hymn. For her, whatever was not Catholic was sacred and true. She said it was now sufficiently proven that the Druids were Buddhist, so all these sanctuaries were certainly of Buddhist origin. Her meditations gave her remarkable indications. She took me sometimes on her "spiritual hikes," as I called them. "If we go this way, that is, in the direction in which this grass-head has turned on itself and fallen," she once said, "and we come to the top of that hill, we may find an old ruined windmill; I can see it as clearly as a cat in the night. We must turn to the left then, and go twenty yards and dig. We may find an ancient stone. I am sure it was a sanctuary." We went up the hill—it was near Saint-Ouen—and the windmill was there; we dug twenty yards away and found nothing. Disappointed, she searched all about the place, as mountaineers do, when they ponder on the direction of the avalanche. She drew deep breaths to find her *chemin de cristal,* and said, "Now I know—it must be at the fountain here." When we washed the stone and dug a little, true, there was a ruin of some sort. I could not say whether it was Roman, Greek or Christian. It was a small circular slab, like marble, and there had certainly been some characters on it at one time, but I could not read them, nor could Madeleine.

She started putting flowers into this fountain. "I am sure it can heal," she said. "Let us try it at Madame Fellandier's: when her son had a stroke, you know, I gave her a cloth, which I had held in my hand for eight days during my meditations. The child sat up for the first time for months, Madame Fellandier told me." This must have been a fact, for Madeleine introduced me to her. The child was up and looked at us with much affection. We had taken him almonds—salted almonds—and his mother opened the packet eagerly and gave us to eat, two to Madeleine and one for me.

"Certainly we'll give your Fellandier a dip in your Roman fountain," I laughed. "Why not, after all?"

No, I could not disbelieve in Madeleine's powers, but she felt she owed them to me. "I was an atheist," she said, "with a horror of the Church. You it was, Rama, with your Brahminism, that gave me the eyes to see."

"To see Buddhism," I protested, and laughed again.

"Look how beautiful the evening is," she said, sitting down on the grass. "How far from the elephant and the bull, Rama! You have been a wonderful friend to me. Promise to be happy."

"I promise," I replied. I must have looked such a fool.

Sometimes she saw miracles as well. The flowers began to speak to her, the marguerites, the daisies, and the horsetails. One day, coming down the hill from one of her expeditions to the Black Madonna, she begged, oh, ever so tenderly, that a little pansy she had found lying crushed on the road would not suffer.

"Some brute," she muttered; "there are such ignoramuses all over the world. They are so cruel that they pluck innocent creatures like these," she said, caressing the flower under the moonlight, "and then throw them down and walk away, as if the world were made solely for man. What if someone did the same with their children, the young ones? And this is the Europe," she continued, sitting on the garden bench, "that has known the horrors of two wars, and Hitler's incineration camps. Lord, Lord!" With tears she dug a small hole, and laid the stem and the two leaves and the blue, open-eyed pansy on the earth. "Rama," she begged, "bring me some water." I brought a jugful of water from the kitchen. "Rama, touch this, please. You have holy hands."

"Holy indeed!" I burst out laughing. "Holy with Brahminic cruelty."

"But it is Brahminic. I know you have power."

"Power or no power, Little Madeleine, give it to me then," I said, and touched the plant, and gave it back to her dispiritedly.

She planted it with many *Hūm-Hūm-s*, *Om-Hrim-s*, and *Mani-padme-Hūm-s*. She laid it first on her frock, and straightened the stem and leaf; then, closing her eyes, she pushed the little broken stalk gently and carefully into the earth. "Today is the ninth day of the moon of Srāvan," she said, "and it is an auspicious day."

I gave water to the pansy. We called it the Buddha's plant, and the last thought of Madeleine before going to bed was to go into the garden and see if the Buddha's plant still flowered under the moon. The pansy looked happy. Indeed, who would not be happy under the Mediterranean moon; and with such loving care about one. In the morning Madeleine woke, and there he was, the Buddha's plant, his face smiling under the magnificence of the sun.

"Oh, be good!" prayed Madeleine, like a child, and gave him water again. We made a small canal round him, and as often as possible we gave him water. Madeleine then went into her room, and brought the sacral water of the Buddha. "This is the best Ganges water," she proclaimed. The pansy was bright, and we were happy with it. Even I grew attached to the pansy. You get attached to anything you create. You create the world, and so you get attached to the world.

"Madeleine," I said, "look, it stays on!"

"Of course it does. And why not? If men recover from wounds in a hospital, why not a plant, a tree?"

"You've heard of Jagdish Chandra Bose and his experiments on weeping trees, have you?" I asked.

316

"Of course. But you don't need an electromagnetic instrument to know plants suffer. Even so, it needed an Indian to prove that plants do suffer."

"And a Bengali," I said.

"What's that now?"

"The Bengalis are a sweet, musical, poetical, large-hearted, sunshine, moonshine people."

"All that sounds very nice," she said.

"And for them the world is all Brindavan—miraculous with peacocks, rivers, lotuses, and dancing men and women with garlands, and the lilting finery of weeping trees."

"And so?"

"And so Santinektan and Tagore and all that *gnya-gnyanerie*. The world has to be made beautiful. They're like the Italians: the world has to be made paradisiac."

"And you, the Southerners?"

"Our home is in Shiva's crematorium grounds. We dance away our momentary deaths—and there is no time for Paradise. Besides, Paradise," I added, "needs space and time."

"In space and time the pansy blooms," she said, and closed the subject.

We gave water to the plant. It flourished with a vigour which made us admire life itself. The leaves stood up, and shot up more leaves. Madeleine's altar table had now a special vessel: a silver tumbler I had had since my *upanayanam* ceremony, which I brought to Europe for remembrance and for reverence of Grandfather Ramanna. Eventually I gave the tumbler as a family present from Hariharapura to Madeleine. This Grandfather Ramanna's silver tumbler gave water to the pansy—and the pansy seemed almost to remember the Himavathy and the Mysore mountains; and the pansy put forth more and more flowers, flowers large as nenuphars. We called in the gardener from Villa Belmont, and he exclaimed, *"Ah, c'est bien étrange, Madame, et encore une pensée!"* And Madeleine said, "Rama, if you stand here in the middle of the night, you will hear a bell, I promise you—just a tingle-tingle bell." And believe me, I felt things turn round me, shapes, eyes, *presences*; sometimes I would turn round and try to see them, but they always seemed to be where I could not see them. They were there; I have no doubt about it whatsoever.

Then Madeleine started looking for wounded caterpillars. "Oh," she said, "how the motorcars crush these slow centipedes. They must go from tree to tree—it is in the very nature of creatures centipedic that they crawl like this. They must go from pine to pine. If man has built a road and cut furiously through the hills, and has invented fast-moving vehicles of battery and combustion, that's no reason why these poor animals should suffer. Poor, poor creatures!" she would say, and lift these hairy, itching things on her lap and arm, and take them across the road and leave them on a pine tree. In fact, some days when she had no class, she would go up the Luberon highway and sit by one of the bedraggled pines, which seemed to specialize in caterpillars.

"The caterpillars eat the tree, so you must kill the caterpillars," I teased Madeleine.

"Oh, no, we should save both." And so she put a large stone under one of the trees and would sit for hours in the *dorje* posture saying her mantras, or would take a book—some Pali book, preferably—and read. She made friends thus with the schoolchildren, who went up there every Thursday; but once when they climbed a tree to see a nest of starlings, how she howled, did Madeleine, and told the *curé* to look after all the children of God, not merely those of man. She convinced the children with Saint Francis of Assisi.

There is no doubt Madeleine developed powers—extraordinary powers. She had by now procured through Lezo, somehow, a Tibetan thighbone Kangling, and she tied bells to it, little bells that also came from Tibet no doubt; she started waving it and sounding it and muttering prayers to herself, chanting *"Hūm— Hūm—Phat."* She started looking fixedly at the sun, and began meditations on the infinity of space. "Do not think of the past. Do not think of the future," she would repeat Nagarjuna's dictum, "and keep your mind in its cool state."

She meditated too, on a red ball, one of those balls you can buy at any big store for children to play with—and then suddenly she would meditate on a stick: the texts said to. So she broke a stick from the holy pine—the one with caterpillars—and she polished it and washed it and gave it an ochre colour, and placing it in the southwest corner of her room she started saying her *japās*. It gave a green and liquid fixity to her look; she smiled with gentleness and her anger seemed to grow less and less. Then, when she had fasted for new moon or eclipse, she would go and throw her sanctified water—always in Grandfather Ramanna's silver tumbler—to the holy pine tree. And the pine tree put forth new green eager needles.

The Buddha, in one of his previous incarnations, had allowed himself to be eaten by a tiger; like the Bodhisat the pine tree, I told Madeleine. This satisfied her, so we called it the Bodhisat Pine, and the caterpillars never seemed happier. Birds, especially ravens, swallows and flamingoes, found the tree very interesting; first for the caterpillars, and because Madeleine fed them with peanuts, rice and wheat. When I told her about the Jains, how they feed ants with sugar, she would secretly take bits of sugar and feed ants also under the tree. When I came home from the library and could not at first find Madeleine, I was sure to see her on her *vajrasana*—for so I called it, "the seat of diamond"—reading away at her book. Sometimes she would look down the hollow valley to Mont Sainte-Victoire; you could see she felt the world was true.

But now and again, she would feel great despair—one saw it in the colour of her eyes. Sometimes they grew quite yellow and she became distant and almost inimical. She seemed to hate everything, food, room, books and all, and she would say, "Oh, Rama, be patient with me; it's only the female nature that must be making monthly demands." Her horoscope was pretty irregular about these events, and I suspected that human biology might have strange variations according to metapsychical convictions. Maybe, and why not?

Her yogic *asanas* helped her; she bought a book on Yoga by a Swami Paramananda, and she was so competent in her locust pose or the swan posture. She also took the Buddhist vow of lying on her right side—the lion position—and said she slept splendidly, needing only five hours of sleep now. Her classes became brilliant, so some of her pupils told me, and the headmistress looked up to her for advice. Colleagues came to ask help with regard to family matters, and very humbly she told them whatever came to her in her morning meditations. Sometimes when the subject was very serious, such as marriage or financial difficulties, Madeleine made many mandalas and sat amongst them. She woke up as in India at three o'clock in the morning, the *brahmakāla*—and sat in meditation till eight o'clock.

Now, one day the holy pansy died—"for like all living things of the eighteen aggregates he had to die," said Madeleine—and he was given a proper funeral. We washed him and put him on a grass bed—curiously enough he had no roots at all, we discovered, after almost seventeen days of life—and cremated him with "*AUM-AUM-AUM — TAM-TAM-TAM — HRI-HRI-HRI — HA-HA-HA*." We buried his ashes under the Bodhisat tree.

The "Black Madonna" appeared to Madeleine after some of her fasts. The divinity gave specific instructions as to medicines, good days and bad days, right people and evil people; and now Madeleine prayed to her, whenever I had fever. "Rama," she said, "you must, must be cured." One day, all of a sudden, she declared: "I'm going on a forty-one-day fast—on Buddha Avalokiteshwara. I had a vision and I am sure I can cure you." And so she started on her fasts and prayers—commencing at dawn, on the seventh day of the month of Ashwīja, when the dew was clear as eyes under the late moon.

Those forty-one days were very moving and important. I could hear Madeleine wake up (she had bought herself a new alarm clock) at two, have her bath, chanting verses in her peculiar round Charentaise accent, and make aspersions to the eight directions of the house, calling on each god and naming his attributes. Then I could hear her stay long, very long, near my door; after which she would suddenly go back to her room, and I could hear her mantras rise slowly, deeply, as though they needed to make themselves familiar with the world, with the night; and then they came out more and more quickly, more and more articulated and grave, till by four in the morning the whole house would be one unanimous sound, vibrant through walls and roof to the kitchen below. One felt that the trees stood stiff, the birds slept awake; one felt that the roads rose up and lifted themselves to the skies, that the cattle looked into sheer space, and the whole of the valley of Aix and the mountains beyond, with those perched lingering lights on the top, were but one single thought, one single experience. And then after a caesura of interrupted silence, the words came quicker and gentler, the mantras became more and more melodious, and little by little the flowers opened to the morning, the Mediterranean sang out its shores, birds spoke, children rose and cried; and man walked back to his journeying work with the spirit of a child, of a happy father, of a new incarnation on a new earth. The morning train could shout as it liked, or the tramcar scream as it turned in the Place Mirabeau; the world was being transmuted—something pink and golden would rise out of the Fire-of-Lotus heart, and Rama would be made whole again.

"Ah, on dirait que toutes les maisons sentent les fêtes," said Madame Jeanne, when she came to work. She knew nothing of Madeleine's *sadhana*. But, I ask you, need one be told when the gods are about, and in Provence?

And that the gods were about, who could deny? One heard strange musical sounds—more like drum-beats than melodious wind instruments—and they seemed to play not all the notes but just three or four, *do, re, fa, ti,* or just *do, re, ti,* as if we had grown subtler, etheric. We played more with each other, Madeleine and I, and sometimes—you must forgive and believe me when I say it—I felt the presence of others playing with us. The red ball went here, went there; the ball stood as if transfixed by someone—the earth moved, one could think, but not the ball: space moved, and not time. Then sound itself became firm and stood on the spot and gyrated; and colours came out, red and green such as parrots have, or blue like the Himalayan hills, and you saw tongues of flame leaping out in the four directions. I could sometimes hear in the heat of the southern sun the Aix tramcars screech away—and yet these flames leapt, they made curves in green and red, turned on themselves and went straight into the ceiling.

Madeleine looked at me and she was so happy. "There, there!" she said. "Listen, that's the music."

The drum-beat indeed was powerful, and as each sound ended another more powerful one rose as if creating mountains, rivers, seas, roads, man. I felt the nervous spiral uncoil from the spine-end, and stood aghast. "Madeleine!" I cried. But she sat on the floor, with her eyes nobly closed. And I went back to the familiarity of my room. Nothing had happened to my room of course, all things seemed in their place; but everything was dusted, laved and cleared. I was afraid.

Madeleine knew no fear. "I am not only Charentaise, I am Saintongeoise," she said, "and we from the Atlantic wilds have no fear."

But her hair grew curly, her skin somewhat parched, and she began to give out odours that seemed, to speak civilizedly, not too pleasant. I felt the smell of rotten flowers, the smell of the carcasses of birds; I felt foul winds, odour of burnt nails and hair and of damp hides. And in the evenings when we walked back home, sometimes I could hear voices, whispers, *pham-phat* sounds. Once I saw a man walking in front of me; he was just like a skeleton—he looked like Mahatma Gandhi, but taller, much taller, and bent, and walking quickly, feverishly, in front of me. Madeleine was pleased with this apparition—it was according to the texts. "On the twenty-second day, you will see the apparition of a man walking in front of you," they said. "Do not be afraid: it is the body in its grossest form." True it was, for Madeleine showed me the text—and I was astonished. Yes, it was, it was true.

The birds became more familiar with us. Some of the sparrows came and sat on Madeleine's shoulders as she walked and fed them. She once sat on a stone and lost consciousness thinking on some *japā*. I waited patiently by her till the moon rose.

"I was in another world, Rama, and what a beautiful world it was. Rama, why must one come back to this?"

"This one or the other, Madeleine, they're both worlds," I remarked, which did not take the discussion any further.

Spirits came, strange, bewildering in their tongues, sounds, sizes and specialities—some to wash and whirl, others to sound nostril and dance; some making noises like the turning of a quern, and speaking as if their voices came from hollows of the bone; some talked in French, others in Hindi or Tibetan, but they all seemed destitute, utterly helpless. I did not see them much, for I just did not care, but could feel them behind doorways, or between the sink and fireplace in the kitchen; they sat on the dustbins, they sounded from trees; they chattered, they talked, they became flame and walked in front of you; small, short creatures, they begged you to have desires, then they showed the red or the pink of your desires—they spoke to Madeleine and to me, but with me they seemed at once arrogant and ashamed. Sometimes I would say to them, "Get out!" If they did not understand English or French I shouted to them in Sanscrit or Kanarese, and these often seemed to have greater efficacy. They leapt like monkeys. And sometimes when Madeleine talked to them in her room, I just wanted to howl, to weep.

But the twenty-ninth day soon came nearer, and the house which was hot as fever began to grow cooler; gentler sounds came, tenderer, and the colours of the spirits became more refined —you saw more mauves and greens, and you often thought them a wisp of cloud or petal of sky-flower. The music had more elevated notes, and the spirits seemed to waft unbelievable perfumes, like those of roses or lotuses. You heard the sound of mountain birds, and they seemed more familiar to you, they came beside you, not in front of you, and had gracious forms. They looked like deer or small, sleek horses. Some floated and flew, like swans musical. Madeleine's delight was deep and grave. She just felt the world was spread out before her, and there was no thought or desire she could not ask that the gods would not accomplish. They came less frequently, however, than the other spirits, but the world changed as from monsoon to the Dussera festival. You could see elephants in procession, the Sword of Kings, and the Lotus of the Throne; and maybe soon, very soon, the Buddha seated on the Jewel of the Nine Rays.

Joy, if I had ever truly seen on Madeleine's face, I saw it then. She marked thirty-one, thirty-two, thirty-three days on her door, as our milk-women do with cow dung on the walls, to show how much milk we have taken. Virtue was flowing back into the world. The "pale-gold light" of the subtle worlds filled the valley of Aix; the earth floated on its own light. With the thirty-sixth day Madeleine looked as if she could last no longer. Her eyes were deep set and she could not eat much. Whatever she ate she threw out, and for a day or two she just drank Vichy water. I added a little camphor and honey to it, quoting the texts to make it taste sweet and wholesome. I gave her honey and hot water constantly. When the thirty-eighth day came, she was unable to walk about. But she smelt like a thousand-petalled jasmine, or like the blue lotus. I liked sitting beside her and feeling the sweet breath of her presence. She looked a saint: I worshipped her.

I gave her the *sainte bouillotte,* but now this too she discarded. It was too artificial, she said. So I strewed some lilies and marguerites on her bed.

"Oh this, this is perfect," she said, "but not lilies, please; they remind me of First Communion." And she continued with her *"OM DHIM—OM GIH—OM JRIH."* She slept very well indeed.

On the fortieth day she would not take the honey and water.

"Then take lemon and water, if you will," I pleaded. "Even Mahatma Gandhi took lemon and water."

"Let me follow my own gods."

I understood and went back to the kitchen.

On the forty-first day she woke up an hour earlier—that is, about one o'clock—and sat in austere meditation till six. I heard no sounds or noises any more. I felt a great, true, compassionate presence in the house. I felt lighter, my breathing improved. At six, while I was in my bath, I heard a strong, singing, super-terrestrial gong go, a long chanting, waving, unsilencing, universal sound. "The Palace of Dhamma is hung round with two networks of bells," say the *Mahasuddasana Suthanata.* The earth became earth, trees became trees, the sound of tramways became normal; the speech of men became crude and simple, the milk of Monsieur Béguin was actual, we paid our electric bills, and the newspapers came in; Madame Jeanne had a headache and smelt bad; when I went down to Aix, I smelt the acridity of tobacco and dust in the air.

That evening Madeleine gave me a bitter orange to rub on my chest, first one, then a second one and then a third. For twenty-one days I was to rub thus, and my fevers and evil breath would be taken away from me. For Madeleine had had a vision between eleven o'clock on the fortieth day and then on the forty-first, it was made clear to her: an Arab doctor with beard and authority appeared to her in her dream. "Twenty-one days and bitter oranges on the chest," he said.

I did not believe it, of course. As days passed, nothing happened. I only saw the birds were even more familiar with Madeleine: sparrows came to eat from her hands, owls flopped near her windows, and she took them back and laid them on some precise tree.

But the tree, it is true—the Bodhisat Pine—put on new shoots, and it was unbelievable. Madeleine gave water to Madame Jeanne for her second child, which had very bad asthma. The asthma stopped; Madame Jeanne herself assured us of this.

Madeleine made me visit the Black Madonna.

"She must once have been a Buddhist Tara, a Druidic Goddess. I now know her name—and even her epoch. Oh, Rama, how wonderful it is to live in the world!" she said, as we sat before the chapel of the Black Madonna.

The Black Madonna, I might say, looked Byzantine, with her long nose, refined hands and dark, slant, Oriental eyes. Looking at the quivering blue of the Alpilles and the Durance flowing white at our feet, I was reminded of *Uttara Rama Charita* and chanted out to Madeleine:

> *Etat tad eva hi vanaṃ punar adya dṛṣṭaṃ*
> *yasminn abhūma ciram eva purā vasantaḥ*
> *āranyakāç ca gṛhiṇaç ca ratāḥ svadharme*
> *saṃsarikeṣu ca sukheṣu vayaṃ rasajñāḥ.*
> *Ete ta eva girayo viruvanmayūrās*
> *tāny eva mattahariṇāni vanasthalāni*
> *āmanjuvanjulalatāni ca tāny amūni*
> *nirandhranīlaniculāni sarittaṭāni.*
> *Meghamāleva yaç cāyam arād api vibhāvyate*
> *giriḥ Prasravaṇaḥ so 'yaṃ yatra Godāvari nadī.*

"What does it mean?"

"*Kim idam āpatitam adya Rāmasya?*" I said, as if I were talking to Madeleine in Sanscrit.

"Which means . . . ?"

"What's happened to Rama?" I answered, and continued,

> *Cirā vegārambhī prasṛta iva tīvro viṣarasaḥ*
> *kutaç cit saṃvegāt pracala iva çalyasya çakalaḥ*
> *vraṇo rūḍhagranthiḥ sphuṭita iva hṛnmarmani punar*
> *ghanībhūtaḥ çoko vikalayati māṃ nūtana iva.*

Madeleine still sat on the slab between the chapel and the road. Now and again a pine-cob fell on the chapel roof, and rolled noisily into the gutter below. The day was very warm for a mountain afternoon in February and singing like the honey bee. I continued to recite Bhavabhūti, as if I were explaining something to Madeleine.

> 'ekaḥ saṃprati nāçitapriyatamas tām adya Rāmaḥ kathaṃ
> pāpaḥ Pañcavaṭīṃ vilokayatu vā gacchatv asaṃbhāvya vā.*

And now Madeleine understood. Even the dead and buried legionaries of Marius, those severe civilized men who fought against the Teutons and conquered Gaul, whose bones must be lying somewhere all about us, they too must have keyed their ears to this grave speech and understood.

"Sapin and sap come from the Sanscrit word *sapa*," I said, as though it were the definition of Truth. The dictionary is often the bible of the inarticulate. Etymology and grammar, I thought, help in the mechanisms of matrimony.

* These are the Sanscrit verses Rama chanted to Madeleine on that February afternoon:

> This, then, is the forest—I see it now . . .
> Both as hermits and householders here have we lived
> For a long, long while, performing our sacred acts
> And knowing the juices of the joys of existence.
>
> This, then, the mountain where the peacocks cry
> And here the valleys with antelope wooded;
> There, with bamboos softly murmuring
> In dark blue tufts, the banks of rivers.
>
> There, where soars Mount Prasravana
> Like a garland of cloud, flows the river Godaveri . . .
>
> Like the burning spread of a rooted poison—
> Like splinters raked by a force unknown—
> Like a healed wound's touch on a tender heart—
> Intense, my pain enfeebles me,
> As if it sprang but yesterday.
>
> Pañcavaṭi, where with her I have spent so long
> As if it were my own true home;
> Pañcavaṭi, the immediate, object of our constant talk.
> But now alone is Rama, and faded his dearest things,
> Heartless would it be not to linger long looking,
> Or leave without deep salutation
>   To Pañcavaṭi.

THOSE WINTER DAYS in Aix seem to have avowed such simple and deep understanding between Madeleine and myself that I can only think of them as having had a lot of warm and powdery sunshine, which bathed the olives to the spread roots and gave the cypresses a sense of singleness, as though they represented a direction, a formula, a principle.

Life outside was full of charm. Monsieur Béguin brought his goats up the path, and he left them to graze while he lay under the olives reading the *Petit Provençal*. Two goats looked up at me now and again with a feeling of kinship and knowingness, and big bellies became flat and the young ones came to play, tottering under the intoxication of being born. I had heard in India that goat's milk was good for weak lungs, so every afternoon I walked out into the fields, and Monsieur Béguin would produce a bottle of the strong-smelling viscous liquid; sometimes he milked the goat called "Gazella" in front of me. How kind and maternal the milk was! Whether it did me good or not I cannot say, but my health never gave me much cause for anxiety.

Dr. Séraphin at the hospital laughed and confirmed me as the perfect specimen of a good patient. "If I asked him to drink three spoonfuls of cod-liver oil, you could be sure he would run down to ask me if I meant the big English coffee-spoon or our small coffee-spoon; in fact he would produce the spoons from his pocket to make sure my instructions were strictly followed. In his country it must be so easy to be a doctor. It must all come from their age-old civilization. Not like the cattle we have to deal with here . . ."

Whether I was a good patient or not, I took my illness very seriously. I did not want to be a problem to Madeleine. We were already enough of a problem to one another.

Madeleine's own illnesses were, if one may say so, somewhat more picturesque. She came back one day with a thorn in her heel, and bandaged the whole thing up so savagely that after a few days it began to smell. "Let the wretched thing suffer," she said; but even so she moaned, quietly, rhythmically, as if she were repeating a mantra. Then I knocked at her door, went down to the kitchen for some hot water and cleaned her wound with boric acid. She had become so shy of exposing any part of her body, that even getting her to stretch out her leg was difficult. She covered the whole of her leg and let me just touch her foot. And when she had a stomach-ache—for she ate so little that her stomach began to give her trouble—she would not let me massage her either. She grew more and more like a young girl and covered up her chest, as though it were a sin to show any part of her body but her two hands and her big, kind face.

"Poor child," she said to me one day, "I make you live the life of an ascetic. You must one day find the right Hindu wife." I did not seem so eager for a wife.

"Madeleine, you have a swollen throat. You must allow me to put some hot towels on it."

"Oh, it's nothing. You know I have had a bad throat since I was a child of three. They say that Mother thought I would have goitre some day. But nothing so serious will ever happen to me. I am not even good enough for disease."

Her food was now measured with the palm of her hand in Indian style. "Three times a day and three handfuls a day," so the Buddhist text said. And whether it was this starvation or the working of her inner spirit, she looked so transparent, elevated.

"When you were in India," she said one day, "I was afraid I would die of those complications. I was frightened they would bury me at the Cimetière Saint-Médard. So on coming here I made a will, and I want you to know—as Catherine knows too—that I'd like to be cremated. You know how complicated French law is on the subject. I wish it would happen, though, when you are still here. Rama, you need not apply to the Préfet des Bouches-du-Rhône any more."

"Oh, don't say such inauspicious things, Madeleine. You know I am more ill than you are."

"That is why I say it. I have prayed night after night, as you said Emperor Baber prayed for his son Humayan, that I be taken away in your place. You are young, you are a man, you have yet to live. When I knew you first you were such a sprightly, vivacious being. It is I who brought all this on you. I am only a log of flesh, and anyone can take my place. But you, you are the head of the family."

"Madeleine! Must you torture me like this?"

"Well then, I shall be silent." She was tucked under her ochre-coloured sheets, and her brown rosary just showed against her pale green-eyed face. The moment had come, I felt, to ask the question that had been lying between us. I made bold and wanted to ask. But she divined my question, I think, and said:

"What is it separated us, Rama?"

"India."

"India? But I am a Buddhist."

"That is why Buddhism left India. India is *impitoyable*."

"But one can become a Buddhist?"

"Yes, and a Christian and a Muslim as well."

"Then?"

"One can never be converted to Hinduism."

"You mean one can only be born a Brahmin?"

"That is—an Indian," I added, as an explanation of India.

"Your India, then, Rama, is in time and space?"

"No. It is contiguous with time and space, but is anywhere, everywhere."

"I don't understand."

"It stands, as it were, vertical to space and time, and is present at all points."

"This is too mystical even for me."

"Would you understand if I were to say, 'Love is not a feeling; it is, you might say, a stateless state, the whole condition of one-self'?"

"I don't. But suppose I did?"

"Can you understand that all things merge, all thoughts and perceptions, in knowledge? It is in knowledge that you know a thing, not in seeing or hearing."

"Yes."

"That is India. *Jnanam* is India."

"But that is the place of the Guru—of Buddha?"

"Well, for me India is the Guru of the world, or She is not India. The Sages have no history, no biography—who knows anything about a Yagnyavalkya or a Bharadavja? Nobody. But some petty King of Bundelkhand has a panegyric addressed to him, and even this is somewhat impersonal. We know more of King Harsha than we do of Sankara. India has, I always repeat, no history. To integrate India into history—is like trying to marry Madeleine. It may be sincere, but it is not history. History, if anything, is the acceptance of human sincerity. But Truth transcends sincerity; Truth is *in* sincerity and *in* insincerity—beyond both. And *that* again is India."

She was silent for a very long time. She was playing with her beads, thoughtfully.

"We are a nation of gamblers," I said.

"Of gamblers? How so?" she asked abruptly, sitting up.

" 'Play not with dice but cultivate thy cornfield,' you know, is a famous Rig-Vedic hymn."

"Oh."

"You remember Dharmaraja sold his kingdom—nay, even his wife—gambling? Even so did Harishchandra give away his kingdom for the Truth. Sri Rama went into exile because his gamble-minded father promised anything she wanted to his young wife, and his young wife gambled for the kingdom of her own son. Recently Mahatma Gandhi said to the British—in the middle of the war, mind you, when the Japanese were at our door—'Clear out and leave India to anarchy. We will know what to do with ourselves.' "

"A strange theory. But like many of your dear theories it sits comfortably on the head of history." After a moment she asked, "From where, though, does this spirit come? You are such a serious people."

"We are so serious, deadly serious, about everything, that we are perhaps the only nation that throughout history has questioned the existence of the world—of the object."

"That may be true. True also that the Chinese were very realistic."

"There can be only two attitudes to life. Either you believe the world exists and so—you. Or you believe that you exist—and so the world. There is no compromise possible. And the history of philosophy—remember that in the eighteenth century even scientists were called '*les philosophes*'—is nothing but a search for a clue to this problem: 'If I am real, then the world is me.' It also means you are not what you think and feel you are, that is, a person. But if the world is real, then you are real in terms of objects, and that is a tenable proposition. The first is the Vedantin's position—the second is the Marxist's—and they are irreconcilable."

"And in between the two?"

"And in between are the many poetic systems: monism, tempered monism, non-dualistic modified dualism, God and Paradise, Islam, etc., etc. . . ."

"Where does Buddhism come into your system, then?"

"The supreme religion of a poet," and I laughed, so loudly that I could have been heard from the cypress or from Monsieur Béguin's meadow.

"I don't grasp what you mean."

"You do," I said, still laughing. "But you do not want to accept it. To have compassion, remember, presupposes the existence of the world. You must have compassion towards some suffering *thing*, so suffering exists and compassion as well."

"But how is Buddhism so poetic?"

"First, we know more about the beautiful and moving life of the Buddha than of any other spiritual figure in India. What do we know of Krishna, let us say? Yet he has more influence in India today than any other figure. Second, the *Jatakas* are among the most poetical stories of mankind. Take the *Sibi Jataka*, for example, and compare it to the *Mahabharatha*. How moving and personal the *Jatakas* seem to the impersonal figure of, say, a Bhisma, a Karna, a Dharmaraja. India believes—and it is from this belief that have arisen not only our philosophies, but our temples, theatres and castles; our grammar, poetics and mathematics; our knowledge of jewellery; even the science of erotics and that fine system of medicine the *Ayurveda*—India believes that to prove the world as being real or unreal is being really objective.

331

To be objective to it is to have a scientific outlook. That is why Lowes Dickinson said we were more like modern scientists than the mystical people we were supposed to be."

"What happens to Buddhism, then?"

"It tries to take more and more of Vedanta into it, so that the Buddha becomes a Hindu *avatara*, and the Mahayana almost a Vedantic system—but a negative one, that is all. What is Indian remains."

"And what is not Indian . . . ?"

" . . . is exported for others' benefit, even unto Aix," I said, and laughed till she laughed too. "And so Lezo can study Pali texts, surrounded by his communist comrade and his little Buddhist baby. You know the baby is called Ananda?"

"You are too clever for me," said Madeleine.

"Brahmins are like race horses: they are either good at their job, or they're sent to the vet to be shot. They are never sent to the common butchery; they could not be. Biology and eugenics are very interesting—you can grow almost anything out of anything. In Russia they will soon grow horses on pear trees, and babies from hyacinths."

"Now, now, don't get childish. One more question, and then Monsieur le Professeur can retire to his room."

"The historian is here to answer questions."

"Then my question is, what was Christ?"

"A poet like the Buddha, and with the great Indian to be banished from the perfect state of Plato. The new civilization has to be a technocratic one. It will have to banish the personal, the romantic, the poetic from life. The true poet sees poetry as poet, and the world as 'I.' "

"Then there is no world?"

"The perfect civilization, then, is where the world is not, but where there is nothing but the 'I.' It is like the perfect number, which is always a manifestation of 1. 1. 1. The Buddhists say the world, the perception is *real*, 'Sarvam-Kshanikam,' that everything is minutous the moment we see it. The Vedantin says the perception is real, yes; but that reality is 'my Self.' And that difference is big enough to drive the Buddhism of Gautama outside our frontiers."

"But what happens when it comes in?"

"It will be treated as a separate caste, and maybe given a compassionate bath, when the wound is painful, at the feet. Love, not compassion, is impersonal."

"Then leave me to my poetic world."

"Yes, I was thinking only yesterday: the miraculous itself is but the dual made manifest, albeit magnanimously. The miracle proves the power it proves."

"I don't understand," she said.

"Formerly, Madeleine, you read Paul Valéry and I read Rainer Maria Rilke. And now you read Rilke—"

"And do you now read Valéry?"

"Yes, I read him a lot in India. Valéry is on the edge of Vedanta. Rilke's angels bore me. Like Tagore's Ganges they are *ennuyeux*. There can never be a Paradise."

"How so?" she asked, spacing herself with a long silence.

"The world is either unreal or real—the serpent or the rope. There is no in-between-the-two—and all that's in-between is poetry, is sainthood. You might go on saying all the time, 'No, no, it's the rope,' and stand in the serpent. And looking at the rope from the serpent is to see paradises, saints, *avataras*, gods, heroes, universes. For wheresoever you go, you see only with the serpent's eyes. Whether you call it duality or modified duality, you invent a belvedere to heaven, you look at the rope from the posture of the serpent, you feel you are the serpent—you are—the rope is. But in true fact, with whatever eyes you see there is no serpent, there never was a serpent. You gave your own eyes to the falling evening and cried, '*Ayyo!* Oh! It's the serpent!' You run and roll and lament, and have compassion for fear of pain, others' or your own. You see the serpent and in fear you feel you are it, the serpent, the saint. One—the Guru—brings you the lantern; the road is seen, the long, white road, going with the statutory stars. 'It's only the rope.' He shows it to you. And you touch your eyes and *know* there never was a serpent. Where was it, where, I ask you? The poet who saw the rope as serpent became the serpent, and so a saint. Now, the saint is shown that his sainthood was identification, not realization. The actual, the real has no name. The rope is no rope to itself."

"Then what is it?"

"The rope. Not as opposed to the serpent, but the rope just *is* —and therefore there is no world."

"But there can be a Beatrice?" she implored.

"Yes," I said, after a long while. "Yes, where I am not. When I can love the self in Maitreyi, I can be Yagnyavalkya."

"Find then, my friend, an Indian Maitreyi. Let me be the woman of the marches."

"*Una vera marchesa?*" I smiled.

"Yes, my Prince."

"He who is," I quoted an ancient text, "not the body, not the mind, nor the sense organs: he, the true Emperor."

The battle at last had ended. I must have sat for a very long time in Madeleine's room, for the moon which I had seen high up in the sky when I came in had set beyond the tower of the cathedral, and the night was musical with the noises of owls, with crickets and the distant sea. On a quiet night, especially in winter, you could hear the sea from where we were, and whether the world was real or unreal, the sea seemed proof of something unnameable. *"La mer, la mer toujours recommencée."*

I went down to the town a few days later, and bought Madeleine a pair of strong country shoes, with crêpe soles on them. And one evening, when the wound was almost healed, while I was dressing her foot, I said, "I have played a trick on you, Madeleine."

"What was it?" she asked, smiling, but weak with so much dieting and lying in bed. Her voice had the gentleness and sorrowfulness that come to those in constant prayer, silence and *askesis*.

"But, first let me tell you a story. It is a story that Ramakrishna Paramahamsa used to repeat a great deal. And it is an old Vedantic parable. It runs thus:

"Once upon a time, and that was a long time ago, there was a very good man. He did whatsoever he undertook perfectly—he was, let us imagine, a Charentais—so one day, when the sun was very hot, he said to himself, the sun is hot here in the courtyard, it is hot there on the road—and he looked farther and he said, it is hot there on the stretch of fields, and hot, too, on the hill. It must be hot in the valley below, and beyond the river and the towns it must be hot too. And beyond the palaces of the city and the fields and the mountains, it must be so hot, hot, in the deserts that be, and the wide, dust-bearing plains. Round the whole world it must be hot. So, said he to himself, I must protect myself from this scorchsome heat. I will cover the whole earth with leather; I will cut and sew, and patch every spot of the round earth with good solid leather. And in this wise I could walk where I would. Thus saying, he went up to the loft, and brought down large chunks of animal hide and started cutting and shaping them. The bull, standing in the yard, gave a loud laugh.

" 'Héo-ho,' he cried.

"The good man said, 'You laugh at me, do you, bull?'

" 'Yes, I do, revered Master. I know what you want to do. You find, like I do, that the whole vast world is very hot, and you want to protect yourself from the heat. So, you want to cover the world with hide!'

" 'Yes, that is precisely what I thought. But how did you know it?'

" 'Well, when I plough the fields, and I drag the cart, the Master does not have to say much to me, does he?'

" 'No, certainly not. You know I want to go to the jackfruit field before I lift my whip, or that I go to the Siddapura or Ramapura fair almost before I jump on the yoke and say "hoy." That is true. But why did you laugh?'

" 'Learned and good Master, I thought how strange that Master should be thinking of covering the world with leather. It will take him all the night and all the day, cutting the hide and stitching it; first in this courtyard, and then on the road with its ruts, on the stretch of fields with their furrows, on the still-standing forests and the sands by the river; and the winter will be gone and then the summer, and the sun will rise and grow hotter and set. The Master will grow old and his children will be born, and they will grow old, stitching and stitching the leather round the earth. And bulls will die, and elephants and horses, too, and sheep, and the earth will take a long time to get covered. It will, of course, be covered with hide, one day after many suns and

335

moons. But if only instead, I thought, the Master who gives me the steel shoes every four months, if only the Master made a pair of nice country slippers, the Master could go in winter and summer, where he would; through furrow or forest, and the sun would not scorch his feet.'

"The good man was so pleased with the beast's answer that he mightily patted and caressed him—thus the bull has the hump and dewlap neck. Then he laughed, the Master did, so that all the trees and the hills laughed with him. The wise man put his bullock to his cart, and went to Ramapura Siddapura and made himself a pair of nice slippers. He could walk where he would, and he was greatly pleased with his freedom.

"And when the bull died he went naturally to the Kailas of Lord Shiva, and became a servant-companion of Nandi."

Madeleine laughed with me, a gentle laugh, that was like the cry of mice or of little rabbits. I had finished washing her feet. Underneath the wound, the skin was getting red and whole.

"And so," I added, coming back from my room, "here are your shoes. I told you India is *impitoyable*. Like the wise bull we laugh at all good men."

"The story is like one of those medieval stories about the *curé* and his wise dog."

"Wisdom, fortunately, is no monopoly of India. But if you start covering the warm earth from Aix—" She burst out laughing this time, till her belly ached.

"—you may need a hundred lives and more. Fortunately you believe in reincarnation," I teased her.

"We Europeans believe in being good," she added, thoughtfully.

"We Indians in being wise."

"Let me remain the Marchesa," she pleaded.

"And I the Brahmin, the bull."

She liked my choice of shoes, however—they were beige with a yellow border—and to honour me she put them on, on the day I was leaving for Paris and London. My main work of research was almost finished, and I only had to consult a few manuscripts at the British Museum and at the Bodleian; then I could start on the thesis, maybe before the vacations began. I put all my papers and important books into my case. I took many warm clothes too; the winter was mild yet, and when it came it might be severer, I thought. My case was very heavy, but Madeleine procured a barrow with cycle tyres from our neighbour, and stopped me from carrying my luggage. "I am the foolish good man," she said. She brought me to the bus stop.

On the way she said, "I have a trick up my sleeve. I will come and see you off at Saint-Charles." So we sat in the bus, warm, very near one another, but with a feeling of the incongruity of destiny.

"The bus isn't bad, is it? Why must we always have such expensive ways, and get in and out of taxis, when there are so many who suffer? Your father was not a Maharaja, nor my father anything but a good bourgeois."

"The bus is all right, but all this smell, and this rubbing against one another . . . ! My olfactory organs, Madeleine, as you know are made of Brahmin substance."

"Whereas I, I am the great-granddaughter of serfs freed by the Revolution. For me human self is rich and warm, and even this smell moves me to tears."

"Yes, Marchesa," I said ironically.

At Saint-Charles I protested against her lifting my heavy luggage. The porters came. I bought myself a first-class ticket.

"Ah, the Maharaja," she said. "You are always a Pasha."

I got into the compartment. In honour of my departure Madeleine had put on the yellow Aurangabad *himru* jacket, that I had brought her from India. Her face was paler against that yellow, but how kind, how true she looked, did my Madeleine, as the train took me away.

> *Devi, devi, ayam paççimas te Rāmaçirasā pādapankajasparçah.*
> Goddess, here for the last time
> Does the head of Rama touch the lotus of your feet.

As the train pulled itself northward, and we passed through Eyguières, Tarascon, Avignon, Orange, there was much spring in the air—though it was only mid-February—and I thought of Savithri. There had been several letters from her—she was now in Assam, and her letters spoke of the rain, and the Bhutiya Nagas and the coffee plantations: "Oh, it's so sad! It rains and rains, as though the earth never had enough water to seep. I hold receptions, and our young and new Republic is growing strong. Ministers, Secretaries of State come and go, and I think, what is this India we are building? Oh, Rama, it makes me sad, sad! Some want it to become like our neighbour China, and others like their foster-mother white England. And nobody wants India to be India. And Nehru is the Hamlet, who knows his madness is intelligent, while others only see ghosts. Ophelia, of course, is dead and buried. Pratap had a fall playing polo in Shillong. Write to me. S." I read it over and over again, and I understood every word of it, every space and contour of her alphabet. With Madeleine everything was explanation. With Savithri it was recognition.

Not Nehru but I was the Hamlet. My madness was not even intelligent. I could have wept into my hands. Instead, I looked at the lovely manor houses, little archways of sudden curve and comprehension, beneath which carthorses dragged hay or manure, while the hens and ducks flew all over the courtyard. I remembered a French poet I had met in a Parisian salon, who had said:

"The best métier for a writer, sir, is to be a level-crossing keeper with squealing children. You only have to show the red and green signals, and that only when the bell rings; then you stand like a deserter before a court-martial, while the children cry from the barrier, making faces, showing fists, and sometimes the *petit monsieur* underneath their pants. It's such fun. You go in the afternoon to the nearest farm, to get milk and sausages, have a brief interlude with the Polish maids—there be many in the French countryside—and go back home to write poetry. There is the ideal life for the modern poet. You must naturally have a fat wife, quarrelling but not too quarrelsome, who does not understand a word of what you write. But in bed she's warm and she will bear the necessary number of children. You have thus three jobs: writing poetry at leisure, letting down the bar when the train bell goes *ting-tong,* and manufacturing the requisite number of children for the State to feed all of us on and well. Then you could write like Baudelaire."

I thought of this middle-aged poet, fervent with poetry in his eyes, but weak with insulin in his system. He was to die very soon, and without his Polonaise or his job.

Catherine was there at the station, and Georges, though I had begged them not to come. "Rama is not my father's client, is he? And yet I go often and fetch Father's clients on some excuse or the other. Besides we have a car." So they took me straight to their flat in the Rue Michel-Ange, though I had asked them to reserve a room in the Quartier Latin.

"You will be far away from the Sorbonne here," apologized Catherine, "but I am the *chauffeur de la maison.* I enjoy going about in Paris. The Parisian is such an intelligent animal—it's a joy to watch him."

The apartment on the Rue Michel-Ange was a large, old-fashioned, rambling, egregious thing, with cupboards everywhere, large corridors and smelly corners. My own room was a small one—next to the kitchen.

"Like this you will be warm, and as long as you are here we

promise not to cook meat. We can always go to a restaurant. And in the morning, as we know you rise early and have your Brahminic bath, here is the coffee and here the milk, and you make yourself perfectly at home."

Georges had grown quiet, distant. His eyes were no more scintillating with vitality, but showed maturity, simplicity and aloofness.

"Well, *mon vieux,*" he said, "Paris is not Aix. There are too many things to do. The student in Paris does less work—he has too many distractions—but he understands things much more quickly. To think that at seventeen they are so clever makes one mad. This generation which has grown up from childhood to youth during the war years is exceptionally brilliant. Perhaps wars are not so bad after all."

Dinner was laid on the table. I found Catherine looking splendid—I was envious that marriage could bring so much fulfilment to anyone. She was gay, and talked of everything with assurance. Oncle Charles was getting old after all: he did not have the same strength he used to, and his phlebitis was worrying him. He might soon have to go to Luxeuil. Tante Zoubie's stroke was not serious, but she would never be the same again. She had just been to her first husband's sister, Diane, who was married to a big-businessman in Brussels, and had a château in Normandy. The sea air, and the atmosphere of receptions, yachting and so on seemed bound to do her good. But she returned more tired than ever. When one grows old, even one's joy seems to diminish.

"One day, *ma petite,* I tell myself," said Catherine, "you too will grow old. Meanwhile, let us be young, don't you think so, Georges?"

"I have news to give you," said Georges, pursuing his own thoughts, and playing with a knife on the table. He was silent for a brief moment, looked at Catherine with adoration and announced: "Catherine will have a baby in five or six months. You are the first person to know it, Rama."

To this day I cannot tell you why, but I felt somewhere I had been washed clean and whole by the Ganges, dipped again and again and made shining with Srāvan Saturday sun. I must have looked very moved, for Catherine put the soup in front of me, touched my head as Saroja might have and said:

"You will look after him, when he grows up, and give him all your wisdom, won't you?"

We must have eaten our soup in silence for a very long time, as the first question after that came not from Catherine but from Georges.

"How is Mado?"

"She's more of an Indian than me. She already knows more about Buddhism than I do."

"I tell you, Catherine, you must learn Russian. You can never understand me without knowing the language of my forefathers. It is in Russian, I have no doubt whatsoever, my most secret thoughts are made!"

"You want to have three children, and you want to have a nice home. And you want me to help you in your work. *Oh, là là!*" said Catherine. "Men will never be satisfied with women."

"To say that before Rama!"

"But Rama is not, is not—" Catherine was trying to find the right expression.

"—a man," whispered Georges, and made us all laugh.

"No, I mean he is not a *man*-man. He is an Indian," she finished, convinced she had defined me.

It must have been past one o'clock in the morning when we all went to bed. Catherine saw me off at the door, and kissed me on the cheeks.

"You are like a prayer—that is what I wanted to say. A prayer, I repeat. You have grown so old—I mean ancient, ancient, Rama," she added, and heaved a large and affectionate sigh. I went to sleep, and for the first time slept very well. I had no dreams. I woke and thought of Madeleine, and knew she must have slept very well too. Pity she had to make her own coffee in the morning, I thought; but I remembered it was a Thursday and she did not work. So I slept an hour more, and woke to Catherine grinding coffee beans in the kitchen.

"This time it will be me," she said, knocking at the door. "Let the Brahmin have coffee in bed. He won't become an animal in the next life for breaking such minor rules. And you say women in my condition are auspicious," she added, "so you will have auspicious coffee, my brother-in-law," and she closed the door behind herself.

As before, I divided my time between the Rue de Richelieu and the Sorbonne. Catherine took me every morning to the Bibliothèque Nationale, and she insisted, for the first few days, that I come back for lunch, driving to fetch me every day. But she soon realized this arrangement could not last very long, so she gave me sandwiches and I used to go and have a chocolate in a quiet café near by. There were always such interesting people about the place, and seeing them day after day I got to know their faces, their specializations. One was researching in Assyriology—into Sumerian texts concerning Kingship and Grammar, among the bilinguals from Assurbanipal's library. Another was copying patterns of Central Asian dress, especially women's dresses, to prove his thesis that Nestorian Christianity was purely of Buddhist origin, for the women had no crosses on their dresses; in fact, to this day they wear a cross resembling the Buddhist swastika. These scholars would talk of their work and I of mine, but strange to say, nobody could help another. Research is always like a man lost in a desert. You can only see stars wheresoever you look. You will always find a star somewhere, and following it through dust and jungle you certainly will come to a kingdom, where you are sure to find a prince, and he has many daughters to marry. If you do the right thing in the right way—that is, if you show your originality by talking of your astronomy starting from your particular star, which is always unique, in position, coloration and behaviour—you can show an altogether different pattern for the whole round sky. It all depends on where you start. And there is always a princess to wed you eventually.

My star, my unique star, was the theory that somewhere in the land between Persia, Turkey and Bulgaria—maybe in the valley of the Euphrates, or maybe a little higher up in Asia Minor, so full of the traces of almost every human civilization—I was certain to find a direct proof of India's link with the Cathar heresy. I studied many texts, and was led mainly by that sort of intuition one develops in research, where almost by just looking at a book (when mind and body are in the best of states), one looks and says, "In this book, in this large and lusty tome, perhaps in the second part of it—no, towards the middle of the third part, will be my precise reference." And almost always you hit on the right information. I had gathered much information in this manner and Georges made fun of me, saying such power of divination must, no doubt, come from my yogic practices.

"You should announce your perceptive capacities on a board at the door of the Bibliothèque Nationale: 'Research through clairvoyance. Twelve lessons, and all mysteries will be solved.' It would be a new job. Nobody has undertaken it so far."

Whether all others had this intuition or not—and many research workers I talked to seemed to possess it to an even greater degree than I did—my finds were important. I looked into the history of the Druzes, that mysterious sect of Arabs who belong both to the Christian and the Muslim fold, and yet have their own priests and their own secret books, which none dare examine. I had however found, first through the works of Gobineau—that extraordinary, if eccentric, imperial scholar—and later in Count Sailly de Mollinfort, whose works on Arab history are a masterpiece of erudition, precision and insight, that there were indeed references to India and Indian wisdom in the Druze texts, *"d'une nature métaphysique,"* he wrote, *"qui nous laissent croire, que le Bulgarisme, l'hérésie Vaudoise, plus tard et plus purement le mouvement Cathare, sont probablement d'une origine directement Hindoue, et pas comme pense Max Müller, un lointain écho des idées partho-boudhiste."* I read all of Sailly on the Druzes, and Morganston, and Wellenby. The latter is a much better scholar than one thinks, despite his unscholarly use of language ("I have no doubt that," or "it is silly to think," and such unacademic language is not permissible in scholarly writing). But after all he was a soldier and an administrator first, though it was he that discovered the Amharic text on Alexander's campaign in India, and edited it so admirably. Well, Wellenby was of much help to me. And then Massignon, with his deep learning and his immense devotion to India.

My thesis made quick progress. But I had to go to the Bodleian for further references to Wellenby; Garraud, in his study of the messianic tradition among the Semites, speaks of some very important manuscripts there. It was also a good pretext, I thought, after nearly a month and a half *chez* Catherine and Georges, to leave them. So I went over to England.

I arrived during those beautiful days in the spring of 1953 when the whole country was getting ready to receive guests from abroad. England had now a lovely young Queen and she was going to be crowned. Even the trees and the earth seemed to have helped the English, so mild and kind the winter was, and so splendid; and soon had spring ushered itself in, bringing bunches of red and yellow and mauve of irises to the great parks. The Londoner looked better dressed and he seemed never to have been more courteous. Everybody who came was going to be the guest of England, and English men and women felt a very personal responsibility for their own behaviour. There was much less drunkenness in the streets and much better taste in the women's clothes, which were British in style and not cheap Dior or Fath. I was happy to see the English thus, in this new mood. There was no triumphant arrogance with them—as in the days of their imperial grandeur—they were more centred in themselves, more sure and more elevated. True, they did not have a clear conscience about Africa, but how relieved they seemed to have "washed their hands of India." I laughed and said to myself, "They have grown more Brahminical."

Oxford was kind and docile, as she ever is, but seemed to have less vitality and purity in the air than Cambridge. Perhaps I had seen Cambridge through Savithri—and was now trying to see Oxford through my own eyes. Anand was at Balliol, but I did not go and see him.

I soon returned to London, where I had very good news. Cooks gave me a letter from Savithri. I always went into Green Park to open her letters; leaning against a tree—there was one spacious plane opposite the gate, not far from the 14 bus stop, that I liked particularly—I rubbed my hands against its trunk, to feel its freshness, and read Savithri's letter. It said that she was coming over to England for the Coronation with her father. Her father felt he had been so loyal to the British that he had to be with them when they were crowning their Queen.

"He feels it a part of his loyalty to himself. The Government of India, of course, has ignored him. He has been sent on no missions, even his privy purse has been reduced. 'How can you fight with minor officials, lack-manner idiots I would not employ as clerks? Such thorough incompetence!' he explodes. He will be happy to be back among his Lord Sahibs. It is sad to see an active man like Father grow old. Even though Surajpur was a small state, with a population of only a hundred thousand, he still did a lot of things. There were at least the elephant and the horses to look after. Then there were such picturesque family quarrels among his nobles and subjects, which he alone could disentangle, knowing all about every single important family, for four, five or even six generations. And when he had had enough of that, he had his tiger-shootings. He enjoyed these enormously. Now they cost too much; besides, who is there left in India to enjoy them? I have been trying to persuade him to go south, on pilgrimage, and visit some Sages. The North is finished. It will soon be like Notting Hill Gate. Your South still has so much beauty, wisdom and purity. Father says he will go to England first, and on his return will make a pilgrimage from Kailas to Kanyakumari. I know he will not do it. But still, I wish Father could find peace somewhere. He would look fresh as a bridegroom if Nehru called him and said, 'Will you be our Ambassador in Tokyo? In Washington?' London, he says, will go to some *khādiwāla,* eating *pān* in Buckingham Palace, and spitting on the floor. Father exaggerates a great deal, but India is not particularly an exalting place today . . . You are my India, and to see you will be my exaltation. Besides, I want Father to meet you, to know you. Maybe you could give him something he seeks. Think of me sometimes. S."

I looked down the green grass and through the mist to the naked orphrey trees. Beyond the road there, and beyond the park beyond, was Buckingham Palace. Somehow I felt grateful, grateful, walking towards it. I walked in the light of a new England.

My research, I fear, did not make very great progress during the next few months. Perhaps the trouble was not with the English climate, as some thought, or with my vegetarian diet, but with some more immediate and occult anxiety. I knew I was losing something and would not find anything again.

And I felt lost in this new, this flowering England, with a feeling of desperation in my lungs. Just as a hunter *knows*— "My father often knows that a tiger is there," Savithri had said, "with the hairs on his toes, as it were, before his eyes or his ears have information"—so did my body *know* of some annihilation before my being knew; the haemoglobules were more intelligent than my mind or my famous intuition. I felt I was sinking, though the X-ray showed no "shadows" of increased activity. Oxford and the damp certainly did not agree with me. I felt I could not go to Cambridge again, so I tried Brighton—and returned to London soon, and even more ill, this time to a hospital. It was somewhere near Euston and specialized in tropical diseases.

Being from India I managed to get in, with the help of our High Commissioner.

They were going to try prolonged bed-rest, and if that was no use, there was always thoracoplasty. The whole thing was a question of breathing well, and they sat me down in the appropriate position and taught me this and that, and how to lie on the right side of my chest.

"Good man," said Dr. Burnham, "if you don't get well soon, I'll give you nice chicken soup," he laughed, "and veal for your dinner." The nurses were very kind and they winked at me. Dr. Burnham, after he'd examined me and my temperature chart, went on, "You must get better, Mr. Ramaswamy. You will."

He was against pneumothorax, and spoke of it with marked contempt. He called it the Indian mango-trick. "You can see the mango but cannot eat it."

"Thoracoplasty," he concluded, "is like the Bank of England. But if you don't obey I'll write to Uncle Seetharamu. Good-bye, *Achchājēe, Namasthé,*" and he went away.

Lord, I must have mentioned Uncle Seetharamu but once, and he had remembered it. What nobility there must be in the hearts of those who bear the pain of others.

Lakshmi (from Cambridge) whom I had accidentally met at India House when I was working in the excellent library there, came often to see me. She was convinced I was a victim of some sort of malediction.

"God knows," she said, protectively and femininely, "Indian palaces are not homes of prayer and virtue."

I was not so dull of understanding, hence I discouraged her visits. But how virtuous she seemed, did Lakshmi Iyengar with her big kunkum mark, and deep-set melodious voice. Madeleine was right: Indian women do not look innocent. They look wise— and virtuous!

Lakshmi never talked to me of Madeleine. For her there were no European women. I think she disliked them, feeling that they were libidinous, always trying to please men.

"You can't press a man to your body, as they do at their dances, and talk of virtue. Oh, I am longing to be back in India."

Lakshmi was doing child psychology and would be going back to the Ministry of Education, in New Delhi. She would look after children's textbooks. Virtue certainly would flood India then.

I hated this moral India. True, Indian morality was based on an ultimate metaphysic. Harishchandra told the truth; and lost his kingdom and his wife, but he found the Truth. I wanted to tell these virtuous ladies of India the story of Satyavrata.

The deer comes—so the story goes in the *Mahabharatha*—leaping, with froth and foam, and whistling with the breath of fear, and takes shelter in the low hut of the ascetic. The hunter, pursuing, comes after, making strange noises and imprecations, but seeing the ascetic falls low before him, and asks Satyavrata, "Learned Lord, have you seen a deer?" Was he going to tell the truth, he, Satyavrata?* "I have five children at home, puling, hungry creatures, and a wife, enormous and distraught; and they be without fire and flesh these six days of the moon. Lord, clear-seeing, compassionate ascetic, I have to save them from starvation and death. The drought has driven all the vulnerable beasts away, and we must lie and starve." Was Satyavrata going to give up the innocent deer to the hunter? No. So he went unto himself and uttered that profound Vedantic truth: *"He* who sees cannot say, and *he* who says has not seen."

* Satyavrata means "He who has taken the vow-of-truth."

Truth is the only substance India can offer and that Truth is metaphysical and not moral. Lakshmi was not India. Lakshmi was the India that accepted invaders, come Muslim, come British, with sighs and salutations. Lakshmi would not read the *Mahabharatha* the whole night, cut her finger, and anointing her Lord with her young blood burn herself alive.

"Page boy, tell me, ere I go, how bore himself my Lord?"

"As a reaper of the harvest of battle. I followed his steps as a humble gleaner of his sword. On the bed of honour he spread a carpet of the slain, whereon, a barbarian his pillow, he sleeps ringed by his foes."

"Yet once again, O boy, tell me how my Lord bore himself."

"O Mother, who can tell his deeds? He left no foe to dread or admire him."

She smiled farewell to the boy, adding, "My Lord will chide my delay," and like an Esclarmonde sprang into the flames.

> N' Esclarmunda, vostre noms signifia
> Que vos donatz clartat al mond per ver
> Et etz monda, que no fes mon dever:
> Aitals etz plan com al ric nom tamhia.

So wrote Guillaume de Montanhagol. The Cathar heroine leapt forward to Paradise, the Rajput princess withdrew into herself and became white as ash. Paradise is the inversion of Truth, and is feminine. It is the elongation of man to his celibate singleness: *"Vidi . . . credo ch'io vidi."* The Holy Grail is the residue of delight.

Virtue is virile. Behind every "virtuous" Indian woman I felt the widow. But we needed real wives, wives in life—as in death. I had too much surquedry to be but Brahmin. The Brahmins sold India through the back door—remember Devagiri—and the Muslims came in through the front. Purnayya sold the secrets of Tippu Sultan and the British entered through the main gateway of Seringapatam. Truth that is without courage can only be the virtue of slave or widow. Non-violence, said Gandhiji, is active, heroic. We must always conquer some land, some country. Ignorance, pusillanimity, ostrich-virtue is the land we shall liberate. That is true *swaraj.* The means is *satyagraha.* Come.

Weak lungs, the doctors say, are bad for nerves. One day, however, I showed Lakshmi the door.

"You think Savithri would have married you? Oh my God, how many men she has turned round her sari-fringe and thrown to the elephants. You men will never understand us women—especially Indian women. Savithri would rather any day have wed a fat, spitting, nautch-girl, cricket-club Maharaja, or a rich *banya* like her sister did—he is a *banya,* though he may be a Minister now—than an intellectual like you, Ramaswamy, a Brahmin. Today in India you can buy anything for rupees."

"Then I shall grow rich and buy myself a wife," I said, and kept very silent. Lakshmi looked into my books, fingered them, read a line or two here and there, rose up and tucked me in, looked through the window, laughed and said:

"Oh, the English, this race of shopkeepers! They will crown a Queen with one hand and count the dollars in the other. They gave independence to India because it suited the Chancellor of the Exchequer and the great Board of Trade."

"I am a monarchist," I said, quietly, pertinently, "and I honour the Queen."

"Funny thing to hear from an Indian," she protested, rising and adjusting her scarf round her neck. I waited for her to put on her heavy overcoat. She had bought it in Prague, she said: "It is so cheap, yet it is made of the best astrakhan."

"I belong to the period of the *Mahabharatha,*" I said. "I have nothing to do with the Board of Trade."

She understood, and left me. She did not come to see me for several weeks. She sent a postcard from Cambridge saying she was busy with her final exams. It suited me that exams were in the summer, and I could go on dreaming of the coronation of Kings.

> In a month mirie,
> Septembre Begynning,
> Baudwynn of Canterbirie
> Come to couronne the Kyng.

349

I started reading Coomaraswamy—that son of an Indian father and a delightful English mother, who characteristically enough spent most of his time in Boston, and eventually died there. The Anglo-Saxon mind does not understand India very well; the best interpreters of India in the West have been mostly French (I am thinking mainly of Sénart, Lévi, Guénon, Grousset, Masson-Oursel, Pryzulski); there have been a few Germans, but very few British. And yet when you have writers like Sir William Jones, Sir John Woodroffe—more Brahmin than any Brahmin—and Coomaraswamy, you feel grateful for those exceptional Englishmen. Even so, it cannot be that the Anglo-Saxon mind understands India so little, but possibly some shy kink in the British strain is frightened of what they name "the imponderables," for who could be more Anglo-Saxon than Thoreau, Emerson, or even Whitman? This Boston Brahmin, Ananda Coomaraswamy, was more of a *smartha,* a true, an orthodox Indian than some tottering old President of the Indian National Congress. India would never be made by our politicians and professors of political science, but by these isolate existences of India, in which India is rememorated, *experienced* and communicated; beyond history, as tradition, as the Truth. Anybody can have the geographic—even the political—India; it matters little. But this India of Coomaraswamy, who will take it away, I ask you, who? Not Tamerlane or even Joseph Stalin.

Woman is the earth, air, ether, sound; woman is the microcosm of the mind, the articulations of space, the knowing in knowledge; the woman is fire, movement clear and rapid as the mountain stream; the woman is that which seeks against that which is sought. To Mitra she is Varuna, to Indra she is Agni, to Rama she is Sita, to Krishna she is Radha. Woman is the meaning of the word, the breath, touch, act; woman, that which reminds man of that which he is, and reminds herself through him of that which she is. Woman is kingdom, solitude, time; woman is growth, the gods, inherence; the woman is death, for it is through woman that one is born; woman rules, for it is she, the universe. She is the daughter of the earth, the queen, and it is to her that elephant and horse, camel, deer, cow and peacock bow that she reign over

350

us, as in some medieval Book of Hours where she is clad in the blue of the sky; all the animals and worlds surround her, and praise her that she be. The world was made for celebration, for coronation, and indeed even when the King is crowned it is the Queen to whom the Kingdom comes—*lactur gens anglica Domini imperio regenda et reginae virtutis providentia gubernanda*—for even when it is a King that rules, she is the justice, the bender of man in compassion, the confusion of kindness, the sorrowing in the anguish of all. Woman is the duality made for her own pools of mirroring and she crowns herself to show that man is not of this kingdom. Man cannot even die. Then must he absorb himself into himself and be being. The coronation is the adieu of man to the earth. Be gay, earth, be beautiful, for man must go.

Woman is the world. Woman is the earth and the cavalcade, the curve of the cloud and the round roundness of the sun. Woman is the space between mansions; those secret, knowing emptinesses from which word goes from house to house and man to man. It is woman that looks out of the window and sees herself in the other, looks at the mirror and sees the light, looks at man and sees her high God; she touches the down of her hair in Piccadilly, and dreams of a world where all is spring, all flowers moving as in the waters, birds.

Woman will sit in a coach and see herself as seen by others; she will wear the tiara and know she is no woman nor known being; she will dream of orb and dove, of annulus and baculus, of the garter and of knights; and she will think of the Abbey, where she will see herself as seen by a thousand years. Woman after woman has sat on the same seat, and has counted the same beads of love. Woman will be on the coin of England, woman will sound as silver all over the world, woman will go round the world and bring the warmth of tenderness to many homes. Many a maid the world over will marry the young man with the red scarf, for the Queen, the Queen will walk through the streets of Adelaide, and will bless the hearts of the chemist's assistant, the minister's daughter, the paralytic at the window. Woman will wander the seas, mount the stairways of many a palace and parliament, for woman is the only meaning of silence over the seas. In the little alleys in London, by parks and by pools, simple virgin grass grew all like words of a saying, and many a child played rejoicing on its birth, for the world would be handed over to a Queen.

Time flowed, and on barques and balustrades man stopped a moment and lived in his own presence. Everything: the towers; the trolley-bus tops; the zebra crossings and their orange lights; the horses of vegetable sellers with their short, restless tails; the electric company's cockney meter-reader; the leaves of eager trees brushed aside, the newspapers' rags that floated on the air; the curse at the pubs, the songs of the Italians: all showed that there was much drink in the air and much sunshine. Men came from all over the globe: the Abyssinians with their curled hair and their white, long togas; the Zambezi Zulus with their split noses and their large masticating faces; the Pakistanis on their white, slim horses; the humble Hindu in his proud tights; the Japanese lady with her large smile; the Togo Islanders, the Canadians, the hearty loud-spoken Australians; the French with their indiscretions, the Germans with their boasts; yes, even the Soviets came to drink of the beer of England. Fruit came parcelled from all the three corners of the world, from Malaya and from British Honduras; peat from the Falklands; pearls from many seas. Kings and Pashas came from everywhere, the lost race of a defeated people, who wanted to know, if knowing will want them from wanting; a great many students and professors came; journeymen to beg or sell; and married couples to believe that one can live one's life and find the meaning of connection in round freedom.

The world gave parties to itself, and everybody felt everywhere, drank champagne at the Prime Minister's party, and drank beer at home. No one was another's adversary, for there was no other and all was simplified, till politicians must have sat and wondered where the next world would be. Politics had lost its acuteness, vulgarity had lost its burthen, and man sang himself a song and went to sleep dreaming of the new birth. The hospitals had never been so full—for London was crowded—but nurse and doctor seemed to know of a common knowledge, in which giving and receiving were not two oppositions of a single act, but two acts of a single living; diseases seemed inappropriate, and some had the shyness of a dog or a thief that has strayed into wide-awakened worlds. Man was simple, simple as the road on which he walked, straight as the pathway of his park; and the sun seemed to come to him with a facility and an assurance, as though the globe were made for each individual, for his elliptical system; the sun came to him, to his face, his eyes, his hands, his breath. Many persons opened their cages and let out their parakeets and their mynas, so that the London trees heard such talk and song as never had seemed permissible; and song linked man and woman over the brow of time, as though death were a superfluity. For a moment everyone looked into himself and found he had nowhere to go. Man was happy, he was very, very happy.

During those days I was reading Thomas le Trovere, that Anglo-Norman poet, to whom England and France were as Tristan and Iseult, and London that beautiful city.

> Lundres est mult riche cité
> Meluir n'ad en cristienté,
> Plus vaillante ne meltz preisiee,
> Melz garnie de gent aisiee.

You could imagine Tristan le Preux moving on the boat, with Iseult, the daughter of the King of Ireland, she, the beautiful, who was to be married to King Mark. And the nephew was bringing her to him, for it was a promise that the young had made to the old and come fire, come water, it had to be respected and obeyed. But the winds rose on the sea, and the sun was hot on the oceans; and one night while they were playing chess they asked Brangien, the faithful, for wine and for more wine to drink. Brangien, the faithful, being full of sleep, it was the potion of love meant for King Mark that she gave unto one first and the rest to the other; and such passions rose in them that not even the waves in the sea would know of such rising and such demand. Just as the castle of Tintagel rounded itself and shone, on the rocks there, in the country of King Mark, in Cornwall, Iseult gave herself unto Tristan, who through fire and forest, through torture and exile, was to be her love. And when he went away and tried to warm his heart through another Iseult, Iseult of the White Hands, no warmth came for there was no love in him. So the ships brought the news of his illness and hopelessness to Iseult of Cornwall, and she took her boat and sped towards him. But when she came Tristan was just dead, and she lay beside him dead. A bramble linked them even in their grave; it rose from the grave of Tristan.

Et de la tombe de Tristan sortait une belle ronce, verte et feuillue, qui montait par dessus la chapelle; le bout de la ronce retombait sur la tombe d'Iseut et entrait dedans. Ce que virent bien les gens du pays qui le rapportèrent au roi Marc. Le roi la fit couper par trois fois. Le lendemain, elle était aussi belle et en tel état qu'auparavant. Ce miracle était sur Tristan et sur Iseut.

Sometimes I thought how beautiful it would be to have a tomb over oneself.

Banners flew in the air, trumpets were tried in the streets, and like thoughts seen in consciousness little aeroplanes returned to their starting points; perhaps in one of them, I thought, looking out of my hospital window, was Savithri. I had not heard from her for a long time, but I knew she was coming. I knew she would come. And no sooner had she come than would I know.

There was about London a restrained effervescence, as though princes, Zulus, soldiers and politicians; theatrical actors, workers on the arches, policemen on horses; the very manipulations of electric lights on houses and towers, were, so to say, interchangeable entities, as though man were discovering himself. To be many is to be one, for when the many speak to the One in the many, one seems to speak to oneself. Objects seem to sink into voices, and voices seem to procreate objects; the streets seem wide or narrow according to considerations of mind, while objects seem to vanish and reappear according to distances and desires. Man gave himself for those thirty days a wide freedom.

The very aeroplanes seemed sure of themselves, like storks when they go a-mating—and nobody thought the Thames could be anything but a river, or that music would not sound wheresoever you touched. Indeed one wondered why every man did not touch every woman and turn her into a monument, and then falling in love with himself (for ever and always does one fall in love but with oneself) he could hook his arm to a statue and walk through London as in a procession, with banners on both sides, and arches everywhere. For it was not that a Queen was being crowned, but that man was discovering his integrity as a being, like the sound in silence, or the swan in the cool, long waters. We were free, so we shone.

> The walls were of cristal,
> The heling was of fine riwal
> That schone swithe brighte.

In the hospital the nurses all seemed reassured, as if the Queen would visit us, would visit every one of us. When they tucked us into our beds, or, when looking at the thermometers, they saw the width of the broad and summery sky, they were sure the Queen would visit us, and would shake hands with us, and with a whisk (made of pink feathers and birch-grass) she would drive away our maladies, pronouncing our sacral name. Yes, she would come and visit us, every one of us, the Queen would, the nurses thought, though they never said it; and the patients sat on their beds at night and asked themselves, were they wondering or was this the truth? There was a Malayan doctor next door who had dengue fever, and who roared in his bed saying some prayer—a Muslim one, no doubt—which seemed like a speech made to one-self: "Calm yourself, my son, my child, the great day of resurrection will come." And you heard trumpets and you saw flags fly. And nobody could die during those days, for there was no space or time for hearses. The horses were busy elsewhere, and man's thoughts were on such important objects that nobody thought of death. That was why every aeroplane flew with the assurance of a train seen in a dream, which goes everywhere inventing its own rails. There are no stationmasters nor accidents in that kingdom, your children are at the station, and the station covered with flowers flies into the air. You felt you could just walk down the parks and the trees would be lit, and that you could talk to anyone and he would speak to you your language. When the train at Euston Station whistled, it was like Uncle Seetharamu's dhobi's donkey braying in the back yard, dreaming it was carrying the washing of a king.

Everything, in fact, lived in the reality, in such a way that each time the lift came up you thought the door would open and anyone, the one person—anyone could only be one—would step out, and you would hear her *jalatrang* voice. Water and vessel produce a sound, and you can hear it many a while.

It seemed to me during those days as though the world had asked itself a question sometime at the beginning of the Ice Age, at the beginning of the first man, and that the answer would now be accorded; that with trumpet and march of soldiery, with the procession of Prime Ministers and Ministers of State, in the assembly of Kings and Prelates, the answer would be given; not as a word, or as a gift, but as a dot, a sign, a recognition. That a spot would be shown, where man concentrated on himself, all in a point; where man, freed of himself, would ultimately know the other, the Truth—that the kingdom of God was interior and well built. "Our feet shall stand in thy gates, O Jerusalem: Jerusalem is built as a city that is at unity in itself. O pray for the peace of Jerusalem: they shall prosper that love thee. Peace be within thy walls, and plenteousness within thy palaces." And like the palace and empire of the *budumékaye,* the six sisters would come and the chamberlain-monkey be thrown into the milk; one would hear sounds, see objects, touch life. The world was not before, the world would not dissolve hereafter, but in the instant is the recreation of the whole; the Te Deum Laudamus will sound, and the bells will peal, whereunto, for an instant, one stopped and became Queen. Everybody was born a King and became a Queen. Everybody was born a King, and became a Queen the instant the second hand had moved on itself—for nothing ever moves, nothing is ever said, one is oneself the Truth.

> Thy blessed unction from above
> Is comfort, life, and fire of love.

Lord, such a Queen shall be crowned, such a Queen shall be crowned, I said to myself and went to sleep.

Then one day I heard, "Thoracoplasty, thoracoplasty." It became the sound of a beautiful song, and whether I called Little Mother or Uncle Seetharamu, they always said to me,

"Thoracoplasty." The operation-table straps said, "How do you do?" and I was all so white. It is good to be white. It is so light to be white. Dr. Burnham said, *"Achchājēe, Namasthé!* I told you, it's solid as silver. I pray for you."

The operation-table straps sang again like clappers of church bells, ether seemed precious and the world re-created out of nothing—the emptiness—and sound was so true. Evil is just part of a lung, and the evil of evil is evil. To awaken is to see the world as a promise made in sleep. Truth is seen inside. When seen outside, reality is as a name given to memory; as a waterfall heard from above, it is light, indeterminate. Man seeks his knowledge in the world but must know it is himself without him. Then the world shines as at a festival.

Death had been made into a poster, and left at the door. He could not come in. Nobody could come in—only the Queen could come in clad in muslin white, single and followed by sixteen maids. She would come by the stone path of the hospital yard, mount up the steps, and all in united silence come along the lit corridors, with red and green lights, and kneel by us and pray. And after prayer she would laugh and we would open our eyes. The temperature charts would go shooting through the window, like evil become birds, and sit on plants, and flower. The Queen would remain with us for a long time, and the world resound with luminous song.

> And with them eke, O Goddesse heauenly bright
> Mirrour of Grace and Maiestie divine
> Great Lady of the greatest Isle . . .

Then she came—she came again, and yet again.

One day she came to me—at that time she used to smoke a great deal—and she said after a long silence:

"Woman should not be."

I said, "Why, Savithri?"

"Woman is coeval with death."

"Which means?"

"Woman is the meaning of death."

"I don't understand," I protested.

"You said: The woman is the world. The truth of the world is dissolution. Or rather Truth can only be because death is. If the world were the world, there would be no Truth."

"Yes, that is so. If oxygen were oxygen or rhinoceros rhinoceros, there would be no Truth. There would be death, and that crown of death the pyramid. But death is not, despite Tutankhamen and his crown. Death itself cannot be, for *he* who says it cannot be *is*."

"Then the woman is Tutankhamen. The woman must die, with crown and pyramid. Or rather the woman must become death. Woman is the disease, the historical lineage of man."

"And man?"

"The Truth," she said, "the Supreme Light. We are the fakers, the makers. We make the falsehood that is life, the trinkets. That is why man has such contempt for us."

"Will you exchange places with me?" I asked.

"Yes, if you like this wretched cloak."

"If you become me, then there is no problem."

"How so?"

"Then you, become me, will be the real Savithri."

"And who's the Satyavan?"*

"The self, the Truth," I said, and heaved a sigh. My stitches seemed sweet and tranquil to feel, they lived their own cutaneous existence. "No, Satyavan cannot die. Man must unto himself be himself and his bride. You remember I told you, all brides be Benares born."

"If Benares is inner, my Lord, the bride too is in Benares."

"Man must die, Savithri, nevertheless."

"There never was a woman. There never can be a woman. When Tristan died, Iseult came. Iseult always comes too late."

"If Iseult had died?"

"Iseult was death itself. When death dies . . ."

"Tristan is born. And there never, never is an Iseult."

"What happens to Iseult, then?"

"She is Tristan."

"Tristan, do not die!"

"Satyavan will not die, Savithri."

* In the *Mahabharatha* Savithri marries, against all odds, Satyavan (The Truthful) and conquers him back from Yama, the God of Death.

358

"Truth must be," she said.

"Why?"

"Because Savithri must live."

"The woman is crowned a Queen," I said.

"How so?" she asked.

"Man rejoices in his own death. For man, death is transcendence."

"And transcendence?"

"Transcendence is splendour. For man, glory is transfiguration. Not Ascension but Assumption is the true nature of the Mother of God."

"And so?" she asked.

"So woman is the sacrifice."

"And what rose out of the sacrifice?"

"The world."

"And of the world?"

"A Kingdom."

"And in the Kingdom?"

"A Queen. Thus man gave himself back."

"So man is eternal—he is deathless," she said. "He is crowned a Queen."

"Indra the deity, the Tristubh metre," I chanted.

> The Panchadasa stone. Soma the King,
> I have recourse to the lordly power,
> I become a Kshatriya.*

> O God, O fathers, O Father, O gods,
> I offer, being he who I am.
> This is my sacrifice, my gifts, my toil, my offering,
> Be Agni here my witness, Vayu my hearer, Aditya
>   Yonder my proclaimer,
> I who am I am I.

The seat of four lions has now the face of a young queen, and Rig-Veda the sound of aftermath.

During those days she came to see me often—she came unannounced, for even the hospital rules seemed to have been

* Of the royal fold.

relaxed during that month, and visitors came in and out as they liked. Only the nurses were often overworked, and one was sorry the temperature charts did not, like some meteorological charts, go marking their own lines. Savithri would come and look long and intently at the chart, take my temperature, making excuses to Sister Jean for her presence, and say, "Today you have less fever, my love," or "Oh, I know I am the fever, I the temperature." And then she would sigh, and as she wiped her eyes the collyrium would trickle down, and she would rub it all away, giving her Bangalore blue sari or the white Lucknow a mark and a distinction of me. "Promise to burn me with this," she would plead romantically. And I would answer:

"Death is feminine and not masculine. So she must burn herself."

Then she would hum some song of Mira which brought peace, perfume and elevation to that hospital room, and the sun seemed to shine the brighter, for a Rajput Queen could sing of Krishna in Brindavan.

"My love, my love," she would say, putting her lips against mine, "how I wish I could suck the sorrow out of these twists," and she would lay her head against mine, and try to feel me.

"You know I don't love you?" she said one day.

"That I know," I said. "For if you did, all would be Brindavan."

"Then why don't you play on the flute, and I leave the cattle and the children and that man called my husband?"

"Don't say, 'that man, my husband.' He is your husband, and you are mine."

"Of course he is. Alas he is."

"Pratap is a very fine person, Savithri. As a husband one needs nothing better."

"But then where is Brindavan?"

"Where there is Krishna."

"And who is Krishna?"

"I, when I am not Rama. Where the mind is not," I continued, "nor the body, there is his home, Brindavan, and there he shines, Lord Muraré."

"Then why this sin of Radha?"

360

"Because Krishna is not Krishna yet. And when he is Krishna there is no Radha as Radha, but Radha is himself. That is the paradox, Savithri, the mortal paradox of man."

"And the paradox is the fever. Lord, what would I not give that this fever should go, this fever that is me . . . Lord, take me, and let me forget the world."

"Savithri, who can take whom? As I once told Madeleine, there where we take there is no love, and there where we love there is no taking. You can but take yourself."

"Quickly then. How can it be achieved?"

"By—by discipleship," I answered, as though I was communicating my ultimate secret.

"Discipleship of what—to whom?"

"Discipleship of Krishna, of the Truth."

She understood. She was silent for a long while; then she shut the window, and putting on her coat she said:

"Rama, I have a question."

"Yes, Savithri? What is it?"

"To whom does one belong?"

"To one's self, Savithri."

"What shall become of her that does not belong to herself?"

"Then must she belong to someone."

"But if she belong to one wholly, or rather almost wholly, and to another she be tied, as a calf is tied to the tether, or as the plane is tied to the radar."

"The plane must accept the direction of the radar, that there be no accident. Either you are a plane and you follow national and international conventions—or you do not fly."

"And no garland put on your wings, and no coconut broken as you make your first flight."

"Yes, that is what I mean."

"So, when the plane refuses the radar, and only loves the beauty of the broad sky, the sea below and sands of Santa Cruz shining in the sun . . ."

"Then must it crash."

"So the plane must obey the radar?"

"Yes, that is *dharma*. The law is *dharma*. To disobey *dharma* is to give pain."

"Pain to whom?"

"Pain to the infinite sky—knowing," I said, smiling, "that the plane is not a flying saucer."

"Pain—what is it?" she asked, intent, stopping near me for a moment.

"Pain," I answered, "is the residue of action."

"And joy?"

"Joy is the identity of love."

"So what shall I become?" She heard her voice choke in herself.

"A wife, Savithri, a wife. A true wife."

"I have not been one yet, you know," she said, laughing. "I have been waiting for Brindavan."

"Wheresoever there be no pain, Savithri, my love, that is where Krishna plays the flute, and the cows come and listen to the music, their faces uplifted, their ears stretched against their wide white shoulders. And the trees will flower and the peacock spread his wings, and the gods will come to see this festival of life."

"And what shall one do with one's pain?"

"Know that to have pain is to give pain. Rejoice, Savithri! Rejoice in the rejoicement of others. That is the Truth."

"You ask too much, my love. Can I still call you that?"

"Yes, my Principle, my Queen, you can. Love is rejoicing in the rejoicing of the other."

She touched me with the tip of her lips as though Truth had been there, just there, and the moment was the whole of Truth. Then she left me. A few days later she left London. The sky was blue with summer in the air, one's lungs felt compassionate towards oneself. "Yes, the Queen has been crowned, the Queen," I said, as my train left Waterloo. The next day I was in Paris, and in a few days I was in the Engadine above the snows. I was happy, very happy. I was white and young as the snows. Snow is the benediction of the earth. It tells you joy is whole, is permanent, and your lungs speak it to you. Oh, the marital air of the mountains, the convexity of spring; the anemones and the blue irises of the Alps; the lavender, the thyme and the rosemary; they seemed like death become white, like blood in the limbs and freshness in one's eyes.

362

Saroja wrote letters and I could understand, Madeleine did not write and I understood silences—words and silences again began to have meaning, and the earth was not the ecstasy of fever, but was solid; with milestones and trees, with the smell of tobacco shops selling picture postcards, the odour of rich, warm coffee, and the smell of Switzerland that makes the room feel the forest and the waters immaculate.

Man is born in pain. His rebirth is solitude, his song is himself. Thus spake Zarathustra, and thus indeed Savithri to Ananda.* Parsifal is the King of the Earth, and he will walk mountains and stand tiptoe on the peaks, seeing wave after wave of iridescent snow; and he will sing unto himself, for singing unto one's self is prayer. And when the planes shine over the Alps, you know they are led away through the mysteries of space into the kingdom where you will never be. Man, tell yourself, tell yourself in the simplicity of the night, you must go as you came, and assure yourself that the Ultimate is the solitude of joy. Rejoice, rejoice in the rejoicing of others, and know that you include the world as joy in the depth of your sleep.

* It may be useful to remind the reader that *Savithri and Ananda* was the name of an opera Wagner wanted to write, which later became the *Parsifal*.

WHEN I CAME BACK to Paris I found Catherine, and the baby so pretty, so happy. It seemed as though happiness was near at hand, could be cut from a tree like a jackfruit, like a *bēl*. I took a room near the Boulevard Saint-Germain, not far from the quay; thus in the evenings I could run down to the river and feel Paris in my nostrils. These October days were very beautiful, with the wind coming from the sea, and not from the north, thus making it seem like a prolongation of the high summer. A single lung seems to make your limbs lighter, your breath deeper and wise. I knew a little, very old restaurant opposite Notre-Dame, Le Coq d'Or, and when I went up, Madame Chimaye always had good *petits pois, salade Niçoise* and artichokes for me.

"*Pauvre Monsieur,*" she said, as though I had to diet because of medical advice—she could not understand vegetarianism on any other grounds. "*Pauvre Monsieur,* he must be well fed," she told the *patronne.* "He already looks so thin. When the north wind comes, he will be blown over the river and get stuck, like some saint, on Notre-Dame." I think she knew, somewhere beyond understanding, more of me than she put into words. "*Allez,*" she protested, "you must be gay when you are in Paris, Monsieur. Otherwise why should your father send you so far? I have a son who goes to school. He's sixteen and he's not bad at his studies. I say, 'Study, my son. But there's time, too, *pour les amusements.* If you are not gay when you are young, you may never be gay again.' Look at all the wars one has. The Americans want to take us to war again. 'And as for the Russians,' I tell my son, 'leave the happiness of humanity to the fools.' There is no happiness for humanity, except in work, in washing bottles, peeling potatoes, or carrying loads at Les Halles. And even if the Bon

Dieu himself should come down, don't you worry, Monsieur, you would still have to pay income tax."

She looked after me, did Madame Chimaye, as though I were some lost *fraticello*. She used to protest against the *patronne* charging me too much.

"Poor student that he is, and so far away from his parents, Madame la Patronne, and how he must languish for his country, his people. It must be such sunshine there, and here the winter weeps like some war widow at the cemetery of Aulnay-sous-Bois. I tell you, Madame la Patronne, we shall have war again this year. Look at the Americans!"

You could not argue with Madame Chimaye. You could not argue with the printed word of a newspaper. There were no duels in France any more: You could say what you liked, print what you wanted. *La France Libérée*—a paper founded in the Resistance by *les braves gens* must speak the truth. So many dead spoke through its columns, said Madame Chimaye. Her husband worked at the Renault Motor Works, and there they knew much that even a Minister would not know.

"What does a Minister know?" was Madame Chimaye's sound argument. "He hardly goes out, except with police motorcycles on either side and his secretary in front. It is his assistants who bring him the information from the whole of France, from the whole world."

Madame Chimaye, of course, knew things through her husband and such terrible things, too, she knew. And he knew them direct from his comrades.

"Oh, the world should never have lean men like you," she repeated, "nor sick. The world should be gay like the people at the Parc des Princes, play while you play and work while you work. Do you know Monte Carlo, Monsieur?" she asked. "There you have so much sunshine that you want to loose all the birds from their cages."

Madame Chimaye had one enemy. It was the man who did business with birds opposite. She hated him more than she hated the Americans. This man had larks, parakeets, canaries, herons, birds of paradise; and he sold grain for them, and medicines for the birds he sold too. He also made lovely cages— "These are the cages of Pekin," he would show his clients, "and these are *cages cambodges,* these *cingalaises;* and these are Arab ones, and these from the *îles martiniquaises.*" You could imprison your birds in lacquer, steel or oak, it all depended upon your purse and taste.

"Better, Monsieur," Madame Chimaye went on, "to be like those booksellers. Look at that friend of mine, Jean there. I have known him for thirty years. He has never grown older, always serving good people like you. And when the young come, foreigners, do you think our Jean would ever sell those horrible novels about naked women? Never, Monsieur, never. I tell him, 'Jean, you should have become a *curé.* You are so virtuous.' 'Ah,' he laughs, 'my virtue ends with my business. I am a tyrant at home. I have two children and a terrible woman; she is Spanish—Andalusian. I beat her sometimes, you know.' Maybe he does beat her; how would I know? My good man, he would touch me only with a feather. Been married for these thirty-one years, Monsieur. Happy as a bird, I am, and my son is happy too. Better sell books, Monsieur, those learned books, and even drawings and medals if you will, but to sell birds . . .! Ah, I would dip that fellow there with a hook in his ankle and his mouth in the Seine. Do they catch birds in your country, Monsieur?"

My friend Jean, the bookseller across the road, used to keep me supplied with my needs. I had just to tell him I wanted this text or that, and he would throw his scarf back and wink his eye; he knew exactly the person who would have it. Thus it was I got my Bédier, Lea, Gaston Paris and others. My work progressed.

I was not in a hurry to go back to India: what was there to go back to, after all? Little Mother had gone to live with Saroja in Allahabad, where Subramanya had now been transferred. She was so happy, for she could take her bath every morning at the Ganges. Sukumari and her husband were both in Bombay. Sukumari had joined the Communist Party. Her letters to me became more and more scarce. I was the arch-reactionary for her, and she hated me with the hate brothers and sisters have for one another when they cannot agree. Besides, Sukumari having married Krishnamachari, her politics became an act of faith, a duty she owed to her happiness. She had to love and worship her husband—she was too much of a Hindu not to worship her Lord. Then must she find an adversary, her enemy. Trotsky is an endocrinal need.

Saroja was moody. Her letters were inconsequent. Only in one letter did she say, "For me life has come to an end. By life I mean hope, work, fulfilment. I expect nothing, except that I long for you. Brother, come back soon."

Working in the Bibliothèque Nationale I would sometimes open Saroja's letter and read it again and again, thinking there must be someone in the world at some point of space to whom I could go with an open free warmth, and clear, tearful eyes. But for that I must have a home, I must get back home. I would then ask Saroja home, and Little Mother would spend six months with me and six months with her daughters. And one day, I said to myself, I would take Little Mother to Europe. She enjoyed sight-seeing; I would show her the Lake of Geneva, I would show her Les Invalides in Paris, and maybe I would take her to London and show her Saint Paul's, the Abbey and the Tower of London. "Oh, no more sea-aubergines!" I was sure she would say, remembering the fish she had been served at the Calcutta Terminus. (Like the wise Brahmins of Bengal, the Cathars too, I now read, could eat these "vegetables of the sea," as the fishes were not born *ex impuro coitu;* for when out of water they die!) I could perhaps persuade Little Mother to come. Maybe even Saroja would come. I was daydreaming. I cleaned my glasses and went back to my bulls of Innocent III. This very wise and good man had to choose between the purity of the heretics and the continuity of the Roman Church. He belonged not to the Church of Christ but to the Community of the Virgin Mary. The woman must rule the world.

I suddenly remembered Savithri's last words, not to me, but to the nurse at the hospital in London. "How men suffer!" she had exclaimed to Sister Jean outside, just before the door was closed; I think she wanted to linger, to say something to someone, to anyone. "How men suffer, Sister Jean! A woman's suffering seems physical: it has a beginning, so it has an end." "You are right, madam," said Sister Jean. "I always prefer women's wards to men's. Women seem to think that once the body is all right, everything is perfect." "And men?" asked Savithri. "Oh, with men, madam—oh, I am not speaking of Mr. Ramaswamy, he is such a good patient, but I mean generally speaking—man has sorrow in him. Every man is like a Christ on the Cross."

Poor Innocent III was such a Christ on the Cross. He paid his dues to the Virgin and founded the Inquisition.

Yes, indeed, how men suffer. The woman's suffering is, one might say, somewhat biological. It has a beginning, so it has an end. But man's suffering is like one of those trunk roads by the Ganges, that the avenue of trees, ancient and, as it were, bent with time, hide from rain and sun. But night comes and penetrates all, night goes through sleeping villages, round customs houses, travellers' bungalows and riverside caravanserais. And there is always a pilgrim, a *pravrajika,* moving—men going with baskets and blankets, women crying, the children asleep; the bullocks unable to drag any more, cars driving them mad, so much the cars hoot. But at break of dawn a parrot may sit on a banyan tree, and eat of its red fruit, and sing. That is all man's joy. Man's sorrow is not to belong to this earth. For him to marry is to belong to this earth, as the marrying of Catherine made Georges a Frenchman. He could now say, *"Nous autres français,"* and with pride. Man must wed to know this earth. "The womb (*bhāga*) is the great Prakriti (nature), and the Possessor of the womb (*Bhagavan*) is Shiva."

In the evenings I often went after dinner to Georges and Catherine. I used to go up the Boulevard Saint-Michel and take the 83 at the Gare Montparnasse, which would take me through Avenue Bosquet, and behind Les Invalides to Place d'Alma. I would linger a while by the river and then take the 63 straight to La Muette. From there I walked down to the Rue Michel-Ange. As I went up the staircase what memories came back to me, of Madeleine, of Oncle Charles and of Tante Zoubie. Letters from Madeleine had become very scarce, and often they would only be to ask some information about a bill I had not paid or about some book I had not returned to the library. She never asked me any more about my health, and of her own news she had nothing to say. "I am no more a person, so why speak of *it?* Of the body's news let the body hear, and of the rest nobody but oneself can tell oneself. So in fact, there is nothing to say. That is why I do not ask anything of you," she had written to me in London. I knew, however, through Catherine, who had friends visiting Madeleine, that she was constantly ill. She had, while pruning a branch of the pine tree in the garden, cut her finger, and the infection had lasted for over six weeks. She tried fasting, and when it seemed all but cured she developed a fever. Then she went on to fruit juice, but it did not bring the temperature down. Eventually she had to take penicillin injections, and she got much better.

Madeleine had by now decided that she would give up even Villa Les Rochers—the garden was too much of a burden. Besides, who was there to enjoy it? She took rooms on Rue Sainte-Geneviève, round the corner, not far from the post office. It was a quiet street, and on the top floor she had, she wrote to Catherine, two very spacious rooms (the landlord was a retired customs officer, and thank God, they had no children!). She had sent some of the unnecessary furniture, including the green chairs, the large spare bed, the two cupboards (ancient eighteenth-century ones, that had come from some English ancestors, they said) to Catherine. "You have a large family—I mean you will soon have a large family, and what does a single person need all this for?" she had written to Catherine. I think Catherine showed me that letter with a purpose. Often it seemed strange to enter the room and find those green plush chairs; I would look behind me to see if the door would open and Madeleine come in saying, "Oh these *professeurs,* these women! They never have any courage. They will fight with each other, but will not stand and fight for a principle. I'm tired of them!" No, Madeleine never had much kindness for women!

Oncle Charles sometimes came over from Rouen. He slept in the room next to the kitchen where I had first stayed. And once in a while he would come up to my new rooms, at the Hôtel des Parcs, Rue de Seine, and try to take me somewhere, anywhere.

"Oh, my daughter, she's like her mother. My first wife was not like Zoubie. She was a *rat d'église,* a smelly fat thing, that went to Mass every dawn, and cooked for her husband and her daughter, dressed the girl up for the Church and the School, and the rest of the time lay on her bed reading the Lives of the Saints. As time goes on Catherine, too, will become like her mother. There is no sap in her; I cannot say, 'Come, let us go somewhere'; she always chooses to go to the Bazar de l'Hôtel-de-Ville to buy children's toys or diapers for her lovely baby. *Au diable*, little round pieces of pink flesh!" said Oncle Charles, and took me first to the Place Clichy, and then to Montmartre.

My own feeling was—though there was nothing to prove it—that since Tante Zoubie's illness, Oncle Charles had other reasons for coming to Paris than to see his granddaughter. I did not think, from a careless remark he once made, that he went to his daughter each time he came down to Paris. Besides, at dinner he always took some mysterious pills out of the same round tube, with no label on it.

"I am not young any more," he explained one evening. "But then there is no reason why I should have such a big belly. I will never be like you, Rama, but I don't want to look like Monsieur Herriot either." From his face I knew he spoke without conviction. "Look, don't you think I have grown much thinner? Oh, I have such a lot of work! When business is bad, people begin to have crooked minds. These bad years mean much more work for a notary. People are so afraid of war. Do you think there will be war, Rama?"

"No," I answered, without much conviction.

After such a conversation I would say, "I will take a walk now, and go back and work," and he seemed always sad to see me go. Poor Oncle Charles, he wanted someone to go with him, so that he could laugh and talk and drink, and maybe take a woman to himself; his companion could always have chosen his own brunette or blonde, and, I imagine, he would have paid for it all. Georges once said that a mysterious woman—a frail, young voice—telephoned every Thursday evening to know if Oncle Charles was at home.

"From her accent I can see she is a woman from a very special *milieu*," said Georges. "She is so courteous, full of such elegant apologies. Catherine thinks it is an act of precaution. Should anything ever go wrong she could always come to the Rue Michel-Ange, and say whatever has to be said."

"They always know whom to approach for the final settlement," added Catherine.

"What is better than a daughter on the Rue Michel-Ange?" continued Georges. "They know the nature of a man or maid from the *quartier* they live in. Besides, they have their own private detectives. Well, poor Oncle Charles—he never had much success with his marriages. One woman was less cultured than he, and the other, the former wife of a future ambassador. It makes one feel so sad and he is such a good man."

But Catherine was worried about the legal consequences. After all, she was the daughter of a notary public.

"*Ah, là là,*" Oncle Charles said one day to me, "I am a crook among crooks, you know, Rama. I am not like your Gandhi, if hit on the right cheek, showing the left. I hit before anyone hits me. All I see every day is how someone wants to protect himself from being cheated by someone else. But when a man calculates that the other will cheat him, it means he would do the same to the other fellow when the time came. There is no love lost, I tell you, in this country. This is the country of Balzac," he concluded, as if he were quoting scriptures.

Sometimes I went with Georges and Catherine to Rouen—going in the morning and returning that same evening, often as late as twelve o'clock, past Pont de l'Arche, Vernon and Mantes. I always felt happy to see Tante Zoubie. True, her face was much disfigured with disease, but that did not make her tell less fascinating stories. Again and again it would be about the Central European diplomat, whose amorous adventures all the chancelleries knew, but who was nevertheless employed by everybody. Then when the war was over and everybody had the original documents to compare, it transpired that he had played tricks on all the governments, now acting the fool, now a drunkard, now a debauchee.

"*Ah, là là!*" said Tante Zoubie, "his love affairs were written on his face. He wore his women as he wore his cuff links or his pince-nez, and hid them when he wanted to. Oh, that grand tradition is gone now. Now you need bawds at your service.

They say that in Egyptian marriages they employ bawds to abuse the bridegroom's party. Like this the bride will be happy: luck is brought by insult, this is an ancient anthropological law. Oh, Rama, the more you travel in space or in time, the more you see the same phenomenon. Man is such a frail, such a foolish creature. If you respect him too much, he will cheat you. If you treat him with condescension, he will obey and insult you. So you must give him a hot bath at one moment and a cold bath at another, as the doctors have advised me. If you ask me who is paralysed, I or the world, I would say I *and* the world. My face is turned this way, but their faces are turned backwards like this, as they say the devil's is. It's just silly to live. And as silly, don't you think, to die? Imagine that that silly woman, la Comtesse de Noailles—I used to know her well, once, *chez* la Duchesse d' Uzès—could write of her terrible solitude in the tomb: '*Moi, qui n'a pas dormi seule, aux jours de la terre!*' I ask you, wise man, is one ever but alone? Tell me, Charles, did you marry me because you were alone? Speak. You married me because you wanted a wife, somebody to sew on your buttons, and wipe your mouth when your saliva ran down your face. *Oh, là là!* marriage is a grand institution. It prepares you handsomely for the grave. You lie by one another, at Saint-Médard, and you are known eternally—do you hear, eternally—as 'Monsieur et Madame Charles Roussellin, Notaire, Rouen (Seine Inférieure).' The Greeks at least wrote elegies. That made death interesting. In life there is a time for everything, love, marriage . . . and then—nothing at all. But now, Notaire, Charles Roussellin." Tante Zoubie laughed. By now Oncle Charles had left the room; he hated to hear about death. "It will come, when it will, as my *huissier* does. Why ask him to come earlier? Why waste the leather on my chair or the wine in my bottles? I know no dog will bark when they carry my hearse away."

Thus the conversation would go on till Georges looked at Catherine, and Catherine looked at me, and we all slowly rose to go. How lonely poor Oncle Charles felt. He would come to the door of the car, and stand with one foot on the running board, talking of coughs and colds or of clients and municipal rates, till Tante Zoubie would shout and say, "Don't catch cold! You haven't taken your coat, Papa." And the car would shake and hum and swing us away—Catherine driving carefully and with authority, while I, seated by her, turned to Georges at the back, and we talked of anything that came to our minds.

Georges's research in Chinese had led him to further very interesting theories about the relation between Nestorianism and Buddhism; he was still working on the Fou'kien stele, and on the connection between the lotus and the cross. His mind, wheresoever it went, took Christianity with it, as mine conspired with history to prove Vedanta. In fact it would seem, speaking objectively, that almost any theory will fit in with most facts, just as almost any system makes it possible to play chess efficiently. The only difference is, in how many cases can you say you really are convinced yourself? It is easy to convince others: you cannot fool yourself. And this, finally, is the only touchstone of good research.

Catherine was happy driving the car, and pointing to some corner of Mantes where she had come with Grandfather, or where she had fallen from a horse at the fair of Saint-Ouen. For her, life was a series of remembered facts. And a good life was one where there was such a series of remembered facts. Death itself when it came would be a remembered fact.

Passing in the night by the Seine, that quiet, self-assured river, which had given kings their strength and the French language its precision, how I fell back on myself, and remembered myself as the other. I would wonder, too, coming back home on those Sunday nights, whether Madeleine would one day let me speak to her again, or whether Savithri had reached India yet—would she be happy, truly happy?—whether the radar had indeed contacted the plane. I wondered what it would be like for Savithri to go back to the Surajpur Palace, with the Nine Musics of the day, the gunfire for the birthday of the Maharaja—he had a right to five rounds—and the parties at night, where the new crude Congressmen and the old vulgar aristocracy mingled for the building of a magnificent India. But it would never be my India, it could never be Savithri's India. It would in fact be nobody's India, till someone sat and remembered what India was.

India is not a country like France is, or like England; India is an idea, a metaphysic. Why go there anyhow, I thought; I was born an exile, and I could continue to be one. My India I carried wheresoever I went. But not to see the Ganges, not to dip into her again and again . . . No, the Ganges was an inner truth to me, an assurance, the origin and end of my Brahminic tradition. I would go back to India, for the Ganges and for the deodhars of the Himalayas, and for the deer in the forests, for the keen call of the elephant in the grave ocellate silence of the forests. I would go back to India, for that India was my breath, my only sweetness, gentle and wise; she was my mother. I felt I could still love something: a river, a mountain, the name of a woman . . .

I wished I could be a river, a tree, an aptitude of incumbent silence.

My work was making a patient and sometimes even a rapid progress. I had just finished my ninth chapter, on the Holy Grail, its historical significance and destiny, and had only two more chapters to finish. When I came, however, to the tenth chapter—it was on Paradise—I had to go very cautiously, for the old professors at the Sorbonne were not only clever men but often conservative and doctrinaire; you had to be sure that every perspective had been foreseen, or you could get into a mesh of futile and often exasperating discussion. I had been at too many *soutenances des thèses* not to know how often the self-evident seemed the least obvious to scholarly minds, especially if they have sat for too long in the same seat, and at the Sorbonne. For them there is nothing more to achieve, except it be the Collège de France—and that does not come everyone's way either. For the rest you go on punctuating your Racine according to historical rules and point out mistakes in the spelling of some text of Pascal, or an Agrippa d'Aubigné, that a former colleague, now dead, had taken some ten or twenty years to edit. For these old scholars, said Dr. Robin-Bessaignac, who was no typical Professor of the Sorbonne, every hypothesis had a way of opening somebody else's grave. The autopsy always proved intriguing. For that matter all bodies do behave differently, whatever their commonplace diseases—which again, Dr. Robin-Bessaignac pointed out, indicated the great significance of individuality; even in death you are different, whether you die of cancer or of heart trouble. But the dead scholar was the particular passion of the Sorbonnards: he smelt bad. "All graves smell bad," said Dr. Robin-Bessaignac, "and they enjoy this delicious humectus of fermenting toxins. It replaces their Dubonnet," said Dr. Robin-Bessaignac, and he was done with the subject.

My tenth chapter was especially difficult because it was going to deal with the metaphysical symbolism of Paradise. According to the Hindu concept there is not only *satya* and *asatya,* Truth and untruth, but also *mitya,* illusion—like the horns on the head of a rabbit, or the son of a barren woman. Paradise, I argued, was the inversion of Truth. To see frankly is not necessarily to see fairly—you can look at a thing upside down. After all, the deer went to drink water at the mirage. The Impossible becomes the beautiful. Love becomes divided against itself, just as Avignon is split into Petit Avignon and Avignon des Papes. In between is the Rhône and the broken bridge of Saint-Bénézet. You can go far into the river, but you cannot go across. Petit Avignon will always be Paradise. It is like Avignon seen in the river: you see the reflection and you enjoy it; you can see it like a child and enjoy it; but put your hand into the water and try to catch it, to palp it, and you have only water in your hand. So does the deer drink water of the mirage or the barren woman have her son.

Heresy, I continued, was the near-Truth seen as Truth. Heresy is romantic, as Petit Avignon is romantic, heresy is the promise of Paradise. Heresy is the masculine turned feminine for protection, for fear of the real—like the solid golden England under Queen Victoria. Paradise is a feminine continuity in a cul-de-sac, it is the deification of death, the immortality of mortality; Paradise, therefore, is full of angels. Eternity is a masculine concept. To accept eternity is to dare annihilation. To be dissolved is not to be reborn. But Paradise is to continue as one is—as a ghost is supposed to be—only not in darkness but in light. Not to dare annihilation but to continue is to affirm the tangibility of the object. In a Paradise created outside of time, isolate and blue, as in some of the medieval manuscripts—with queens, gardens and palaces, and turrets; white horses, storytelling pygmies, the unicorn, and angels trumpeting; with the river of Paradise flowing as milk— you create the isolation of love. You keep your body pure for Paradise, *come la carna gloriosa e santa*. You jump into fire and become pure, because you will go to Paradise. So Paradise becomes the fulfilment of love.

> On a green emerald
> It carried, the desire of Paradise:
> It was the object called the Holy Grail.

Turrets, blue skies and the music of angels are promised. So you isolate your love and put her into a turret, into a palace. You can go as far as the end of the broken bridge, and look at Petit Avignon. And standing on this side you can sing ditties. Being un-deflowered the virgins in Paradise will be exalted. Their bosoms will be full, their limbs straight and lovely, and on their heads will be crowns. There is no pain and there is love. Meanwhile you go, on horse and foot, to fight the Turk. The Holy Land shall be free. There be many lovely women there. You might marry them, give children to them and return heroes with booty, with your limbs stilled of passion. Then lay your sword before your Lady, and offer her your worship. She smells it, and you sing to her.

> Sans coeur suis et sans coeur demeure
> Je n'ai membre, ni pied, ni main.
> Sans amour en amour demeure,
> Vivant, faut-il donc que je meure.

That is the perfect picture of Paradise.

To be orthodox, to be a *smartha*, I said to myself, is to accept the real. Stalin is orthodox; he is crude and smelly like some Jesuit father, he the product of a seminary. But Trotsky promised us beauty, promised us Paradise. There is a saying that when Trotsky was talking of the beautiful world revolution, Stalin was making statistics of the bovine riches of Soviet Russia. He wanted to know whether the peasants had enough to eat and drink, and their children had enough milk.

Again, Bonaparte turned the French Revolution and made it

realistic. He built roads and bridges, started a military academy, established jurisprudence, innovated the system of education and turned Robespierre's Republic into a total human experience. ("Robespierre himself," said Péguy, "that Royalist.") But Bonaparte went wrong when, after changing his world, he established himself as the cause of the change; from the Consul Bonaparte he made himself the Emperor of the French. From an impersonal revolutionary he made himself into a hero; as a person, an ego, he entered history. This he knew to be improper, which explains his desperate desire to be crowned by the Pope, to be sanctified, to recover the impersonal—the thief of the Absolute, to become identical with the Absolute. And thus on to the Emperor N.N.N.N. . . . Otherwise Napoleon would have ended, almost as Hitler did, on the bunk of a dugout.

The Cathar, the pure Hitler, who ate only green vegetables, lived in some Montségur (remember Tristan and Parsifal) and ended in the crudity of his own myth. He married Eva Braun: that had to be his death. Paradise ended on that bunk.

Beatrice, O Beatrice is beautiful in Paradise. But what an impossible tyrant she becomes. It is she who wants to show the Truth to Dante.

> Apri gli occhi e riguarda qual son io;
> tu hai veduto cose, che possente
> sei fatto a sostener lo riso mio.

She who should see light through him, now wants to show the light to him. It is the inversion of Truth. Where the world cannot annihilate itself, whether it be in Buddhism or in Christianity, it has to make the world feminine. Just as progeny is through woman, child after child, generation after generation, you may have as many paradises as you care to have. Buddhism went to Tibet, and gave itself many paradises. Tantra entered Hinduism, and worshipping the women, made the world real. Man became thus the everlasting, the superman, the slave of himself, and all such supermen must end in stink and on the bunk of a dugout. Eva Braun showed the world was real. The ogre, the superman Hitler, inventor of the gas chambers and the concentration camps, died a simple man. Almost an anonymous person. Ravana was defeated by his ten heads. The miracle must for ever end in emptiness.

But the *smartha*—some Innocent III—knows this world is intangible, and all worlds therefore are intangible, and turns his vision inwards. Paradise vanishes *where* you are—the *interior intimo meo* of Saint Augustine. And the world continues as it is. The two are not distinct experiences, but it is experience seen as the totality of Experience. Whether you see the world or you do not see the world you *are*.

Writing this I am reminded of a very moving story of Radha and Krishna:

"One day Radha had a very possessive thought of Krishna. 'My Krishna,' she said to herself, as though one could possess Krishna as one could possess a calf, a jewel. Krishna, the Absolute Itself, immediately knew her thought. And when the Absolute knows, the knowing itself, as it were, is the action of the act; things do not happen according to his wish, but his wish itself is his own creation of his wish, as the action is the creation of his own action.

"So, Durvasa the great Sage was announced.

" 'He is on the other side of the river, Lord,' spake the messengers, 'and he sends his deep respects.'

"Then Krishna went into the inner chambers and said to Radha, 'Radha, Durvasa the great Sage is come, my dear. We must feed him.'

" 'Oh, then I will cook the food myself,' said Radha, and Krishna was very happy at this thought. So he went back to the Hall of Audience, and not long after, Radha came in with all the cooked food. 'Yes, the meal is ready, my Lord. And I will take it myself to Sage Durvasa.'

" 'Wonderful, wonderful!' exclaimed Sri Krishna, pleased with the devotion of his wife to the Sages.

" 'I'll go and come,' said Radha, and hardly had she gone to the palace door when she remembered the Jumna was in flood. No ferryman would go across. She came back to Krishna and begged, 'My Lord, how can I take the food? The river is in flood.'

" 'Tell the river,' answered Krishna, 'Krishna the *brahma-chari** wishes that the way be made for you to pass through.'

"And Radha went light of heart, but suddenly bethought herself it was a lie. Who better than she to know whether Krishna be *brahmachari* or not? 'Ah, the noble lie, the noble lie,' she said to herself, and when she came to the river, she said, 'Krishna, the Lord, the *brahmachari,* wishes that the way be made for me to pass through.'

"And of course the river rose high and stood still, but suddenly opened out a blue lane, small as a village footpath, through which Radha walked to the other side. And coming to the opposite shore, she thanked the river, and saluting the great Sage Durvasa, in many a manner of courtesies and words of welcome, spread the leaf, and laid him the food.

"Durvasa was mighty hungry and he ate the food as though the palm of his hand went down his gullet. 'Ah, ah,' he said and belched and made himself happy, with curds and rice and many meats, perfumed and spiced with saffron, and when there was nothing left in leaf or vessel, he rose, went to the river and washed his hands. Radha took the vessels to the waters, too, to wash, threw the leaf into the Jumna and stood there to leave. Then it was she suddenly remembered, the river was in flood. Sri Krishna had told her what to say while going and not what to utter while coming back.

"Durvasa understood her question before she asked—for the Sages have this power too—and he said, 'Tell the river, Durvasa the eternal *upavasi*† says to the river, "Open and let Radha pass through to the other shore.' "

"Radha obeyed but she was sore sorrowful. 'I have seen him eat till his palm entered his gullet, and he has belched and passed his hand over his belly with satisfaction. It is a lie, a big lie,' she said, but she went to the river thoughtful, very thoughtful. 'River,' she said, 'Durvasa who is ever in *upavasa* says open and let me pass.'

"And the river opened a lane just as wide as a village pathway, and the waves held themselves over her head, and would not move. She came to the other shore and returned to the palace in

* The celibate, or he who has taken the vow of celibacy.
† He who fasts.

heavy distress. 'Yes, nature is a lie, nature believes and obeys lies. Lord, what a world,' she said to herself, and going into the Hall of Sorrowing, shut herself in and began to sob. 'Lord, what a lie the world is, what a lie.'

"Sri Krishna knew the cause and cadence of this all, and gently entered the Hall of Sorrowing: 'Beloved, why might you be in sorrow?' he said.

" 'My Lord,' she answered, 'the river believes you are a *brahmachari,* and after all who should deny it better than me, your wife? And then I go to Durvasa and he eats with his palm going down his gullet, and he says, "Tell the river, Durvasa who is ever in *upavasa* asks you to open and let Radha pass." And the river opens herself, makes a way large as a village pathway, and I pass over to this side. The world is a fib, a misnomer, a lie.'

" 'The world, my dear, is not a lie, it is an illusion. Besides, tell me, is my body your husband, Radha?'

" 'No, my Lord.'

" 'Is my mind your husband, Radha?'

" 'No, my Lord.'

" 'Then what is it you mean when you say to yourself, "Krishna, my husband"?

" 'Assuredly something beyond the body and beyond the mind —the Principle.'

" 'And tell me, my love, can you possess that, can you possess *it*?'

" 'No, my Lord, how can I possess the Absolute? The "I" is the Absolute.' And she fell at the Lord's feet and understood, and lived ever after in the light of the Truth."

To be free is to know one is free, beyond the body and beyond the mind; to love is to know one is love, to be pure is to know one is purity. Impurity is in action and reaction: what is born must die, what has form must vanish and stink. La Charogne of Baudelaire was a fact; La Charogne was a fact to accept, so that Cézanne could paint the mauve and violent sky of Mont Sainte-Victoire. You need not take *consolamentum* and jump into the fire to be a Cathar, for what are you but a Cathar? Everyone, beyond his body and beyond his mind, is a Cathar. The Ganges dissolves all sin. Even the ashes of the dead that the fire has burnt must dissolve in the Ganges and have absolution.

> *Sakala kalusha bhangé svarga sopana sangé*
> *Taralata rangé Devi Gangé prasida*
> Dissolver of blemishes
> Companion of the Waters
> Dancing and sparkling Ganges I worship.

Benares is everywhere where you are, says an old Vedantic text, and all waters are the Ganges. To realize this is to be a true Cathar. The rest is heresy.

But I had such a tender heart for the Cathars, as I had for the Buddhists, that I felt I must go down south, and see in the light of the Languedoc the truth of this truth, so to say. Yet the Church too had its truth—you must remember what a kind and gentle Christian even Innocent III was. On the other hand, how could one condemn those who, with such beauty in their eyes and their faces lit with a divine conviction, jumped down the precipice at Montségur, or shut themselves up in the caves of Orolac, the Holy Grail in their hands? Death itself to them was life.

The Cathar, the Saint, wants to transform the world in his image—he the supreme anarchist. The Sage knows the world is but perception; he is King, he, Krishna the King of Kings. The one cannot be many, but the many can be one, and the one thus transcended to its non-dual source, the *ekam advayam,* the one-not-two, is Truth. (In between is the moralist, the Republican of Ferney, with one foot in Royalist France, the other in Zwingli's Switzerland, in the contemplation of the lake, memoryful.) Brother, my brother, the world is not beautiful—you are beauty. Be beauty and see not the beautiful, my Parsifal.

I went down to Montpellier again, to that very lovely arched town of Henri IV, took a room on Boulevard Ledru-Rollin, just off the recurrent aqueduct of Le Peyrou. Wandering backwards and forwards through that light and clear air, wandering to Béziers to see the Black Church again, going to Sète to see the Cemetery, taking a train and going to Carcassonne, feeling the earth, and looking at the faces of the men and women of Languedoc, I understood much that no history could say. There was great kindness in the sunshine, a keen perceptivity about the cypresses, the oaks of the *garigue*; some love had passed by there, that had no name as yet, and had hallowed the land. The minstrelsy of Languedoc had made modern man, as Denis de Rougement explained, and the troubadour was the forerunner of Paul Valéry. The Lady had to be, for the Cemetery of Sète to have meaning. The Mediterranean had to be, for happiness to be. In that sunshine, in the touch of that volcanic earth, man could believe in his own realistic eternity. Greece made life real. Montségur made death real. To believe in death is to commit suicide—the Cathar Bernard Bort refused *consolamentum* because he thought he could not die: *quia non putabat mori*. Life that prolongs itself beyond death, beyond all deaths, is orthodox, is the real law. "Never at any time am I subject to Death," says the Rig-Veda. The only real illusion, *mrityu, mara,* is Death. Man seeks for ever the death of Death.

You can live in life and think on death. Can you be in death and think on life? La Charogne proved the soul. Valéry fulfilled Bertrand de Born:

Lumière! . . . ou toi, la mort!

Instead of life being turned into death, death had to be integrated into life. The cemetery proved the Mediterranean, with its serrated cypresses going upward into the light of the hill, the silly tower of the church, and its empty bell, showed the wide, blue, free Mediterranean was the norm, the reality. The Mediterranean is inclusive of Sète. *"La mer, la mer toujours recommencée."*

The acrid, crusted Languedoc did not have the rolling, self-assured sweetness of Provence. The Rhône divided them, blue-green, Mother Rhône. And where the Rhône met the Mediterranean rose the stub, collected Church of Saintes-Maries-de-la-Mer, where Marie-Madeleine had landed, and where the gipsies still come to crown their king. Farther away, where the Mediterranean turns inwards, withdraws with an intimate tenderness into the land, and curves again to make the castellated hilltops of

Liguria, is Italy; there man believed himself to be whole, and so invented the Paradise where the acorn grows. I had shut myself in, and tried to isolate myself in the present of separated existence. Mother Rhône, sister to Ganga, flowed on the other side. Madeleine's kingdom was not my world; her trees, virgins, Buddhist pigeons were not of my understanding. I lived among the unicorns. I wrote letters to Madeleine and I had no reply.

The days were filled with many splendid things. As the sunshine had given me an instinct to see, to discover, I went into libraries, families, monasteries and found manuscripts and stories of the Cathars, for Catharism is a very living tradition in the Languedoc; and I marvelled at the sheer magnanimity of their faith. I did not hear from Savithri for a very long time. Then came just a line, sent on by Cooks from Paris: "The radar, Rama, has landed the plane where it should. Forgive me. S." The Ligurian coast seemed to shine with a greener brilliance than I had ever known before. Paradise, I thought, does, does exist . . .

One very cold winter evening early in January, when the snow had fallen, and the whole world seemed re-created, I went back to Aix. It was moving to hear the long lamentations of the Marseille streetcars, to smell the rich, soaplike air of the city, and slowly, desperately seek back the hills, the mountains, from which so much sweetness, so much purity once had flowed. The Buddha might have passed there, so cool and tender the landscape looked, and it was as if the stones were but elephants that had knelt, as the Compassionate One passed by, offering their homage, kneeling with their trunks between their legs. The Buddha had touched them, and such was their love of the Lord that "Let his touch remain," they said, and so became stone. And in between the legs of the elephants, where they laid their trunks, little altars were built by the Goths, and then by the Romans and the French, first in adoration of the sun and moon, Apollo, Zeus and Diana; and then time turned them into chapels of the Virgin, the Mother of God. I could have knelt as the bus swung upwards. Holiness is wheresoever love is.

I entered the Cathedral of Saint-Sauveur and wandered into myself. How such a structure seems to mirror one's own mystery, the memory of one's self, the picture of one's being. The dead live in the towers, they say, and the dead speak in compassion to us. Father, mother, brother, husband or son: speak, that we bear kindness to one another, that we revere one another, for in death there is no reverence. Death is a shadow, a despair of light.

I knelt, I do not know for what, and hid my eyes from myself. I did not weep, I did not sing, I did not know. I knelt that happiness might be. That the dead might pardon us for our mistakes, for we are poor fools, thinking that the Rhône divides mankind. Love was born on those *garigues* of Provence, and love lights us when we pray.

Love shines as the instinct in the step, where we move. The snow has fallen again. We leave our footsteps behind telling love we have loved. The post office may be there and may not take letters—for someone, they think, has cut the bridge on the Rhône —but where chevaliers have walked, and have conquered kingdoms for their ladies, why could not a Brahmin, a simple foolish soul, go up the steps and see the light on the second floor of Villa Sainte-Cécile? I go up the steps, I the husband of Madeleine.

There were irises on both sides of the pathway. The snow had bent them, the snow overflowing the orange trees. I rang, where my name still was, "K. R. Ramaswamy," and Madeleine came down the staircase. She was light of foot, though she was still round; her fat had not diminished. Like the moon in a theatre, there was a crescent somewhere in the sky, and an abundant purity about the stars. Madeleine opened the gate.

"It is I," I said. *"C'est moi,* Madeleine." She did not seem surprised. She did not look happy; she did not look hesitant. "May I come in?" I said, as she walked back up the garden. I closed the gate behind me. She held the door wide ajar, for me to come in.

It was a strange house, it was someone else's house. There were wheelbarrows on the landing, and bottles and two bicycles. I went up the stairway. The rooms were bare. Almost all the furniture was gone, it seemed. There was the same low bed, covered with a yellow bed-cover. There were many *chakras* and mandalas on them, like one sees on Tibetan *tanakas*. The table was richer with a few more *vajras,* a few more demons and a very beautiful big Avalokiteshwara. There were red hibiscus in the water, and at the foot of the Avalokiteshwara. I sat in the only chair in the room, still one of the plush chairs that had come from her mother. She sat on the floor, squat like a Hindu, and took the rosary from the table. The room smelt of something familiar —it smelt of sandalwood.

"Why did you come?"

"To see you."

"You cannot see anything but the eighteen aggregates."

"But eighteen aggregates can see eighteen aggregates," I said, laughing.

"Then it is no business of mine," she said, and started counting her beads. I sat there, in the smell of sandalwood. In the inner picture, of Indra and Prajapathi, of the Buddha that was, and the Buddha to be, I saw mountains, rivers and snows, animals and mankind walking backward through history, as in a film, as in some ancient story. I could see Madeleine kneeling before an ascetic and saying, "My Lord, are you a man or a divinity?" And the yellow-robed one answered, "May I know what I am, lady? I am but a wanderer, a minstrel, a mendicant." And she gave him, she in the infinitude of her compassion, a home and a bowl, hot water to wash in and cool, cool water to drink. She rubbed him, did the lady, with many sweet-smelling unguents, and bathed him in the love of her tears; her hair grew long and curled and black, for her love was so simple in devotion, and she rose and she sat, as though love was a gesture, a genuflexion, and she parodied herself out of existence, remembering the love she bore the ascetic. And she lived a long and intent life, in world after world, bathed herself and combed her hair, washed herself and prepared herself, as though for a wedding; but when the earth came and the light of trees and rivers, the intelligence of Plato, the directness of Descartes, she gave herself a name and a station, and prepared herself for a festival.

Festival is only the commemoration of what is not; you worship the non-existent to prove that you exist. You worship yourself in your birthdays, saying time is eternal. You worship your son knowing you will die. You worship your husband the Lord, knowing he is a fool, a thief, a non-existent Brahmin, "made of the eighteen aggregates of Nagarjuna." True, the snow is pure and white in the garden outside; true that the sun must shine some day on the footsteps that have been left behind; true, too, that the Buddha has passed this way, and that elephants have knelt; and that the Black Virgin of Saint-Ouen still cures dread diseases —three circumambulations with a stick of oak, and four *"OM— JRIMs,"* and a draught of the juice of red dandelion with honey, and eight narrow nights on the white carpet asleep—and the next morning, what you give cures, what you say heals. But love, my love, cannot be healed, cannot be said. It must go as it came. It must not linger, it must not name, it must die; for it was made of the eighteen aggregates. Love that is love remains, like those hibiscus in the crystal; the water reflects them, as my eye reflects God. Look, look into it, my Brahmin, and see me. *"Apri gli occhi e riguarda qual son io."*

There was no word spoken, and all was said. You just see the counting of beads. Then you rise and say to God, even unto the Buddha Himself, many, many angry things. "Lord Buddha, my Lord, O you abode of Compassion, O you who talked even unto the courtesan Ambapalli and partook of the meal of Chunda, the untouchable, do you hear me? May love be as fat-bosomed as the olives in Aix be ancient." (*"Ah, cela vient du temps des Romains,"* said Scarlatti, as though, being Italian, he still was a Roman, and as though he had conquered France.) Lord Buddha, did you make the cypress grow grey, and the skin so pale? Must one shine only because one is desperate, that man and husband had to take the steps out of the garden, counting the marks he'd made on the pure winter snow? Must the bead be the ladder of intelligence? Must truth grow fat with fasting? It smells bad, Lord Buddha, it smells very bad, that the Kingdom of earth be shut in with a garden gate.

India, my Lord, is a vast and lost land; a beloved land of many mountains and cliffs, of cedars and deodhars, of elephants and tigers, of pigeons that sing and owls that hoot. We grow mangoes in India, Lord Buddha, and the women of my country worship trees. Buddha, Lord Buddha, quit the sanctum, come through vision and dream; come like that statue of you, brought to London in some British Governor's box, which came night after night with tears in its eyes, and body grown fat with fasting, saying,

386

"Send me back, send me back, send me back to my own land";
till one day the lady sent the Buddha away and all was peace and
brilliance in the air of Brighton. Buddha, Lord Buddha, do not
traffic with the Black Virgin; do not sing those Tibetan mantras;
do not fast, do not preach, do not count beads; open the door and
walk out to the India that is everywhere about, marking the
footsteps on the snows.

The river Rhône flows like the Ganges, she flows, does Mother
Rhône, into the seven seas, and she built herself a chapel, that the
gay gipsies might come and sing and worship Sarah in her sanctuary. Ships go, rushing ships go now to India, to far India,
to quick India. Go there, Mother Earth, go there, Mother Rhône!
Do not devastate your being with fast, tear and prayer. India
is the Kingdom of God, and it is within you. India is wheresoever
you see, hear, touch, taste, smell. India is where you dip into
yourself, and the eighteen aggregates are dissolved. Even Bertrand
de Born I take with me. I would take even Péguy to my India.
Come . . . Mother, Mother Rhône . . . !

I must have gone round and round the post office six or seven
times, then I went down to the Place de la République and
jumped into a taxi. I said "Tarascon"—and what a night of love
it was, with the moon and the snow, and then the Rhône.

I went back to work. I now understood why the boat of Iseult,
which carried the white sail first and then the black, was seen
by the people of Loonois as though the black came first. Iseult
with the lovely hands had to remain a widow. The potion of
love was made of the eighteen aggregates. The limb and the
lip spoke to one another. King Mark was not fooled, he was wise
and he knew, knew that being a King, a Principle, he could not
admit sin. Where sin is admitted death is true. Tristan took
Iseult of the White Hands as bride, but he did not take her
maidenhead. Between adultery and virginity is the river Rhône.
The gipsies who marry and dance at Saintes-Maries-de-la-Mer
know there is no sin. When you have a Gipsy King, and the long
road, you play with life distributing destiny cards to yourself.
King or Queen, Diamond or Heart, they are so many dimensions
of one's living. But when you live in dimension itself, the world is

yours. You reap and you enjoy, you breed children and you grow fat, you live in a palace or you give away prizes at a football match ("Savithri Prize at the Allahabad Football Finals," I had read in some Indian newspaper, and seen Savithri giving away a prize to some sturdy fool), but love is continuous with dimension, love is the light of space. Objects are articulated in space, so go right, go left, go north, go east, you cannot go beyond yourself. Love, my love, is the self. Love is the loving of love.

Harmonieuse Moi . . .

The train came from Sète, and took me away through the night and by the Rhône, to the severe clarity, the austere benignity of Paris.

I HAVE NOW TAKEN a room off the Boulevard Saint-Michel, just where the Rue de Vaugirard goes up by the Lycée Saint-Louis. My room is on the seventh floor—I had long been waiting to live up here, and had asked for it week after week at the hotel. Now, I have it. It's a small mansard room but from my window the whole of Paris lies spread like a palm-leaf fan under me. Beyond the terrace of the Lycée Saint-Louis line after line of walls, towers and coloured chimneys rise into the air, and then suddenly down below you see the green Seine under the bridges, and to the right, as though abruptly put aside, the parvis of Notre-Dame.

> Et nous tiendrons le coup, rivés sur notre rame,
> Forçats fils de forçats aux deux rives de Seine
> Galériens couchés aux pieds de Notre-Dame.

Behind me I can feel, though I cannot see, the history—almost the architecture of time—out of which the garden and the Palace of Luxembourg were born. I often walk there, breathing the clean sane air of the park, and see the children play about, setting their ships to sail all over the waters. They must indeed wander through many lands, encircle many continents:

> Vaisseau de pourpre et d'or, de myrrhe et de cinname,
> Double vaisseau de charge aux pieds de Notre-Dame.

And when I am tired, I come and sit by one of those stiff chairs that seem especially reserved for lovers, by the Medici fountain. The water drips and seems to make us forget time, as if it were a cravat pulled loose to one side. For here, woman whispers to man seated on the lap of the sun. I close my book and go down the Boulevard Saint-Michel, feeling that between the top of the hill and the parvis of Notre-Dame is the real sanctuary of Europe.

"When we speak in universal terms of class and category, do these terms correspond to realities existing outside the mind?" asked scholars at the beginning of the Middle Ages. "When we speak of the species *man* and the species *animal,* do these terms awaken ideas of *collection?* And does the idea of *collection* correspond to a reality outside the mind, or is it a mere concept of the mind? And if these terms or universals are not mere concepts, but do correspond to realities, what is their nature? Are they corporeal entities? And further, what is their mode of existing? Do they have their being outside the sensual domain, that is, outside the individual, or do they lodge within?" Thus and for a thousand years, through Abelard, Saint Thomas Aquinas and Dante, and all the monks and poets, going down the centuries, through the alleyways and hard earth of the Sorbonne, you feel the Western world has breathed and shaped itself; and he who walks in Paris here, walks somewhere in the steady light of recovered Truth.

Now and again, when I am stuck in my work and I can dip into silence and find nothing to say, nothing to sound, to illumine me, I seek over the walls for an answer, I seek through the space above the river for an answer, I look at the twin towers of Notre-Dame. I say a prayer to the Mother of God, at such times: *"Marie pleine de grace, Mère de Dieu."* And she always knows and she always answers, for the womb of the world is She.

And when I have shaped a sentence to my satisfaction, word after word repeated back to silence, rediscovered through a backward movement and made whole, reverberant and true, I leave the authenticity of it on the page, and wonder that these round and flat shapes could name meaning as they do. I shiver at the thought that one can speak. I repeat some verse from a troubadour, and then tell myself that only half a century ago, perhaps, Verlaine walked these very streets, drunk, and not knowing how to say his own name. It is good to forget's one's name, it makes one a saint.

So much of Paris rises up, evening after evening, as I sit in this room and work—ghosts, dignitaries, crusaders, kings, poets—that I want to get out, to walk out where no man has ever walked, no one has ever borne his own torture.

J'ai plus de souvenirs que si j'avais mille ans.

Then I go down the steps, ring up Georges from the bureau of the hotel, for I have no telephone in my room, and when they say come—they always do—I jump into the 83 bus at the Gare Montparnasse, linger a little by the river as usual, then cross over and take the 63. Down La Muette I walk as if I were in Hyderabad or Mysore, and the street were one that father and son we had walked, so personal it has become. It is always Catherine who opens the door, with her splendid rich smile—as if one could possess happiness with the same certitude of holding a baby in one's arms.

"Vera is sleeping," she said one day, knowing Vera had become a great friend of mine. "She's had fever, you know, Rama, and I was so frightened. But Georges said it was nothing, just the effect of the temperature outside going up and down in a way that even our adult bodies are not strong enough to bear. Tell me, how are you?"

Georges was standing behind me, as I removed my coat; I could feel him take my scarf and hat, and hang them on the rack. "It's nice to see you, Rama. How terrible to think France is becoming like Russia. It has been twenty-five degrees below at Luxeuil. Can you imagine it! In the Luxembourg even old men have begun to take to skating."

"Georges will not allow me to do any *patinage* in the Bois. But when I see men and women carrying skates I want so much to go, and say, 'Gee' like that, and swirl and fall on myself. I love snow and all that is white," Catherine said. "White, snow-white, is my colour."

I went in and we sat on the green plush from Aix. Oncle Charles had been very ill.

"When the strong fall ill, it's like a bull falling—you need three other bulls to help you out of it," said Catherine, "not like a horse. Georges falls ill and rises as if it were a game he was playing; I never can believe in his illness. Tante Zoubie is so worried."

I promised we would go there the week after. And then Catherine gave me a letter from Madeleine.

Madeleine spoke of my visit to her. "It's all like a ghost story," she wrote, "Rama, India—and the world. Contemplation is the only truth one has. I pray that I be forgiven for my sins—my ignorances, the Buddhist text would call them. By the way, Cathy, before Rama leaves for India, don't you think it would be wise for the legalities to be settled, once and for all? My own future is settled. I want nothing: what I earn teaching will suffice me for a lifetime. So I have been thinking that Vera, and others who will come after her, should have everything. Anyway it all belongs to the family, my properties in the Charente, in Rouen, and even that plot of land in Saint-Médard. I will just keep mother's house at Saintongel. Just a spot to call my own, that is all; and that again only as long as I live.

"I am sure it would also be wise to give Rama his freedom. He must marry someone younger from his own country. He will be happy with an Indian woman, I have no doubt. I know talking like this is painful, but truth has some day to be faced. In any case Rama must go back to his family; his lungs cannot bear our climate any more. Besides, why would he want to stay in France? Nowadays divorce has become so easy. You could perhaps tactfully put it to Oncle Charles. Better still, why don't you consult someone there, while I consult someone here?"

It was, of course, the inevitable, and by the inevitable nobody has yet been surprised: you know what is going to happen before surprise dawns on you. So quite simply I accepted to go to a lawyer in Paris. Georges knew of a very able Russian-born advocate, who would make everything easy. Meanwhile Madeleine went to see a notary in Aix, and a letter came from a Maître Charpentier, asking me to consult a colleague of his. And on a Saturday, only the other week, we went over, Catherine and I, into some obscure district off the Rue Saint-Denis. Past the Porte Saint-Martin and the Boulevard Sébastopol was a little lane.

"You know what these streets are, do you, Rama?"

"No," I said.

"You are so simple and innocent that I am sure you will never have heard about this quarter." I understood. "Formerly," said Catherine, "the police used to insist on cards; now these ladies have the same profession, only they need not pay any municipal tax."

It was the day after that terrible March storm, you remember. The wind had blown away chimney pots, wireless wires, laundry hangings, and papers out of offices; even children's toys and old chairs had been thrown into back yards. It howled through garage doors, through school archways, and sang in the chimneys. Through windows and chimneys birds had been blown in, leaves, handkerchiefs. In these back alleys of the Boulevard Sébastopol they had not cleared up everything.

"It smells of spring," said Catherine, as she parked the car. "Wrap yourself up, Rama. Nothing is so treacherous, we say, as the winds of March."

Yes, spring seemed to be in the air. We wandered to and fro, along the Rue Saint-Pierre, looking for the house number. We could not find 17 anywhere, so we looked in at a locksmith's, a round, portly man with an apron, who came out and showed us the narrow entrance to the building. We went up the smelly, dark staircase, and wondered why it was not lit.

"*Ah! là là,*" said someone coming down, "it's not enough to be blown at hot and cold, now the electricity must also give us the go-by. Funny, funny this country. You pay income tax through the nose, and you don't have light to see beyond it." He held a match against my face, to convince himself I was another man. When he saw Catherine, he thought the world even funnier. "You never can say what the world will be," he concluded at the bottom of the staircase, "white or dark. What do you say to that, Pierre?"

Higher up, the afternoon sky gave some visibility through the skylight. Maître Sigon was there.

"The lights have all gone," said his secretary from behind the counter, "but please sit here, Monsieur and Madame." And she planted a lit candle behind us. "Monsieur Sigon has a client at the moment. He will see you immediately." We sat for ten miserable minutes, and we did not seem to have anything to say to one another.

"To think that everything must end in darkness, even when spring is in the air," I said, eventually, and added, "The law is the death of truth."

"Don't condemn me so easily," pleaded Catherine. "Where would I be if Oncle Charles had not piled up money by counting on the crookedness of mankind?" Somehow this gave me an assurance, a feeling of positive goodness—life flowed deeper in the bowels of existence. "You must have a son this time, and soon," I said, to assure Catherine of my goodwill.

"Oh, it's enough to have one, for the moment. By the time you come back from India I shall have a second one, I promise."

The wooden door behind me opened. Maître Sigon, a little round man, with a pince-nez and a black ribbon to hold it, called us in. A white round spot of light—a kerosene lamp, such as we have in India when babies are asleep—lit the green baize of Maître Sigon's desk. He looked up at me, asked my name, father's name, mother's name, date of birth, and assured himself that everything sent by the *notaire* from Aix was correct. "You married Madeleine Roussellin, on February tenth, nineteen-forty-nine, at the Mairie of the Seventh Arrondissement. Is that right?"

"Oui, Maître."

"Now, you ask for a divorce."

"No, not I, but Madeleine Roussellin does."

"Yes, yes," he said, looking first at the paper in front of him, and then at me, unconvinced. "We men are so virtuous, Monsieur. It's always the women who cuckold us," and the storm was on me before I knew. I brushed it away with a broomstick. Catherine looked at me, as if to say, "What can one do? They are like that, the *huissiers* of Paris." But I still felt I could not let such vulgarity pass unnoticed.

"So you do not love your wife any more, Monsieur?" continued Maître Sigon.

"I never said that, Monsieur."

"But you have to say that. That is the law. Do you think they are *copains* of ours at the bench, and will arrange our affairs as nicely as you'd wrap a present, and offer us an aperitif after that?"

"I am a foreigner, Maître," I reminded him, "and I do not know French law."

"I know French law, Monsieur. Yes, of course, you are a foreigner. You are an Indian." Saying this, he told himself, that since Indians were inferior, what did it matter when he spoke ill of France or not? You could shout at your wife before your servant at home, but you kissed her hand when you went out. For Maître Sigon, India had not yet been free. It was a colony far away, where bananas grew, and men sang funny songs, like a *mélopée*. It was the country of the Buddha: it was the country of Lakmé.

"You are a student," he said, after a moment's silence.

"Yes, Maître, so I am."

"Living in the Rue de Vaugirard."

"Yes, that is so."

"You can sign here. You can say you seek divorce for '*incompatibilité de tempéraments*.' I hope you get the divorce, Monsieur. Oh, French justice is not so bad. It's a little odd, rather like this building is, like this light. This light, now, Monsieur, have a good look at it. It has seen three generations of *huissiers*, just as this building has seen three generations of Sigons. Once a *huissier*, always a *huissier*, is a very good proverb, I tell you."

"This lady," I said, as though to give myself some dignity, "this lady, the cousin of my wife, is the daughter of a *notaire*."

"Ah, I thought so, Mademoiselle, when I saw your face. Ah, I can smell a *notaire* like I can a good Burgundy. Where would France be without her *notaires*? We do not make laws like those pompous politicians at the Palais Bourbon; we keep laws functioning, that is all, and you know that is a great deal. We protect the child from the greedy grandmother, we protect the woman from her husband, we protect virtue from being sold like the girls in the opposite street. We make the continuity of France."

"Yes, I know," I said, very proud. I had heard the same discourse from Oncle Charles.

"Well—Mademoiselle," said Maître Sigon.

"No, Madame," I corrected.

"Madame, will you kindly sign here, as witness. Funny, what the world is coming to," he said, looking up at me. "Formerly, if a wife separated from her husband—for divorce in the time of my grandfather was a very difficult business, what with the Church and all—I was saying, when you separated, you swore enmity to one another. If you saw her brother, mother, sister, cousin, you looked away, Monsieur, you turned your face away; and if they came too near, you looked up insolently, you insulted them; you swore from the opposite corner of the room. You even sent your card for a duel. Now, Monsieur, cousins come to sign for one another. Now, the cuckold and the lover both sit at the same table, and play bridge. Oh, Monsieur," concluded Maître Sigon, "the world is changing, changing too rapidly for me."

Not having made much impression on us, he rose and said, "Monsieur, say what you will. You go to fifty other notaries in this city; they will say, the storm has come, it has blown away my car, my house, even my wife, and they will close their offices and go to a cinema. I belong to the older generation: even if there is a storm there is always a light. Is that not so, Henriette?" He turned to his secretary. She was middle-aged all right, and her check overall gave her an air of respectability.

"We work whether others work or not," she confirmed. "Maître Sigon is always here, ill or well. At nine-thirty he is here, before the postman is here. Even before I am here," said Madame Henriette, smiling. She wanted to please.

"Her aunt," said Maître Sigon, "her good aunt, was brought up in our house. We saved her from an orphanage, and that was after the wars of 1870. She served us well at home. And now Madame Henriette is such a faithful secretary. I tell you, if I die she can run this office. That is France, Monsieur, that is France."

The lamps outside were lit, but in the building the electric connections had still not been made. The little kerosene burner continued to spread its yellow light on the green tablecloth. Madame Henriette had a pen in her hand as she opened the door.

"By the way, Madame," said Maître Sigon, as if he had suddenly remembered something. "You never told me the name of your excellent father, my colleague. You have signed here, 'Catherine Khuschbertieff.'"

"My father is Maître Roussellin, because my cousin is Madeleine Roussellin."

"Of course, of course," he said, "that is true. And he is from Rouen, did you say, Madame?"

"Yes, Papa's *notariat* is in Rouen. Rue Saint-Ouen."

"My regards to Maître Roussellin, your excellent father, Madame. Remember, France is mainly run by its *notaires* and *huissiers.* Our red seal," he said, unhooking the seal from its peg, "this rules France. *Au revoir, Madame, au revoir, Monsieur.* Madame Henriette will lead you down the staircase. The candle will be of help—otherwise you might do the wrong thing with one another, and have to come back again to me. *Au revoir, Monsieur.*"

The candle-light lit parts of the staircase here and there. Once at the bottom we shouted, *"Merci. Au revoir, Madame Henriette,"* and the light disappeared. The locksmith was still hammering at something—he also had a little oil lamp. The cold wind blew on our faces. Spring was coming.

"*27.3.54.* Yes, I say to myself, 'I must leave this world, I must leave, leave this world.' But, Lord, where shall I go, where? How can one go anywhere? How can one go from oneself?

"I walk up and down this mansard, and say, 'There must be something that exalts and explains why we are here, what is it we seek.' And suddenly, as though I've forgotten where I am, I begin to sing out loud, *'Shivoham, Shivoham,'* as if I were in Benares, on the banks of the Ganges, sitting on Harishchandra Ghat and singing away. In Benares, it may still sound true—but here against the dull sky of Paris, this yellow wallpaper, with its curved and curling clematis, going back and forth, and all about my room . . . I say, 'Clematis is the truth, must be in the truth.' I count, one, two, three, simply like that, and count 177 clematis in my room. 'If I add a zero,' I say to myself, 'it will make 1770 and they would cover ten mansard rooms.' I look out and count the number of windows in the Lycée Saint-Louis. It has eighteen windows: one, two, three, five, eleven, eighteen windows. And I say, 'If they had clematis on their walls, how many would there be? Each room there is about three times the width of my room.' My arithmetic goes all wrong, for I must subtract one wall out of every three, and that's too complicated. I roll back into my bed. *'Hara-Hara, Shiva-Shiva,'* I say to myself, as if I were in Benares again, then *'Chidānanda rūpah, Shivoham, Shivoham,'* I began to clap hands and sing. The Rumanian lady next door again knocks to remind me I am in Paris. I go out, with my overcoat on, wander round and round the Luxembourg Gardens by the Rue d'Assas, feeling that three times round anything you love must give you meaning, must give you peace. Buses still go on the streets, and students are still there *chez* shining, mirrored Dupont. I wish I could drink: 'It must be wonderful to drink,' I say to myself. The students get drunk and are so gay. That Dutch boy, the other day, was quite drunk; he sat in the hotel lounge, with his mouth on one side, and started singing songs. If you don't feel too warm at heart, you can always warm yourself in the Quartier Latin. You never saw more generous girls in the world. Existentialism has cleared the libido out of the knots of hair. Wherever you go, girls have rich bosoms, fiery red lips. They don't need cards—not because the gendarme does not ask for them, but because girls have grown too pure. Purity is not in the act but in the meaning of the act. Had I been less of a Brahmin, I might have known more of 'love.' "

"29.3.54. I go down the Boulevard Saint-Michel, stand before the lit fountain and come back. I am sure I am much better. I go round the '100,000 Chemises' shop, who know their arithmetic. I see that a cravat costs 1,990 francs, the good ones—shoes cost twice as much; the best one four times in the next shop. There is a brawl on the corner of my street, and I look at everyone, thinking as if I am not looking at them, but I am counting them. 'One, two, three, four, five,' I say, and one threatens to beat four and four threaten to beat me. Fear is such a spontaneous experience— I slink away, I run and run till I reach my hotel. I think it was a political battle of some sort. A group of Moroccan and Indochinese students were having a brawl with some elderly Frenchman. Then I understood. They thought—the fat, threatening Frenchman thought—that I must be a Tunisian. You must fight for something. You cannot flow like the Rhône, dividing Avignon into the Avignon of the Popes and Petit Avignon.

"I get my key from the concierge and come up to my room. I feel the room to be so spacious, so kind; I could touch the sky with my fingers. You can have 177 clematis in your room and yet touch the sky of Paris. A Brahmin can touch anything, he is so high—the higher the freer. I look at the carefully arranged manuscript of my thesis. It has 278 pages. It has been finished for over a week. Dr. Robin-Bessaignac said it is very interesting, very very interesting indeed, but blue-pencilled several passages. One in particular, in my preface, made him laugh. 'History is not a straight line, it is not even a curved line,' I had written. 'History is a straight line turned into a round circle. It has no beginning, it has no end—it is movement without itself moving. History is an act to deny fact. History, truly speaking, is seminal.'

" 'You don't know our professors,' Dr. Robin said. 'They would hide behind their notes if they saw a girl with too much rouge on her lips. Besides, my friend, there is an ancient tradition in this country: Beware of too much truth. We French live on heresies. If only poor Abelard had ended with a question mark and not with a *"Scito Teipsum,"* he might have walked Paris uncastrate, and be canonized a saint by now. You must go to the end of philosophy, go near enough to truth—but you must end with a question mark. The question mark is, I repeat, the sign of French intelligence; it is the tradition of Descartes, that great successor of Abelard. And as for anything imaginative . . . There's a famous story about Sylvain Lévi, the Orientalist, you know. He had said, and that was seventy good years ago, something about Kalidasa's plays. His books ended, as all good literature ended in those days, with a noble sentence, rounded like one of Mallarmé's. Would you believe it, the thesis was refused: he had to write it again. I do not want to see your thesis refused. I know what they will say. "This is supposed to be a thesis on the philosophical origins, mainly Oriental, primarily Hindu, of the Cathar philosophy. But it is too poetic. It lacks historical discipline!" Get someone—preferably a professor—to help you to remove everything that does not end in a question. Can you find one?' he asked me. Of course I know one. Who could be more helpful to me than good Georges? I often discuss my thesis with him, and I have read him bits of it. He does not say whether it would be suitable or not as a thesis: he is happy at my defence of Catholicism, and finds my logic inescapable. Here and there, however, he has suggested a few corrections. And then, somebody has to translate the whole text into French. I wonder whether

Georges would do. Good Georges, of course, agrees. I must give it to him tomorrow."

"2.4.54. I roll and roll in my bed. Not that I am ill; no, I am not so ill. In fact the doctors are very satisfied with the state of my lungs; hardly any complications with my ribs or my chest, they say. I could, in fact, stay in Europe if I cared. But why should I? What is there to do? I think of Saroja. She is not happy, but she is settled. I think of Little Mother going and dipping in the Ganges every morning. And now, this year, with the Kumbha Méla and the sun in Capricorn, she must be very happy. Could I give Little Mother such joy if I were back? What can a poor professor in Hyderabad do? At best I could take her on a pilgrimage once in two years. There is nobody to go to now: no home, no temple, no city, no climate, no age.

> *Kashwam koham kutha āyatha ka mē janani ko mē tātah?*
> Who are you and whose; whence have you come?

"Wheresoever I am is my country, and I weep into my bed. I am ashamed to say I weep a lot these days. I go to bed reading something, and some thought comes, I know not what—thoughts have no names—or have they?—and I lie on my bed and sob. Sometimes singing some chant of Sankara, I burst into sobs. Grandfather Kittanna used to say that sometimes the longing for God becomes so great, so acute, you weep and that weeping has no name. Do I long for God? God is an object and I cannot long for him. I cannot long for a round, red thing, that one calls God, and he becomes God. It would be like that statue down the road. I asked someone there, 'What is this statue, Monsieur?' He was surprised and said, 'Why, it's Saint Michel!' Since then I have known why this road here is called Saint-Michel and that Saint Michel kills a dragon. Being a Brahmin I know about Indra and Prajapathi, but not about Saint Michel or Saint Denis. I will have to look into the *Encyclopédie des religions*. And that's not too helpful either. God, in this *Encyclopédie,* has sixty-two pages, and they do not illuminate my need."

"5.4.54. No, not a God but a Guru is what I need. 'Oh Lord, my Guru, my Lord,' I cried, in the middle of this dreadful winter night. It was last night; the winds of April had arisen, the trees of the Luxembourg were crying till you could hear them like the triple oceans of the Goddess at Cape Comorin. 'Lord, Lord, my Guru, come to me, tell me; give me Thy touch, vouchsafe,' I cried, 'the vision of Truth. Lord, my Lord.'

"I do not know where I went, but I was happy there, for it was free and broad like a sunny day and like a single broad white river it was. I had reached Benares—Benares. I had risen from the Ganges, and saw the luminous world, my home. I saw the silvery boat, and the boatman had a face I knew. I knew His face, as one knows one's face in deep sleep. He called me, and said, 'It is so long, so long, my son. I have awaited you. Come, we go.' I went, and man, I tell you, my brother, my friend, I will not return. I have gone whence there is no returning. To return you must not be. For if you are, where can you return? Do you, my brother, my friend, need a candle to show the light of the sun? Such a Sun I have seen; it is more splendid than a million suns. It sits on a riverbank, it sits as the formless form of Truth; it walks without walking, speaks without talking, moves without gesticulating, shows without naming, reveals what is Known. To such a Truth was I taken, and I became its servant, I kissed the perfume of its Holy Feet, and called myself a disciple.

"This happened, this happened so long ago—Oh, as long ago as I have known myself be. Ever since being has known itself as being I have Known It. It is the gift that Yagnyavalkya made to Maiteryi, it is the gift Govinda made to Sri Sankara. It is the gift He made to me, my Lord. May I be worthy of the Lord. Lord, my Master! O thou abode of Truth."

I GO SOMETIMES to see Catherine and Georges. While Georges corrects my manuscript, and puts it into the acuity, the brilliance of the French language, I often sit by little Vera, and speak to her my truth. For Vera, with her seven months, can understand more of it than I could ever make Georges accept. Truth is to be recognized when told—as the beauty of a flower is recognized. Truth has such a perfume too. When I go into Vera's room she smiles, and her little eyes know who I am. She sees beyond me.

I am so happy with Vera that even when the maid is there I tell her, "Go to a cinema, enjoy yourself. I will look after the baby." And sometimes I send Georges and Catherine away to see a play or go and hear music. They see that I am really happy, and they let me be with their daughter. And when I am alone I sing to Vera—I sing her Sankara and Bharthrihari, and tell her one day she shall know there is somewhere to go. For now I know the name of Him to whom I have to go, though I have always known Him without knowing His name. So to Travancore I will go, I tell Vera, "I will go there, Vera, and think of you."

Sometimes so deep is my joy that I dance about the room and sing of the Truth. I show His picture to Vera, for I have a picture now—and have bought His books too—and say, "Look, look, Vera, this is He! Can you see Him? It is He, the Guru, my Lord."

It was Georges, good Georges, who had originally taken me to the Rue de Boulainvilliers. "There are some Vedantins in Paris, too," he said. "Would you like to meet them?" I was happy. I met an Indian who knew me, and knew my family; he talked too much. But the Frenchmen and the Frenchwomen—and one or two English people as well, and an American—they all made a deep impression on me. That had been long before I went down south, soon after leaving London. I had carried His books to the

Alps and had read them again and again. They convinced me, but I had to *know*.

Now, I think I *know*, but I must go, I must go to Travancore. I have no Benares now, no Ganga, no Jumna; Travancore is my country, Travancore my name. Lord, accept me, vouch that I be where I should. How can I ever, ever tell Georges? Will he understand? Would Madeleine, with her *vajras* and her *chakras*, understand this simple, this ever-lit Truth? Truth indeed is He, the Guru. No, He is beyond definition. He is, and you are not.

Now, when I am singing Sankara, how my eyes fill with tears, and I drop them on Vera. "Vera, do you see?" I say, and cover her cheeks with my tears. I sing to her the Kanarese cradlesong I sang often to Sridhara:

> The Swan is swinging the cradle, baby,
> Saying "I am That," "That I am," quietly.
> She swings it beautifully, baby,
> Abandoning actions and hours.

Georges and Catherine went this evening to see *Oberon*.

"What gorgeous scenery!" Catherine said. "And how rich and appreciative the audience. But what was true a hundred years ago is true no more. Kings and queens have to talk differently, be different. The President of the Republic was there, and so was Prince George of Greece. But Paradise, Rama, the Paradise of Oberon . . . ?"

"All you need's a donkey," said Georges, tired.

"Come, I will make you some nice warm chocolate. Chocolate or coffee, my children?" said Catherine, very happy.

"The children being very wise," said Georges, "they will take chocolate."

"How was Vera?" said Catherine. "You don't need to go to India for a job, Rama. You look after Vera. Vera loves you: she is so quiet when you are here. And you can write your abstruse theories. I will give you back your small room. And Georges will drink chocolate and translate your clever ideas."

"I promise to stay if you will have a baby before I go," I said jokingly.

"Now, now, Rama, you may have more intuition than you think you have." This from Georges.

403

"Ah, là là!" said Catherine. "A Brahmin after all."

"Do you know what a Brahmin is, Catherine?"

"No, what is it?" She came back, having gone halfway to the kitchen.

"A Brahmin is he who knows Brahman. That is one definition," I said. "There is another, a roguish definition. A Brahmin is he who loves a good banquet."

"You certainly do not belong to the second category, poor dear. Rama, what shall we do when you are gone? You have become so like one of us. We will be lost."

Georges looked at me. He looked so sad.

"We must have been brothers in a past life," he said, as though to explain everything. Catherine must have heard it, through the kitchen wall. For she came back and said:

"I must have been your wife. That is why Vera knows you. Marriages are made in Heaven, they say, don't they? Sometimes they are made on earth."

Georges and I went back to the kitchen with her. I said, "Catherine, I will tell you what: marriages are made in Benares."

"Georges, let us go to Benares," she said.

"And what about the dead bodies, and the pyres, and the famous crocodiles that some French author saw with his own four eyes?" I laughed. She had read about the crocodiles in some book and was convinced Benares had only floating dead bodies, beggars and many cremation fires. She had also heard that seven miles away was Sarnath. That was where the Buddha had turned the Wheel of Law.

"No, let us go to Travancore," I said.

"Now, what is this new place?" protested Catherine.

"I have been telling you and myself a lie, all these years. My real home is in Travancore. Benares is there, and there you have no crocodiles nor pyres."

"It's opposite Ceylon," said Georges, in geographic explanation; like me he was a born professor.

"I will make chocolate for two in Travancore. Travancore, Travancore, there's magic in that name!" said Catherine.

And we went back to the plush chairs. The chocolate was very good.

404

ACKNOWLEDGEMENTS

The dignity and precision of Sanscrit are so difficult to convey in translation that I have taken the liberty of using all the well-known translations to make my own versions of the texts quoted. Chief among the translators I am indebted to are: Sir Monier Williams, A. B. Keith, Max Müller, the monks of the Ramakrishna Mission, Dr. A. K. Coomaraswamy and, of course, Sir John Woodroffe. Sir John Woodroffe's translations are so authentic that almost never have I had to correct them.

The French version of Rainer Maria Rilke's poem on the Cathedral is by Professor Angelloz.

I have finally to thank my original English publisher, the House of John Murray, for the deep understanding they have shown of my book. The present text owes a great deal to their unfailing care and help.

R. R.

GLOSSARY

This short glossary is for those quite unfamiliar with India; but I have not explained here all the Indian terms used, lest by overemphasis I disturb that growing intimacy between reader and book for which I hope.

Arathi: At the end of worship camphor flame is shown to the face of the deity. Sometimes it is also waved round the face of the deity.

Banya: Of the third or merchant caste.

Bhang: A strong intoxicant whose chief ingredient is hemp.

Choli: A woman's bodice.

Coconut: It is sacred in India and is often used as an offering at worship.

Dharma: The Law by which society is governed linked with the Transcendental Law.

Dhoti: An Indian male garment worn round the legs. It is a long piece of cloth, often with a filigree border.

Ganga: Sanscrit name for Ganges. She lives in Shiva's hair.

Ghat: Usually the stone steps that go down to the waters of a sacred river or tank. It has also come to be associated with the mountain ranges in India going down to the Eastern and Western Seas and they are thus called the Eastern and Western Ghats.

Ghee: Clarified butter.

Karma: The Hindu concept that you pay here for your past deeds, good or bad.

Kirtana or Kirtanam: A holy song composed by a mystic or philosopher.

Kudtha: A skirt. It is usually decorated with flower designs.

Kunkum: A sacred red powder used by married Hindu women to mark their auspicious state. The kunkum is placed just above the meeting of the eyebrows.

Krishna: Hero of the *Mahabharatha*, Prince and Sage. His main teachings are contained in the famous *Bhagavad-Gita*.

Mantra: Sacred syllable or syllables first uttered by a Sage, which repeated (by others) take effect on the appropriate plane. An incantation.

Nandi:	The sacred vehicle of Shiva.
Pandal:	A bamboo and coconut-leaf ceremonial hall.
Prasada:	Offerings to the gods returned to man sanctified.
Rama:	Hero of the famous epic *Ramayana*. Rama is Prince of Ayodhya, whose wife Sita was stolen by Ravana, the monster king of Ceylon (Lanka).
Sātwic:	The purest of pure.
Shiva:	The ascetic God, who married Parvathi, daughter of the Himalayas. Shiva, as symbol of the Absolute, dances over the monster of ignorance.
Sri Sankara:	The famous philosopher of the Classical Age of India. He may have lived anywhere between the fourth and the eighth centuries. He propounded the ancient theory of non-dualism—Advaita Vedanta.
Tilak:	Sacred mark of sandal or kunkum, etc., on the forehead.
Tulasi:	The sacred balsam. In Hindu households this plant is grown in the middle of the courtyard and worship is made to it.
Upana-yanam:	Initiation ceremony to attain Brahminhood, at which the young Brahmin is given his sacred thread.
Vina:	The most subtle and sacred of Hindu musical instruments. The *vina* is supposed to be of very ancient origin.